5/82   DC1   S

Cadell, Elizabeth
A lion in the way

                              13.50

DUE

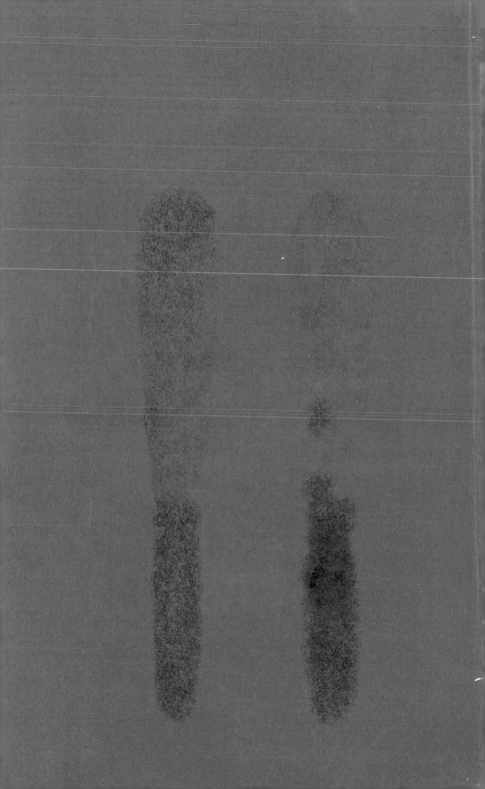

A
LION
IN THE WAY

A
LION
IN THE WAY

Elizabeth Cadell

WILLIAM MORROW AND COMPANY, INC.
New York   1982

Library of Congress Cataloging in Publication Data

Cadell, Elizabeth.
    A lion in the way.

    I. Title.
PR6005. A225L5   1982   823'.912   81-16928
ISBN 0-688-01098-9   AACR2

Printed in the United States of America

First Edition

1 2 3 4 5 6 7 8 9 10

BOOK DESIGN BY MICHAEL MAUCERI

PART ONE

1913-1914

The *ayah*, middle-aged, overweight, indolent and by nature opposed to haste, was soon left behind. She did not, however, abandon the chase. Hooking her toes more firmly into her velveteen slippers, she proceeded at a shuffle, directing angry screeches at the thin, long-legged child disappearing into the distance.

"Oh *baba*! Oh Anlee *baba*!"

Annerley ignored the cries and the appeals. She knew why the ayah was incensed. Instead of going to the triangular grass plot known as Levett Gardens, to which every afternoon during school holidays local children, accompanied by their ayahs or bearers, went to play, she had decided to pay a visit to a friend. She had slipped the leash. She had turned right instead of turning left and was now on her way to see Shareen Prebdel, thus depriving the ayah of an hour's gossip with her cronies in the Gardens.

Annerley had two close associates, each of them claiming to be her best friend. She saw no reason to grade them, but she knew that if she had to choose, Shareen Prebdel would be her choice.

It was the Prebdel mansion to which she was speeding now. Speed was necessary because she had to reach the gate, pull the bell rope and gain admission before the ayah caught up with her. Once the gate closed again, the ayah could do nothing but settle herself in the shade of a tree and spend the waiting interval abusing the *durwan*.

Annerley could have sent her away; the Prebdels had more than one carriage available to take her home when she was ready to go. But she was here without permission, and she would like to time her visit so that she could get home at the end of the hour she was supposed to have spent in the Gardens. The ayah would report the matter on their return home, but the fact of being scolded by her grandmother did not disturb her; all she wished to avoid was a fuss that would reach the ears of her father and bring about a tightening of the rule against too-frequent visits to the Prebdels.

But for the moment, the ayah was outside, unable to argue or to interfere, and Annerley was inside on the broad, palm-lined, gravelled drive that bisected the beautiful grounds. Ahead, some distance away, was the house, white, two-storied, pillared, with a flat roof and terrace-like balconies onto which opened the long windows of the principal rooms.

It had been built in the late eighteen-eighties by Shareen's grandfather, Amrit Prebdel, shortly before his marriage. He was an industrialist—probably one of the most influential, certainly one of the richest, men in Bengal. He had brought his bride to the house and today, in 1913, they were still living in it. Also resident were their four sons, their sons' wives, their innumerable grandchildren and a horde of distant relations, dependents and hangers-on.

Amrit's oldest son, Zumeer, had been born a year after Amrit and his wife had moved into the newly built mansion. Amrit had decided to send him to England to be educated, and the boy had been entered at a preparatory school in Sussex. From there he had gone on to Harrow and thence to Cambridge. After graduating, he returned to India—and Amrit realized that he had sent away a small Hindu boy and had received in return a tall, handsome, suave, polished Englishman. Divided between pride and dismay, he decided that he would keep his three younger sons in India. One foreigner in the family was enough.

There had been a long-standing engagement between Zumeer and the daughter of a wealthy family in Lahore. Though he had seen no more than her photograph, Zumeer had agreed to the betrothal. On his return, she was sixteen, and to the infinite relief of his parents, he declared himself ready for the wedding. He put aside his English dress and manners during the ceremony, and after it brought his bride to Calcutta.

The northeastern corner of the house was allocated to the newly wed pair, and Zumeer, taking possession, announced that his style of living would in future be western. His sons would be educated in England; his house would be run on English lines. There would be English furniture in all the rooms; meals would be served at regular hours on a table and not at irregular intervals on trays, and would consist of English menus varied by occasional Indian dishes.

Things had not worked out quite as he had planned. The English furniture arrived and was placed in every room—except the three or four occupied by his wife. She had shown no opposition to her husband's plans, but it now appeared that she would rather recline on divans than sit on Chippendale chairs. Moreover, she did not care for regular meals or for English food, and would adhere to her lifelong habit of eating and drinking when she felt hungry or thirsty.

The sons who were to be educated in England failed to materialize. His wife bore two children only: a boy and, three years later, a girl. The boy was in due course sent to his father's old schools, and reports filtering in from relations in England indicated that he was becoming as Anglicized as his father. His sis-

11

ter's education had been placed in the hands of a series of governesses and tutors, but though all these were English, Shareen had remained obstinately Hindu.

Annerley, walking up the drive toward the house, could see no sign of life other than the gardeners moving among the flower beds—but she had often seen these grounds when they were graced by elegant women in saris or flowing gowns, by tall Englishmen in impeccable suits or Indians wearing well-tailored, high-necked tunics and snow-white leggings. She and Shareen had watched the guests from the balcony outside Shareen's room, and had listened to the band playing airs from popular operettas. Today there was no reception, but she could hear issuing from the central courtyard of the house a familiar babel of voices, and could picture the animated scene. The courtyard, spacious, marble-floored, reached by steps from the surrounding verandahs and from the balconies above, was the heart of the house, where life was lived in the open and where several generations of the family gathered.

The sights, the sounds had become familiar to her during the past four years—ever since, at the age of nine, she had come to know Shareen Prebdel. Here, for the first time, she had been accepted by a cultured Indian family and had learned something of the Indian way of life. She spent almost as much time in this house as she did her own. She no longer felt an outsider; she was one of them, a daughter of the house.

Following the drive as it curved round the building, she came to the part of the house occupied by Shareen's parents. The outlook now was of more smooth lawns, a lily pond, trees giving patches of cool shade. She could see in the distance the tennis courts on which Shareen had been expected to become, under professional coaches, a champion. She could glimpse the blue shimmer of the swimming pool which had been provided for Shareen's practice sessions of swimming and diving. Pool and courts and coaching had all proved useless; Shareen, like her mother, detested physical exertion in any form. The pool was left to the troops of cousins, children of Zumeer's brothers and their wives.

Waiting on the drive at the foot of a flight of steps was Mrs. Prebdel's gleaming landau, its top open, its luxurious interior and cool, freshly laundered seat covers visible. Mrs. Prebdel was coming down the steps. Following her came an ayah carrying a small parcel, a bearer carrying nothing and a plump, grey-haired Bengali lady who acted as housekeeper. A small boy, son of the bearer, brought up the rear, ready to run back and fetch anything that had been forgotten.

Annerley knew that in the newly constructed garage adjoining the stables was a motor car—a proud, high carriage on wheels, recently imported with its attendant chauffeur from England—a sight so novel in this city of carriages that all eyes followed its slow, stately progress through the streets, and groups gathered to gaze at it, awestruck, when it stopped. Shareen's father used it daily and had frequently taken Shareen and Annerley for drives, but his wife, after a brief trial, had reverted to her open victoria and her closed landau.

Annerley paused to watch the process of embarkation. The *syce* sprang down to open the door of the landau. Mrs. Prebdel came gracefully down the steps on high-heeled sandals and raised a ring-bedecked hand in a languid gesture to Annerley. Her sari was of pale pink diaphanous material, with a wide silver edging. On her arms were several delicate gold bangles. On her forehead was painted a small crimson circle.

"You are going to see Shareen?" she called from the door of the carriage.

"Yes, Mrs. Prebdel."

"She will be glad to see you. She is there, inside. Go inside, go."

Her English had a singsong quality that was absent from the speech of her husband and daughter. She had no claim to beauty —her face was too thin, her nose too arched, her large, dark eyes too prominent—but she was exquisitely groomed and she had an air that Annerley described to herself as queenly.

She waited until the carriage drove away. There was no fear that it would go through the main gate and give the ayah an opportunity to slip inside. It would glide behind the handsome, glossy horse through the north gate, now being opened in readiness by the durwan's son. She watched until it went out of sight and then turned and went up the steps and into the house.

Her father, Edwin Brooke, who coached Indian students wishing to enter English universities, had for a short time been one of Shareen's tutors. It was this engagement that had led to her first visit to the house. Learning that Edwin had a daughter of Shareen's age, Zumeer had invited him to bring her to one of the lessons. The visit, in the view of the elders, had not been successful; the two children had scarcely addressed a word to one another and had expressed no desire for further meetings. But since that day, Annerley had been a frequent visitor. If she failed to appear for two or three days, a *chaprassi* in the picturesque Prebdel livery—scarlet tunic and cummerbund and white leggings—would appear at her house with a peremptory note from Shareen. Annerley would initial the letter book and the chaprassi would stand respectfully waiting for an answer. This she scribbled hastily, anxious to see him depart, for his kingly appearance and bearing looked embarrassingly out of place in the dusty, drab, treeless compound of her father's house in Seymour Street.

Annerley's grandmother, Mrs. Devenish, fearing that too many visits would put a strain on friendship or hospitality, had attempted to impose a limit of three visits a week. This decree Annerley thought unnecessary, while Shareen considered it unwarrantable interference; they continued to see one another as often as they wished, but as Shareen seldom bestirred herself to make the journey to Seymour Street, it fell to Annerley to maintain communication.

Shareen's room was on the upper floor. Annerley crossed the hall and went up a wide, curving staircase. Through the arch that gave entrance to Shareen's room she saw the ayah—not, like hers, a limpet-like attendant, but one whose sole function was to

14

look after Shareen's dresses. She surveyed Annerley with disapprobation.

"Why have you been running in this heat, miss-sahib? Look at you, wet with perspiration and your hair sticking to your cheeks. Why so much haste?"

It was early April, and signs of the approaching hot season could already be felt. Only last week, at this time, it had been cool. Now the heat lingered, only giving way to the cooling breezes of the evening. Soon it would be May, and Shareen would go with her parents to their house in Naina Tal or Musoorie and return only when October was well advanced. It was an annual deprivation, and Annerley had reconciled herself to it.

"I'm not hot," she told the ayah.

She spoke the fluent, ungrammatical Hindustani that most English women and children used when addressing domestic servants; she had spoken it before she learned to speak English. It was the present limit of her linguistic powers. Her father, on his arrival in India, had taken Urdu lessons from a *munshi* and spoke grammatically, but the servants had difficulty in understanding what he said, and applied frequently to Annerley for enlightenment.

Shareen's room opened onto the balcony. It was very large, its floor of polished red stone, its walls white. Curtained arches led to the bathroom and to the small room used by the ayah as a workroom. The furniture consisted of a chintz-covered sofa and two cane-seated chairs. Only the bed conformed to the Indian pattern, being a low wooden frame with wide strands of webbing.

There was no sign of Shareen.

"She is in the governess's room," the ayah said. "She is being fitted for her dresses. She is in a very bad temper. Come; you will see."

They went out to the balcony and walked along it to the adjacent room. In a far corner, on a mat spread on the floor, two of the *dirzhee's* assistants sat cross-legged, busily working sewing machines. The dirzhee, a venerable gentleman with a flowing white beard, in spotless white shirt and *dhoti*, was endeavouring to make slight alterations to the dress he was trying on a thin, dark, restless and impatient child of Annerley's age.

"Hurry, will you?" she was shouting. "And I won't have it shorter. It's too loose here and it's too tight there and when my mother sees it, she'll make you take it away and do it all again."

"But miss-sahib," the old man protested, "if you will only let me—"

"I won't stand here any longer. Go away. I'm going to take it off."

But the ayah had fetched reinforcements. The governess, Miss Severn, entered. Her expression was reproachful, her manner authoritative.

"What is all this?" she inquired. "Shareen, kindly don't shout when you're addressing servants."

She was forty, built on generous lines, with large hands and feet and a vast, untethered bosom. She feared the sun and wore her topee whenever she stepped out of the house; round her forehead was a permanent broad pink line left by its lining. She had held this post for three years—longer than any of her predecessors. She could not subdue her turbulent charge, but she usually succeeded in calming her.

"How can you be dressed properly, Shareen, if you won't allow the dirzhee to fit you?"

"I told my mother I don't want dresses made by dirzhees. I told her twice. Why didn't she listen?"

"The only dresses you have made by dirzhees," Miss Severn pointed out, "are your morning ones. Now let's see what all this fuss is about. You mustn't be so impatient. We always have this argument when the dirzhee comes to fit you. I shall be thankful when you stop wearing English clothes and go into saris; then we shall have no more trouble. Let me see. . . . Yes, the dress is a little too short. Tell the man he'll have to let it down a little."

Shareen told him, not politely.

"Have you offered Annerley a cool drink?"

"No."

"I don't want anything, thank you," Annerley put in. She was seated on a rug near the door. "I can't stay long—and my ayah's waiting."

"Let her wait," said Shareen. "Why didn't you tell her to go home?"

"I'm not supposed to be here. I didn't ask my grandmother. She thinks I'm playing in the Gardens."

"Oh, she's so stupid, so *silly*," Shareen said in exasperation.

Miss Severn was on her way out of the room, but she paused in the doorway for the exchange of courtesies which she never omitted, designed as they were to demonstrate to her pupil the exquisite manners of the English.

"Your grandmother is well, I hope, Annerley?"

"Yes, thank you."

"And your father?"

"Yes, thank you."

"Please give them my regards."

She swept out, and Shareen looked at her retreating back with a contemptuous snort.

"So polite, oh my goodness me. Good morning, Miss Brooke, your father is well? Oh, so glad. And your mother? She's dead? Oh, so sorry. And your brothers and sisters? You haven't got any? Then good-bye for now."

"Stop being silly," Annerley requested. "And keep still or you'll get pins stuck into you."

While the adjustments to the dress were being made, she studied her friend. Shareen was tall and thin, not delicately made like her mother, but big-boned, which gave her a gaunt look. Annerley had to admit that she was not pretty—her nose was too arched, her mouth too large. But she had beautiful dark eyes and her skin was like brown satin. Her hair, long and very thick, was worn in a tapering plait. She had a loud voice and a loud laugh which successive governesses had tried in vain to reduce in volume. Her temper was ungovernable.

Her wardrobe was full of elaborate dresses and expensive shoes, offering a great contrast to Annerley's simple cotton frocks —for festive occasions adorned with a sash—and her shoes, which were made by Chinamen in their row of shops in Bentinck Street. Being measured for them was merely a matter of standing in her stockinged feet on a piece of cardboard while a Chinaman drew a pencil line round each foot. Her hair was very fair; it was short and wavy and needed no more than a comb drawn through it to make it tidy.

Following Shareen back to her room after the fitting, she told her that she had seen her mother going out.

"She's gone to visit Mrs. Dutt," Shareen said. "She wants to see the baby."

"Baby? A baby—already?" Annerley exclaimed in astonishment.

"How, already? She got married a long time ago—more than a year. You should remember; your father went to the wedding."

"No, he didn't. He was asked to go, but he didn't because he thought she was too young."

"Young? Fourteen too young to be married? Sometimes you're so *childish*, Annerley." She threw two cushions onto the floor and sank down beside her. "She had been engaged since she was eight years old." She reached over for a bowl of pistachio nuts, and they began to eat them. "My aunts want me to be engaged, but my father won't allow it."

"Engaged!"

"I'm thirteen. My cousin Gulab got married when she was thirteen. I wouldn't like to wait till I'm old, like English girls."

"Engaged who to?"

"I don't know. They didn't tell me. But I think to Starup Gupta."

"Who's Starup Gupta?"

"The Alipore Guptas."

"Who are they?"

"You've never heard of the Guptas who live in that palace in Alipore?"

"No."

"My goodness, Annerley, you don't know *anybody*."

"Not many Indians, no. Not as many as my father does."

"Even if he and your grandmother don't go out much, they ought to tell you about people—important people. Even if you never meet them."

Annerley let this pass. She let most provocative remarks pass. Her nature, like her father's, was one on which the seeds of envy, hatred or uncharitableness did not flourish. It was this quality that had attracted the two widely differing, uncontrollable children who were her closest friends. She could seldom be roused to retaliation, and her tolerant, if-you-say-so attitude killed argument. There was about her a certain detachment; she was content to watch life from the sidelines. In this house, during her visits to Shareen, her senses were alive to the brilliance and richness and colour of the surroundings, but her appreciation was untinged by envy. She recognized that this was a way of life far beyond the means of her father; she had long ago accepted without question the fact of his comparative poverty. All she was concerned with on her visits was the unpredictable, temperamental, ever-interesting Shareen.

"This Starup," she asked. "He's important?"

"Not him. Only his father."

"But do you know him? Do you like him? Do you want to be engaged to him?"

Shareen gave a lazy shrug.

"How do I know?"

"If you don't know, who knows? Don't pretend, Shareen. You must have *thought* about it, at least."

"Why should I think about it? First they'll choose Starup and then they'll change their minds and think of someone else. What's the use of thinking about something that isn't going to happen?"

"But—"

"It isn't as though it was all settled, like my brother's engagement."

"Your brother's? But he's only . . . how old?"

"He's sixteen. Since he was eleven, he's been engaged."

"Who to?"

"A girl in Allahabad."

"Does he know about it?"

"Are you quite mad? Know about it! Do you think he didn't agree?"

"But he wasn't here when he was eleven. He was in England."

"He met her before he went."

"But he was just a . . . a child!"

"He was old enough to know whether he liked her. And he did, so it's settled. Did you ask your father about going to Musoorie with us?"

"Yes."

"What did he say?"

"He said no. That's what I came to tell you."

Shareen sent the bowl of nuts flying and turned on her, her eyes blazing with anger.

"I told you! I told you he'd say that!" she shouted. "I *said*. I said to you that you should let my father ask him, and then he would have said you could come."

"No, he wouldn't. Because we're going to Darjeeling."

Shareen stared at her, the anger on her face changing slowly to astonishment. She sat trying to decide whether Annerley had spoken seriously. Deciding that she had, she measured the significance of the information. For as long as she had known Annerley —this would be the fourth hot weather of their acquaintance— the Brookes, father, daughter and grandmother, had remained on the plains. Shareen's father had explained that Mr. Brooke was unable to afford the expense of a sojourn to a hill station. His refusal to allow Annerley to accompany the Prebdels on their annual visits to their houses in the hills was regarded by Shareen as sheer vindictiveness.

"You're really going?" she asked. "All three of you?"

"Yes."

"How long will you go for?"

"Only until the monsoon."

"Only then? That's worse than not going. How can you come back in June, in the heat? It'll be terrible."

"No, it won't. It's never so bad in the monsoon."

"You've never come with us," Shareen said bitterly. "Never. We ask you and ask you, and what does your father say? Always no, no, no. He wouldn't even let you come to Delhi with us for the Coronation Durbar, do you remember that? Even my mother said you should have been allowed to come because you would remember it all your life, the king and queen and the processions with elephants and silver *howdahs* and big umbrellas with gold worked on them and . . . and everything. The king and queen came all the way from England to show themselves, and you didn't see them."

"They didn't only come to show themselves. They came—"

"You don't have to teach me why they came, thank you very much, because I know already. They came to say that Calcutta wasn't going to be the capital any more, only Delhi. But you didn't go—and now you're going to Darjeeling even though we asked you to come with us to Musoorie. What's in Darjeeling? Only snows, and you can see the snows from other places. If you had come with me, you could have ridden my ponies and we would have gone for picnics every day and . . . and things like that. But no, your father prefers to take you to Darjeeling. He wouldn't let you come and have lessons with me. He wouldn't let you come and share my governess. No, you had to go to that silly convent. Why did he send you there when you're not even a Catholic? And look at the girls you make friends with there. Not best friends, like me, but still, you like them. And who are they? Nobody."

"They're nice."

"How can you *say* that? They're not nice. Look at that Moira Fenwick. Do you know why her father and mother had to send her to the convent?"

"Yes."

"You don't know everything about her. You think she went

21

because nobody's governess would teach her, she was so disobedient—but before that, she was in England and she ran away from two schools. *Two*. Did you know that?"

"Yes."

"And still you go with her? Still you allow her to say she's your best friend? She's not your best friend, and you can tell her so to her face, from me, so there."

"Don't shout."

"I'm not shouting. I have to shout because you don't listen to anything I say. I've told you before you shouldn't be friends with her. She's rude to everybody and she's got a bad temper."

Annerley nodded. There were bad tempers and bad tempers. Shareen, dissatisfied with a dress, shouted at the dirzhee. Moira, whose sartorial standards were even higher, had put the offending garment on the floor and jumped on it.

"You'd like Moira too, if you knew her," she said. "But all you do is listen to stories about her."

"They're not stories. They're true. But you still go to her house and she goes to yours and sometimes you even don't come here because you're with her. You wouldn't have come today if she hadn't been away at that rajah's wedding. Moira Fenwick's bad enough, but look at that other girl, the one who lives next door to you—that Edna Fernandez. How you can even *speak* to her, I don't know."

"As she lives next door to me, and as she's in my class at school, I can hardly *not* speak to her, can I?"

"Your grandmother should forbid you. Do you know that those two sisters of hers go out with *men*? They go to dances at hotels without even their mother. Did you know that?"

"Edna doesn't go."

"Because she's only fourteen. Wait till she's sixteen, like her sister Myrtle, or seventeen, like her sister Ruby, and you'll see. If you had come to have lessons with me, you wouldn't have had to be with that Edna. But you wouldn't come."

"I couldn't come. My father wanted me to go to school."

22

"He did it on purpose, just out of spite. I tell you to your face: I *hate* him. So."

The ayah, performing a token tidying of the room, clicked her tongue in disapproval at this exhibition of temper. Annerley was unmoved. Shareen had wanted something, Shareen hadn't been able to get it, Shareen was cross.

"Why don't you take Anlee Miss-Sahib to see how Virendra baba is walking?" the ayah suggested. "His brothers and sisters didn't walk until they were one year, but he is only eleven months and already so advanced. Go and see him."

Annerley got to her feet.

"Come on, Shareen."

"Why? You've never seen a little baby walking before?"

"Not this little baby. And I've got to go home. We can stop and see Virendra on the way."

They did not go by way of the balcony. They went downstairs and through the house, going through room after room, leaving western influences behind them. Now there were pictures of Krishna on the walls and little statuettes of Hindu goddesses; divans instead of chairs, brighter colours.

When they reached the courtyard, Annerley paused to look at the scene which never ceased to fascinate her. There were carpets spread here and there on the black-and-white marble floor. Women in beautiful saris reclined against cushions. Small children balanced precariously on miniature bicycles, toddlers tumbled against their ayahs, servants in white uniform carried round silver trays of food to the shelter of the verandah, where it would be safe from the kites that swooped silently from the sky and snatched unprotected morsels. On the trays were small bowls containing rice, gram, rice with mince, rice with sultanas, Indian sweets swimming in syrup. The only men to be seen, apart from the bearers, were merchants displaying silks and embroideries. The women of this household did not go to the shops—the shops came to them.

There were aunts to be greeted, small brown bodies to be

picked up and hugged. It was difficult for Annerley to make herself heard above the medley of sounds and the snatches of Hindi and Bengali and Gujerati and Punjabi. Virendra was not walking; he was eating, seated on a miniature armchair and concentrating on the spoonfuls of semolina gruel that his ayah, squatting beside him, shovelled into his mouth.

Shareen walked with her to the gate.

"When will you come again?"

"On Friday."

"Then come early."

The distant pool looked inviting; Annerley would have liked to suggest bringing her bathing suit—but she said nothing. Swimming was a delicate matter. Her mornings throughout the convent holidays were spent with Moira Fenwick at the Albion Swimming Club, but membership was not open to Indians. It would not do to mention swimming.

When the gate was opened, the ayah rose and resumed her complaints. The durwan responded with a lecture about letting the Miss-Sahib run through the streets in the heat, and added that there was no hardship in sitting comfortably in the shade while she was waiting.

Walking homeward, they reached the end of the well-kept residential district and turned onto a street that became narrower and ended in a bazaar. Signs of European occupation vanished; to right and left were hovels fronted by stalls.

"Again you come this way," the ayah protested. "This is dirty way."

"It's quicker," Annerley pointed out.

It was also, in her opinion, more interesting. On the stalls were fruit, grain, vegetables, cloth, pots and pans, cheap jewelry, sweets half-hidden under swarms of flies. Pariah dogs nosed through the debris, half-naked children played in the dust. The open drains, the foul smells did not worry her. She passed a *bisthi* with his goatskin bag filled with water; a Sadhu, naked and painted; diseased beggars, women carrying earthenware jars on their heads. Her grandmother objected to her going this way, but her father, on their walks together, penetrated the most unsavoury alleys and byways—to show her, he said, that all Indians did not live like the Prebdels.

The bazaar gave way to a series of narrow lanes. Threading a way through them, they reached a piece of waste ground. As they crossed it, Annerley saw a short distance ahead a pin-*wallah*, one of the *dhobie* fraternity entrusted with the pressing of expensive or fragile dresses. On the dress hanger, folded over the pin-wallah's arm to prevent the hem from touching the ground, she recognized her grandmother's best evening dress—an elaborate gown with the discreet decolletage that Mrs. Devenish allowed herself on rare, formal occasions. It had a draped bodice and a long, flounced skirt and was decorated with a sprinkling of sequins. She must, Annerley concluded, be going to a rather special dinner, which meant that the ayah would have to help her to dress and so would be too busy to complain about the visit to Shareen.

They entered a wide, tree-shaded street—Seymour Street. Here, on the upper story of number 5, Annerley lived with her father and her grandmother. At the end of the street—number 10—lived the Fenwicks. She did not pause at their gate; she walked on until she reached the gate of number 5. She was home.

2

When Edwin Brooke had heard, some twelve years ago, that the upper story of a house in Seymour Street was being offered at a very moderate rent, he had hesitated before going to inspect it. Urgent as was his need for accommodation, he knew that the street, though far from fashionable and at one end beginning to run to seed, still retained a certain air of respectability by reason of the fact that the houses along it faced a wall behind which stood the elegant mansions of Park Place; some reflected glory found its way over the wall and was duly included in the Seymour Street rents. The low figure at which number 5 was being offered must indicate, Edwin thought, some fault in the drainage or some defect in the structure.

But on inspection, he could find nothing wrong—and the accommodation was exactly suited to his needs. There was an entrance hall with three green-painted doors with louvered shutters screening the lower flat. Upstairs, there was a narrow verandah on three sides, from one of which a steep wooden stairway led to the cookhouse and the servants' quarters in the compound below. On the fourth side was a room built over the porch—a large, rectangular, high-ceilinged apartment with wide windows that allowed a current of cooling breezes to flow through.

At the head of the staircase was a drawing room which Edwin planned to use as a dining room; the room over the porch would be the living room. There were three bedrooms; three somewhat primitive bathrooms and a small room in which he could give lessons to his pupils.

The flat had been empty for two months. Before this time, there seemed to have been a succession of tenants who came and went with mysterious speed. Edwin asked the landlord the reason for this.

"It has been misfortunate," explained Mr. Lobo. "One tenant had to go away to England. Another one, a werry nice gentleman, was transferred up to Delhi at very short notices. Then another gentleman—"

"Who lives downstairs?"

"A French lady. Her name is Madame Roubaix. She is very old. She does not have visitors, so you will not have incoming and outgoing, see? nothing like that. You will take the place?"

"I'll let you know," Edwin said.

He made a survey of the street. It was wide, and shaded by gold mohur trees which in season blazed with scarlet blossoms. The houses along it were all flat-roofed but varied greatly in size and style. Number 5, at the halfway point, seemed to mark the dividing line between the rich and the ramshackle. On one side —up to number 10 at the end of the row—the houses were well kept and stood in pleasant gardens. The last two, numbers 9 and 10, were imposing mansions. But from number 5 downwards, the picture was less reassuring. There were no gardens; instead, there were compounds on which nothing grew but a central bed of ferns or cannas. The gates were wide enough to allow the entry of carriages, but it was unlikely that any privately owned vehicles had ever driven through them. Number 4 was shabby; on its verandah a Eurasian woman in a bedraggled dressing gown was supervising a row of dirzhees who sat cross-legged before their sewing machines, working busily. In the compound were two young children, dark-skinned, pretty; a younger child was in the arms of a blowzy Madrassi ayah.

Outside number 3 was a board: *Benjamin Stanley, Court Photographer*. Beyond the board was a seedy bungalow and a compound littered with what Edwin took to be the backgrounds for sitters: facades of Swiss chalets, boards depicting beaches. The last two houses, numbers 1 and 2, were derelict and obviously due for demolition.

Edwin took the flat. Moving into it with his infant daughter, his widowed mother-in-law and four servants—ayah, cook, bearer and sweeper—he discovered almost at once why Mr. Lobo had so substantially reduced the rent. Madame Roubaix proved to be a retired opera singer who, though past her eighty-fourth year, had retained most of the force and carrying power of her voice. She began singing each day at about ten o'clock, tuning up with a series of piercing Mee-mee-mee-mees. By midday she had launched into her first aria. She ate and rested between the hours of two and four, and then began singing again. High C's, tremulous but sustained, were wafted up to the flat above until nine-thirty, when Madame went to bed.

There were other sounds in the street—noisy children, itinerant vendors, incessantly barking dogs—but Madame Roubaix had been trained to make her voice carry. After enduring her concerts for a week, Edwin paid the singer a visit. He knocked on the central door downstairs and when it opened, found himself confronted by a witch-like figure draped in an elaborate nightgown.

"Good evening," he began. "I—"

"You are from upstairs, the new tenant. I have seen you. Now, like all those others before you, you have come to tell me that you do not like me to sing and that you wish me to stop and have no music in my life. You are wasting your time, Monsieur Whatever-is-your-name. To sing, this was once my whole life, and until I am dead I shall go on singing. You cannot stop me. Nobody can stop me. The landlord, that Lobo, he also tried, but

28

as I pay my rent regularly each month, he can do nothing. Let me inform you, *monsieur*, that you are privileged to hear my singing. Once, I sang with the greatest names, the greatest voices. I was paid a fortune to sing—now I do so for you for nothing. Excuse me."

The door banged with a rattle of shutters. Edwin went upstairs, settled himself on his cane-seated long-sleever in the porch room and admitted defeat. But here was one tenant, he resolved, who would not be driven out.

Madame Roubaix did indeed sing until she died. When that event occurred, some four months after Edwin's arrival, he was torn between relief and compassion. It was good to know that he would no longer be regaled with off-key excerpts from *La Tosca*, but he thought it a sad, lonely end for the once-famous singer. He attended the funeral on the following day, and met a white-haired, hollow-cheeked gentleman who introduced himself as Madame's estranged husband and lost no time in removing her furniture and effects from the lower flat.

When the last load had been carried away, Edwin sent for the landlord, to whom he made a proposition: he would rent both the upper and lower stories on a long lease, and he would do some decorating, if he were given permission to furnish and let the lower flat to tenants of his own choosing. Mr. Lobo raised no objection. A month later, four young men moved in downstairs and the lower flat became a chummery. Its membership had changed through the years, but there were still four members. Each had his own bearer, but shared with the others the services of a cook and a sweeper. Two of the men were at present on short leave up-country; two were in residence.

Annerley, following the pin-wallah through the gate, encountered one of the two on his way out. His name was Charles Crowther. He was a bachelor of twenty-two and had fair, curly hair, laughing blue eyes and a way with women. He paused to greet Annerley.

"Hello, little Miss Skinny-shanks. Been taking the air in the so-called Gardens?"

29

"No. I went to see somebody. Are you playing your match tomorrow?"

"Yes. Coming to watch me get beaten?"

"I don't suppose I can. Unless my father takes me."

"Well, ask him. He ought to be playing himself. He's getting old and lazy. Tell him so from me."

She smiled. She liked him very much. The youngest member of the chummery, he had come out from England a year ago to join an insurance firm, and had almost immediately surrounded himself with a circle of friends as heedless and as irresponsible as himself. He consistently overspent his salary, most of it going on the entertainment of Eurasian girls of the flashier type. He would have been dropped by discriminating hostesses if it had not been for the fact that, as well as being the nephew of a bishop, he was a first-class tennis player and a useful cricketer. These twin talents ensured him invitations to houses that would otherwise have been closed to him.

"There's time for a tennis lesson," he told Annerley. "Go and change your shoes."

She ran upstairs to her bedroom, kicked off her sandals, put on a pair of tennis shoes and reached up to take her father's old tennis racket from the top of her wardrobe. From her grandmother's room issued a request for the ayah to be sent to her.

"I want her to help me with my dress, Annerley."

"I'll tell her, Granny."

Her father was in the porch room, lying back on his long-sleever.

"I'm going to have a tennis practice with Mr. Crowther," she called. Then she ran downstairs, pausing halfway to send the ayah to her grandmother's room.

With Mr. Crowther—known to almost all as Charlie—she walked to the back of the house. Here, on one side, were the cookhouses and the servants' quarters; on the other was a large coachhouse—unused, since Edwin could not afford to keep a carriage. It served instead as a repository for two motorbikes owned by the chummery members, and two bicycles belonging to

Annerley and her father. The floor was of beaten earth; the far wall was long and high and windowless. Against this, Charlie had taught Annerley tennis. She spent much of her time sending balls against the wall, aiming them at marked points above the line that Charlie had drawn at net height.

"Go on—let's see you hit number eight three times in succession," he said.

She was using her father's old tennis balls. His racket was too heavy for her, and she lacked strength and stamina, but she had learned timing and accuracy, and Charlie, watching, expressed his approval.

"Not bad, not bad. If you keep it up for another ten years, you'll be able to knock spots off your father."

He wheeled out one of the motorbikes, mounted and then paused.

"I was at a dance last night," he told her. "Who do you think I danced with?"

"I don't know."

"Guess."

"How can I guess?"

"It was one of your teachers."

She had only one teacher who was not a nun.

"Miss Highfield?"

"Yes. Pretty, isn't she?"

Annerley agreed that she was. Miss Highfield, recently out from England, had big brown eyes and a pink-and-white skin that was as yet untarnished by the Indian sun.

"I think I made quite a hit with her," Charlie boasted. "You can give her my love if you like."

He rode away. Annerley went up to her bathroom, stepped out of her perspiration-soaked clothes and threw some cans of cold water over herself. Then she dried, put on a much-darned *tussore* kimono and went to join her father in the porch room.

The green-lined split-bamboo blinds, let down each morning to keep out the heat, were now rolled up. There was very little furniture in the room—her father's long-sleeper, two cane-seated

31

armchairs, a round low stool, a table, a bookshelf. The floor was of polished wood. The other rooms had crazy-china floors, smooth, cool, colourful. The bathrooms had floors of red stone. They were equipped with large bathtubs and flushing lavatories, but although there were two taps over the bathtub and the basin, only cold water flowed from them. Hot water, needed only in cold weather, was heated in kerosene drums in the compound and carried up by the sweeper.

A cool breeze had begun to stir the leaves of the trees in the road. The bed of cannas, which lent the only touch of colour to the compound, was beginning to look less listless, as though grateful for the drop in temperature. In the well-tended garden of number 6 a *mali* was watering the flower beds. On the flat roof of number 3, the four Stanley boys, sons of the Court photographer, were putting up a tent in preparation for spending a night under canvas. From downstairs came the voice of Mr. Leeson, one of the chummery members, shouting for his shaving water.

Edwin's coaching was over for the day. He had bathed and changed into the soft white shirt, white drill trousers and black lightweight jacket that were his usual evening wear. He called to the bearer to bring iced tea; it was the drink that at this time of the evening he found most to his liking. With slices of lemon, he thought, it was more refreshing than mineral water, less potent than whisky.

Annerley dragged a chair to his side and sat down. The bearer brought the tea and asked her if she wanted anything; she shook her head and he went away, leaving her alone with her father.

Edwin Brooke was forty. He had come to India at the age of twenty-four, to join a newly opened educational establishment named Canning College, which was situated in Simla. Its well-advertised aim was to provide, for Indian boys between the ages of thirteen and seventeen, an education based on the traditions of the leading English public schools.

Enough money had been raised by its founder, Mr. Connolly

—who was also the headmaster—to buy and equip an imposing building which had once belonged to a maharajah. Classrooms had been furnished, cubicles installed, a spacious gymnasium set up. Assistant masters from England were engaged—Edwin among them. All that was needed was pupils.

Brochures were sent to discriminating parents. After a time, however, it was found that the recipients tended to look not at the school's amenities but at its astronomical fees. When the first entrants, all sons of the wealthy, had been installed, the demand for places fell rapidly and then ceased altogether. In vain was the standard of the entrance examination lowered to a level at which only the half-witted could fail to answer the questions; in vain were scholarships offered and fees lowered; there was no response. It became clear to everybody, including the owner, that the gap between income and outgoings would soon become unbridgeable.

When the college closed, Mr. Connolly dealt fairly with his staff. They were paid for the full two years of their contracts, and were given their fares back to England. Most of them returned there—but Edwin had other plans.

"Got any particular job in mind?" Mr. Connolly asked him.

"No."

"You're a first-class teacher. There are schools in Calcutta who'd be glad to take you on. I could get in touch with them, if you're interested."

"Thanks, no. I thought perhaps I might . . ."

"Might what?"

"I want to stay in this country."

"I'm not surprised. It gets into some people's blood. But you'll need a job."

"Yes. I thought I might go down to Calcutta and set up on my own. I'd like to coach boys—girls too—to enter English schools or universities."

"Well, why not? I've just said that you're a good teacher. You've got something that many teachers haven't got: a way of stimulating your pupils into working. They like you, so they

33

work for you. But you'll need a bit of capital to shore you up while you get onto your feet. I suppose you'll be able to find it?"

Edwin said that he would, but he knew that there would be very little money coming in to augment his small store. He had all his life been dependent on his mother. His father had had little money of his own; his mother had held the pursestrings. She had been generous when she approved of the object on which money was to be spent, but if she was opposed to a scheme, she refused to contribute. Edwin had, since the age of fourteen—when his father had left his mother—battled to win from her a regular allowance, however small. She had never given in. When, shortly before leaving for India, he refused to become engaged to the girl she had long had in mind for him, and chose a fiancée for himself, her rage led to a quarrel that he felt was final. Since leaving England, he had written several letters giving brief news of himself; she had sent no reply.

The move to Calcutta accomplished, Edwin took another bold step: He sent for his fiancée. He had to send her the fare; she was the only child of an impoverished country parson. They would have to live on his earnings and on the small income left to him by his father. His earnings were at present meager, but they gradually increased, and by the time—a year after his marriage—that his first child was expected, he and his wife felt that they could afford to move out of the small, airless flat they had occupied since their wedding.

Shortly before the baby's arrival, Edwin's father-in-law died. His widow, left almost penniless, was obliged to leave the parsonage in which she had lived for so long, and her letters showed that she was incapable of planning a new future for herself. Edwin spent most of his scant savings in bringing her out to Calcutta. It was to be a visit that would span the birth of her grandchild, and give her time to decide what she wanted to do.

The baby was born—a daughter. She was twelve days old when her mother died. Edwin was left a widower with an infant daughter, a grief-stricken mother-in-law and very little in the way of funds.

The first necessity was a change of residence. Settled in number 5 Seymour Street, his mother-in-law, Mrs. Devenish, showed the first signs of pulling herself together. Her sense of duty revived, and she attempted to get the small establishment into running order. She knew no Hindustani, and her only previous experience of servants had been an aged general maid, but she did her best to order meals, supervise the making of the baby's bottles and maintain quiet in the house while Edwin gave his lessons. There was no talk of her returning to England; she felt that she was needed here, and was only too willing to stay.

Relations between her and Edwin were smooth, but not intimate; not only his days, but also many of his evenings were given to his pupils, and he had from the first made it clear that he would not take part in the social life of the neighbourhood. His interests, outside his work, were first and foremost his daughter; next came his exercise—cycling, swimming, tennis and morning gallops on the Maidan with Annerley. To buy a horse would have been beyond his means, but the bony beast he rode had once belonged to an aged judge who on retirement had raffled it. There had been no need to buy ponies for Annerley; year by year, children going to school in England had to leave theirs behind. These had either been given to friends, or sold for trifling sums; thus, from an early age, Annerley had been in the fortunate position of always having a horse to ride. When she outgrew ponies, there were neighbours in Seymour Street who kept horses and welcomed help in exercising them.

Between Edwin and Annerley there was a close bond which had its roots in the similarity of their dispositions. He looked at her now as she sat beside him.

"Had a good day?" he inquired.

"Yes. I went to see Shareen. I didn't tell Granny. I wanted to tell Shareen we were going to Darjeeling and so I couldn't go with them to Musoorie."

"And she screamed, stamped her foot, tore her hair—or tore yours—and called me harsh names?"

"Sort of."

"Your other friend also displayed signs of displeasure when she came an hour ago and found that you were at the Prebdels."

"Moira came?"

"Yes."

"I didn't stop at her house because I thought they weren't back from the wedding. What did she want?"

"Help with her holiday essay."

"She always leaves it until the last day. Did she show it to you?"

"She did. I wasn't impressed."

"Didn't you help her with it?"

"I gave her a few pointers, yes. But she went away unappeased."

It was odd, he thought, that her two closest companions should be so headstrong. Or perhaps it was not odd. She led a quiet, perhaps a dull life; she probably got from Shareen Prebdel and Moira Fenwick the drama, the tempests, the fireworks lacking in her own existence.

Annerley was watching the lizards on the wall. There were five, and they frequently engaged in battle. One of them shed its tail and it fell with a soft plop onto the floor.

"Is Granny going out?" she asked. "I saw her dress coming with the pin-wallah."

"Or the pin-wallah coming with her dress. She's going out to dinner."

"Who with?"

"Canon Tremblett and his wife."

"That's a long way. Will she go in a *gharry*?"

"No. They're sending their carriage for her. Did you see Mr. Prebdel when you were at the house?"

There were several Mr. Prebdels—Amrit and his four sons—in the house, but the only Mr. Prebdel who concerned Annerley was Shareen's father. She saw him seldom, but when she did, his good looks, his urbanity and charm dazzled her and reduced her to speechlessness.

"No. He wasn't there," she answered.

36

Edwin was not surprised. That was a house of women. The men were usually elsewhere—at their offices, their clubs, their racing stables.

"When are they leaving for Musoorie?"

"I don't know, exactly. I was eight, wasn't I, when we went to Darjeeling before?"

"Just on. How much of it do you remember?"

"Everything. The night train first, and then the Toy Train from Siliguri. And feeling cold, and the hill coolies carrying heavy trunks with straps round their foreheads. And the hill ponies. What were those shortcuts called, when we used to nearly slip down the side of the hills?"

"*Pugdundies*. What else do you remember?"

"The train stopping at stations for meals, and we'd get out and go into the big dining room with all those long tables and white tablecloths, and lines of bearers waiting, and then all the passengers trying to get the soup down in a hurry, and get the bones out of the fish, and then the bell ringing to tell people it's time to go into the train again."

As she was speaking, a carriage entered the compound, circumnavigated the bed of cannas and came to a stop in the porch below. Mrs. Devenish came in to say good-night. She looked so regal that Edwin sketched an admiring bow.

"You look charming," he said.

"Yes, Granny, you do look nice," Annerley supplemented.

"Thank you, dear. Thank you, Edwin. Annerley, you'll do as the ayah tells you, won't you?"

"Yes, Granny."

"Good-night, Edwin. Don't keep her up late."

"I won't. Good-night, Alice."

He called her, at her request, by her name; she had not wished him to call her Mother, and he understood why. He sat listening to the sounds of her departure—her slow, careful footsteps on the stairs, her polite greeting to Mr. Leeson as she passed him in the hall, the jingle of harness, the crunch of wheels as the carriage drove away.

She had not, he thought, changed very much since her arrival in the country. Tall, thin, nearing sixty, she had retained her fresh complexion and smooth skin. She knew little more Hindustani than when she had arrived, and her talent for housekeeping was negligible, but she was not required to do more than order meals, inspect the cook's purchases when he returned from the bazaar each morning, and supervise the boiling of the milk and the drinking water. She was too mild to exert any authority, but she had a quiet dignity that made the servants respect her. There had been few changes of staff since the move to Seymour Street. Cooks had come and gone, but the bearer, Abdul, who had been in Edwin's employ since his arrival in India, was still the mainstay of the household, loyal to Edwin and slavishly devoted to Annerley.

Edwin had watched with interest and a touch of compassion his mother-in-law's initial efforts to become what she understood to be a memsahib. She had begun by having visiting cards printed and had left them in the little black boxes affixed to the gates of those in the social swim. Cards had been dropped in return into her own black box, but that was as far as the response went; no invitations followed, no pleasant associations were formed. Edwin's teaching schedule made it impossible for him to escort her to functions. Without a carriage, without dresses suitable for grand occasions, with a personality so colourless as to be dull, she had roused no interest in any of the European women living in the neighbourhood, most of whom were many years younger than herself. All she had to offer were good manners and a guileless disposition. Her circle of acquaintances now embraced a few Englishwomen and a number of Eurasians who, though they spoke of England as home, had little or no connection with that country. She went out to sewing parties—she was an excellent needlewoman—or to teas or at-homes. Now and then—as tonight—her position as the widow of a churchman brought an invitation to dine with one of the cathedral dignitaries.

The saving that she considered essential for thrifty living was made from the money that Edwin gave her for household expenses. For her own disbursements she used, as far as it would stretch, the minuscule income her husband had left her. Though it was not possible to save any of this, she had her own methods of keeping down her expenses. Her fear of having to pay dentists' fees led to her urging Edwin and Annerley to clean their teeth after every meal, as she did her own. To ward off doctors, she advocated a weekly dose of quinine and an occasional dose of fruit salts. Oculists were unnecessary: every two or three months there appeared a *babu*, tall, gaunt, dignified, in spotless white shirt and dhoti, followed by a coolie bearing a tin box containing spectacles with a variety of lenses. Seated on a chair on the verandah, Mrs. Devenish tried on pair after pair until she found lenses to suit her, and then paid the modest sum asked. Hair was washed weekly in carbolic soap, which also served as toothpaste. Cosmetics were never dreamed of.

The ayah came in to tell Annerley to get ready for her dinner. Edwin said that it would be served with his own. Freed from the last duty of the day, the ayah departed down the wooden stairway to her quarters below, to be seen no more until six o'clock the next morning, when she would take tea and fruit to Annerley and Mrs. Devenish.

A companionable silence reigned in the porch room. Annerley broke it with a question.

"If Granny hadn't wanted me to be called Annerley, what would you have called me?"

"By your mother's name—Rosalind. But your grandmother didn't want that."

"Because it would have reminded her too much?"

"Yes. So she asked if you could be called by your mother's other names—her full name was Rosalind Anna Lee Devenish. So you became Annerley."

"And you didn't mind?"

"No. I wished I'd thought of it myself."

They fell silent once more. Again it was Annerley who spoke. "What are you thinking about?"

39

"I wasn't exactly thinking. I was listening."

"Listening what to?"

"To the sounds I can hear when I close my eyes. Sounds I used to hear in my mother's house in Norfolk."

"Such as what?"

"The lap of water. The distant mooing of cows. The rooks high in the trees. The chimes of the church clock in the distance. The sound of hooves in the paddock."

He heard other sounds which he did not mention: his mother's voice, never raised but always cold, uttering contemptuous criticisms of himself or of his father. He did not speak of his mother, and Annerley never mentioned her; she seemed content with one grandmother.

"Listening," he said, "makes one want to go back—in a way."

She said nothing. She had closed her eyes and she was listening to sounds which were as familiar to her as the sounds he had recalled were familiar to her father. She could hear the fluting of the snake charmer as he passed the gate. In the distance was the rattle of the monkey man. She could hear what the neighbours were doing, since every window was open wide to the cool air. Mr. Leeson was shouting for dinner to be served. Ruby Fernandez, next door, was playing on a tinny piano her version of the latest dance tune. The Stanley boys, at number 3, were enacting, with bloodthirsty cries, an Afridi raid. The chummery gramophone began to play a wheezy version of "I'm All Alone." A Sikh fortune-teller was calling offers to read palms. From number 8 came the sound of a Mozart trio played by Monsieur and Madame Maule and their middle-aged daughter, Celeste. Overhead, the electric fan hummed. In the compound, servants chattered. These were the sounds that made up her life, and she had no desire to change them for the mooing of cows or the cawing of rooks. Some time soon, she knew, the distant cloud that threatened this happy existence would come closer. Some time soon, the decision would be made: school in England. She had accepted the fact that one day she would, like other English children, have to leave India. But everything in her rebelled at the prospect.

"Dreaming?" Edwin asked.

"No. Thinking. About school."

"The convent?"

"No. England. Do I have to go?"

"I'm afraid so. Eventually."

"Why?"

"Why?" He pondered. "It's hard to explain why. There are so many factors involved."

"What factors, specially?"

"Climate, for one. Things grow too fast out here. Health: you need a more bracing atmosphere. Education, English-style, with English girls. English games. English food."

"But you won't be there, you'll still be here, and you said there wasn't enough money for a boarding school, so then what?"

"There's a hope that I might be able to arrange for you to be a day girl. Will that make it any better?"

"It might. Why can't I stay here with you?"

"I'd like it just as much as you would. But it wouldn't do."

The last three words, spoken quietly but with a kind of unanswerable finality, told her that there was no appeal. She would have to go—and when she went, everything pleasant would come to an end. She would no longer be able to go barefoot in the house, or wear cool cotton frocks or sit on the steps of the porch watching a snake charmer, or drink the milk of young coconuts, which Abdul, with a flick of a knife, opened for her. It would be hard to leave Abdul behind. He had taught her how to ride her bicycle, how to wind *pugrees*; he had been friend, guardian, playmate since her infancy. He could tell stories far more exciting, far more dramatic than the tepid tales told by the ayah. There would be no Shareen, no sitting on the Prebdel verandah watching the aunts choose saris. There would be no mangoes, no papayas, no pomaloes or passionfruit or pomegranates, no long pods pulled off the tamarind tree near the cathedral. No Diwali festivals, with every building, great or humble, outlined in glimmering lights. No raids by monkeys on the bunches of bananas her grandmother hung on the verandah railing. There would be no monsoon, with the compound flooded to a depth of two feet and the Stanley boys floating over in zinc tubs to play warships. No more tennis with Mr. Crowther, no more rides with her father or with Moira, no launch trips up to the Botanical Gardens. No more roller skating in the big tent on the Maidan ...

There would, of course, be one or two compensating factors. For one thing, no topees. And no ayah trailing everlastingly behind. And in England, she could keep pets. She would be able to have a dog—she was not even allowed to stroke one here, because dogs were liable to get rabies, and anyone who had been in contact with them had to go up to the Pasteur Institute in Shillong and have syringes pushed into their stomachs. Dogs, cats, rabbits ...

She heard her father speaking.

"I know you don't want to go. But it won't be too bad."

He wondered, as he spoke, what he would do without her. She had been a good companion. She was sensitive, undemanding, sensible, ready to laugh with him. But he had to send her away. He had no great faith in the English system of education, but he believed in building on a firm national basis. One saw too many hybrids out here.

He thought, glancingly, of his mother. Her overriding aim in life had been to get her own way. All her good qualities—and he admitted that she had many—had been submerged, drowned in the desire to rule. And because both her husband and her son had possessed peace-loving natures, they had allowed her to rule, except in matters too near or too dear to their hearts. Her husband had at last left her and had died away from her, alone but content. Her son had left her. She lived alone in the beautiful old house, ruling her servants and her tenants, her large fortune destined to be divided among distant relations she considered more deserving than her son. Annerley would never know her, never see her or visit her. It was a pity, but he thought that the loss was his mother's.

They went to table. Annerley's appetite was small, and nobody had been able to persuade her to vary her limited menus. She sat down now to rice, *dhal* and a boiled egg, followed by banana fritters. As usual when they ate alone, she assumed the role of hostess.

"I'm so glad you were able to come, Mr. Brooke. How is your nice daughter?"

"She's very well, thank you. Thin, but healthy. This is delicious soup—won't you try some?"

"I don't like soup, thank you very much. Will you take water or whisky?"

"A small peg, if I may."

"And how is your mother-in-law?"

"She's very well."

It was extraordinary, he thought, how little impact his mother-in-law had made on the household. For this, he had never ceased to be grateful; he did not think that he could have endured a woman of strong personality constantly in his house. She had few definite views, and most of these were weakly sustained. She was not a good organizer, and became confused if there were too many things to deal with at once. But she was not a chatterer; she could sit, silent and absorbed, head bent over her needlework, without uttering a word. She was colourless, but she was restful.

Mrs. Devenish seldom approached Edwin on any but domestic matters, but there were times—as on the day following her visit to Canon and Mrs. Tremblett—when she felt impelled to step outside these limits. She asked him after lunch to give her ten minutes that he had free before the arrival of a pupil. Annerley was spending the day with Shareen Prebdel.

Edwin followed her into the porch room and waited until they were settled in their chairs.

"Something's worrying you," he said. "Is it money?"

"No. No, it isn't money, Edwin."

"Then?"

Her hands were clasped nervously on her lap. She spoke hesitatingly.

"You do know, Edwin, that I never interfere unless I feel it to be absolutely necessary?"

"Yes, I know. Has anything happened?"

"No, no. At least, nothing has happened, but . . . it's just that when I was coming in last night from the Trembletts, I saw something that . . . that made me a little uneasy."

He waited. Her feelings of uneasiness were usually aroused by some disturbance in the compound: the sweeper might be shouting at his wife, or the cook quarrelling with the chummery cook.

"When I was getting out of the Trembletts' carriage," she went on, "I saw someone, a kind of shadow, hiding behind one of the porch pillars. I thought it was probably one of the cook's children—it wasn't a tall figure, it was rather small. But as I came up the steps into the hall, I recognized one of the Fernandez girls—the eldest, the one called Ruby. As I got to the top of the stairs, I looked over the banister and I saw her slip into the chummery." She paused. "It was half past eleven. I don't like mentioning it, but I thought the matter over and felt that I must refer it to you."

The information was no surprise to Edwin. He was aware that since Charles Crowther had joined the chummery, there had been a marked change in the type of visitors entertained by the four members—and a sharp deterioration in the style of entertainment.

"You see, Edwin," the mild voice was going on, "things are a little different now. If you remember, you and I discussed long ago the wisdom of having young men as tenants. But we decided that those first ones were very nice young men—and besides that, it would be years before Annerley was old enough to have anything to do with them. But I haven't felt easy about her friendship with Mr. Crowther. Seeing that girl last night made me decide to talk to you about it."

Anger stirred in Edwin. He had every sympathy for healthy young men living in a city in which they met few Englishwomen and even fewer unmarried girls—but he knew that gossip about the chummery had begun to circulate, and he had been coming reluctantly to the conclusion that he would have to go downstairs and make some kind of protest. He had tried to convince himself that it was no business of his, but the fact was that they were his tenants, and if he did nothing to check the nocturnal visits of women, it would be said that he was condoning them.

He spoke in a calm tone.

"I'm glad you brought the matter up, Alice. I'd like to think it over."

"You don't think I'm making too much of it?"

"No, I don't. Certainly not."

"If I hadn't actually seen her going in, I might have . . . well, perhaps I wouldn't have . . ."

"You were quite right to mention it. Leave me to deal with it."

Deeply relieved to have passed on the responsibility, she took up her needlework. Edwin went to his pupil, putting the matter at the back of his mind. It was not going to be allowed to stay there for long.

School reopened on Monday.

The convent stood at the junction of two wide roads, so there was space enough for a reasonable volume of traffic to circulate, but there was not space enough for the innumerable vehicles that brought the pupils to school every morning and came back to take them home in the afternoon. There were private carriages, open and closed; there were gharries—first, second and even third class. There were landaus and there were box-like conveyances known as office-jauns. There were chariot-like carriages owned by rajahs, with two postillions in scarlet tunics.

In addition to the wheeled traffic, there were two converging streams of children on foot, followed by ayahs or bearers carrying their charges' satchels. There were flower-sellers seated on the ground against the church wall, and sweet-vendors and cake-vendors. A babel of voices rose in English, Hindi, French, German and Bengali. There were girls in western dress and girls in eastern dress, girls in expensive outfits and girls in reach-me-downs.

Annerley came early, on foot. With her, inevitably, came Edna Fernandez. Mrs. Fenwick had issued a permanent invitation for Annerley to come in the carriage with Moira, but the invitation had not been extended to Edna, and Annerley had preferred not to drive away and leave her behind.

There was no sign of Moira when they reached the convent. Annerley took her satchel from the ayah and handed over her hated topee.

"I'll carry your satchel, if you like," Edna offered.

"No, thank you. I wish you wouldn't always say that. I've told you and told you—people can carry their own things. You're not a servant, are you?"

"I'm bigger than you, and my books are lighter. I don't offer anyone else, only you."

This assumed humility was something that Annerley found it hard to put up with, but she knew that all three Fernandez sisters were impervious to snubs. Their mother was a widow—stout, ignorant and easygoing—who augmented her dressmaking earnings by playing the piano during performances at a cinema. Her head and shoulders visible to the audience, she watched the screen and provided appropriate music—slow waltzes for the love scenes, harsh chords for the entrance of the villain and stirring passages for the cowboy-Indian encounters. Her two elder daughters, Ruby and Myrtle, had attended the convent, but had left it when the nuns began to make inquiries about their out-of-school activities. Mrs. Fernandez made no objection to their leaving. She answered criticism of her daughters by stating that all young people should be encouraged to enjoy themselves, and if young men wanted to run after her girls, she saw no reason to discourage them. Her house was open to all—especially to young Englishmen who missed the home and family they had left behind. The Fernandez family welcomed them and sought to cheer them up. Charles Crowther was more welcome than anybody.

Annerley, when younger, had sometimes gone to the house at the earnest pleading of Edna, but she had found the assembled family too boisterous and too unruly to make the visits a pleasure, and had gradually ceased to go.

She and Edna waited now in the shade of the great archway that led to the convent. The assembly bell was ringing before

Moira appeared. The Fenwick carriage drew up; Moira stepped out, took her books from the syce and dismissed him.

"I thought I was late," she said. "How long have you been here?"

The question was addressed to Annerley. Edna might not have been present for all the notice Moira took of her.

"We've been here ages," Annerley answered.

"Then let's go in."

She was a year older than Annerley, taller by half a head—and already a beauty. Slender rather than thin, she had shoulder-length auburn hair kept in place by a ribbon. Her face was rather long and had an expression that in someone older could have been called world-weariness. Her brows were arched, giving her a look of faint surprise; her mouth drooped in what could be taken for contempt. When with grown-ups, she rarely spoke unless directly addressed; if she had to answer questions, she did so briefly and laconically.

She had from early childhood been the victim of selfish or irresponsible adults, and had developed for them a hatred to which she gave vent whenever opportunity offered. Her father, Francis Fenwick, was a senior member of the government. He and his wife both possessed substantial private incomes, and their house at the end of Seymour Street was the scene of a succession of receptions. Neither parent had ever shown any desire to assume the responsibilities of parenthood. Their son, Mark, and their daughter, Moira, had from birth been consigned to the care of those their parents considered trained and equipped to deal with children. Mark was now sixteen. He had been sent to England at the age of eight, and seemed to have settled down without giving any trouble. But Moira, sent at the age of nine to an expensive boarding school in Essex, had lost no time in getting herself expelled, and had also walked out of the next establishment in which she had been placed. Unable to find a third school willing to receive her, her parents had been obliged to bring her back to India with them. She had been sent to the convent, and had been on the point of removing herself when she became friendly with

Annerley Brooke and decided to stay. Her free time was spent as much as possible at number 5. Shareen Prebdel was her loathed rival for the possession of Annerley.

The nuns had begun by attempting to deal with what they called her insubordination, but they had run into serious difficulties. Her loaded replies to lectures were not crude, schoolgirlish answers that could be labelled impertinence and punished; they were delivered in a soft, well-bred and polite voice, so that it was some moments before their import became clear to her hearers. Her Madonna-like appearance acted as a trap to those who did not know her. The nuns had endeavoured to exercise patience. Mother Baptist had given her a holy picture to hang on her bedroom wall; Moira had jumped on it. Her father's position and his conciliatory contributions to convent charities deterred the nuns from expelling her; they ended by praying for her and walking warily round the minefield.

Mrs. Devenish tried to like her, if only because most people found it impossible. Moira in her turn seemed to make some attempt, when in conversation with her, to conceal the fact that she considered all old people better off dead. Edwin saw little of her, but his feeling was that with parents like hers, she could have turned out even less cooperative.

The lunch hour at school—tiffin time—was passed in the long, stone-floored corridor, open-sided and more like a cloister, that connected two of the convent buildings. After the Angelus, when the whole school gathered to say, or not to say, the responses, the boarders went to their dining room and the rest of the school streamed out into the corridor, one side of which had been prepared with long trestle tables on which bearers had spread cloths and were waiting to serve lunch to their young mistresses. The food, carried in aluminum tiffin-carriers, was almost the same all down the line: mince fried in potato, curry and rice and dhal, followed by fruit. Conversation was not possible while the clash of crockery continued; only when the bearers had cleared the tables and departed could girls gather in groups to exchange news.

Moira had little to say about the rajah's wedding that she and her parents had attended. The only thing she had liked was the procession of elephants.

"How's your friend, Shareen?" she inquired. "I suppose you've been seeing her?"

"Yes."

"Rather you than me. Did you ever know her brother?"

"No. He went to school in England before I knew her."

"I got a letter from my brother. He said he'd talked to an Indian boy at his school, and found he came from Calcutta. His name was Prebdel. Chandra Prebdel. Now they're friends. I would have thought Shareen Prebdel would have told you."

"She would have, if she'd known. When did you get the letter?"

"Yesterday's mail."

Edna, standing by, made no contribution to the conversation. In Moira's presence she was invariably silent. Later, though, walking home with Annerley, she became talkative.

"If you like," she offered, "I'll tell you a secret."

"No. I hate secrets. A secret is only for one person," Annerley objected. "If two people know it, it stops being a secret."

"It's a secret if you don't tell. It's about Ruby."

"I know. You told me. A man gave her a silver watch."

"This is a different secret. She's going to get engaged."

"What's secret about getting engaged? She'll go round telling everybody."

"No, she won't. He said she mustn't."

"Who said?"

"The other person. I can't tell you who. But you know him. He lives close to you."

Annerley could think of nobody living close to her who could possibly have become engaged to Ruby Fernandez. The eldest Stanley boy might have been socially suitable, but he was only fourteen. Her interest evaporated.

She parted from Edna at her gate and was in the compound

when she heard her name. Turning, she found to her surprise that Shareen was walking towards her.

"I called you when you passed the Fenwicks' house," she complained. "You didn't stop."

"I didn't hear you."

"I was in our carriage. My mother went to talk to Mrs. Fenwick, but I didn't go because that Moira was with her. My mother came to talk about my brother."

"Moira told me he'd made friends with her brother."

"I don't see anything for my mother to get excited for over that, but when she read my brother's letter, she came to see Mrs. Fenwick and ask if Mark Fenwick could spend the summer holidays with my brother. With my uncle, I mean. My uncle lives in London, but he's got another house in . . . I forget what the place is called, but it's got a river near it, and so the boys can sail. Chandra's mad about sailing."

Annerley walked back to number 10 with her. When she returned to her own house, she found waiting in the compound a chaprassi she recognized. He was almost as smartly turned out as the Prebdels' messenger. He had come from Park Place and had brought a letter for Edwin. Annerley, going upstairs, found her father penning a brief note in reply. He handed it to the bearer and resumed his interrupted tea.

"Invitation," he told Annerley. "Or rather, a summons from Lady Parrish to appear for a drink this evening."

"Will you go?"

"Of course. Didn't I say it was a summons?"

When he walked over later, he was wearing a suit—Lady Parrish did not encourage informality. As he went, he noted the marked increase in heat since the week before. He paused at the gate of number 6 to exchange a word with his neighbour, Mr. Ronson, who was lying at ease on his verandah, his wife on a wicker chair beside him. On his retirement some years before, they had gone to England to start a poultry farm, but they had soon returned, and were now dividing their time between Calcutta and Ootacamund and between golf and gin. Selfish, self-sufficient, they seldom invited anyone to their house. Their sole contribution to neighbourliness was to organize occasional river picnics on their commodious launch. They were both lean, both sun-scorched, and each year grew more leathery.

"Evening," he called to Edwin. "Off to a party?"

"No. How's the golf?"

"So-so. How about you and Annerley coming to the Botanical Gardens on Sunday? Launch leaving Outram Ghat seven o'clock sharp, drinks on the house."

"We'd like it; thanks."

"Bring the old lady," suggested Mrs. Ronson.

Edwin said that he would ask her, and walked on. Number 7 was brightly lit, and from the busy movements of servants it looked as though visitors were expected. Mr. and Mrs. Cole-Hardy, unlike the Ronsons, always had a house full of guests. He was a quiet, unassuming man who worked in the Port Trust. She was small, wiry, hard-drinking and hard-riding. She kept four horses and two syces and was in great demand for organizing *gymkhanas*. She was fifty, the daughter of a wealthy sporting parson in Leicestershire. Each September she departed for England, to arrive in time for the cubbing season. She returned at the end of the hunting season, her conversation solely of masks and brushes, runs and kills, and largely incomprehensible to her listeners. She paid occasional visits to Mrs. Devenish, explaining that the possession of a clerical husband and a clerical father made a bond between them. Mrs. Devenish bore the visits meekly and counted stitches when the details of hunts became too gory.

Edwin would have liked to walk past the house unseen, but Mrs. Cole-Hardy had sharp eyes.

"Hey!" she called. "Come back, Edwin, you."

He came back.

"Been wanting to see you," she told him. "There's a rumour going round that you're off to Darjeeling—right?"

"Quite right."

"Good. It's time you all had a change. What I'd like you to do is bring me down a supply of tea. I'll tell you what kind and I'll give you the money when I've worked out my sums. Will you do it?"

"Of course."

"Thanks. How about coming in for a peg?"

"Sorry, I can't."

"I suppose you're on your way to pay a call on Lady High-and-Mighty?" She sniffed contemptuously. "Did you read that bit in the home papers about her brother being a member of the Cabinet?"

"Yes."

"She'll treat us more like dirt than she did before. You're privileged, I dunno why. Oh, by the way, tell Annerley I've got a nice new mare she can try out if she wants to."

"Thanks."

Number 8 was in darkness. This, he remembered, was a concert night at the Conservatoire, and Monsieur and Madame Maule, who for twenty years had been teachers of the violin and whose daughter taught the piano, would not have dreamed of missing it. Annerley had for a time been a violin pupil and for over a year had struggled to get past the first painful stages. At length, Monsieur Maule told Edwin that perhaps she had better take up the piano instead. Mademoiselle Maule had not waited a year; before it was half over, she had informed Annerley that God had given her many gifts, but music-making was not among them. The piano lessons ceased.

Number 9 was closed and shuttered, its tenants being on leave in England. The Fenwicks' house was dimly lit; they were seldom at home in the evenings.

He reached the corner and turned into Park Place. When he reached Lady Parrish's house, he was shown into a beautiful drawing room that had so little of India that it reminded him of his mother's house in Norfolk. Lady Parrish entered a few minutes later, tall, elegant, tightly corseted, in a long, elaborate gown, her hair in a smooth knot behind but frizzed round her forehead.

She was in her middle forties and still handsome, though her skin showed the effects of twenty years of Indian sun. She was the widow of a prominent member of the Political Department who had died as the result of a riding accident. He had left his widow a substantial income and, on his death, it was generally expected that she would sell her furniture, take train for Bombay and embark on the next homegoing mail boat. Instead, she had decided to stay in India and turn her spacious house into a residential club—the membership, it was well understood, to be of the most exclusive kind.

The venture had been from the start successful. The impeccable service she provided for the members was matched by the perfection of her own household arrangements. She left mundane duties to a competent Swiss housekeeper, lived in her own suite of rooms and rarely met the other occupants of the house.

She saw a good deal of Edwin, however. On their first meeting, which had been in this room before he moved to Seymour Street, she had claimed a distant cousinship. She had visited his house in Norfolk and knew that he and his mother had quarrelled. She deplored his refusal to humble himself and seek forgiveness.

She seated herself on the sofa. A Goanese butler poured whisky for her and for Edwin, served the drinks on a small silver tray and withdrew. Edwin spoke when the door had closed.

"You decided on a Goanese, after all?"

"Yes. I know you'd rather I employed one of those tall, princely *khitmagars*, but I preferred Joseph, if for no better reason than his perfect command of English. How is your mother-in-law?"

He smiled. After an initial invitation extended from a sense of duty, she had behaved as though Mrs. Devenish did not exist. She had explained to Edwin that entertaining her might seem to his mother to be taking sides—accepting the fact of his marriage to Mrs. Devenish's daughter. He took this, as he took many of Lady Parrish's pronouncements, without comment.

She put her glass on a table at her elbow and spoke in a businesslike tone.

"This isn't a friendly occasion, Edwin. I've brought you here to lecture you."

"Oh?" He took a low chair facing her. "What about?"

"About your daughter. About Annerley. She went back to that convent today, didn't she?"

"Yes."

"Do you know that several people gave children's parties during the holidays, and she wasn't invited to a single one?"

"I didn't hear about the parties. I don't think she did, either."

"That's just the point, Edwin, and you know it. Don't hedge. I told you, when you took that dreadful flat, that you were ruining your chances of getting into the right set—the set you belong to. What's worse, spoiling your daughter's chances of meeting the kind of children she should meet. Who, for God's sake, are her friends?"

"Well, they—"

"Don't tell me. Let me tell you. Chief among them, of course, is the Prebdel child. If you want her to have Indian friends, then of course the Prebdels are all right."

"You've taken a load off my mind."

"Don't try to be funny. Moira Fenwick is all right, too—socially, that is—though I've told you before that I don't consider her a suitable friend for Annerley. It's no secret that she ran away from two schools in England and that every governess here refused to take her on. Her parents talk of taking her to England when they go on leave. I hope they can find a school to her liking." She picked up her glass, drank, and resumed. "The people I'm really talking about are those dreadful Fernandezes. I've talked to you about them before, not once, but many times. I've warned you—and now I'm going to tell you something that you won't be able to ignore. It concerns the oldest daughter—the one they call Ruby."

Where, Edwin wondered, did she pick up her gossip? She would not listen to her servants, of that much he was certain. Her friends kept her informed on social and political matters, but who among them would be interested in the Fernandez family?

"Perhaps you know," she went on, "what I'm going to say."

"My mother-in-law said that she had seen Ruby Fernandez going into the chummery one night last week. Is that—"

"I'm surprised she noticed the incident, and even more surprised that she brought it to your notice. I would have said that she would have followed her usual practice of looking the other way."

"You don't know her very well, Barbara. She—"

56

"She's the kind of person who's called harmless, but I don't think she's harmless at all. She shares with you the responsibility of bringing up Annerley, but she exercises no authority whatsoever. She should be firm, someone a child can lean on, turn to. And is she?"

"No. But she's kind, she's good, and loves Annerley. That's enough for me."

"It isn't enough for your daughter. Edwin, you've got to send Annerley home. She's thirteen; she should have gone years ago. Do you know what people are beginning to say?"

"I'll have a guess: that I'm keeping her for selfish reasons."

"And aren't you?"

He hesitated. He had asked the question of himself, many times, and had never succeeded in finding an answer. Who knew what lay behind his reluctance to send his daughter away? How many of his reasons for keeping her here were valid? How many sprang from his fear of losing her?

He left his chair and turned towards a side table.

"Can I pour myself another drink?" he asked.

For answer, she drained her glass and held it out to him. He refilled it and his own.

"I suppose you're going to tell me," she said as he went back to his chair, "that she's very happy here?"

"You don't see much of Annerley," he said slowly. "You can't really judge—"

"All I need to know is that she's at an age when English children are better away from this country. On healthy grounds alone—you have to admit that she's far, far too thin."

"She's fit enough. I think it's fair to say that I would have sent her home earlier if there had been any relations there who could have kept an eye on her or given her a happy home."

"Isn't it even fairer to say that you found boarding school fees beyond your means? And isn't that a reason for trying to get back onto good terms with your mother? Why should all her money be spent on others? She could pay the fees and Annerley could spend her holidays in that lovely house of yours."

"No." He spoke with decision. "No on both counts."

"Pride?"

"No, not pride. My mother has her good qualities, but bringing up young children. . . . No. For what it's worth, Annerley has been happy out here. She—"

"Happy? I don't doubt it. Children out here are happy because they have things their own way. They're spoiled by the servants, they're followed round by those awful ayahs . . . why go on? What they need is the English climate, a good English school—and some discipline. They have to learn to conform to English ways."

"Annerley will learn. All I want to do is see to it that the transition is gradual. I know, and you know, how miserable some of the children from here have been after being left behind in England."

"The longer you leave it, the more miserable Annerley is going to be. Why don't you face it? She's got to go." She paused. "And so, if I may advise you, has Charles Crowther."

He leaned back in his chair and gave a sigh.

"Yes," he agreed. "Something's got to be done. He's becoming a problem."

"He's been too stupid to heed warnings. I was very kind to him when he first came out, as you know. I invited him here, I invited nice English girls to meet him when I could find any; I asked him to tennis parties and I would have gone on being kind to him if he hadn't begun to run after Eurasian girls. He's been seen several times taking them to places in which—how shall I put it?—they're not welcome. I spoke to him like a mother and tried to explain that the firms out here didn't want their young men to get involved with the kind of friends he was picking up. He didn't take the slightest notice. It won't be long—please keep this to yourself; I know I can trust your discretion—before he'll find himself on his way home—for good."

Edwin said nothing.

"It's sad," she went on, "to think of a nice boy like that spoiling his chances in such a reckless way. To become entangled

58

with that Fernandez family is really going too far. Though to be quite honest," she added, with the touch of fairness she sometimes injected unexpectedly into her more waspish remarks, "those three girls are exceptionally pretty. I can't say I've had a close view of the mother, but she couldn't have contributed anything to their looks. They must have had a very handsome father. But what neighbours, Edwin! Another reason for getting Annerley away."

She paused, and he looked at her with a smile.

"Lecture over?" he inquired.

"Yes. I don't suppose you've listened to a word. And I don't suppose you'll act on anything I've said."

"On the contrary," he told her, "I've listened so carefully that I've decided to send Annerley to school in England."

She frowned.

"It's nothing to joke about. This is a serious—"

"I'm not joking. I'm perfectly serious. If you hadn't asked me to come round this evening, I would have come on my own account. I wanted to talk to you—about Annerley's school."

"You mean you want me to recommend one?"

"No. I've already chosen one."

She gave a skeptical lift of her eyebrows.

"Really? Which fortunate establishment is to be given the honour of—"

"I'll tell you in a moment. First of all, tell me something: Did you ever meet at my mother's house, or did you ever hear her speak of, a man named Stephen Holt?"

"Yes. He was your great-uncle, wasn't he?"

"No. My mother always called him Uncle Stephen, but in fact he was no relation. He took no notice of me throughout my life, or his life; he only saw me twice, and didn't seem to be unduly impressed. I thought he had died long ago, but he only died four months ago. He left me a house."

"His house?"

"Not his big house in Chester, no. This is a cottage he built down in Devonshire, because his wife wanted a warmer place to spend the summers, and wanted it near the sea. I don't think they used it much. They invited me down there once. Now it s mine."

"Did he leave you any money with it?"

"No. When I got the telegram telling me I'd inherited the cottage, I said nothing to my mother-in-law or to Annerley, because a plan had sprung to my mind. I knew the cottage was near Exeter—on the sea side of it. On the other side, about fourteen miles inland from Exeter, there was a school. A very good school."

"You must mean Mardon Abbey."

"Yes, I do."

"You're not going to tell me that you want to send Annerley there?"

"Yes."

"Surprise on surprise. For a man who said he couldn't afford school fees, you've hit on a—"

"As a day girl. I've always had the school in mind. It was my mother's old school. I know a good deal about it and about its standards. Annerley's extremely intelligent. I wouldn't mind seeing her go on to Girton or—"

"She hasn't got to Mardon Abbey yet," Lady Parrish said dryly. "I take it you can afford the day-girl fees?"

"Yes."

"Then where is she going to live? Or . . . is this where Stephen Holt's cottage comes in?"

"Yes. I want to go to England with Annerley and my mother-in-law and settle them into the cottage."

"Leaving Annerley to be looked after by Mrs. Devenish?"

"Yes. She could run the house."

"With servants, I trust."

"Not resident servants. There wouldn't be room for them."

"Would she agree?"

He hesitated.

"She'd agree, but how willingly, I don't know. She's been

happy out here. But with Annerley in England, there'd be nothing to keep her in India."

"So it's all settled?"

"No."

"Then what is the hitch?"

"There's a waiting list. A long one, I wondered if you would . . . I'd like to ask your help."

She sat looking at him in amazement.

"Ah. At last, at last, at last you're going to ask me to pull some strings. When I offered to do so over that splendid teaching job you could have had in—"

"We're talking about Annerley."

"I'm talking about you. For a man with a splendid brain like yours, you're . . . I don't want to sound harsh, so I'll choose a mild word: unrealistic. I suppose I could say idealistic, but you're too practical to be called that. To take just one example: your pupils. You coach young men and women whose parents could make you rich, and what do you do? You collect reasonable fees, and only the fees, and you get them through their vital examinations but you refuse the small tokens of gratitude they offer you."

"I wouldn't refuse them if they were small."

"To the people with the kind of wealth those people have, they're very small indeed. Some of your pupils are the sons or daughters of influential Indians who could—"

"—make me rich. But to return to Annerley—will you help me?"

"You want me to pull strings?"

"No. Not exactly."

"Then?"

"As I said, there will undoubtedly be a waiting list. If I write and make my application for Annerley to be entered, even as a day girl, I shall get a courteous reply telling me that there are no vacancies for the next three, four, six, eight years. You agree with that?"

"I most certainly do. So?"

"So I shall feel that there's nothing more to be done. As a schoolmaster, I shall feel bound to respect—"

"Do you call yourself a schoolmaster?"

"I was a schoolmaster once. And—"

"And having got this courteous reply, you would choose a school to which no girls were waiting to go. Is that what you're saying?"

"No. I'm trying to tell you that after thinking it over, I felt that the best thing would be for me to make the application, but that, with your help, it might be accompanied by, or bolstered up by, some letters from people whose interest would count for something. Do you follow me?"

Her eyes opened wide. She looked at him as though she had never seen him before.

"Whatever made me think," she asked slowly, "that you were . . . what did I call you?"

"Unrealistic. Idealistic. And before that, egotistic."

"I take back the unrealistic. Let me see if I understand you. You write an application, and some extremely important people of my acquaintance underwrite it. Is that it?"

"By and large. All I need is someone who can vouch for the quality or the value of the work I do here. I've been lucky—I've had some brilliant pupils through my hands, and some of them are doing well at English universities. That ought to put my daughter into a category offering a hope that she'll do well in the school, and on that hope they might accept her. I could, of course, send them a list of my successful pupils, but nothing will carry as much weight as some independent recommendations. Will you help me?"

"I'll see that someone does."

"Thank you."

"Does Annerley know you've chosen a school?"

"Neither she nor her grandmother know anything about the cottage or the school—yet. I don't want to tell them until things are fixed. I'm relying on your discretion, as you told me you relied on mine."

"I hear you're going up to Darjeeling."

"After getting the news about the house, I felt we could afford a change. And it'll fill in time while this matter's being straightened out." He rose to take his leave. "When do you leave for Simla?"

She had never spent a hot weather on the plains. Her usual escape was to Europe, but sometimes she accepted invitations to stay with friends in one or another of the hill stations. She told him now that she was not, after all, going to Simla; she had been offered the use of a houseboat in Kashmir.

"Belonging to the Sinclairs—you know them, they live next door to the Fenwicks. They decided to stay in England until October, so they can't use the houseboat they rented, and offered it to me. It's quite large—there would have been room on it for you and Annerley."

She walked with him onto the balcony, and then down the steps and into the garden—a shortcut back to Seymour Street.

"I wish I could understand," she said, "how a man like you—still young, good-looking—can live the life of a . . . a Benedict? No, not a Benedict. A Benedict succumbs, doesn't he?"

"In the end, yes."

"I hope you won't. But if you do, I shall expect to be the first person you tell."

He smiled.

"I'll remember," he promised.

He walked home slowly, her last words in his mind. He knew that he did not want to form permanent ties with any woman. His marriage, though brief, had been passionate and infinitely satisfying; the happiness that he had experienced during that year he did not expect to feel again. When desire occasionally stirred in him, he could not bring himself to seek alleviation. Memory was still strong—strong enough to hold him faithful to that last ideal.

For some days after his meeting with Lady Parrish, Edwin saw nothing of Charles Crowther. When he did, he could detect nothing in his demeanour that indicated the smallest anxiety about his future. Nor did James Leeson, employed by the same firm as Charles, and his closest friend, show any sign of uneasiness. Their comings and goings—to their office, to pay visits, to play tennis or golf—continued without interruption.

Then one evening, when Edwin returned from seeing one of his pupils off to England, James Leeson came into the hall and stopped him.

"Could you spare me ten minutes, Mr. Brooke?" he asked.

"Of course. Here, or upstairs?"

"Down here, if you don't mind. I'm alone. Come in."

They went into the large, plainly furnished drawing room. There were some armchairs with shabby covers, walls hung with rather moth-eaten hunting trophies, and an assortment of books, photograph albums, newspapers, magazines and writing pads put into as much order as the bearers could contrive in the absence of the owners. The windows were shuttered against the heat.

"I know you like tea with ice," James said, placing a chair for Edwin. "Can I order some?"

Edwin accepted gratefully. Before sitting down, he took off his jacket and hung it on the back of the chair.

"Well?" he asked.

James shouted over the verandah to order not one but two teas. Then he turned to face Edwin.

"Not well, Mr. Brooke," he said soberly. "Trouble. Have you heard any rumours?"

"If you're talking about Charlie, yes. Any truth in them?"

"He's been sacked." He paused to steady his voice. "He's been given the boot. They warned him. They warned him more than once, but all he did was laugh. Not exactly in their faces, but still, they knew he wasn't going to toe the line. I talked to him. All his friends talked to him, but it wasn't a damned bit of good. I pointed out that getting a good job in a good firm and then chucking it up was madness. It *is* a good firm. I've only been in it for a couple of years, but that's long enough to know that the prospects are bright. But Charlie wouldn't see it."

"Is his dismissal quite definite?"

"Yes."

"How has he taken it?"

James hesitated.

"I don't know, exactly. I don't know whether he believed they'd really throw him out."

The bearer brought in the tea, went to the icebox and returned with a jugful of ice and a sliced lemon. When he had put out glasses and gone out, James spoke again.

"The truth is, Mr. Brooke, Charlie should never have come out here. He doesn't understand the country. He wouldn't listen to the old hands. His view was that he wasn't doing anything he hadn't been doing when he was in the head office in London, and that in any case, his private life was his own affair. But as you know, things are different out here. When he met the Fernandez girls . . ."

He stopped, poured tea and carried a glass to Edwin.

"What you probably think," he said, "is that we've been entertaining girls like the Fernandez sisters. That isn't quite true. They were Charlie's friends. Charlie asked them here because he thought we'd enjoy their company. And we did, in a way. If he'd stopped at that—if he'd just invited them here, he might have kept his job. But he seemed to go out of his way to put the boss's back up."

"Do you know if he has any plans?"

"No. His mother lives in London. She's a widow, but I don't think she's short of money. And he's got two sisters—they're not married; they're both hospital nurses. He hasn't any brothers. What he'll need, when he gets home, is someone to give him a leg up, and as far as I can make out, there's nobody but an uncle who's given him up as hopeless and won't have anything more to do with him."

"Do you think he'll try and get another job out here?"

"No." James spoke with certainty. "He's got it in for most people out here. He doesn't like what he calls their hypocrisy. He says the whole bunch of the English out here are snobs incarnate. He hated, from the moment he came out, what he called the caste system—not the Indian one, but the political and mercantile and social one. He didn't see, couldn't or wouldn't see why he had to kowtow to dull, stupid women just because they happened to be the wives of some high official or other. From the first day he arrived, from the first contacts he made, he began to put people's backs up. I've made myself hoarse trying to talk some sense into him—it was no good. And he's going, and I'm sorry. Some people . . . isn't there a saying about being one's own worst enemy? That applies to Charlie. We're going to miss him."

There was silence for a time.

"I'll miss him, too," Edwin confessed. "He's a nice young fellow. When is his notice up?"

"He's only been given a week. The firm's been generous—he's got his pay for the next six months, his passage home and a lump sum to pay his debts. It won't cover them all."

"Does he owe much?"

"Not more than the rest of us. Tailors, mostly—his suits, his hot-weather kit, that kind of thing. He paid his share of the rent."

"Perhaps if he came out again in a couple of years, when he'd grown up a bit . . ."

James shook his head.

"He'll never change, Mr. Brooke. With a lot of fellows, this kind of . . . of devilry, I suppose you could call it, is a kind of top layer. Even if it goes deeper, you feel it's something they'll outgrow. But Charlie's set. He's got definite ideas on most subjects; they're not the ideas most of us can agree with, but he's had them since he began to think, and right or wrong, he'll stick to them. I'm glad I've talked to you. I know you like him, and I wanted you to know the news before it got round. The firm's being very decent about trying to keep it quiet until he's out of the country."

There seemed nothing more to say. Edwin, feeling more depressed than he had for some time, made his way upstairs. He told his mother-in-law the news, but asked her to say nothing to Annerley.

"She'll find out," Mrs. Devenish prophesied. "They seem to hear everything in school. But of course I'll say nothing."

"She'll miss him. He's been very kind to her."

It was not long before the matter became generally known. Charles made no attempt at concealment—but he hesitated to tell Annerley that he was going. They had been good friends. Besides giving her tennis lessons, he had frequently made his way upstairs to fill in an idle hour by playing card games.

She was not at home when he went upstairs to see Edwin two days after James and Edwin had had their talk. Mrs. Devenish told him that Edwin was with a pupil, but would soon be free. He sat down to wait, and she resumed her sewing, looking up from time to time as if about to speak, but failing to find anything to say. She longed to sympathize, but did not know how to frame the sentences. Charles did not help her. When Edwin came into the room, she murmured something inarticulate and went quietly to her bedroom.

"She's upset," Edwin explained. "We all are. I've put off telling Annerley because she'll take it hard." He pushed forward a chair. "Sit down, Charlie. Any plans for the future?"

"I'm not much of a planner, Mr. Brooke." Charlie sat down, accepted a beer and waited until the bearer had poured it out. "I'm not worried about the future. I'll go home, people will click their tongues for a time and then things'll go on as they were going before I came out here."

"Will you miss India?"

"The country, yes. Its people, yes. The people who are currently ruling it, no. If I hadn't been sacked, Mr. Brooke—and this is the truth—I couldn't have stuck much more of it. Right from the start, I found all the protocol irritating. Big fish in a small pool, that's what most of them are. So-called memsahibs coming out from Brixton or Balham to lord it over the natives. *Burra* sahibs looking down their whisky-reddened noses at anybody who wasn't eligible for the Bengal Club. The whole thing was . . . well, take the reason I've been chucked out. What did I do? I got friendly with a bunch of Eurasian girls. Why? Because I liked them, and because there weren't any white-skinned damsels available to play with. Play is the right word. I like girls. I had an unlimited number of them to have fun with in England. I like their company. I like looking at them, I like taking them out and watching them enjoying themselves. I knew there was some prejudice out here, but I didn't realize for some time how deep it went. It was only when my boss had me up and talked to me like a Dutch uncle that I knew what I was up against."

"You see, Charlie—"

"Don't think I'm trying to alter the rules. I'm not. All I believed, all I still believe is that you can mix on a level that doesn't do any harm. I had no more idea of marrying any of these girls than I had of getting tied up with any of those girls in England. No man could get married on a salary the size of mine —especially when you've subtracted what I've spent out of it. To go on river trips, to go dancing, to enjoy a social evening in one of their homes—where was the harm?"

"Charlie, I've nothing against—"

"I know you haven't. The thing I like most of all about you, Mr. Brooke, is the way you've brought up Annerley—natural, happy and absolutely free from prejudice. How long can you keep her like that? Even those friends of hers, that Indian child and Moira What's-her-name—even they make a wide circle round the Fernandez girls, and other girls like them. Why? Afraid of catching spots? A hundred years ago, high-ranking English used to marry equally grand Indians."

"That's true. But in the past fifty years—"

"I know. The boss explained it all. Undesirable mixture, best not to get involved, et cetera and et cetera and so on. Well, before I go, I'd like to put on record that I've had a lot of nice clean fun with Eurasian girls, and a lot of kindness from their mothers. I made it crystal-clear from the start that I wasn't husband material. I even told them how much I had in the bank, to underline the point."

"Yes, Charlie, but—"

"And shall I tell you something else, Mr. Brooke? The whole business boils down to a simple matter of geography. You know, and I know that most of these girls, transferred to a provincial town in England, would be regarded merely as attractive brunettes. I know at least three families near my home in which the mother, once no different from Ruby or Myrtle Fernandez, settled down with an English husband and made a good wife and mother, with nobody aware of or worrying about any so-called mixture. As I said, geography. And speaking of geography reminds me to ask you if you'd mind if I didn't tell you which route I'm going to travel home by. I don't want anybody to know. People will ask, and they may ask you; if I don't tell you, you won't be able to tell them. The reason is that I hate being seen off. I don't want to slink away, don't think that—I don't feel I've done anything wrong—but I'd rather cut out the farewell scenes."

."You haven't much choice of route," Edwin pointed out. "Mail boat from Bombay or City Line from here."

"City Line. It's cheaper than mail. I don't suppose I'll ever come East again. Or I might—"

He stopped. Annerley's footsteps could be heard in the hall. She came up the stairs, came to a halt at the entrance to the porch room, saw her father and took a step forward. She was breathing quickly.

"The bearer says—"

She saw Charles and stopped abruptly. Then she turned to him and spoke in an unsteady voice.

"Is it true, Mr. Crowther?"

Charles had risen and was putting his chair back into its place beside the long-sleever. He answered calmly, without hesitation.

"If you mean have I got the sack—yes, it's quite true, Annerley. My boss says I've been a naughty boy, but he used stronger language. It's very short-sighted of the firm to let me go, because I would have made a good burra sahib, in time."

"I don't understand. What did you *do*?"

Edwin knew that she was close to tears, and knew also that she would not allow them to fall. She had never cried easily.

"What I did," Charles said, "was take no notice when I was told how to behave. In England, I had an office life and a private life. Out here, offices keep what they call a benevolent eye on their employees out of working hours. I don't like it. I don't like it at all. I told them so, out loud, and they said go away and stay away. So I'm going."

"When?"

"In a week. Which doesn't leave me much time, so I think it would be a good idea if you put on your tennis shoes and come down and have a last lesson in backhand drives. Hurry, before the light goes."

She turned without a word and went into her bedroom. Awaiting her return, Charles stood staring blindly out of the windows. Edwin said nothing.

The tennis session did not begin well; the wall seemed out of focus. At last Annerley shook the tears angrily out of her eyes and began to put into her shots all the grief she was feeling. There had been other nice men at the chummery, but there had never been anybody like Charlie. If she had had a brother, she would have liked him to be just like him; kind, laughing, patient, never-failing fun. She knew, in a confused way, why he was being sent away; snatches of talk, half heard, recurred to her and gave her some clues. But reasons were not important; all that mattered was that he was going.

When they finished the practice, they walked slowly back to the house.

"If I wrote letters to you, would you answer them?" she asked him.

"I'll write to you from every port the good ship *City of Trieste* stops at. And I'll send you postcards. And when you come to England, which you're bound to do, you must come and meet my mother and my sisters, and if you're in school, we'll go and visit you and see if they're treating you properly, and complain if they're not. I'll take you packets of biscuits—I used to take biscuits to bed with me and eat them after lights-out."

They were in the hall. She turned towards the stairs.

"Good-bye, in case I don't see you again," she said.

"Never, never say good-bye," Charles enjoined her. "Only say good-bye if you don't like someone; then you can say it and sound as though you really mean it. But if you like someone, you don't say it at all because you're going to make sure that you meet them again soon. So no farewells."

Without farewells, she went slowly up the stairs and into her room.

She did not see him again before he left, nor did she speak of him to her father or her grandmother. She kept her eyes averted from the green doors as she went through the hall. Looking through the newspaper that her father had left on the table in the porch room, she read that the *City of Trieste* would leave Kidderpore Docks on Thursday. Three days.

Moira brought up the subject next day at school. Edna Fernandez was absent—down with fever, her mother had called to Annerley.

"I suppose you've heard about Mr. Crowther?" Moira asked.

"Yes."

"Why didn't you tell me? I only heard last night, when my father and mother were talking about it. They said he deserved to get the sack."

Annerley turned on her.

"Oh really? And what do they think they know about it?"

"Well"—Moira sounded taken aback—"they know him. They met him. They liked him at first, but then they didn't because he had such funny friends."

"Such as who?" Annerley asked coldly.

Moira stared at her.

"What's the matter with you? Are you upset or something?"

"No. I just wanted to know who the funny friends were."

"You know as well as I do. Those Fernandez girls, chiefly. Or maybe only Ruby. She went about with him a lot, so I bet she's sorry he's going. Why hasn't Edna come to school today?"

"She's got fever."

"Why did you get angry just now?"

But Annerley's brief, uncharacteristic spurt of anger had died down. It was no use trying to defend Charlie, she decided. People would say things about him, against him, and it would be no use getting into arguments. He had gone, or almost gone; perhaps she would see him one day in England, perhaps not. By the time she got there, he would probably have forgotten her—or she might have forgotten him.

She was reminded of him on the following evening, when the ayah came to tell her that Ruby Fernandez was at the gate and wanted to speak to her.

"Tell her to come upstairs," Annerley said.

"She say no, she won't come; you go." The ayah, who was practicing English in the hope of one day being taken to England with the family, assembled a few more words. "She say not long time keeping you."

Annerley went down to the compound. The swift transition from day to night had taken place; the lights were on in the chummery. By the lamps on the gateposts she could discern Ruby Fernandez' thin figure.

"Why don't you come upstairs?" she asked as she reached her.

"No." The voice sounded unfamiliar. "No. I don't want anyone to hear."

"Why not?"

"Because . . ." She put out a hand and took Annerley's arm in a painful grasp. "Annerley, I want you to help me."

Annerley waited, not unduly disturbed by the hoarse urgency of Ruby's tone. The Fernandez girls frequently injected drama into everyday events. She thought she had never seen Ruby looking so pretty—her narrow, almond-shaped eyes were shining under the light, the contours of her face were softened.

"I want to ask you something, Annerley. Perhaps you don't know. I asked your father—he didn't know, but perhaps he was only saying that to put me off. I asked Charlie's bearer—he wouldn't tell me anything. I looked on the luggage, but they didn't have any labels yet. But I must know! Annerley, I must find out!"

"Must find out what?"

"What ship Charlie's going away on. Or what train. I must know."

"Why don't you ask him?"

"I did. He wouldn't tell me. He hates being seen off, he said, so he didn't tell anyone on purpose. He wouldn't listen to me when I begged him."

"If he said he didn't want anybody to know, why do you go round asking people?"

"Because I've got a special reason. A reason I didn't want to tell him. A reason I haven't told anybody, not even my mother. I think your father knows what ship or what train, and I think you know, too. Please tell me, Annerley. *Please!* If he asked you not to say, I swear I'll never tell that you told me. I swear. I swear on Our Lady. Please tell me, Annerley."

There was silence. A coolie passed on the road, pushing a handcart. The ayah came down to the hall and peered into the darkness to see what was delaying Annerley. Two gharries rolled past, the second one carrying Mr. and Mrs. Stanley.

Ruby came nearer, and Annerley took a step backwards.

"Listen, Annerley. I didn't want to tell you, but if I don't, you won't believe how important it is for me to know." She paused and then spoke in a whisper. "Annerley, I'm going to have a baby. *His* baby..."

Complete disbelief leapt into Annerley's mind—an instant reaction based on her knowledge of all three Fernandez girls. They were all liars, and now Ruby was lying because she thought that making a claim so wild would get her what she wanted. Yes, it was a lie. It was what her father called shock tactics—to force the information out of Annerley. And shock it certainly was, for although she heard enough at school and from the servants to have picked up some of the facts of life, no girl she had ever known or had ever heard of had ever been accused of anything more than flirting.

"I don't believe it," she said. "If it was true, you would have told him."

"I couldn't, not at first. I didn't want to. Then when I knew for certain that he was going away to England, I said to myself that I ought to tell him. And now his bearer pretends there aren't any luggage labels, and your father won't tell me anything —and Charlie isn't here. The bearer says he's gone to stay with a friend until he goes away. What I think, Annerley, is that he's running away. He must have guessed what I want to tell him, and he's run away."

The idea of Charles Crowther running away from Ruby Fernandez was almost as ludicrous, Annerley thought, as her claim to be having his baby. But the two assertions added up to a picture of Charlie that she did not care to face. She wanted him to be able to defend himself. She did not want him to go away leaving Ruby to spread lies about him. And the only way she

74

could think of to give him the chance of stopping the lies was to
let Ruby see him, and let him deal with Ruby.

"You know how he's going, don't you?" Ruby flung at her.

"Yes, I do."

"And you're not going to tell me." Ruby burst into sobs. "I
knew before I came here that you wouldn't. You're going to keep
it to yourself, and you'll tell everybody at school what I've told
you, and—"

"The *City of Trieste*," said Annerley.

Without another word she turned and went into the house.
She had no doubt that she had been right in giving the information. She had not been asked by anybody to withhold it; she had
betrayed no confidence. Anything, anything, she thought, was
better than letting Charlie go away without the chance to silence
Ruby Fernandez.

Edwin, in the porch room, looked up from his book as she
entered.

"The eldest Miss Fernandez?" he inquired.

"Yes."

"Did she want anything special?"

"Yes. She wanted to know what ship Mr. Crowther was going
on."

"But you don't know which ship, do you?"

"Yes, I do."

"Did you tell her?

"Yes," Annerley said. "I told her."

Edna Fernandez was away from school for six weeks. She spent these in hospital with typhoid fever, and it was reported that during this time her life had been in danger.

But it was not these facts that accounted for the interest which met her on her return to the convent. She had been eagerly awaited because she was the only person who could supply the answer to the puzzle that had kept everybody guessing during her absence: Where was her sister Ruby?

Ruby had vanished. Her disappearance coincided with the departure to London of the *City of Trieste*, and Mrs. Fernandez had informed inquirers that her eldest daughter had married Mr. Charles Crowther and gone with him to England. But there were several factors which kept the gossips from swallowing this information. Mr. Crowther had been seen to leave unaccompanied. The date and place of his departure having been revealed at the last moment by a member of the ship's company, he had been seen off at the docks by his friend Mr. Leeson, two other members of his firm, the entire band of the revue currently playing at the Empire Theatre, by Mr. Edwin Brooke and his daughter Annerley, and by several unidentified young ladies of dusky complexion. Ruby Fernandez had not been among them.

Furthermore postcards sent by Mr. Crowther from the first port of call—Madras—mentioned the weather and stressed his enjoyment of the journey, but said nothing whatever about a wife. This, Mrs. Fernandez explained, was because he was keeping the marriage a secret until he had presented Ruby to his family.

It was not possible to apply to Myrtle for information; she had gone to stay with cousins at Ranchi. Those anxious for further details had therefore had to await Edna's return from hospital.

She came out two inches taller than she had been before her illness. Her head, which had been shaved, was now covered with a mass of tight, dark curls. She attached herself to Annerley and Moira with newly acquired poise and confidence, and corroborated her mother's story: Ruby had married Mr. Crowther shortly before the ship sailed. She had kept to her cabin—first class—until the ship reached Colombo. The other passengers had not been informed of the marriage. The newlyweds would live in London, close to Mr. Crowther's uncle, who was a bishop.

Nobody believed a word of this, but unfortunately, nobody was in a position to disprove it.

Edwin had his own view of what had taken place, but did not impart it to Annerley. And for reasons she found it difficult to define, she had said nothing to him or to anyone of Ruby's claim to have been pregnant. She had not believed her; now she wondered if perhaps she had been speaking the truth.

No enlightenment came from Charles on the further stages of the voyage. He wrote from Port Said to both Edwin and James Leeson, and sent a postcard to Annerley, but he made no mention of Ruby.

"All the same, Mr. Brooke, I'll swear she went with him," James said to Edwin over drinks one evening in the chummery. "We didn't see her, but I'll lay any money she was on board. I've been making some inquiries—a girl booked a last-minute passage, but the name wasn't Fernandez. That doesn't mean anything.

All I'd like to know is whether Charlie knew anything about it beforehand. What do you think?"

"I'd say he didn't."

"So would I. Hiding her away doesn't sound like Charlie. But she couldn't have stayed hidden all the journey—so why not tell us?"

"Did the girl book a first or a second-class passage?"

"Second."

"Then he mightn't have seen her. There wouldn't have been any mixing."

"Charlie would have done his own mixing. But perhaps her idea was to keep away from him until the ship got to Tilbury. Then she'd go to him and . . . what's that expression?"

"Throw herself on his protection?"

"That's it. And you know Charlie. He'd take her on. He'd marry her." He leaned back in his chair and sighed. "Lord, what a mess!"

Edwin made no comment. He was thinking of Charles's views on the geographical limits of colour prejudice. Ruby in Seymour Street. . .Ruby in England, where untravelled or uninformed or undiscriminating people would take her at her own valuation. . . .

"Any comment from Annerley?" James asked. "She must have heard all the rumours."

"She hasn't said anything."

"Like you, Mr. Brooke. You don't say much, either. All of us down here have always wished we had your knack of keeping out of unprofitable arguments. Charlie thought a lot of you. That's why I can't understand his saying nothing, to you or to me. He and I were good friends; I don't like being left to sift the evidence from the sheaf of lies that Mrs. Fernandez has been shelling out. Do you suppose she knows any more than the rest of us?"

"Yes. Ruby had to tell her, or she might have gone to the police to report a missing daughter."

"What's your view, Mr. Brooke? Did she go with him?"

"I don't think she went *with* him. I think she went after him.

But I don't know how she managed to get the money to pay for her passage."

"That wouldn't have been hard. Mrs. Fernandez has a brother in Ranchi who sends her money. It's supposed to pay the rent, but most of it went on the girls' backs. Yes, that's the answer: Mrs. Fernandez gave her the fare. Why not? She knew Charlie pretty well; she'd know that whether he married Ruby or not, he'd see she was all right. If she hadn't given Ruby the money, why would she be going round looking so pleased with herself? The only one of the family who seems to have kept out of it is the middle girl, Myrtle. She always had more sense than the other two."

Mrs. Devenish's views were usually tepid, but in the affair of Ruby Fernandez she surprised Edwin by coming down strongly on the girl's side.

"I'm not going to blame her if she went with him, Edwin. Who knows what promises he may not have made her? I only hope that things will turn out well for her in the end. But I'm sorry there has been all this fuss. Somehow, I think that it has made Annerley change her opinion of him."

The gossip died down. At the convent, the Fernandez affair was forgotten in the excitement of preparing a concert to welcome Mother Superior, who was coming on a visit from the parent house in Ireland. At the chummery, it was decided not to fill Charles's vacant room. And from Ranchi came Myrtle Fernandez wearing an engagement ring; she was to marry her cousin Victor Millet, a young doctor who had done his medical training in Edinburgh and who had already been offered a partnership in a practice in Calcutta.

The Prebdels left for Musoorie. The Fenwicks were as usual going up to Simla, but shortly before they were due to leave, Mrs. Fenwick came round to see Edwin. She came in the middle of the morning—a time, she told him, when she hoped to catch him between pupils.

Mrs. Devenish was out visiting Madame Maule. The bearer led the visitor to the porch room. She looked very pretty, Edwin thought as he entered; her white muslin dress with its long, full skirt and its fichu collar gave her a misleadingly unsophisticated look. She was hatless; her lace-edged sunshade had protected her along the few hundred yards of shady street. It was some time since he had seen her, but he was struck once again by the freshness of her appearance. Nobody could say, in her case, that loose living led to listless looks.

He had never liked her. He liked her husband even less. Rumour had long been busy with regard to the two, but they conducted their affairs—if affairs there were—with a discretion that foiled any observers less well informed than Lady Parrish.

"I'm disturbing you, Mr. Brooke. I hoped you might be having a morning break. Don't you allow yourself one?"

"Not as a rule. Won't you sit down? Can I offer you anything to drink?"

"No, thank you." She gave him the sweet, half-shy smile that he described to himself as a smirk. "I'll try not to keep you long. The fact is"—another shy smile—"I've come to ask you a favour."

He waited. She did not look like a suppliant. Under the beguiling manner he sensed confidence.

"Before I ask it," she continued, "I must clear up one or two things you may not know about Moira. Do you know, for example, that she ran away from two perfectly good schools in England?"

"Yes, I'd heard that."

"My husband hasn't many relations, and Moira's aunts and uncles on his side are rather old. But my own two sisters are perfectly charming, and they offered to look after her during school holidays—but she proved too much of a handful. So you see where that leaves me?"

"I see that it's a difficult situation, yes."

"Her brother, Mark, has never given us the slightest trouble, during school terms or during holidays. But Moira . . ." She sighed. "It's only since she met your daughter, Mr. Brooke, that she has given any sign of settling down."

"They're good friends," Edwin agreed.

"Annerley—you must believe this—is the only real friend Moira has ever bothered to make in her life. Which is why I'm going to ask you this favour."

Once more, Edwin waited. His habit of not filling in pauses disconcerted many people, but Mrs. Fenwick gave no sign of uneasiness.

"My husband and I were going to take Moira up to Simla with us," she went on. "But we heard yesterday that my husband has been invited to go up to Gilgit, to join an expedition—and of course he's terribly keen to go. He's talking of nothing but the roof of the world, and untrodden snows, and he's particularly anxious not to refuse, because he says this might be the only chance he'll ever get of seeing . . . I think he said the source of the Indus, but I don't know much about geography, I'm afraid. It's a form of holiday I would never consider for myself. I have every respect for those women who go off with their husbands on *shikari*, or exploring, but for myself . . . no."

"You'll wait for him in Simla?"

"No. The Goodsons—you know them, of course? He's in the Finance Department—have invited me to join them on their houseboat in Srinagar. And here is the favour, Mr. Brooke: there isn't room for Moira. Would it be possible for you to take her up to Darjeeling with you? I realize it's asking a great deal, but I'm certain she would refuse to go anywhere with anyone else. If Mrs. Devenish would kindly agree to keep an eye on two girls instead of one. . . . Naturally, we shall expect you to treat this as a business arrangement. Moira must be a paying guest. And I would send her ayah with her."

"Does Moira know about this?"

"She . . . well, yes. I told her about the invitation to Kashmir this morning, and said that I was going to ask you . . ."

He sat considering the matter. He knew, and knew that she knew, that he could hardly refuse. Her husband's plans were made; her own plans were made; Moira was being farmed out. In a case of this kind, he thought, the best thing to do was to put

81

aside his opinion of the parents and think only of the child. He liked her; Annerley would be glad to have her; the rest was unimportant.

Some of her complacency had seeped away. She spoke with genuine uneasiness.

"You're our only hope, Mr. Brooke. I could, of course, give up the trip to Kashmir, but that would leave Moira feeling that she had been the cause of my losing. . . . You see what I mean?"

"I would like to talk it over with my mother-in-law before giving a definite answer," he said. "As far as I'm concerned, Moira will be welcome to join us."

"Of course you must talk to your mother-in-law." A shade of patronage had crept into her tone. "I hope she won't raise any objections."

"And please, no ayah. How long do you plan to be away?"

"Until October—but my husband will be back before you return, and he will look after Moira." She held out a hand. "Thank you so much. I do hope we can come to some arrangement."

He accompanied her down the stairs. She opened her sunshade and glanced at him from under it—an arch look which he felt was entirely wasted on him.

He opened the gate.

"You shouldn't be out in this heat."

"I know. But I had to come and see you. I'm longing to get to a cooler place. You won't be long in deciding, will you?"

"I hope you enjoy Kashmir. You'll probably be running into Lady Parrish."

She shook her head.

"No. She's going to Simla."

"No. Kashmir. Like you, she changed her plans."

Her gentle manner vanished.

"I know she's a friend of yours," she said coldly, "but she's no friend of mine. I hope you're mistaken about her going to Kashmir. It would certainly ruin my holiday. Good-bye."

He watched her out of sight, graceful under the sunshade;

then he went up to his waiting pupil. Seating himself to resume the interrupted lesson, he wondered how much thought Mr. Fenwick was giving to matters of state. Walking the untrodden snows was all very well, but he might walk them with less enjoyment, Edwin thought, if he could hear some of the political views expressed by his Indian pupils and their parents. More and more he felt that their attitudes were becoming militant.

He was aware that his social detachment, his disinclination to mix with his own countrymen or to join clubs from which Indians were excluded, had given the Indians who met him the feeling that he stood in the middle of the road, in a position to see both sides of what he was beginning to think of as the Indian problem. They were beginning to talk to him more openly of their views—and after listening to them, he found it more and more difficult to understand or tolerate the uninformed, casual attitude of the majority of the Englishmen he met, who seemed to him to fall into two groups: those who were convinced that the British would rule India indefinitely, and those who conceded that self-rule might come, but not in the foreseeable future.

When the lesson was over, he discussed Mrs. Fenwick's proposal with Mrs. Devenish. As he expected, she expressed pity for Moira's plight and said that she would be glad to look after her in Darjeeling.

He found that Annerley knew nothing of the Fenwicks' change of plan.

"Didn't Moira say anything to you at school?" he asked.

"No. I'll go and ask her why she didn't."

She walked to number 10. Moira was having tea in the garden. She was lying on a rug in a shady corner of the lawn, beside her a low table on which were toast and cakes and cool drinks. She ordered a fresh supply for Annerley.

"Why didn't you tell me about your mother asking if you could come with us to Darjeeling?" Annerley inquired.

Moira, rolling over to make room on the rug, gave a lazy shrug.

"What was there to say? She was going to ask your father. I just waited to see what he'd say, that's all."

"Well, he said yes, only you're not to bring your ayah. Ours isn't going, either."

The bearer poured out two glasses of cloudy, pale-green lime-and-barley, dropped in extra ice and handed them on a small tray to the two girls.

"I'm glad you're coming with us," Annerley observed between sips. "Lucky your father was asked to go to Gilgit."

"It wasn't luck. I made it happen."

"How could you make—"

"Ever since you said you were going to Darjeeling, I wanted to go too. But I knew you wouldn't ask me because we were going to Simla."

"What's wrong with Simla? You would have liked it."

"No, I wouldn't. My father and mother would have been out going to parties all the time, and I would have been stuck with the ayah. I would have been in the way. I'm always in the way. They don't say so out loud, but I know what they're thinking. So what I did was—"

"Was what?"

"Colonel Falcon came to have dinner, and after dinner they all sat on the verandah and I heard them talking, and I heard my father tell Colonel Falcon how much he would have liked to join his expedition that was going to Gilgit. Colonel Falcon said he hadn't asked him because he knew he was going to Simla, and they said what a pity it was. The next morning, I said to my mother that my father wanted to go to Gilgit and she said was I sure Colonel Falcon would take him, and I said yes, and she said in that case, she'd tell the Goodsons she'd go with them to their houseboat in Kashmir, but if she did that, where would I go? And I said she should go and ask your father to take me with you to Darjeeling. So now it's all settled."

This explanation at an end, she drained her glass. This was not the first time she had told Annerley about her methods of threading her way through the selfishness of her parents. Anybody else, she knew, would have been shocked, would have accused her of cheating—but not Annerley. She uttered no criticism; she might sometimes say that she didn't like the methods —but she would never tell anyone else.

When she spoke again, it was on another subject.

"My mother's going to be friendly with Mrs. Prebdel now."

"Because of your brother being friends with Chandra Prebdel?"

"Yes. She'll expect me to be nice to your friend Shareen, but I won't." She got up and refilled the glasses. "Do you know if Edna Fernandez is going to be in the play at school?"

"Yes."

"Then I'll tell them I won't be in it."

"Have they asked you?"

"No, but they will. They think I look like a Christian martyr. Why do they always choose plays about martyrs? I'm sick of Romans and Christians, and I'm sick of those finales when the martyrs go to heaven and the mosquito net comes down in front of them and they look holy and everyone in the audience claps."

"Not everybody. Some people cry. Don't you remember when Edna was St. Philomena?"

"Yes. Sickening. I hate all school plays. They were always having them in that first school I went to in England."

"Shakespeare, I suppose?"

"No, worse. We did *The Blue Bird*—in French. And bits from what they called the classics. I don't know how I stuck it for as long as I did. But the second school was worse. The uniform!" She shuddered. "Blouses and skirts and ties like men, and on Sundays awful dresses with tight sleeves and sort of sailor collars. And hard straw hats like men, only with huge brims like cartwheels. I used to feel ashamed, walking to church. And the food! Wait till you go to school in England, and then you'll find out. You're not allowed to leave it on your plate, you have to eat it. That's why I left. Then my aunts said they wouldn't have me anymore, and my parents had to bring me back to India with them, and a good thing too. You know what I've decided?"

"No. What?"

"My mother keeps saying to my father that you ought to go away to school soon. When you do, I'm going to try to go to the same school. Then even if it's awful, we'll both be there and it won't be as bad as being alone."

There was silence. The bearer cleared away the food and the drinks. Mrs. Fenwick came out of the house, got into the waiting carriage and was driven away.

"Have you heard," Moira asked, "that Mr. Crowther was very keen on Miss Highfield?"

"I only know he met her at a dance once. He told me."

"Well, he wanted to take her out, but my mother told her she shouldn't go with him because of his bad reputation."

Annerley sat up, her cheeks flushing with anger.

"She shouldn't have said that. She had no business to—"

"Don't worry. I don't suppose he cared much. Now she's going out with Mr. Leeson. Did you know that?"

"No, I didn't."

And how anyone, she added to herself, could like Mr. Leeson better than Charles Crowther, was something she would never understand.

News of Charles came the following week in letters to Edwin and to James Leeson. He did not write to Annerley. Edwin took his letter downstairs, and met James on his way up.

"You've had a letter, too?" he asked Edwin.

"Yes."

"Come downstairs—I'm alone."

"How much," Edwin asked when he was seated in the chummery drawing room, "did he tell you?"

"Here, read it," James said.

They exchanged letters and there was silence as they read them.

"So you see," said James at last, "He married her. We thought Mrs. Fernandez was lying, but she wasn't."

"Let's say she was anticipating," suggested Edwin. "I like his phrase for his mother's departure from London—'riding out the storm.' Though it isn't quite what he means. I think she merely removed herself to see how his two sisters were going to react."

"Imagine moving in with them!" James said in wonder. "Can you see Ruby as a housewife, sharing a kitchen with her two sisters-in-law?"

"I don't think Ruby will spend much time in the kitchen."

"They *like* her, Mr. Brooke. Did you note what he said, not in your letter but in mine? They *like* her. They think she's got Italian blood, and they like her pretty Welsh accent." He paused. "A chap like Charlie," he went on thoughtfully, "hadn't much chance against a clan like the Fernandez, had he? Mother provided the passage money, Ruby got on board, kept out of sight until the ship was well on its way, and then came out with a fairly strong conviction that he'd marry her. Which he did."

"Which he did," repeated Edwin. "We'll have to write and wish them luck. I'm glad Charles has found a job."

"Will he earn much as a games teacher in a prep school?"

"It's a living. And it's a good school. With a wife and two sisters to keep an eye on him in the home, and strenuous exercise to keep him busy at the school, he might yet become a reformed character." Edwin rose. "There are rumours," he added, "that this matrimonial bug has spread."

James turned an unbecoming brick colour.

"Oh, you've heard? We've been trying to keep it quiet, because she's only been out a few months. She's not on contract at the convent, or anything like that, but she didn't want the nuns to feel she was leaving them. Not that she is. We might get engaged, but we won't be able to get married for . . . well, for years. Two, at any rate."

"Well, congratulations, anyway."

"Thanks, Mr. Brooke. By the way, I hope you have a good holiday in Darjeeling. I suppose you'll tell Annerley about Charles?"

"Yes."

"Didn't he even write her a postcard?"

"No. I suppose this wasn't the kind of news he felt he could put on a postcard."

He told Annerley and Mrs. Devenish the news when he went upstairs. Mrs. Devenish's comment was that, taking everything into consideration, Mr. Crowther had acted rightly in marrying Ruby. Annerley did not comment.

The time came for preparations to be made for the move to Darjeeling. Trunks were brought out and aired, bedrolls opened; Mrs. Devenish packed bottles of disinfectant to use in the train lavatory. The hot weather was at its peak, but nobody complained; they would soon be in the mountains.

The holiday began badly. In the night train, Mrs. Devenish, Annerley and Moira shared a second-class compartment in which, to their relief, the remaining two berths remained vacant. Farther down the train, Edwin was in a two-berth compartment with a portly priest. The heat was almost unendurable, and even Mrs. Devenish's stock of disinfectant was insufficient to quell the odours from their lavatory.

At Siliguri, in the foothills, breakfast was interrupted by a search for a missing bedroll. The day-long journey from Siliguri up to Darjeeling in the puffing little Toy Train, higher and higher, round hairpin bends and over precipitous gorges, with scenery becoming more spectacular every moment, enchanted Edwin and the two girls, but the jerking and shaking made Mrs. Devenish feel sick and dislodged her hat, causing it to slip frequently over her eyes. She bore these discomforts without complaining; they were temporary annoyances and would end when the journey ended. But she had forebodings that the presence of Moira in the party would make difficulties. Annerley was amenable enough, but if Mrs. Devenish found it necessary to give orders or impose prohibitions, she knew Moira would go her own way, doing exactly as she pleased. And after weeks in her company, she feared that Annerley would pick up, would catch, some of that casual, insolent manner, that complete ignoring of authority.

When they reached Darjeeling, they disembarked and stood with their luggage around them while Edwin studied the sketch map that Mr. Lobo had drawn to show the position of the house to which they were bound. It was called Jupiter Lodge, and had been rented from Mr. Lobo, whose ancient mother had owned it and in which she had lived until her death. Having ascertained its position, Edwin summoned three Tibetan coolies, saw the luggage safely suspended from straps round their foreheads, installed Mrs. Devenish in a rickshaw and proceeded on foot with Annerley and Moira.

The house—very small, and built of wood—occupied an isolated spur which jutted from the mountainside some two hundred feet below the town. Its design was simple—a long, glass-enclosed verandah divided into two, drawing room and dining room, overlooking a view which could claim to be one of the most spectacular in the world. The snow-clad Himalayan peaks seemed to hang in the sky, dwarfing the mountains at their feet. Kinchenjunga towered above them, second only to Mount Everest in height and majesty.

Behind the verandah were three small bedrooms and three smaller bathrooms. The view from these was not of majestic snows. The lodge was built almost against the mountainside, so that no sun and little light penetrated. Vast boulders overhung the windows, looking as though at any moment they might be dislodged and come crashing down to obliterate the building.

A short distance away was a hut, seemingly the home of several Tibetan families. Diminutive hillmen, beautiful, powerful-looking women in long, heavy skirts and woolen blouses with bead necklaces, earrings and nose rings; red-cheeked, incredibly tough children ranging in age from three to thirteen, came out and disappeared again into the dark interior. The cookhouse was a lean-to; Mrs. Devenish, attempting to enter in order to assess its equipment, found it full of cooks or cooks' assistants, and retreated.

But housekeeping proved to be no problem. Food appeared when called for. Coolies toiled up the hillside with large, conical baskets full of fresh vegetables. Bread was prepared in the dark, odourous cookhouse and baked in an adjacent bread oven. Goat's milk came in buckets, and with it enormous slabs of butter and small, smelly cheeses. Meat was provided by the innumerable scrawny, undersized chickens that scratched between the lodge and the huts. Water came cascading down the mountain-side—straight off the snows of Everest, Edwin said when he cupped some in his hands. And service was offered by all the inmates of the hut indiscriminately. The dining table was laid in a new and strange way. The youngest children brought eggs in small, grime-encrusted hands. Washing was seized, pounded under the cascade and hung between poles to dry beside the fluttering prayer flags. From dawn to dusk the picturesque Tibetan figures busied themselves to make the tenants comfortable, and everywhere could be seen the wide, happy, inextinguishable grin of the hill dwellers.

Freed from domestic duties, the visitors could spend their days amusing themselves. Mrs. Devenish sent for a rickshaw and was carried up the precarious path to the town, where she made a timid entry into the club, hoping to be accepted as a temporary member. The first person she encountered was Mrs. Tremblett, who, on a holiday without her husband and feeling lost and lonely, greeted her with unexpected but gratifying warmth, and took her under her wing. Thereafter, they spent their days together.

Edwin, Annerley and Moira clambered up the almost perpendicular mountainside to the town's stables, where they hired three small, sturdy, inexhaustible hill ponies. These, with their syces, appeared each morning at the lodge; the syces were dismissed and Edwin led the girls on exploratory expeditions. Carrying packets of sandwiches which grew larger and larger as the days went by and their appetites increased, they spent their days riding up and down hair-raising slopes, lying on sunny mountainsides, or splashing in icy waterfalls. They found their way to the shops, but not to those frequented by Mrs. Devenish; they wound their way down to the bazaar, to the stalls kept by grinning Tibetan men and incredibly old, gnarled, wrinkled Tibetan women. They bought sweets floating in syrup, hot from huge black frying pans. They bought delicate silver bracelets and long bead necklaces and strangely shaped cowbells. They paid a courtesy visit to the convent, encountering on the way a priest who was going to hear confessions, astride a shaggy pony, his cassock tucked up to free his legs which—like Edwin's—dangled almost to the ground. Each evening they returned to the lodge, guided by the smoke from the fires on which their bath water was being heated. Then they gathered round the dinner table, clad in layers of the warmest clothing they had brought with them, shivering in the bitter cold that filled the rooms when the sun had gone down. They piled coats on their beds; even these were not enough to keep them warm, and they ended by using the rugs from the floors. It was a strange, wild life, a holiday such as none of them had ever had before, and which they hoped would never come to an end.

But end it did. Edwin paid the wages that were due, supplementing them with *largesse* dropped into countless horny, outstretched hands. Their progress to the station, past the bazaar, was slow, hampered by frequent stops to say good-bye to their newly made friends. They took their places in the Toy Train and waved until the last smiling face was out of sight.

They returned to Calcutta to encounter violent monsoon storms, with high winds and rain that poured down and turned streets into streams. Horses splashed by, drawing gharries whose wheels were hub-deep in water. Insects came in swarms, mosquitoes found their way into mosquito nets. Cool breezes alternated with warm, moist ones; the clothes in the wardrobes were damp to the touch, and white whiskers grew overnight on shoes. In every sunny interval, however brief, sheets and garments were carried outside and spread over enormous baskets overturned on glowing charcoal braziers. The Stanley boys came floating perilously in their tubs and offered to do battle, but this year Annerley was not disposed to play. Her budding bosom could be hidden under dresses, but in wet, clinging garments it was embarrassingly visible.

Moira's ayah, and the other Fenwick servants were at number 10, awaiting the return of Mr. Fenwick. The only sign he gave was a telegram addressed to Edwin stating that he had been held up and would return as soon as possible. Moira spent most of her time with Annerley.

It was another three weeks before news was brought to Edwin that Fenwick Sahib had returned. A few hours later, Mr. Fenwick appeared at number 5. The bearer led him upstairs; he accepted a drink, thanked Edwin and Mrs. Devenish for their kindness in looking after his daughter, apologized for the long delay in returning—owing, he assured them, to circumstances quite out of his control—and then said he must go home and deal with his accumulated mail.

On his departure, Mrs. Devenish voiced an uncharacteristically strong opinion.

"I don't like him, Edwin."

"Nor do I. He's a cold fish, I think."

"And what a father! Not one word—did you notice?—not a word about Moira, not a question as to how she got on while he was away—nothing."

"Perhaps he feels more than he shows."

"Can you wonder Moira is so . . . so. . . . What help could she ever have got from him, or from either of her parents? I feel very sorry for her."

"So do I."

He spoke absently; there was something besides Moira and her father on his mind. The latest mail had brought the information that Annerley had been accepted by Mardon Abbey. Now came the necessity of breaking the news to her and to her grandmother.

After thinking it over, he decided that the best time to choose would be on Sunday evening, after the evening service at the cathedral. Their attendance at this, though not regular, was frequent. Mrs. Devenish went because she wanted to keep up what she called her worship. Edwin and Annerley went because they enjoyed listening to the organ and the choir, and liked joining in the hymns. They usually walked there and back, sometimes making a detour to cross the Maidan and go through Fort William to watch the shipping along the Strand.

But on the following Sunday, Edwin led the way home by the most direct route, and then took the unusual step of pouring himself out a peg of whisky before dinner. After the meal, the three returned to the porch room; only then did he announce that he had something to tell them.

"Something good, or something bad?" Annerley asked.

"Neither." He was lying back on his long-sleever; they were seated on either side of him, Mrs. Devenish in her usual chair, Annerley on the low stool. "Neither good nor bad. It concerns your future."

"Oh."

There was a pause. Edwin was aware that the atmosphere had become tense. Mrs. Devenish slowly laid on her lap the embroidery she had picked up.

"You both know," he continued, "that one of the difficulties about deciding on a school for Annerley in England was the fact that I wasn't able to afford the fees of a good boarding school. If we had been living in England, I would have chosen a day school. You know I believe very strongly that education is something that should be shared equally between parents and teachers. But we're not living in England, and it seemed to me that there was no way of my being able to arrange for Annerley to be a day girl. Even if my mother and I hadn't quarrelled, I wouldn't have considered asking her to act as guardian. She is a good person, but hasn't the . . . the knack of dealing with young people. Apart from my mother, there was nobody to whom Annerley could go."

He paused. Nobody spoke.

"Then," he continued, "a solution fell out of the sky. At the end of March, an uncle died. He was one of those old family friends that are given the title of uncle, but who in fact are no relation. His name was Stephen Holt. He and his wife—they had no children—lived in Chester, but they built a small cottage down in Devonshire, in a village called Torring, a few miles from Exeter, because they wanted to spend their summers near the sea. It's this little cottage which has been left to me. I stayed in it once, for about a week, but that was a long time ago, and I'm afraid I don't remember much about what it was like. He didn't leave me any money, but he left me something which I value much more—the means of arranging that Annerley could go to school as a day girl."

Once more he paused; once more nobody had anything to say.

"My idea is this," he went on. He turned to address Mrs. Devenish. "If you, Alice, would agree to live in the cottage, Annerley could go every day to a school not far away from it: Mardon Abbey."

Mrs. Devenish stared at him, frowned and then shook her head.

"I'm afraid, Edwin, that you'll find it impossible to—"

"If you're going to say that getting a place in the school would be difficult, you're right. That's why I said nothing about this plan until I was certain that they would accept Annerley. They did. They have. She is to go in the spring term next year."

A third time, he waited for comment that did not come.

"This could only come about," he told Annerley, "if the cottage could become, as it were, our second home, with your grandmother running the house and looking after you, and you going to school every day."

This time, Annerley filled the pause.

"Where would you be?" she asked.

"Me? I would be out here, working. Teaching as usual. I'm too well known as a coach, too established, too . . . I think the time has come when I can say, thank God, too successful to hope to earn as good an income anywhere else. I would like, in some ways, to live in England, but I can earn money out here, so I shall stay. I'll take you both to England and settle you into the cottage. I plan to go on home leave every two years, so as to be able to spend every alternate summer with you."

"How long would you stay when you took us to England?"

"I could stay until July." He turned to Mrs. Devenish. "Well, Alice? What do you think?"

She had picked up her work and was bent over it, but the needle was not finding its way into the right places. She was very pale. Like Annerley, she had known that something of this kind was bound to come. Now it was here.

She had never, in all her years in India, spoken of England without leaving strangers with the impression that she was homesick. She was not of a nature that could pursue a deliberate policy of deceit, but when the genuine pangs she had felt during her first months in India had ceased, her manner retained a wistfulness which made people feel that she was making a sacrifice in staying to devote herself to her grandaughter. The truth—she faced it now—was that she dreaded leaving. This house had become her home. In it she had a position of authority; within her restricted circle, she was respected, even looked up to. She loved the sun, bore with the monsoon, enjoyed the three or four months of cold weather. She did not feel the heat unduly; the rheumatism that had troubled her in England had left her. The things she had here—leisure, servants—she had never had before. Life in England, as she had known it, was cold and uncomfortable. She would be returning to a strange part of the country, to a house she had never seen. She felt she was too old to make new friends, too old to adapt to new conditions. But there was no appeal against Edwin's decision; he was right to send Annerley to school, and right to expect her grandmother to make a home for her.

She looked at him and spoke quietly.

"Of course I shall be happy to make a home for Annerley," she said. "I think you've been very lucky to get her into Mardon Abbey. But . . . you said the spring term."

"Yes. Early April. September's the beginning of the school

year, but that meant her spending another hot weather out here."

"There won't be much time," Mrs. Devenish pointed out, "between our arrival in England and Annerley having to start school. If you could have allowed yourself time to show her something of England before she had to—"

"That," Edwin said, "I would have liked to do, but I worked it out in terms of money. I have to be back in July. But I'll be able to take Annerley to school and see her in. It's a splendid school."

"What's so special about it?" Annerley inquired.

It was better to talk. She could think afterwards, when she went to bed, when she was alone, when she could cry if she wanted to. But crying . . . she had cried when Charlie Crowther went away, and it hadn't helped much.

Edwin reached out and took her hand lightly in his.

"Some good advice coming," he told her. "When you're up against anything in life that you can't dodge, the first thing to do is to release all your disappointment or rage. Rail against fate. Cry out to the gods for help, for justice, for alleviation. Cry out loud, if you can find a place suitable for crying out loud. And then . . . then, when you've spent your disappointment and rage, turn your eyes to the other side of the coin. Take a clear look at the situation and make yourself look at it from a new point of view—the fellow-on-the-other-side's point of view. I don't expect you to like the idea of going to England—not yet. How could you? If you were happy at the idea of going, wouldn't it mean that you hadn't been happy out here?"

Two tears rolled slowly down her cheeks. She shook them away.

"This house," he went on quietly, "mightn't look much of a place to . . . well, say the Fenwicks or the Prebdels. But the three of us have been happy here. It has been a real home. This is in large part due to your grandmother, Annerley. She could have gone back to England after your mother died, but—"

"No, I couldn't," Mrs. Devenish broke in. "How could I,

Edwin? How could I have done anything but what I did—stay and look after my daughter's baby? What would I have done in England? What was left for me there?"

And what, her look seemed to add, would there be for her now?

Edwin released Annerley's hand, took some papers from the table beside him and handed them to her.

"A school prospectus," he said, "and some old exam papers they've sent to give you an idea of what they'll expect from you. I'll be interested to know if you find them difficult."

She was glancing through the prospectus.

"It looks very big."

"You asked what was so special about it. The answer is that it's a school that takes in intelligent girls and turns them into well-informed women. If you're going to say that this is what all schools do, you'll be wrong."

"How did this school know that I was an intelligent girl, if I am an intelligent girl?"

"They took my word for it. My word as a teacher. I've no doubt they made some inquiries about me—they'd know where to go, because I told them. I also told them that you would be prepared to sit for their entrance examination, but they . . . well, as I said, they took my word for it. So you can't let me down."

"Those other girls who went to England to school, don't you remember? They wrote and said they found it very hard to keep up with the others in class."

He smiled.

"Many of those other children who went to school in England had spent their time out here with parents who didn't keep them up to scratch," he said. "Think how lucky you've been, having a father who could guide you through all those mazes of mathematics."

"Do these fields"—she held out the prospectus open at a page —"belong to the school?"

"Yes. Playing fields. Just look at those girls—Amazons."

"Do I have to wear those clothes?"

"You'll find them warm and practical. Day girls—see page 18—can have a midday meal at the school. Also tea, if they stay late for any reason."

She closed the prospectus and looked at him.

"Is it . . . is it absolutely definite?" she asked.

"Yes, Annerley, it is. Absolutely."

That being established, there was nothing left for her to do but make the best of it. And also, she found when she went to the convent next day, to make the most of it. For the interest roused by her plain, unstressed statement of her impending departure took her by surprise. She had been prepared for strong reactions on the part of Moira and perhaps even Edna, but the general expressions of regret were totally unexpected.

"Of course, we knew that you would go soon," Sister Philippa said at the end of the morning classes. "Mind you remember your convent teaching."

"Yes, Sister."

"It's a pity your father won't be with you."

"He will at first. He's going to England with us. With my grandmother and me."

"I'm glad to hear that. I don't doubt he'll stay for the summer. If you get a chance, you must try to get over to Ireland to visit our House. You must write to us, you know. We don't like to lose touch with our girls. Remember that, won't you?"

"Yes, Sister."

Edna said she had known all along that Annerley would go off to school in England, and then offered to tell her a secret.

"Oh, secrets! Why don't you just say a thing, and not say it's a secret all the time?"

"Well, this *is*. It's a secret because I don't want my mother to know about it, because she'd get upset. Ruby said in her letter to me that she's going to send for me to go to England. Not now, but when I'm a bit older. So I'll see you there."

"Did she say you'd go to school there?"

"No. I'm not going to school anywhere after I leave here."

Moira's feelings were expressed not in words but in actions.

The day after hearing Annerley's news, she came over to number 5 with a note from her father. It was addressed to Edwin, asking if he could drop in for a drink and a chat that evening, or any other evening that suited him.

Edwin was inclined to send a reply to the effect that he would be too busy for the next few months to pay visits. It was one thing to answer a summons from Lady Parrish; it was quite another to wait upon Mr. Fenwick. But he went that evening, because he guessed what Mr. Fenwick wanted to talk about, and felt that it could be better said while Moira and Annerley were out of the way, doing their homework together.

He wondered, as he went, when there would be news of Mrs. Fenwick's return. Moira knew nothing; she received brief letters from her mother, but nothing in them had given any hint of when she would rejoin her husband and daughter.

The Maules, Monsieur and Madame, were at their gate, mackintoshes over their arms, waiting for the umbrellas their daughter insisted on their taking with them.

"What use are umbrellas?" Monsieur Maule grumbled to Edwin. "If it rains, you know how it will be; of what use a *parapluie* in so great a *precipitation*?"

"Here, take them." Their daughter had returned. "Take them, but you are foolish to walk. If there is much rain, you must call a gharry and go in it, is it understood?"

"Yes, yes, yes." Monsieur Maule gave his wife an arm and they walked on beside Edwin. "You are not going far, I hope? You have no umbrella."

"I'm only going to number ten."

"Ah. Madame Fenwick is not there. Only Monsieur. And the little girl. I think. . . . Ah! It comes!"

It had begun to rain. The wind, which had been strong, rose suddenly to gale force. There was a short, sharp altercation between Monsieur Maule, who wanted to go on, and his wife, who wanted to turn back. She won, and when they turned for home, Edwin turned up his collar and sprinted the rest of the way to number 10.

The verandah was awash. Mr. Fenwick was in the drawing room and beckoned Edwin inside.

"Thanks for coming," he said. "Sit down. What'll you drink?"

Edwin said that he would have a *chota* peg, and studied his host while it was being poured out. He had always thought he had a strong resemblance to a fox—reddish colouring, sharp features and narrow, watchful eyes. He also suspected him of having much of a fox's cunning.

"I'm going to have a burra peg; I need it." Mr. Fenwick poured it out and handed Edwin his glass. Then he seated himself in one of the cane-seated, cushioned chairs. "Have you any idea what I want to talk to you about?"

"Yes," said Edwin.

The other man studied him for some moments.

"You're a strange fellow, Brooke," he said. "I wouldn't call you a hermit, but you certainly don't come out much from your cave. You don't teach all the time, do you?"

"Not all the time. But I've got a busy schedule, and I found at the start that I couldn't mix pupils and parties. Some of these young chaps come at all hours."

"Are they all Indians?"

"Yes. The English boys go home very young. I get the young Indians aiming for Oxford or Cambridge. I've had some rewarding results. It may sound narrow, but I find it fascinating."

"That's why I called you a strange chap. I wouldn't say you were using all your functions, would you?"

Edwin smiled.

"Perhaps not." He shook his head when Mr. Fenwick began to refill his glass. "No more, thanks. I haven't much time, so . . ."

"So you want me to come to the point. Well, the truth is that I want your help."

Asking favours must run in the family, Edwin thought. First the wife, now the husband.

"Well?"

"It's about Moira. You know, of course, that she walked out of two schools in England?"

"Yes."

"You must also know that her relations washed their hands of her. That's why we had to bring her back with us. The convent idea worked because your daughter Annerley happened to be there and Moira happened to like her. But now there's a new complication."

He walked to the door and stood staring out at the trees swaying in the wind. Then he turned to face Edwin.

"What's coming," he said, "is pretty private, but I have to tell you. I'm confident, from the little I know of you, that you'll keep it to yourself."

He paused. If he expected reassurance from Edwin, he did not get it. After some moments, he resumed.

"Has anyone ever told you that my wife and I don't get on?"

"No."

"That proves you ought to get out more. But I would have thought that your friend Lady Parrish would have had something to say on the subject. As I said, my wife and I don't get on. I might add that from the first year of our marriage, we ceased to get on. Now we've decided to separate."

This time, Edwin had a comment.

"I'm sorry about that."

"We should have made the decision long ago. The trouble was that we both wanted to stay in this country, and we didn't see how I could survive a scandal. You know what my job is. I would have had to resign. But the situation is now changed; the man my wife is leaving me for is in Malaya. So she and I are going to England at the end of October. We'll tell people I'm taking leave. I shall come back here, but she won't. She will go to Kuala Lumpur. And Moira—now I come to the point—Moira will have to be put in a school in England, and this time, she'll have to stay in it. But if she doesn't, then what in hell are we going to do? The solution seemed to come when Moira informed me that Annerley is going to school in England in the spring. That's correct, isn't it?"

"Yes."

"She told me what the school was, but I've never heard of it. It occurred to me that if Moira can get into it, my problem's solved. She'd be a boarder, of course. Annerley, I understand, is going as a day girl?"

"Yes."

"Could you tell me exactly where it is?"

"Fourteen or fifteen miles from Exeter. Inland, not towards the sea."

"I suppose there's a long waiting list?"

"Yes."

"Had Annerley's name been on it for long?"

"No."

"Then how . . . ? No, don't tell me, let me tell you. You're in the profession, isn't that it? You're one of them. Clergymen seem to have a special entree, too. I might be able to pull some strings."

He got up to refill his glass. He held out a hand for Edwin's, but Edwin shook his head.

"No, thanks."

His own glass refilled, Mr. Fenwick turned from the table and spoke.

"What do you think yourself, Brooke? How much chance is there of Moira getting in?"

"In the spring?"

"In January. You can be as frank as you like."

"Then . . . I'd say there was practically no chance."

"Why not? I said I'd pull strings."

"The school has a very high academic standard—unusually high. They took Annerley because she's clever."

"But they won't take Moira because she's not. Is that what you're going to say?"

"Yes."

"That's not my experience of the way institutions are run. I'll write to them and see what they say. If they won't take her, I'll have to find some other school that will. But running away from

102

two of them has put her on a kind of blacklist."

He paused, stared at the whisky in his glass, drained it and poured himself out another. Edwin would have taken his leave, but stayed where he was because he knew that the other man had a further request to make. It did not come at once. Mr. Fenwick returned to his chair and sat slumped in it, his expression moody.

"I envy you your happy relations with your daughter," he said. "I suppose my wife and I could have done something to get closer to our two children. The fact is, I didn't want children. I'm not a family man and I never pretended to be. I think the early stages of childhood are unrewarding for most fathers; by the time Moira had begun to be interesting, it was too late to make friends. She'd grown independent, self-sufficient. Too independent; I suppose you've noticed that the only orders she obeys are the ones which square with what she wants herself?" He got up once more and moved restlessly round the room. "I don't know what it is about your daughter that has this extraordinarily calming effect. Do you know?"

"I can make a guess. Annerley has a way—unusual in a child of her age, I think—of taking people as she finds them. Their faults, or their oddities, don't seem to worry her. I suppose this is partly due to the fact that I tried to keep her free of prejudice. Living as I do on the fringe of the Eurasian community, I knew she'd make friends with our neighbours, and I decided to let her mix without . . . well, as I said, without prejudice. Children don't create it—it's passed on to them by their parents."

He stopped. Why pursue the subject? It was his own lack of prejudice, his own willingness to accept his humbler neighbours, that had driven a wedge between him and men like Fenwick. Their views were too wide apart to admit of any bridge. He decided to help him towards his second objective.

"If Moira doesn't get into this school . . ." he began.

"I was coming to that. This, in fact, is what I most wanted to see you about. I've explained my situation. How much chance is there of Moira spending her school holidays with Annerley and your mother-in-law?"

"Very little." Edwin answered without hesitation. "Mrs. Devenish isn't young, and isn't of the temperament that could manage a difficult child. The cottage they're going to live in is small, only large enough for two. The summer holidays . . . those would be all right. The children would be out of doors and near enough to a beach to go and come on their own. But Christmas and Easter would be impossible; I wouldn't like to ask my mother-in-law to undertake it."

"I see."

Mr. Fenwick's tone had become frigid. Like wife, like husband, Edwin thought; neither of them likes being thwarted.

He rose. The other man made no attempt to detain him.

"I'll write to the school and let you know what happens," he said as Edwin reached the door. "But I think it'll probably be all right; I did a bit of electioneering in Devonshire last time I was on leave, and helped the candidate to win his seat. He owes me something, and he has a lot of pull."

Edwin nodded, crossed the rain-splashed verandah and then turned back with a question.

"How much are you going to tell Moira?"

"About her mother and myself? As little as possible for the present. But these things have a way of getting round. I'll tell her that I'm trying to get her into the school. I'll also tell her that we're going to England in October or November. With your permission, I'll add that she can spend the summer holidays with Annerley."

Edwin returned with relief to his long-sleever. Moira was still at the table in the porch room, but the schoolbooks had been put away and a pile of other books had taken their place.

He smiled to himself. Annerley had just discovered reading. The room in which he gave lessons was book-lined, and she had always had freedom to choose what she wanted to read, but it was only recently that she had begun to examine the shelves and take down the books. She was now trying to convince Moira that reading could offer more than instruction. She was not finding it easy.

"But it's *fun*, Moira. These aren't like the books you have to read at school."

"I know that. I just don't like reading, that's all."

"How do you know if you don't try? *Try* it. You can skip the dull bits."

Moira chose two books, thrust them into her satchel, and got up to leave.

"Have you been talking to my father, Mr. Brooke?"

"Yes, I have. About schools."

She went down the stairs. Annerley saw her off and then returned to Edwin.

"Is she going to the school I'm going to?" she asked.

"Her father's going to try to get her in."

"If I can, why can't she?"

"A small matter of academic standards. Before they accepted you I had to give them my assessment of your standard of work, and your capabilities. You're not a genius, but you're a worker, and of course you've had the inestimable advantage of a brilliant father to keep you up to scratch. Moira's intelligent, but she's been content to sit at the bottom of the class drawing animals in her exercise books."

"She draws beautifully. And paints, too. She's doing a whole zoo. You've only seen her tigers and lions, but you should see—"

"Drawing a zoo, even a whole zoo, isn't going to get her through examinations—unless they're examinations to see who can draw the best zoo."

"She said she would have worked harder if the teachers had been any good."

"That's merely the bad workman blaming the tools."

"She said her father was going to ask you about holidays. Did he?"

"Yes. I refused—on your grandmother's behalf and for your

grandmother's sake—for Christmas and Easter, but said the summer would be all right."

Annerley's disappointed expression indicated that she thought the inclusion of Christmas and Easter would have made the matter even more all right, but she said nothing more on the subject.

7

The answer to Mr. Fenwick's application to Mardon Abbey came in the form of an entrance examination paper which was sent to the convent. The nuns asked Edwin if he would proctor, and on his agreeing, sent him the sealed envelope. He asked Moira to come to the house at a quarter to eight on the following morning.

He led her into the room in which he gave lessons. Besides bookshelves, it contained nothing but a large table at which he sat, and three small tables for his pupils. At one of these he settled Moira with a pen, ink and a sheaf of lined paper. Then he broke the seal of the envelope, opened the examination paper and carried it to her. In the brief glance he was able to give it, he saw that it was well beyond her capability.

"You've got two hours," he told her. "It's a general paper. Fix on the questions you can answer, and put down all you know."

He returned to his seat. She read the questions, raised her eyes and met his glance, and he saw that she realized that the standard was too high for her. After that single look, she bent her head and began to write.

He sat preparing his morning's lessons, but his mind was on the lonely figure seated at the end of the room. She probably knew by now that her parents were going to separate. She knew that throughout the winter she would be a new girl in a new school—not, as this examination must have shown her—the same school as Annerley. She had nobody in England, perhaps nobody in the world to whom she could turn for sympathy or security. Anger burned in him as he thought of her parents and their refusal to interest themselves in the problems of their daughter.

The two hours passed slowly. When he told her that time was up, she put down her pen, blotted the last sheet, shuffled the papers together and brought them to him. He gave her a friendly smile.

"How did it go?" he asked.

"I couldn't do it. I only did two of the questions."

"Which were they?"

"The geography ones."

He was putting her answers into the envelope provided for them. She stood silently watching him seal it.

"It's a waste of postage, really, to send them back," she observed quietly.

"Not necessarily."

"Do they make an examination more difficult when they don't want somebody to get into the school?"

"No, Moira, they don't."

"Annerley didn't have to take one."

"Only because I gave them my disinterested assessment of her work. They accepted this because I'm a professional teacher and was bound not to mislead them."

"She's clever. I'm not. She and I won't be together."

"If you're not, does it matter very much, so long as you can meet in the holidays?"

"Only the summer holidays. My father told me. He said you know about him and my mother."

"Yes." On an impulse, he took one of her hands into his.

"Yes, Moira, I know, and I'm more sorry than I can tell you. But you must try and think of it from their point of view as well as your own. A man and wife . . . things can go wrong."

"I'd rather they were apart than together. They fight all the time."

Her tone was calm, almost detached. He felt shaken by pity.

"Shall I make you a promise?" he asked.

She waited. Again he was struck by her unchildlike demeanour.

"I told your father that you could only come to us in the summer holidays. The reason for that was because Mrs. Devenish is old, and won't have any bearers and cooks and ayahs to work for her in England, and so might feel that two children were too much for her to manage. But I promise you this: that if you find it difficult to settle down at school, if you're lonely or not very happy, you can consider our home as your home."

"Only in the summer?"

"Not only in the summer. We shall be in England at the end of March. You will have our address. I shall be there until the end of July and I will help you in any way I can. After July, I shall hand you over to Annerley. That's a promise. Shall we shake hands on it?"

He rose, and they shook hands solemnly.

"Thank you, Mr. Brooke."

She said no more, but he knew that he had managed to communicate to her some of his feelings. She had a hard and lonely winter ahead of her, but she could now look forward to the spring and to the coming of friends who could make up in some part for the inadequacy of her parents.

He took the examination paper to the post that evening, but before leaving the house, he sat down at his study table and wrote a covering letter. It was brief, and he did not reread it before putting it into an envelope. It might prove to have been a waste of his time, he thought as he stamped it, but on the other hand, it might be read by someone who was prepared to take a chance.

He returned to the house. Mrs. Devenish was in the porch room.

"Have you made up your mind, Edwin, how we're going to travel to England?" she asked him.

"City Line, I think. It's a long way round, but you and I both came out to Bombay; going by City Line, we'll be able to see a few more ports. It'll take a week or so off my time in England, but I think it'll be worth it."

"What ports would we stop at?"

"Madras. Colombo. Then across to Aden. Suez, Port Said and then into the Mediterranean to Gibraltar. Then to Tilbury. There's not much deck space in the second-class part of those boats, but I'm told they're quite comfortable."

She said nothing. He thought that she was thinking of the journey, but when she spoke, it was on another matter.

"Are you sure, Edwin, that I can make a success of running the cottage and looking after Annerley?"

"Quite sure. I'll be there to help you to settle in, or settle down. There's only a bare minimum of furniture, so we might be a bit uncomfortable until we buy any extra that's needed. I've written to the lawyers—Holt's lawyers—to ask them to let me know whether the place is in good condition. I think it must be—the Holts occupied it every summer, and someone in the village had a key and went along every now and then to see that everything was all right."

"It's going to be strange to be without a hot sun, and . . . and everything we've got used to here. Is it a large village?"

"It was a very small village when I saw it, but a place can change a lot in fifteen or twenty years."

"Do you mean to write to your mother to tell her you're going to England?"

"Yes. She won't be interested, or if she is, she won't say so."

"How can she bear not to see her grandchild?"

"How can she bear not to see her son? If you knew her, you'd realize that she can bear it very well indeed."

"You shouldn't speak against her. She's your mother, after all. She's all alone in that large house. It is large, isn't it?"

"Yes."

Far too large, his father had thought when he moved into it on his marriage. Far too large for a couple with one child who looked like being the only child. But it had been owned by his mother's family for two hundred years and more, and she had planned that her son would marry a woman of her choice and go on living in the house and bring up his children there. But her son had rejected the woman and the house and had gone out of his mother's life, as his father had done before him. Now she was alone, but he did not think that she was repining. There had been no repining when his father left. A hard woman. An upright, God-fearing, dutiful, arrogant and bitterly obstinate woman. His mother, after all.

He was roused from his reverie by the sound of footsteps. Mrs. Cole-Hardy was on her way up the stairs, her strident voice proclaiming her arrival. Edwin, murmuring excuses about pupils, retreated to his study and closed the door.

"Hello, Alice. How are you? Can't stay long. Yes, wouldn't mind a peg if you've got one. Make it a burra—I've just been exercising a devilish difficult horse."

She was in jodhpurs and a short-sleeved white shirt which, soaked with perspiration, clung to her thin body.

"You'll catch cold," Mrs. Devenish protested. "Let me send the ayah for a wrap."

"No. Never catch cold. Whisky's splendid warmer. Where's Annerley?"

"She's walking in the Prebdel garden. She'll be back in time for dinner."

"Wish I had one or two of those Prebdel horses. I'd give my ears and whiskers for that last one they bought. But I'm not a millionaire, like Zumeer Prebdel."

"When are you leaving for home?"

"Next week. End of. Got a berth on the mail boat. I usually

wait until the beginning of September before going, but I'm taking an extra two weeks to go to Newmarket and look at some ponies my father's thinking of buying. Marvelous old chap, he is. Going on for eighty, and still never misses a meet. You've heard the rumours about the Fenwicks, I suppose?"

"Well . . . "

"Not well at all. Mrs. Fenwick isn't back yet. I'm no gossip-monger, but I know what's going on round me. I'm sorry for that girl of theirs, Moira. She gets into a lot of trouble for back-answering, but most of the time, all she's doing is reacting against adult rudeness, like that time, if you remember, when that silly cow of a woman, Mrs. Tremblett—sorry if you like her, I can't stick her—when she met Moira at a children's party and said she didn't like the way she did her hair, and was she trying to pretend she was Alice in Wonderland? And remember what Moira said, polite as you please?"

"Well, it was . . . "

"It was the solemn truth. She told Mrs. T. that the way *her* hair was done, those plaits coiled like snakes round her ears, made her look like a sheep with mumps. And so they did, and if you noticed, Mrs. T. didn't go round with snake-coils any more after that. There ought to be more children who speak up. All the same, I'm glad I didn't have any. I don't think it was my fault that I didn't; Cole-Hardy may look virile, but—"

"Would you . . . may I offer you . . . "

Mrs. Cole-Hardy's empty glass was already out-held. The speed at which she disposed of one, two and sometimes three large whiskies never ceased to astonish Mrs. Devenish. Her adoption of jodhpurs for riding and the fact that she rode astride were further matters that she endeavoured to overlook.

"Decided when you're all going off home?" Mrs. Cole-Hardy inquired.

"Very early in March."

"You'll feel the cold, I expect. I like it. Does me good. Have to grope to see where my nose is sometimes when I'm hacking out to a meet, to make sure it's still on my face. How long is

Edwin thinking of leaving Annerley at school in England? I expect it depends on whether she decides to be one of those girl graduates or not. She's got the brains for it. The only thing is that if she came out here after she left school, she'd have the time of her life, so many nice young men, so few nice young girls. She'd be snapped up in no time. What's Edwin going to do all by himself out here for the next few years?"

"He's going to try to get home every second year."

"That still leaves him on the loose for too long. Though he's a strange chap; doesn't seem to hanker after women."

"Could I offer you . . ."

"Thanks. I must make it a quick one; if I keep dinner waiting, my husband gets peevish. All stomach, that man. I only came round to remind Annerley about exercising my horses while I'm away. Well, I must be off." She drained her glass and went to the door of Edwin's study. "Come out and say good-bye, Edwin," she shouted. "You may not see my ugly mug for a long time."

He came out and said good-bye and then accompanied her down the stairs.

"Couldn't get your mother-in-law to say anything about the Fenwicks," she confided, "but I suppose you know what's going on?"

"Yes."

"A pretty pair. She's a flighty piece and he's a pompous ass. Every time I see him, I want to bare my teeth and take a bite. Well, good-bye, Edwin. See you sometime, I expect."

He watched her out of sight and then rejoined Mrs. Devenish.

"Good sort," he commented.

She agreed, and they thought, in their differing ways, of Mr. Cole-Hardy, soon to be left alone. Edwin remembered, and Mrs. Devenish tried not to remember, that he would not be lonely. There was solace in a little flat overlooking Chowringhee in which he had long ago installed a stout, sensible, French-born widow named Amelia. He would not miss Mrs. Cole-Hardy.

The monsoon made a lingering departure. The weather became drier, but hotter; it was the time of year that Mrs. Devenish found most trying. She endured uncomplainingly prickly heat and restless nights, and longed for the cold weather.

It came, as always, with a swarm of green flies. For two evenings, the lamps in the street were obscured by clouds of the tiny insects. Myriads of them entered the house, dropped into the soup at dinner, settled on the plates and on the food and formed a screen through which the servants had to brush a way. They were a nuisance, but they were welcome; they were harbingers of cool days to come. Winter clothes were taken out of their zinc-lined trunks and aired. The mornings became chilly, the evenings cold. And an answer came from Mardon Abbey to Mr. Fenwick.

He took it to number 5 and showed it to Edwin. When he entered the porch room, letter in hand, Edwin knew at once that the news was good; it was evident in the other man's triumphant bearing and the near-sneer on his face.

"Something I thought you'd like to see," he said, and handed the letter to Edwin.

Edwin read it. It was not long and it was not warm. It said merely that although Moira's entrance examination results had not reached the required level, it had been decided to accept her on special terms. She would be admitted in January, for one term only. If her school work, and her deportment, were satisfactory, she would be enrolled as a permanent pupil.

"Remember what I told you?" Mr. Fenwick did not attempt to conceal his contempt. "I said I'd get her in. If you know the right strings to pull, you can get past all that waiting-list nonsense. That's just window dressing."

"I'm very glad she's got in."

"I never doubted she would. She hasn't Annerley's brains, of course, but you can't fill a school of that size entirely on merit. There's money involved, too." He held out his hand for the letter and Edwin returned it. "So there you are. You used your method, I used mine. No, I won't stay, thanks. I left a peg on my verandah."

Moira took the news with no sign of pleasure, and with so little show of interest that Annerley came near to anger.

"Don't you understand that you're jolly lucky? Don't you understand that this is a good school? Don't you understand that we'll both be there?"

"We won't be in the same class. And I'll be a boarder and you'll be a day girl. They don't mix much. I know; I was in those other schools."

"They can't stop us from seeing each other, can they? And they won't have separate buildings for separate classes."

"They might. I'll find out when I get there."

"Listen, Moira. If you don't stay in this school, if you decide that you don't like it, and run away, don't you understand that we'll never be together, not for years?"

"Yes."

"So you've got to like it."

"No I haven't. I've just got to stay in it, that's all. I've got an idea."

"Well, what?"

"There's not much time left, but if you asked your father to . . . well, to coach me, to give me some extra lessons in the subjects

I'm worst at, do you think he would? Then I might be in your class."

Annerley hesitated.

"He will if he can. He's awfully full up. Would you mind if it was before breakfast, or some time like that?"

"I wouldn't mind if it was in the middle of the night. Will you ask him?"

"Yes."

The same idea had occurred to Edwin, but the only free time he had was at eight in the morning. Moira could take it or leave it.

She took it. It was a trying period for both pupil and teacher. Edwin, accustomed to dealing with exceptionally clever adolescents, found Moira's slowness and apparent lack of response baffling. But he was too good a teacher to fail to rise to the challenge—and he was unprepared for the amount of study that Moira did in the intervals between lessons. She gave up her morning rides; she gave up skating and swimming and the tennis sessions she had begun to have with Annerley. She separated what she found easy from what she found impossible, so that Edwin was able to concentrate on essentials. It began to seem to both of them that this was a fight, and they were in it together.

Mr. Fenwick offered no thanks, but he offered a fee, which Edwin refused. His reward, he told himself but did not tell Mr. Fenwick, lay in the undoubted progress made by Moira before the time came for her to leave for England. He had lifted her over some kind of hurdle. She had learned how to learn.

Mrs. Fenwick returned at the beginning of October. A week later, the Prebdels came back from Musoorie. Shareen appeared in one of their carriages and bore Annerley back to their house.

"You said you'd be back on the third," Annerley told her. "This is the tenth."

"My mother kept delaying and delaying. I wrote eight letters to you, but you only wrote six to me. Can you come tomorrow and spend the whole day?"

"Yes. Why don't you ask Moira, too?"

Shareen's voice was high with astonishment.

"Ask Moira Fenwick? Ask her to my house?"

"Why not? Mrs. Fenwick's come back from Kashmir, and she and your mother were going to be friends, remember?"

Shareen waited until they were on their way up to her room before replying.

"They're not going to be friends anymore," she said.

"Why not? The Fenwicks are going to England next month, and they could take messages and parcels and things to your brother."

"My mother wouldn't ask them."

"Why not?"

"Haven't you heard what's happened?"

"No. What's happened?"

Shareen sent the ayah for lemonade and pistachio nuts. Then she spoke in surprise.

"You mean Moira didn't tell you anything?"

"Anything about what?"

"About her father and mother."

"What about her father and mother?"

"You simply don't know?"

"I don't know anything special, if there's anything special to know. If there had been, Moira would have told me."

"But she hasn't, so she isn't your best friend as she's always saying. And she must know about it, because her father wrote and told her brother. If he told her brother, then he'd tell Moira too, wouldn't he? That's how we knew about it—Mr. Fenwick told his son, Mark, and then Mark told my brother Chandra and Chandra wrote to my father and mother and told them."

Annerley spoke in exasperation.

"Look, I don't know what you're talking about. Why don't you stop this your-brother my-brother her-brother, and just come out with whatever it is?"

"What it is, *is*, they're going to England together—Mr. and

117

Mrs. Fenwick and of course, naturally, Moira. But when they get there, Mrs. Fenwick is going to run away with another man."

"Run away with. . . . You're making it up."

"If you don't believe me, go and ask Moira—go on."

"Don't shout."

"I'll shout if I want to. Why should you call me a liar?"

"Will you calm down and please tell me . . ."

She stopped. Shareen had already told her. Mrs. Fenwick was going to leave Mr. Fenwick and go off with someone else. So where did that leave Moira?

When she left the Prebdels' house, Annerley stopped their carriage at the corner of Seymour Street, got out and dismissed it. Going into number 10, she saw that visitors were present, and went round the side of the house to effect an entrance by the method that she and Moira had long ago devised. She whistled softly outside Moira's window. It opened, and Moira handed out a chair. Climbing onto this, Annerley stepped into the room.

"I knew you'd come," Moira said.

"How did you know?"

"Because you went to see Shareen Prebdel. I knew she knew, because my father told Mark and Mark told Shareen's brother. So he told the Prebdels."

"They knew, yes. Does my father know?"

"Yes. I suppose he thought I'd tell you."

"Why didn't you?"

"Because I thought it might not happen. Often, when they've had a quarrel, they've said they'll go away and leave each other, but they never did, so I thought that this time, they mightn't. It was only when my mother came back that I knew for sure."

"Is it going to make any difference—I mean when you get to England?"

"No. I suppose she'll go off when we get there, and my father'll see about taking me to the school and everything. Then there'll be just one term before you come. But I've made up my mind about one thing: if they want to send me to my aunts for the Easter holidays, I won't go. I'll stay at school."

"Can you do that?"

"Yes. The prospectus says so."

There seemed nothing more to say. Annerley left, as she had come, by the window.

Edwin was alone; Mrs. Devenish had gone with Monsieur and Madame Maule to a concert. Annerley joined him in the porch room.

"You knew about Moira's mother and father," she said without preamble. "I wish you'd told me."

"I left Moira to do that."

"She says she's going to stay at school for the Easter holidays."

"Not a bad idea."

It was almost dark in the room, but when the bearer came in to switch on the lights, Annerley sent him away. Edwin called him back and ordered drinks—whisky for himself, lime-and-water for Annerley. When the tray was on the table beside them, Annerley filled the glasses. Then she curled up in a chair, and out of the darkness came the first question she had ever asked Edwin about his mother.

"You quarrelled with your mother, didn't you?" she asked.

"Yes," he answered. "I did."

"You've never told me about it."

"No. There seemed no point."

"Was it because you didn't want to remember?"

"No, that wasn't quite the reason. If you had shown any interest in the subject, I was prepared to tell you anything you wanted to know."

He sat silent for some time, letting his mind go back over the years. When he spoke, it was in a quiet, reminiscent tone.

"I suppose there wouldn't have been a quarrel—at any rate, not a serious, not a final quarrel—if my mother hadn't made up her mind to choose a wife for me—a girl who lived not far from us, the daughter of a family we'd known for years. She was two years older than I was, well brought up, well educated—and she had a good deal of money. Money matters a great deal to my mother. Not the money of the newly rich, but money inherited and passed on and used to run great estates, money to give dignity to great names. She herself had inherited her uncle's fortune —a very large one. Added to the fortune she inherited from her parents, it amounted to a very large sum, and gave her, at the age of eighteen, a good deal of responsibility. And a great deal of power."

He paused. So long ago, so far away. And now he was recalling that old history for his daughter.

"Go on," prompted Annerley.

"Power," he repeated. "She was a person of simple tastes, so she didn't use the money to buy things she wanted. What she used it for—at first, I think, unconsciously, but later with a full knowledge of what she was doing—was to make people do what she wanted them to do."

"You mean . . . sort of bribing?"

"No. Not bribing. She was open-handed and gave freely— while people did what she thought they ought to do, or what she wanted them to do. If they didn't, she withdrew her financial support."

"I see. She wouldn't give you any money because you wouldn't marry that girl she wanted you to marry?"

"It went rather further than that."

"Didn't she like my mother?"

"She never saw your mother. She refused to meet her. She accused me of having jilted—do you know the meaning of jilted?"

"Yes."

"—Of having jilted the girl she'd chosen for me. But I had never got beyond the point of mild friendliness with the girl. Whether things would ever have got beyond that point, I shall never know—because when I was twenty-two, I met your mother."

Again he paused, but this time she waited for him to resume.

"I went to stay with a friend from Cambridge. He lived in a very small village in Somerset—a kind of toy village, very picturesque, with a few houses, a smithy, a little shop or two—and a church. A very small church next to a disproportionately large parsonage.

"When Sunday came, I was taken to Morning Service. The parson was rather old. His wife, I had been told, was some years younger than he was. They had only one child—a daughter. The mother and the daughter were sitting in a pew just below the pulpit.

"I was sitting at the back of the church and could only see the backs of heads. But my friend and I were asked to take round the plate for the collection after the sermon. He began at the front and worked down the pews on one side. I started at the end row on the other side, and worked my way up towards the altar. As I got near the front pew, I wondered whether it was customary to ask the parson's wife and daughter to contribute. Were they exempt? I didn't know. I stopped in front of them and held out the plate."

This time, the pause was very long.

"Did they put money in it?" Annerley asked at last.

He came out of a reverie.

"Yes. It must have been difficult for them, because I was moving the plate from side to side without knowing what I was doing. My eyes were on Miss Devenish. When I came to myself and turned to walk up to the altar, I left my heart at her feet. Will you believe that?"

"Yes."

"She was beautiful—as you will have seen from her photographs. But it was something more than beauty that I saw. She was the gentlest creature who ever walked. You can see something of that gentleness in your grandmother—but on your mother, it was a kind of . . . a kind of bloom. She had spent almost all her life in that village. She had gone to a day school eight miles away, but she had left when she was sixteen because she felt that her father needed her help.

"The parsonage was, as I said, very large. It was also very cold and very uncomfortable. There was only one servant—very old, very deaf, not very useful.

"I saw, on that first visit, as much of your mother as I could. I said nothing about my feelings, but when I went away, I knew that she liked me, perhaps more than liked me. When I got home, I told my mother that I had met the girl I wanted to marry.

"She didn't take it well. She asked questions, and didn't like the answers. And so it was left for a time. I filled in the interval looking for a job—and dreaming. I used to carve our names on trees: Edwin Anson Brooke, Rosalind Anna Lee Devenish. When I got the job I was after, I changed the Devenish to Brooke. Rosalind Anna Lee Brooke."

Once more, silence.

"So you got the job—and then?"

"I told my mother that I had one, and that I was going to ask Rosalind Devenish to marry me. She gave me an ultimatum: marry her, and she would refuse to see me again. The house, and the money I was to have inherited, would go to my cousins. The news didn't disturb your mother, because I had from the beginning guessed what might happen, and had presented myself as a man who would probably have no money but what he earned."

"Go on."

"I had signed a contract to come out to India and teach in a school in Simla. Your mother and I wanted to marry before I left England, but we felt it would be wiser for us to wait until I could send for her. The school job didn't last long—a pity, because a lot of money and a lot of hope had gone into it. When it closed, I came down to Calcutta and began to earn my living coaching students. I sent for your mother, and she came out—not to Seymour Street; we couldn't have afforded it then. A year later, you were born and we knew we'd have to move, especially as your grandfather—your Devenish grandfather—had died and it was obvious that your grandmother would need a long rest and a change before settling down to live on her own. She came out

122

just before you were born. And twelve days after you were born, your mother died."

The light from the servants' verandah shone in and gave a dim, ghostly illumination. The men in the chummery shouted for their dinner. From Annerley's bedroom came the sound of slaps as the ayah attempted to trap between her palms a mosquito that had got into the mosquito net.

"Didn't your father have any money?" Annerley asked.

"Very little. Like me, he was a teacher. When he married, my mother persuaded him to give up teaching and help her to run the estate. She had a lot on her hands: a very large house, extensive grounds, servants, a home farm, tenant farmers, the marketing of some of the estate produce. My father did his best to help her, but gave up when he found that all she needed was someone who would carry out her orders. In the end, he left her. I used to go and visit him, and I always told my mother I'd been, but she appeared not to hear. She never asked how he was. And she didn't go to his funeral."

He stopped. They sat on, dreaming. It grew chilly. At last Edwin came back to the present, switched on the lights and said that it was time Mrs. Devenish was back.

"Do you often write to your mother?" Annerley asked.

"Often? No. When I do, she doesn't reply. I shall write and tell her you're going to school in England. I don't think she'll show any interest. She meant what she said when I left: she didn't want to see me or hear of me again."

She uncurled herself from the chair and went into her bedroom. Edwin, left alone, stood with his unfinished drink in his hand, thinking of his boyhood.

November brought Lady Parrish. Edwin did not wait for a summons; he set his pupils an examination, put Mrs. Devenish in the study to proctor, and walked to Park Place.

She joined him in the drawing room, wearing a long gown in a shade of apricot, with a full skirt but a clinging bodice. This, and her careful makeup, suggested to him that she had dressed for a special visitor, and he did not think that it was himself. He decided to make his stay brief.

"Did you enjoy yourself?" he asked her.

"I think so. I'm not sorry to be back. Most of the nice people had left, and I got lonely."

"That doesn't sound like you."

"I think I'm getting to a peculiar time of life. I'm restless. Once or twice I thought I was actually falling in love. Absurd, isn't it?"

"I can't imagine you with only one man. I like to see you surrounded."

"I like to be surrounded. I hope I'm not going to do anything foolish. Ring that bell, will you, and let's have a drink."

He rang, and the drinks were ordered and brought. Then she spoke irritably.

"I've let myself in for organizing another fête. Why couldn't they have found someone else to do it?"

"Because nobody can charm as much money out of people's pockets as you can. Why didn't you refuse?"

"Because the Viceroy asked me."

"Blackmail, no less." He raised his glass. "I've come, of course, to thank you."

"What for?"

"For what you did for Annerley."

"It's all settled, is it?"

"Yes. We go home in March and she joins for the Easter term."

"And her friend, Moira Fenwick, will already be there."

"Yes. You heard about that?"

"I did. I also heard the news about her parents. It didn't surprise me. The other piece of information I picked up was how their daughter got into the school."

"Fenwick pulled strings, so he told me. He doesn't believe in waiting lists."

"Whether he pulled strings or not, he didn't get her in. You got her in. Don't sit there looking innocent."

"They sent an entrance paper for Moira to—"

"Yes, yes, yes. But you know perfectly well that it wasn't her answers to the entrance paper that got her into the school. What got her in was your covering letter. It was a good letter, I was told. You put her case very well."

"However it was done, I'm glad they accepted her. She's coming to us for the summer holidays. Fenwick wanted me to agree to her spending all her holidays with Annerley, but I thought that would be too much for my mother-in-law to handle."

"You were right. You seem to think she'll make a good house-keeper and guardian, but I confess I don't."

"She'll be all right. She—"

"Yes, I know; great sense of duty. You forget she's got used to being waited on. Anyway, you'll be there long enough to see how she gets on."

She emptied her glass and he rose to refill it.

"You know all about Charles Crowther, I suppose?" she asked.

"He wrote fairly detailed letters to me and to young Leeson. It all seems to have turned out well."

"For that girl, yes. The whole business was a wicked waste. He could have done so well for himself out here, instead of which he got himself sent home and ended up with a good-for-nothing Eurasian girl."

"Good-for-nothing? That's rather sweeping, isn't it?" he protested. "Besides being very pretty, she had a certain charm, and she showed some courage in leaving her home and taking a chance on Charles."

"He was a weak fool. She's welcome to him. Have you written to tell your mother you're going home?"

"I will do, before leaving."

"You're travelling first class, I hope?"

"No. Second."

"Oh Edwin, you make me so angry! Money, money, money. You need it, she has unlimited amounts of it, and you refuse to ask her for any. Is asking so difficult?"

"Not difficult; impossible."

"Oh . . . pride!"

"Not entirely. I've tried to explain before that she's not a woman who responds to appeals. She despises people who make them. All I want from her is—or was—a brief note telling me she was aware I had a daughter; that's all. I can understand her determination never to mention my wife, but I would have said that she would at least have commented on the fact that I was a father. I don't want money from her. Taking it in the past was as hard for me as it was for my father—but we were both dependent on her. My father, because he had given up his independence on his marriage; myself, because I didn't want to break away until I'd got my degree."

"So you won't even see her in England?"

"Not unless she says she'd like to see me. Which she won't."

"When will you be back?"

"July."

She did not speak for some time. When she did, it was in a different tone.

"Do you ever think," she asked, "that you might find it difficult to get back here?"

He looked at her uncomprehendingly.

"Get back to India? What's to stop me?"

"Well . . . shall we suppose for a moment that there's a war?"

"War?" He put down his glass. "Have you heard anything?"

"From my influential brother in the Cabinet? No. But I read the home newspapers, and I like to use my brain, and I think the Germans are preparing for war. Don't you *feel* the unrest? Morocco, the Balkans . . . don't you feel at all uneasy?"

"You think the Kiel Canal's being widened so's they can send battleships through it?"

"Since you ask me, yes. I do. I'm not speaking lightly, I'm speaking seriously."

"Are you suggesting that we're heading for an early war?"

"We're not heading; we're being headed. If it does come, what will you do?"

He frowned.

"If I'm in England, I'll offer my services in some way. I don't suppose I'd be considered very useful, but they'd find something for me to do."

"Well, let's hope I'm taking too pessimistic a view and that you'll be back in July."

When he left her, he walked home slowly and thoughtfully. She certainly read the English newspapers and she certainly used her brain, but it was equally certain that she kept in close touch with her brother in Whitehall, and frequently echoed his views.

A mood of depression seized him. Life without Annerley . . . and the threat of war . . .

There was a large crowd at Howrah Station to say good-bye to the Fenwicks. Edwin was there—unwillingly, but he felt that he had to take Annerley. Mr. Fenwick, festooned with garlands, stood among his English and Indian colleagues. Mrs. Fenwick, smiling, gracious, was beside him, the picture of an affectionate wife.

Annerley, apart with Moira, was giving her some last words of advice.

"Remember what I said—you've got to stay at the school, whether you like it or not."

"All right. Oh, wait a minute." She climbed into the compartment and came out holding her topee—not the round, elastic-tethered kind with cotton covers worn by most English children, but an expensive, helmet-shaped one with a soft white finish. "Here. You can have this."

"Your topee? You'll need it."

"No, I won't anymore. It's nicer than that awful one you wear. Try it on."

Annerley removed her own and tried on Moira's. It was light and comfortable, and suited her.

"Does it look all right?"

"Yes. You look nice."

"Sure you don't want it anymore?"

"Yes. Wear it now."

"What'll I do with my own?"

Moira's answer was to take it, put it on the floor and jump on it.

"There. You can say it got squashed."

Bells were ringing, latecomers were struggling through the crowd and attempting to find empty seats on the train. Vendors of *pan*, of cigarettes, of tea, made last bids for customers. Coolies carrying luggage on their heads fought their way to the owners and ran along with the moving train, hands outstretched for their fees. The figures at the windows were borne away; the crowd on the platform began to disperse. When Edwin and Annerley got to the station entrance, Mr. Cole-Hardy's landau was waiting, but Edwin did not expect to be offered a lift—he knew that it was waiting to convey Mr. Cole-Hardy to his Amelia.

On Christmas morning, the annual procession of Edwin's pupils and their parents, carrying garlands, was followed by the arrival of coolies carrying gifts. This ceremony had in years gone by caused Annerley a great deal of anguish, for her father refused all expensive offerings and accepted only a small gift from each basket, sending the rest away. Expensive dolls, toy bicycles or cars—all these had returned the way they had come, as had the cases of whisky, the bottles of champagne and the cigars. Edwin allowed Mrs. Devenish to keep one or two of the baskets containing fruit. The donors pleaded, argued, protested; Edwin remained firm and the donors departed. Honour was satisfied.

On the afternoon of Christmas Day, Annerley walked to the Prebdels' with the ayah following her with Shareen's present—a book for which she had sent to England, with delicately executed illustrations of Hindu mythology which she felt would have an artistic if not a religious appeal. Shareen, after having studied the little Hindu goddesses in her mother's rooms; having inspected the pictures of the Sacred Heart hanging on Miss Severn's bedroom walls; having watched the Christians walking in tributaries to the English church and the Scottish kirk; having each evening seen kneeling figures bowing their heads on prayer rugs and Buddhist priests in their saffron robes carrying begging bowls, had ended, like her father, by rejecting totally all forms of organized religion.

But the illustrated book was not so much a Christmas present as a peace offering. Annerley had not seen Shareen for more than a week. This unusually long separation had been caused by the fact that Mrs. Devenish had accepted an invitation to Myrtle Fernandez' wedding without realizing that Shareen's birthday was on the same day. Shareen's rage at discovering that Annerley would arrive late at her party by reason of having to attend the wedding had been so violent that Miss Severn had threatened to leave, and even Annerley had felt it wise to stay away in order to allow her anger to cool down.

She left the ayah at the gate, walked up the drive and turned the corner of the house. When she entered the hall, she came face to face with Shareen's father.

She stopped. As always, the sight of him seemed to freeze her tongue. She thought him the very perfection of manhood. Her father was good-looking, a handsome English gentleman—but Mr. Prebdel's noble head, his features, the smoothness of his dark skin, his splendid figure—all these appeared godlike. He was not, today, in the western suit he habitually wore; he was in Indian dress—close-fitting white trousers and a long, black, high-collared, beautifully cut coat.

"Hello, Annerley. Shall I say Happy Christmas?"

She made an effort to unloosen her tongue.

"Thank you. The same . . . I mean, thank you. I brought . . . I came to see Shareen."

"Will you go to her room? I'll send a message to tell her you're here."

"I'll go up."

"Will you give my good wishes to your father?"

"Yes, I will. Thank you."

"Are you looking forward to going to England in March?"

"No. Not much."

"You'll like it when you get there. Have you heard from Moira?"

"Yes. She wrote from Bombay, and then from Aden."

"Shareen will miss you when you go. But perhaps she'll come to England with me—I have to go in May."

Annerley went upstairs. When Shareen joined her, she gave her the book in its wrapping.

"Don't open it now. It's only a book. Thank you for the scarf you sent me. Did you knit it?"

"Some of it. Miss Severn did a lot."

"I saw your father downstairs. I like him in Indian clothes."

"He only wears them when my mother's relations come to see us. Have you found out yet what ship you're going to England on?"

"Yes. The *City of Portsmouth*. Your father said he's going to take you to England when he goes in May."

"But you'll be stuck in school, so what's the use?"

"We could see each other. I'm sorry I haven't come over for so long, but I didn't want to be shouted at. If you want to know, I don't want to go to the wedding—but I've got to."

"You mean that truly, that you'd rather come to my party?"

"Of course I mean it. Do you want to hear what presents I got in my pillowcase this morning?"

"Yes."

They settled down to the recital.

The wedding, as described by Mrs. Fernandez, was a big splash. Cheated of an opportunity to launch Ruby, she had decided to give Myrtle a memorable send-off. Invitations were sent to a host of friends and relations; carriages were borrowed and beribboned. A cousin in the catering business provided food and drink at a generous discount. Mr. Stanley charged a nominal fee for the photographs, and the bridegroom paid for the marquee that was erected in the compound. The bride was in white satin and was attended by four bridesmaids dressed in pink.

Victor Millet, the bridegroom, was tall and somewhat stout, with a pleasant smile and a calm ease of manner. His years in Edinburgh had given him poise and improved his accent, and it was generally felt that Myrtle had been lucky to catch him. His gift to the bridesmaids took the form of bird-shaped brooches. Edna, showing hers to Annerley, said that on the return of the couple from their honeymoon, she was going to stay with them in Ranchi. At the end of the year, Doctor Millet would move to his practice in Calcutta.

Mrs. Devenish returned to number 5 in a pensive mood; the wedding was the last function she was to attend before the departure to England. Nothing remained now but to get ready to leave.

There was much to be done. The upper flat had been let to Mr. Leeson, who was to marry Miss Highfield in April and occupy it until Edwin's return. The rooms had to be emptied of personal belongings. Packing cases were made to contain things that would be needed in the cottage in Devon: sheets, pillowcases, blankets, tablecloths and—carefully inserted into the folds of the blankets—the cherished ornaments that Mrs. Devenish had brought with her from England. There was also cutlery, and Annerley's books. In trunks marked "Wanted on Voyage" were put the warm clothing which would be required when the ship entered cool waters. Light clothing went into cabin trunks.

Annerley watched the calendar and got into bed each night feeling as though she had taken a step nearer the edge of a precipice. She lay staring at the ceiling and reminding herself that she was, after all, English; England was her country and she must do her best to like it. But the letters sent back by girls who had been sent to England had not been reassuring. And schools apart, there was the climate, which was cold and damp and which even in summer could not be relied on.

And above all, life in England meant life without her father. He would be there until the summer holidays—but after that? How many months would it be before she saw him again? It was better not to count.

During the last two weeks before the ship sailed, Shareen gave up all pretense of not minding being left behind. She appeared daily in the carriage, came up the stairs and sat watching gloomily as luggage was strapped and labelled. Her parting present to Annerley was practical—a small fur muff and a fur neckpiece that Miss Severn said was called a tippet.

"I don't suppose you'll ever use them," she said.

"Yes, I will," Annerley assured her.

"No, you won't. Miss Severn says that girls in England use them when it's snowing, but look how old-fashioned she is. I don't suppose anyone uses them anymore. You won't even remember who gave them to you. I don't think you'll ever think of me ever again."

"Shareen, don't be silly. Your father's bringing you to England in May—he said so."

"If you tell your father you hate it over there, will he bring you back here?"

"No. He wants me to do well at school so's I can go on to Oxford or Cambridge. He says it's very important for women to—"

"Yes, you told me. But my mother says it's all rubbish. She says you'll get married. If you could marry someone who was going to live in India, you could marry them and come back, and then you and I could be friends again, only with husbands and babies."

This possibility seemed to uphold her until the *City of Portsmouth* edged away from the docks at Kidderpore and began the journey down the Hooghly. Annerley, standing at the rail with Edwin and Mrs. Devenish, looked down at the receding crowd and tried to pick out through gathering tears those who had come to see them off: Edwin's pupils, their parents, Shareen and

Mr. Prebdel, Mr. Leeson and Miss Highfield, Mr. Cole-Hardy, Mademoiselle Maule. And, weeping copiously, Mrs. Fernandez with a dry-eyed Edna.

The ship glided slowly down the river. From the garlands which had been hung round Edwin's neck by his Indian friends rose a scent of mingled rose and jasmine. Darkness fell. Edwin and Mrs. Devenish went down to their cabins, but Annerley remained on deck, watching the lights of Calcutta disappearing into the distance. Only when the city was at last out of sight did she turn from the rail and go below.

The *City of Portsmouth,* 16,000 tons, carried many more first than second-class passengers. Annerley shared a two-berth cabin with her grandmother. Edwin was in a four-berth with two businessmen and one of his Indian students, who was bound for Oxford.

There were no children of Annerley's age in the second-class part of the ship, and as far as she could see across the intervening well deck, none in the first-class section either. Until the ship left Madras, she was left very much to herself. Her grandmother sat in a shady corner of the deck and knitted mufflers designed to keep out the English cold. Her father took her walking a mile or two round the deck every morning, and then settled down with a book. She was asked to join the glee club, but had to confess that she was not musical. She spent most of her days in the small canvas swimming pool rigged up in the stern of the ship.

But when she was observed beating her father at deck tennis; when the quoits she aimed fell thudding without a single miss into the bucket; when the wooden discs slithered along the deck and stopped on the line marking the highest points, she began to be much sought-after. When the list for the games competitions was put up on the notice board, there was a rush to engage her as partner.

The sea was smooth, the sun shone more and more warmly as the ship neared Colombo. Edwin took Annerley, Mrs. Devenish and the Indian student to dinner at the Galle Face Hotel. The Indian ocean was glassy, almost oily. Breezes became cooler, friendships were formed, flirtations began. The grass widows found Edwin attractive, but the years had taught him how to elude without offending.

The hours spent ashore at Aden were interesting, but too hot for enjoyment. Mrs. Devenish had not wanted to leave the ship, but it was taking on coal, and staying on board was all but impossible. She returned exhausted; Annerley dragged a deck chair for her to the coolest spot on deck and settled her in it. In the Red Sea, the heat forced them to follow the example of the other passengers and have their mattresses carried up to the deck every night. The fact that the men slept on the port side and the women on the starboard gave Mrs. Devenish some degree of reassurance.

Suez brought relief from the heat—and then came the part of the voyage that Annerley was to remember with pleasure for the rest of her life: the slow journey through the Suez Canal. She hung over the ship's rail, hour after hour, staring entranced at desert sands, palm trees and camels that looked near enough to touch. When darkness fell, she went with her father to the bow of the ship and watched its searchlight slicing a wedge out of the blackness ahead. She was interested to see outward-bound ships tying up in order to give precedence to homegoing ones, and was willing in her turn to give precedence to the homeward-bound mail steamer, which passed so close that passengers shouted messages over the intervening space.

The ceremony of throwing topees overboard at Port Said did not amuse her. Mrs. Devenish was keeping hers as a reminder of

India; Edwin kept his because he would need it again in July on his way back. Annerley refused to part with the one Moira had given her.

There was a strong wind blowing as the ship left the port. It was noticeably colder—a foretaste, Edwin said, of colder climes.

It proved more than a foretaste. The ship ran almost at once into high seas. The weather steadily worsened. The waves ceased to play and became menacing, until it was plain that storm conditions were ahead. Passengers disappeared from decks, from the dining saloon and from the public rooms. Day by day, the ship rolled and pitched more violently, until at last the stewardess gave up all pretense and confessed that she had never known anything like it.

Less than a dozen passengers remained on their feet in the second class, and on the first-class side, even fewer. Among those unaffected were Edwin and Annerley. Edwin had never been seasick. Annerley had experienced some initial doubts as to whether she would succumb or not—but the sight of her grandmother, almost unrecognizable, dishevelled, moaning and retching and striving in vain to retain some remnants of dignity, drove her back to the lounge, her feelings divided equally between compassion and embarrassment. Once there, she forgot seasickness in the wonder of watching gigantic waves hurtling over the ship's side and streaming away in angry froth. All decks were out of bounds. The passengers in the dining saloon were placed together at one table. Annerley made frequent trips to the cabin to minister to her grandmother, and answered an appeal from the stewardess to help look after children whose mothers were too ill to attend to them.

The fancy-dress ball was cancelled. The ship's concert could not take place. Mr. and Mrs. McFie would not give their amusing skit on a French couple in England, Mrs. Rearsley would not be heard in the ballads which had gone down so well in the Club at Bareilly. The Pierrot costumes, the pirates' outfits, Mr. Bell's authentic toreador costume which had won the first prize on several voyages—all these lay in the cabin trunks, unwanted, unworn.

The stop at Gibraltar was long enough to bring some measure of relief to the sufferers. Some, indeed, managed to keep on their feet as the ship rounded the Cape of St. Vincent. Thereafter, they vanished again. The Bay of Biscay did its dreaded worst. The English Channel was calmer, but the weather had a last surprise in store; the ship docked at Tilbury in a raging blizzard, and Annerley's first steps onto English soil were made not onto a greasy dock but onto a carpet of almost untrodden white. The bleak official buildings wore a mantle of snow: the cranes went to and fro looking like aerial cabins at a ski resort. It only needed, said a disgruntled porter, a couple of ruddy reindeer.

There were few farewells; the passengers had been separated too long for friendships to ripen. It was almost impossible to recognize, among the furred and booted figures, those lightly clad forms which had graced the decks during the early part of the voyage.

At the end of the jetty waited the boat train to London. Annerley's first glimpse of the city was of lovely, white-clad buildings. Only inside the stations—first Victoria and then Paddington, where they caught the train to Devon—was there evidence of drabness or dirt. But the sight of English men and women performing tasks which all her life she had seen assigned to servants or to coolies, filled her with amazement and embarrassment—men shovelling snow, women pushing heavy barrows. When she saw a friendly, florid woman attendant stepping into the station lavatory to wipe the seats, she wanted to apologize for using them.

She was bewildered by the extent of the city. Charles Crowther lived here—but if they went by bus—one of the puffing red omnibuses with passengers on the upper deck holding heavy tarpaulins over their knees to protect them from the cold —it would take more than an hour to reach the district in which he was living.

They had a carriage to themselves. As they progressed westward, the snowy scene changed. The white blanket disappeared; green fields came into view. Annerley, wiping the vapour from the windows, looked out into a world of red-roofed houses and neat farmhouses and prosperous-looking towns.

Exeter. Only another few miles to go. A crowded station, but nobody to meet them, nobody to offer a welcome. Outside, thin, cold sleet.

A porter, his uniform damp, his peaked cap sodden, heaved their luggage onto a barrow and led them to a train that was standing on the branch line. This, Edwin told Annerley, was the line on which she would travel to and from school. On taking his seat and paying the porter, he wished he had withheld the observation, for the carriage, a third-class one, had damp, stained covers, a cracked mirror, two scribbled-over views of local beauty spots and a floor littered with biscuit crumbs.

But the countryside through which the train carried them was green and soft and gentle. Edwin recited for his companions the county's many claims to fame: junket, cider, clotted cream, villages noted for their beauty. This was not his part of England; this was not the county in which he had been born and bred, but it was the one that Annerley would come to know best.

The sleet stopped. They knew that Torring was the third stop, but when they reached it, they were taken unawares—this surely could not be a station? There was a tiny platform which appeared to be growing out of vegetable plots; a small, open-sided building which might have been a school cricket pavilion. An ancient, bent, bearded figure stood gazing at the train as though he had never seen one before—could he be a porter? He was. He was also the station master and he was also, it transpired when they had hurried out of the train and got their luggage out, the authority on local affairs.

"You be the owner of Holt Cottage, that's right, zur," he told Edwin. "I'd known you wur to come today. Young Bernie Bray's up at the house, and you'll find it all straight. His grandpa wur to come and meet you wi' the cart, but he's not here, so he must be late, but he won't be long. Young Bernie's got the fire going, and you'll find milk and bread and butter and my missis sent up a bit o' cheese she made and Mrs. Cornell, she's postmistress, she sent up some letters. And here's old grandpa."

The newcomer looked about the same age as the porter. He brought the farm cart in which he had arrived to the edge of the platform and got down to snatch off his woolen cap and shake hands with the new arrivals. His small, twinkling eyes told them that they were being welcomed, but the sounds coming through the gaps in his teeth were more whistles than words. He helped Edwin and the porter to load the luggage, assisted the two ladies into the cart and dusted the narrow bench on which they were to sit. Then with Edwin on the front seat beside him, he took the reins and drove into the green, wooded silence ahead. Through the trees they saw a sight with which the last five weeks had made them all too familiar: the sea.

The road was rough, but the distance from station to village proved to be little more than half a mile. They drove out of the wood to see small, red-roofed buildings, and Annerley discovered that nothing had been left out of the scene she had painted in her imagination. There was a village green—tiny, but it was there. There was a duck pond and three ducks. There was a toy church, and an inn with a hanging sign that looked almost too pretentious for so humble an edifice: the Commodore. Everything was on a miniature scale—a butcher's, a baker's, a grocery store which doubled as post office, a little house with items of haberdashery in the front window.

They reached a turning. The horse turned into it unasked, toiled up a short, steep incline and stopped in front of a cottage. They had arrived.

Edwin realized that he had forgotten almost everything about the place but its site—and even that, he saw had been confused in his mind, for he had thought it some distance from the sea, whereas it stood a mere field's width away. There were no trees to break the force of the gale that had begun to blow.

Someone was running across the sodden field—Annerley. Freed at last from ayahs, from restricted decks, narrow corridors,

140

cramped cabins and musty-smelling railway carriages, she was speeding, hat snatched off, hair flying, scarf wind-whipped, to the uneven, unsubstantial wooden palings that marked the cliff's edge. She stopped and stood outlined against the spray that dashed up from the sea; Mrs. Devenish's gasp of alarm was carried away and lost in the swaying branches of the trees beside the cottage.

Edwin took her arm and turned her towards the house. She gestured towards Annerley, and he shook his head. He took her inside, left her in the tiny hall and went to help with the luggage. From inside the cottage came a boy of about fourteen, in rough, patched clothes and stout boots. He swung a cabin trunk effortlessly onto his shoulder, grinned at Edwin and went back to the house.

Edwin waited for Annerley, ushered her inside, waved his thanks to the departing grandfather and grandson, and then closed the door.

He was almost afraid to look round him. His memories of the site and even the size of the cottage had been misleading. He had thought of a rather roomy dwelling with a distant sea view —but he was standing in a doll's house with the sea a stone's throw away. He did not see how the three of them could fit into this space. There was a low roof with dormer windows, and an upper story reached by a staircase so narrow that only one person—a thin one—could go up or down at a time. In the hall, by stretching out his arms, he could touch the wall on one side and the front door on the other.

He entered the living room, and his misgivings vanished. Whatever lay beyond or above, this, the heart of the house, would make up for all the rest. A log fire crackled in the brick fireplace; a table was spread with a blue checked cloth on which had been placed bread, a dish of yellow butter, a pot of jam, a pitcher of milk, slices of cold beef, cheese, and a low earthenware jar of Devonshire cream.

They warmed themselves at the fire, and then they went upstairs. There were two bedrooms—and a cubbyhole. The rooms were small, but had windows facing the sea on one side, fields and woods on the other. The cubbyhole had a window unhappily reminiscent of a porthole, but proved to open onto a sea view. There was room beside the bed for a small table and lamp.

There was no electricity. A bathroom downstairs was supplied with water from a hand pump connected to a well at the back of the cottage. The kitchen had a flagged floor and a wood-fed stove. Outside, there was a small tool shed and two empty rabbit hutches.

Mrs. Bray, wife of the owner of the Commodore, mother of the boy Bernie, daughter of his grandpa, arrived to welcome them and to apologize for not having been present when they arrived. She was a sturdily built woman with a hearty voice and a cheerful manner. She did not have to tell Edwin and Mrs. Devenish that she was not a Devonshire woman, the accents of London could be clearly recognized. If they wanted anything, she told them, they had only to ask. She had known this cottage since it was built and she had looked after it for many years. There was wood in the tool shed, enough to start with; more would be brought by Bernie when they needed it. There was a grocer to supply stores, but she would send up their bread and dairy produce every morning. The pump at the well was easy to work, but Bernie would leave filled buckets at the kitchen door on his way to work in the mornings. She had lent them some things: crockery, cutlery; they could return them when they had unpacked their own. This room—she waved a red, chapped hand round it—if you kept it warm, sent up a good bit of heat to the rooms upstairs, so they never got too cold, but if you wanted, you could light the fires in the bedrooms, the way Mr. and Mrs. Holt liked to do. And that was all for now, she'd better get back to the customers at the inn. Her niece Dorcas, funny name, but it was common in these parts, would come in every morning and do the rough. She was seventeen; she'd been in service in Exeter but hadn't settled. No, there was nothing to pay just now; Grandpa would see to that when he came up tomorrow or the next day.

She bustled out. The cottage was theirs. Outside, the wind howled. Some of it came through the gaps in windows or doors, but Mrs. Devenish was already making neat rolls of brown paper to act as draught-stoppers. Annerley was in the kitchen. She had filled the kettle and brought down some of the large stock of tea Mrs. Devenish had brought from India. She warmed the teapot, put in the tea, poured on the boiling water and noted with pride that this was the first domestic task she had ever performed.

Darkness fell as they sat down to table. Boiled eggs supplemented the meal; toast was made at the fire. There were no curtains to draw, but the blackness and the wildness outside merely accentuated the comfort within.

Mrs. Devenish had been allotted the largest bedroom, cozy and warm, with a fire lit by Edwin. He also lit a fire in his own room. Annerley closed the door of the cubbyhole, undressed and snuggled under the blankets, her feet on an aluminum hot-water bottle for which Mrs. Devenish had knitted a pink woolen cover. She remembered that she had not cleaned her teeth, went down to the bathroom, brushed them and sprang into bed once more. She would have forgotten her prayers if her grandmother had not come in to kiss her good-night and reminded her. Her eyes were closing. She got through an appeal or two to the Almighty before they closed altogether.

Bless us all, bless those we left behind, let school be all right, don't let Shareen be sad. . . .

It would be nice to see Moira again. She was spending her holidays at the school; she must be there now, wondering how soon they would come. . . . Bless the poor and the sick and . . .

There were only nine days between Annerley's arrival at the cottage, and the date on which the school opened. There was no time for any apprehension; there was a list of clothing to be bought and marked and, if necessary, altered to fit.

It was a long list. Many of the items had been crossed out as being applicable only to boarders, but there still remained shoes, outdoor and indoor, stockings, galoshes, gloves, and the school uniform of dark green skirt, white blouse with a dark green and white stripe, and a round, dark green felt hat with a green and white striped band and the school badge. Name tapes, thanks to Mrs. Devenish's forethought, had been ordered from India and had arrived with the first letters received at the cottage.

The visit to the school took place three days before the beginning of the term. On getting out of the train at Exeter, Edwin led Annerley towards the adjoining bus station to board a bus that would leave them at the school gates. They were intercepted, however, by a tall young woman in a neat mackintosh and a brown felt hat.

"Mr. Brooke?"

"Yes."

"How do you do? My name is Williamson—Miss Williamson —one of the school secretaries. The headmistress sent me to meet you. This is Annerley? How nice to see you. Do come this way, will you?"

They followed her to the station entrance. A neat groom sprang down from the seat of a pony-and-trap, surrendered the reins to Miss Williamson and took his place behind the three passengers.

"The bus," Miss Williamson explained, guiding the pony skillfully towards the road, "goes to the school, but only after making a rather tiresome detour." She glanced at Annerley, who was seated next to her. "Are you finding England very cold?"

"Yes. But I don't mind."

"Good. Your friend, Moira Fenwick, doesn't like it at all, but she's looking a very different person from when she came to us. Pink cheeks."

"How is she?" Edwin asked.

"You must ask her that yourself, Mr. Brooke. I can only tell you that she's looking forward to seeing you. She is to be allowed to have lunch with you, but we would like her back at the school by half past three."

There was no sign of Moira, or any other pupil, when the trap drew up in front of the imposing flight of steps that led up to the front door. The size, the extent of the building was already known to Annerley from the photographs she had seen in the school prospectus sent to Edwin, but no photograph could convey the beauty of the setting. In front were sloping lawns, shrubberies, wooded paths leading to a spacious park. When they entered the hall, they could see through the central corridor a vista of playing fields and tennis courts.

Annerley was asked to sit down and wait on one of the sofas in the hall. Edwin was led away by Miss Williamson. A few moments later, a girl of about sixteen came running down the stairs and addressed Annerley.

"You're Annerley Brooke. Hello. I'm the Head Girl, Avis Lind-

145

say, and I'm to show you round the school. Ready? Let's start at the top."

She was tall and thin, with wavy hair tied back with a dark green ribbon. She was brisk and confident and alert. She was not wearing the school uniform.

"These are the junior dorms and the senior cubicles—but you won't be interested in those; you're a day girl, aren't you? These are the practice rooms—they used to be downstairs, but someone had the idea of changing them to up here because once everybody's out of the dorms and in the classrooms, the practicing can't be heard. Bathrooms. This is the staircase we use—we're not allowed on the main staircase except on special occasions—as now. Right at the end is the San, but that won't interest you, either. Now we go down. Classrooms—I always think they look a bit creepy when they're empty. You can hardly make your way along this corridor when the girls are changing classes—awful noise, but not the noise of chattering; no talking allowed during class changes. Science labs. Common room for the visiting staff. And here's the recreation room we use during holidays—by 'we,' I mean the girls who stay at school because their parents are away or dead or travelling or something like that. That reminds me: you know Moira Fenwick, don't you?"

"Yes."

"She's waiting to see you, but you won't be allowed to see her until you've seen the headmistress."

"Do you mind staying during the holidays?"

"No. It's fun, rather."

"How many of you stay?"

"During the Christmas hols, only eleven. Easter hols, twenty-two. We're looked after by the senior matron and one of the school secretaries—this hols, it was Miss Williamson. Now we go down to the ground floor. Most of it is for staff—headmistress's room, teachers' common room and—in here—the assembly hall."

Annerley gazed at it from the threshold. At the far end, a plat-

146

form. Row upon row of chairs, neatly aligned. On the walls, portraits of capped and gowned women.

"And this end—this way; we're not allowed to go through the hall—is the gym. It's rather famous. I mean, the equipment is better than most schools have. Are you keen on gym?"

"I've never done any."

For a moment, the Head Girl's composure faltered.

"Never done gym?"

"No."

"Goodness. Where were you at school?"

"At a convent."

"I suppose that accounts for it. Here's the dining hall."

Tables, endlessly long. Serving hatches. More portraits round the walls.

"The day girls have lunch at school—tea too, if they have to stay late."

"Yes, I know."

"You'll be coming by train, won't you?"

"Yes."

"The school brake meets the trains, but it only waits at the station for ten minutes—unless the trains are late, of course. But they're usually punctual except when there's snow. Want to see any more?"

"I don't think so. Thank you for showing me round."

"Pleasure. We take turns. I don't suppose I'll be seeing you much—I'm in the Matriculation form and we don't mix much because we're too busy swotting, but I hope you'll like the school and settle down all right."

"Thank you."

She was back on the sofa at the foot of the staircase. A short while later, Miss Williamson came to lead her to the headmistress.

While she had been looking round the school, Edwin had been shown the latest examination results.

"Impressive, I think you'll agree, Mr. Brooke," said the head-mistress.

"Very impressive. I congratulate you."

"The credit must go to my staff." She laid the papers aside and leaned back in her chair. "I'm very glad to have this opportunity of talking to you. Before we get to your daughter, may I say a word or two about Moira Fenwick?"

He smiled.

"Is it necessary? She's still with you—doesn't that say everything?"

"It says a good deal—for her and for us. If you hadn't written that covering letter . . . "

"It was unorthodox. It was . . . well, out of line. But I felt that you ought to be told the true position."

"Her true position. It won't surprise you to know that her parents are by no means the only parents of that kind that I have to deal with. To be honest, I long ago lost interest in unsatisfactory parents; I find it more interesting, and certainly more rewarding, to study the effect they have had on their children. The effects are never the same. They can even differ between members of the same family. For example, Moira Fenwick reacted by withdrawing into herself. Her brother—I took the trouble to make inquiries—appears to have shown no signs of insecurity. Did you know him?"

"Not well. He was sent to England very early. But his father told me that he had always been easy to deal with."

"His schoolmasters like him. They find him cooperative. I can't say that Moira has exactly cooperated, but she has worked hard. I didn't realize for some time that she was working towards an end: to catch up with your daughter, to be placed in the same class. Whatever the end, her work has been steady and satisfactory. Out of the classroom, she hasn't shown much interest in her fellow pupils or, come to that, in the school."

"Is she going to be put into Annerley's class?"

"No. She's going into what we call the parallel class. They'll be together for gym, and of course they'll see each other during the mid-morning break, and at lunch."

He made no comment; it was what he had expected.

They went on to talk of Annerley's work, and then the head-mistress pressed a bell on her desk. Miss Williamson appeared.

"Will you take Mr. Brooke round the school, Miss William-son."

"Certainly, Miss Harding."

"And please," added the headmistress, "bring Annerley Brooke to see me."

It was not, on the whole, a bad interview, Annerley thought when it was over. Questions, of course, about her work. And information on which class she was to be in—not the same as Moira's. The only difficult part had been to try and ignore the fact that under the questions and the information, a pair of keen grey eyes assessed her. She was being examined and docketed and she would be filed, but she would never see the file.

And after the interview, at last, Moira.

Edwin took them to lunch in Exeter. He chose a quiet restaurant, led them to a table, said that he would go and buy a news-paper, and left them to talk.

"Parallel classes," Moira said. "But I'm going to be allowed to come out and spend one weekend a month with you. My father gave his permission and so did the headmistress and so did your father."

"Tell me about school."

"There's nothing to tell. It's just the usual clang clang, get up, clang clang, go to breakfast, clang clang go to classes, clang clang put on your cloaks and go outside for ten minutes' brisk exercise, don't dawdle, Moira, now a nice run, come along, come along, now deep breathing, one-two, one-two, clang clang more lessons, clang for lunch, for games, for tea, for prep, for supper, for bed. That goes on every day, day after day, till you feel you've swal-lowed a bit of clockwork and have to be wound up all the time.

And then they say isn't school wonderful, you must enjoy every minute, and please don't run away."

"You didn't, thank goodness."

"I nearly did, several times. I ticked dates off on the calendar, waiting for you to arrive—that helped."

"Don't you like the place at all?"

"Not much. It's different for you—you can get out and go home every day. What do you look like in the uniform?"

"A bit awful, really. I don't care how I look, but I hate heavy clothes. Remember those cotton dresses we wore in India?"

"Yes."

"Where are your parents?"

"My father's in Switzerland. My mother went to Malaya but she didn't like it. I knew she wouldn't. My father knew too; he said she wasn't cut out for rubber plantations. She went to Australia. Now she's in Melbourne."

Annerley wanted to ask whether the rubber planter had taken her there, but decided not to.

Edwin returned and they ordered lunch. He found Moira far more talkative than she had been in Seymour Street, and thought that perhaps she had waited for Annerley's arrival before giving rein to her tongue.

The school pony-and-trap, the groom at the reins, awaited Moira at the station.

"Thank you for the lunch, Mr. Brooke."

"I hope we'll have many more together."

She was driven away. Edwin and Annerley walked towards their train.

"Do you think she's changed?"

"One can't tell. She was always well behaved . . . on the outside. She's certainly going to be a beauty."

"But she was always pretty. Even people who didn't like her had to admit she was pretty."

They had a carriage to themselves, and for some time they sat silent, watching the scenery, each occupied by thoughts that were not on the present, but on the future.

He turned to look at her at last.

"Well," he asked, "what do you think of your new school?"

Clang clang, go to classes, clang clang, time to go home. The months while her father was here. The years when he would be in India . . .

"It seems very nice," she said.

PART TWO

1914-1918

In May 1917, a troopship carrying a detachment of British and Indian troops to the Mesopotamian theater of war was torpedoed and sunk in the Mediterranean. Eighty-four survivors were picked up by the crew of a Greek ship and taken to Patmos, where they were interned. Among their number was Major Edwin Brooke.

The reactions of the inhabitants of Torring to this news varied widely. Some shared the mingled relief and anxiety of Annerley and Mrs. Devenish, but there were others who expressed the opinion that Major Brooke need never have volunteered for service abroad; he should have stayed in his job at Aldershot and not got himself sent all the way to Greece, leaving his daughter and the old lady on their own.

That they were on their own was due to the swift and enthusiastic response that the young men and women of the village had given to the call to arms. On the outbreak of war, they had departed with a promptness that had led Edwin to suspect that they had been impelled not so much by patriotism as by a desire to escape from an existence in which the highlights of leisure pursuits were whist drives, or the weekly cinema show given at the church hall. Whatever the reason, their going brought about several changes in Mrs. Devenish's way of life.

On her arrival in England three years earlier, she had assumed the duties of housekeeper at the cottage. They were not heavy. The cooking was done by a young girl from the village; the cleaning was done by Mrs. Bray's niece, Dorcas. The washing was carried away to be done by the village laundress, seventy-year-old Mrs. Scaife. Bernie Bray or his grandfather provided wood and water. Annerley stayed at school for lunch and for tea. Edwin spent the weekdays looking up old friends in various parts of the country, returning only at weekends. Mrs. Devenish was left with ample leisure, and made frequent trips to Exeter to change her library books or to have lunch in her favourite café near the cathedral. She sometimes thought regretfully of the bearer or the ayah, and she missed the colour and variety of Seymour Street, but on the whole she was content with life.

The change in conditions as the war progressed was gradual and at first painless. Dorcas left to go into a munitions factory, but the cook was able without much difficulty to do the extra work. Bernie Bray added three years to his age and went away to enlist, but his grandfather continued to fill the water buckets and leave a supply of logs. But when the cook left and no replacement could be found, it became necessary for Mrs. Devenish to do the work. Her tasks were made easier by the fact that Edwin was now in the army and seldom came home, so that the only cooking required of her was a boiled or scrambled egg for Annerley's breakfast and a light dinner when she returned from school in the evening.

It was the light dinner that revealed to Annerley the inadequacy of her grandmother's domestic skills. She had grown used to the slow deterioration in the order and cleanliness of the cottage. She helped to bring in wood and water. She made her own breakfast and took early-morning tea up to Mrs. Devenish before leaving for school, so she did not think it too much to expect at least a snack when she got home. But all she found on her return each evening was a mess of preparation and her grandmother, scarlet-cheeked, agitated, poring over a recipe book. Her curries were messes of meat or vegetables floating in yellow liquid. "I didn't like to overdo the curry powder, Annerley dear." The rice was a soggy, sticky ball. "It seemed a shame to wash all the goodness out of it." Her puddings were unidentifiable. "I don't know why it didn't rise; perhaps I should have warmed the oven first."

Soon Annerley decided to cook the dinners on her return from school. She had also to cook for Moira when she came for the permitted weekend.

"What I can't understand," Moira commented, "is why she can't even cook an egg properly. Didn't you tell me she once lived in a large parsonage with only one servant? She must have had to do *something*, mustn't she?"

"It was a long time ago. I suppose she's forgotten."

They were in the kitchen, frying eggs and bacon for Sunday breakfast.

"Perhaps your mother did all the work."

"Perhaps."

"If I've got to spend my weekend helping you to do the cooking, you'll have to keep her out of the kitchen. Why can't she even do a simple thing like washing spinach without leaving bits of sand in it?"

"Ask her."

"I would if I didn't think she'd get upset and take to her bed. Funny, in India I used to think she wasn't a bad old lady, as old ladies went. Quiet and dignified. And shy, but at least she looked *capable*."

"I think she was too long in India to be able to—"

"—Live without slaves?"

"Yes. She's too old to—"

"Age hasn't got much to do with it. Take my father: he's young enough to be her son, but while he was in England, he was as bad as she is—convinced that if he shouted 'Qua hai,' a slave would appear."

157

Annerley, making coffee, spoke absentmindedly.

"It's rather sad, I suppose, in a way."

"It's also rather convenient. Here she is in her room, dressing up to go to Morning Service in Exeter, and here we are—slaving. Does she like her bacon crisp or clammy?"

"In between."

"Then here it is. You can ring the bell."

Annerley rang it, and filled in time before her grandmother's appearance by reminding Moira of Mrs. Devenish's usefulness in other spheres: knitting for the troops, making bandages, helping in the communal kitchen in Exeter.

"Yes, yes, I know all that," Moira said impatiently. "She could hardly sit and do nothing, with a war going on, could she?"

"You don't give her enough credit."

"You give her too much. And you've given her nearly all the bacon—give me another slice."

Annerley gave it to her and took off her working overall, revealing the blouse and skirt that made up her invariable day-time wear. Her skirts became longer, her blouses slightly less plain; she had two dresses which served for afternoon or evening. Her hair was still short and wavy, needing no more than a brush night and morning.

Moira was at all times, as in the past, perfectly turned out. She would rather die, she frequently told Annerley, war or no war, than be badly dressed. Her hair she now wore in a thick plait, doubled back and tied at the neck with a narrow ribbon.

It was Moira who was most affected by the news of Edwin's internment. Since his arrival in England before the war, he had shown unfailing interest in her progress at school. He had obtained permission for her to bring her books to the cottage at weekends, and had patiently coached her in her weak subjects. In return, she had worked with a zeal that had surprised her teachers, and her Matriculation results had been almost as good as those obtained by Annerley. The strength of her gratitude and devotion to Edwin was something that not even Annerley guessed.

With Matriculation behind them, there had arisen the question of their future. Annerley's presented no problem; she was to continue her studies in the hope of getting a place at Somerville College at Oxford. Moira had her own plans: having vindicated Edwin's faith in her abilities, she decided that her schooling should now end. She was eighteen and she wanted to do some kind of war work, in however humble a capacity.

After the divorce of her parents, her mother had remarried and was now living in Australia. Her father had married a wealthy widow who had turned her Dorset mansion into a hospital for wounded officers. When he had brought her down to the cottage on a visit, both Moira and Annerley had been reminded of Mrs. Cole-Hardy, for the new Mrs. Fenwick was lean, tough, wiry and devoted to horses. She was not at all the woman, Moira confided to Annerley, that she would have expected her father to choose.

"Why not? She's the right age for him."

"But she's not in the least like my mother."

"Perhaps that was the reason he chose her."

"Perhaps. But I seem to remember reading somewhere, or being told, that men usually stick to one type. I wish she had children of her own—I've got a feeling she's going to try and be a mother to me."

But any maternal feeling the second Mrs. Fenwick possessed proved to be reassuringly practical. She agreed at once to Moira's leaving school, and in no time had her in nurse's uniform, attached to the hospital. After the war, she told her husband briskly before he returned to India, she would bring Moira out and let her take her pick of the inexhaustible supply of eligible bachelors.

Her stepson, Mark, claimed whatever credit there was to be had for the marriage. He had enlisted at the age of nineteen. Wounded in the spring of 1917, he was sent back to England, where he found himself in a large Dorset house-turned-hospital in the care of a middle-aged widow whose common sense, strength of mind and no-nonsense approach to life he felt would make a good anchor for his loose-footed father. Whether it was these qualities or her considerable fortune that attracted Mr. Fenwick was not known. Mark planted a seed, tended it and, while it grew, spent all the time he could at the cottage in Torring.

His first arrival, two months after the news of Edwin's internment, was by ambulance, unannounced, and at midnight, the driver having lost the way. He had been warmly welcomed. For Mrs. Devenish he represented male support, so sadly lacking since Edwin's departure. For Moira he was an ally, supporting her in her decision to take up nursing as a profession. And for Annerley he filled a lack that she had not known existed: a brother.

He was tall and broad; his hair was a darker auburn than Moira's, his features a masculine version of his mother's. He was loosely knit, a somewhat clumsy mover, energetic in spite of crutches and a serious leg wound; sensible and light-hearted. His visits revitalized the cottage, and turned it upside down.

His plans for the summer were clear-cut: he was, he said, going to engage two rooms at the Commodore.

"Two?" Annerley asked.

She was swinging lazily in a hammock that he had slung between a tree at the side of the cottage, and another whose branches hung over the woodshed. Moira was lying on a rug on the grass; Mark was in a chair with a leg rest, his injured leg outstretched. It was late June; the weather throughout the month had been almost uninterruptedly warm and sunny.

"Two," he confirmed. "One for myself, the other for Prebdel."

"Prebdel? Chandra Prebdel? Shareen Prebdel's brother?"

"The same. Now in his second year at Oxford."

"Can you live away from the hospital?" Moira asked.

"For a time. The ambulance would fetch and carry me when they wanted to see me. My leg's going to take some time to get itself right, and there's nothing they can do to hurry it, so we'll all have a wonderful holiday, with cider and clotted cream and so on. Somebody's got to help me to negotiate those steps down to the beach, but if I'm not killed on the way, we can have some picnics and try to forget there's a war on. I don't suppose the accommodation at the Commodore will be up to Prebdel's standards, but it'll do him good to rough it for a change."

"What's wrong with a tent?" Moira asked. "Not for you, with your leg in plaster—but for him?"

"If he ever entered a tent," Mark said, "it would have to be one of the kind used by desert sheiks, with Persian rugs and silken hangings and perfumed with the scents of Araby. You should see his rooms at Oxford. His trouble is that he's got too much money."

Annerley, lying against the hammock cushions, gazing at the sky, said that nobody could have too much money.

"Oh yes they can," Mark said. "Money corrupts."

"Bosh," said Moira. "You're always generalizing."

"In a general way, money corrupts," Mark repeated firmly. "In this particular instance, the process of corruption has barely begun, but a chap can't go on for too long treating himself to everything he fancies. It's unhealthy. He's already at the stage of seeing that everything he orders is of the highest quality. His clothes, for instance—but you'll see. I warned him long ago that he was turning into a tailor's dummy. A dandy, in fact."

"He can't be a dandy in a bathing suit," Moira pointed out.

"His beach wear will be impeccable. He'll go into Exeter every morning to be shaved. He'll bring his own towels, which came from the mills at Cawnpore and were specially made and initialled for his family." He paused. "But you knew his family," he told Annerley. "I don't suppose he'll be much of a surprise to you. He's looking forward to meeting you—you figured very largely in his sister's letters. Do you still hear from her?"

161

"Yes. Often."

"She was a spoilt little brat," Moira remarked. "I hope she's changed."

"She wasn't spoilt," Annerley said. "She had a bad temper, like you, and she liked her own way—who doesn't—but she didn't get it all the time. She just had a strong character, that's all."

"How could you judge, at twelve or thirteen?" Mark asked.

"I didn't judge. I saw a lot of her, for years, and I got to know her well and I liked her. I'm sorry she never came to England."

There was silence, broken by Annerley with an inquiry as to whether it was her turn to make the tea.

"Yes, it is," Moira answered.

"If my leg wasn't in plaster," Mark said virtuously, "I'd do it."

"I'm sure you would," Annerley said dryly.

"I certainly would," he assured her. "I'm not like my sister, who always insists on my-turn, your-turn."

"If I hadn't refused to do other people's turns at the hospital," Moira told him, "I would have had a hard time of it. If you do someone's duty once, you find yourself doing it forever. So you don't do it."

Annerley put a foot on the ground to stop the hammock, and climbed out. She went into the kitchen, lit the oven, mixed scones, put them in to bake and then filled the kettle. Through the small, diamond-paned window she could see Moira lying on her stomach, chin propped on her hands, reading. Mark's eyes were closed; she thought he had fallen asleep. His face, seen thus, unguarded, showed the frown caused by the constant nagging pain in his leg, pain that at other times was concealed under his carefree manner.

He was not asleep. He was musing on the differences between his sister and Annerley, and wondering what had kept them good friends for so long. Perhaps it was this very contrast that explained it—his sister, so withdrawn, so uncompromising, so . . . he rejected the word cold, but there was certainly no warmth in the manner in which she responded to friendly advances, or to male attentions. She had outgrown her habit of uttering unwelcome home truths, but she still had an edge on her tongue. That she was very pretty could not be denied—even prettier in her nurse's uniform. That she attracted men was even less in question, but he knew few who could stand up for long against her unflattering lack of interest.

And Annerley? Not as pretty—but she had a way of staying in the mind. She had a fund of humour that was deep, but kind. She was, in her way, no more approachable than Moira, but this was because she was enclosed in a quiet, contented life of her own. She was perhaps not the kind of girl who turned men's heads, but she was, in his opinion, the kind of girl that men married. He might, he thought, even marry her himself in a few years, if he survived the war . . . if the war ever ended, and if he survived to see the end.

Annerley carried out the tea tray. Moira got up and dragged a folding table from the shed. Mark sat up to count the scones.

"Do we divide these by three, or by four?" he asked.

"Three. My grandmother won't be back from Exeter until this evening. She's having tea with her knitting group."

"Tell her," he requested, "that she mustn't knit me any more sea-boot socks. I'm not in the Navy, I don't wear sea boots and at the moment I've only one foot to put into them."

"Don't stop her from knitting," Moira begged. "The more she knits, the less time she has for trying out cooking recipes. If she were my grandmother, I'd lock her out of the kitchen—but you know what Annerley is."

"I don't know yet," Mark said. "I'm learning. Which of you is going to book those rooms at the Commodore?"

"Why have you left it as late as this?" Moira asked him. "Getting rooms anywhere in this village is going to be practically impossible. They'll all be booked by holiday-makers. War or no war, this is still Devon-glorious-Devon, and it still fills up in summer."

"I'll go down and see what Mrs. Bray has to offer," Annerley said.

"And you'd better inspect what she offers," Mark warned her. "I like a sea view. Prebdel won't mind the view, but he'll expect a high standard of comfort."

"Which he won't get at the Commodore, and serves him right," Moira said. "What time is the ambulance coming to fetch you this evening?"

"Seven. It's too early, but Annerley didn't invite me to supper."

"I'll go back with you. I'm on early duty tomorrow."

"I wish," Annerley told her, "that I was doing some useful work, like you."

"You're doing what your father wants you to do. Have you heard from him lately?"

"Yes. Two letters, both so heavily censored that there was practically nothing left to read. There's time for us to go down and talk to Mrs. Bray about those rooms, if you want to."

"All right. What happens," she asked Mark, "if she gets nervous about having an Indian living in the house?"

"Tell her he's a rajah. He looks like one."

Mrs. Bray was running the inn while her sergeant husband bawled commands at raw recruits on a distant parade ground. She began by telling Annerley and Moira that every available guest room—there were only five—was booked to the end of the season. Annerley, after professing disappointment and agreeing that her application should have been made months earlier, asked whether all the bookings had been confirmed. They had not. Then, said Annerley, perhaps two of the rooms might be offered to a wounded officer and his friend from Oxford, who was an Indian and who would make a perfect guest once he had been allowed to bring his room up to his standard of comfort.

"If my rooms aren't good enough for him," Mrs. Bray said indignantly, "you can tell him— What is he? A rajah or something?"

"Almost," Moira answered. "I promise you, Mrs. Bray, that when you've had him for a week, you won't want him to go away. The only thing that'll disappoint you is that he doesn't look or sound or behave like a rajah or like an Indian, because he's been in English schools since he was fifteen. My brother said he'd like a sea view, but if that nice front room isn't available, he'll have to do without a view."

"Come upstairs," invited Mrs. Bray.

Two rooms were allocated on condition that two weeks' rent would be paid forthwith. Moira produced the money, and they inspected the room that was to be Mark's. It was not large, but it had two windows, one giving a view of the fields, the other looking onto the road. Chandra's room was larger and overlooked the sea on one side, and on the other, the hen houses and rabbit hutches that filled what before the war had been the inn's tea garden.

"Got them?" Mark asked on their return.

"Yes," said Moira. "At the expense of two unfortunate guests who thought they'd made a firm booking."

"What's Chandra's room like?"

"A bit bare."

"Comfortable bed?"

"If we'd felt the bed," Moira said irritably, "we would have been thrown out by Mrs. Bray and we wouldn't—or you wouldn't—have got the rooms. I suppose your exigent friend has stayed in an old English inn before, and knows what to expect?"

"I'll bring him down to look at this one on Thursday."

They did not come on Thursday. On Friday afternoon there was still no sign of them. Annerley, after walking down to the Commodore and finding that there had been no message from them, returned to the cottage, piled cushions on the hammock, selected a book and settled down to read.

She found, however, that her mind turned persistently to her father. Closing the book at last, she gave herself up to musing. His letters were censored, but surely they would not have deleted harmless references to his future—and hers? She had not been able to find a single sentence that touched on what he proposed to do when the war ended. Would he come to England, or would he return to India? It was difficult to think of him in Seymour Street without her. And how long would it be before she saw Seymour Street again?

Roots. What were roots? She had never put down any in this country. She had never been able to feel that her home was here, that she belonged here. On the other hand, it did not seem sensible to say that her roots were in India. She knew that she could not claim to know anything about the real India—the country, the people, the religions. All she knew, all she could be completely certain of was that her life out there had been almost magically happy. Lying here now beside a field bordering the English Channel, her eyes closed, she could recall a medley of sights, smells, sounds which transported her to the scenes of her childhood. She could believe that Shareen Prebdel's chaprassi was standing in the compound of number 5 Seymour Street waiting for a reply to one of her letters. Ruby Fernandez was playing the piano. Mr. Leeson was shouting for his shaving water, Charles Crowther was puttering out of the gate on his motorbike, Abdul was waiting to serve dinner. The gharries rattled by, drowning the plaintive notes of the snake-charmer's flute. Her father lay on his long-sleever, her grandmother sewed, the monsoon rains poured down, flooding the compound. The Stanley boys in their zinc tubs . . .

Where were the Stanley boys? What would she find if—when —she went back? India was vast and varied, and she knew only one tiny fragment of it. What was there to go back to but her childhood? And childhood was over, the life she had led as a child was over, merged into this land of mists and fogs and— sometimes—glorious days like this one to prove that the climate was not wholly malignant.

Childhood . . . Moira was here. Shareen was in India, in her own land, her own home. The latest photographs she had sent showed that she, too, had grown up. No longer in western dresses, but in delicate saris; tall, thin, elegant, facing the camera with the fearless, direct look which Miss Severn had thought so unladylike.

Her musing was interrupted by the sensation of slipping. The hammock was descending slowly to the ground. With an impatient exclamation, she got up, found that the rope on the shed side had become unfastened, and retied it to the tree. Then she climbed once more into the hammock.

She had read a few pages of her book when she became aware that the hammock was once again on its way to the ground. This time, her annoyance was voiced more strongly. Struggling out, she turned to deal with the rope.

She took a step forward—and then halted abruptly. For a few frightening moments she could almost believe that her thoughts on India had been too vivid—for the man she saw leaning negligently against the door of the shed, hands in the pockets of his trousers, might have been Shareen Prebdel's father. She could almost, as in the past, feel her tongue stiffening, her powers of speech leaving her. And then, with a wrenching effort, she brought herself back to the present. Not Shareen's father. A young man, but made in the same image—the same tall, slender figure, the same dark, smooth skin and large, dark, long-lashed eyes.

Not Shareen's father. Shareen's brother. Chandra Prebdel.

He spoke, and even the voice was the same: low, unhurried, faintly amused, the accent that of a cultured Englishman.

"Miss Annerley Brooke, I presume?"

He was wearing a white, open-necked shirt, grey flannel trousers and a blazer—all as impeccable as Mark had said they would be.

"You're Chandra," she said.

He straightened, and raised a hand in salutation.

"You can't say we're strangers, can you?" he asked.

"No. When . . . how did you come?"

"I drove. With Mark."

"Drove what?"

"My car. He proposed my joining him in the ambulance, but I

167

convinced him that he'd fit into the car, crutches and plaster and all." He came forward and stood before her. "I think I startled you."

"Only for a moment. I thought you were your father. Where did you leave Mark?"

"At the inn."

"Did you see your room?"

"No. I thought that could wait. I wanted to come here and meet you."

"I'm glad you did. Why don't we sit down?"

She waved a hand towards the seats, and he stood inspecting them. A rough wooden bench that doubled as chopping-board for logs. A deck chair whose striped canvas had a rent in it. An old-fashioned steamer chair, wooden, with a leg rest, onto which Mark carefully lowered himself when they sat in the garden. His eyes rested finally on the bench, and she had a strong impression that he was waiting for someone to dust it for him.

"I think," he said, "I'll borrow one of your hammock rugs, and sit on the grass."

He went back to retie the rope. She stood watching him.

"A bad way to knot it," he told her. "If you'd done it properly, I couldn't have got it loosened."

She was looking at his hands. They, too, were like his father's —long-fingered, supple.

"A bad way to begin an acquaintance," she answered. "Suppose I'd come down with a thump and injured my spine?"

"Would I, did I, let you down with a thump?" He rejoined her. "I did not. I took the utmost care. Shouldn't I go inside and pay my respects to your grandmother?"

"She's in Exeter. We ought to go and help Mark fix up about his room."

"Mark, when I left him, was doing his own fixing up. He was also entertaining a group of small boys who had followed him into the inn to find out exactly what was wrong with his leg. I told him I wanted to see you. When I don't return, he'll know we're making friends."

She was in the hammock. He stretched himself on the rug—a slow, easy, lazy movement. Lying on his back, arms behind his head, he looked very much at home.

"I was sorry to hear that your father had been interned," he said. "I remember him quite well, though I only met him once or twice."

"You've met Moira, of course?"

"Only recently. Her first, her very first remark to me was that she had never cared for my sister. I said that, regrettably, my sister's letters showed that she had not cared much for her, either."

"Isn't that what's called starting off on the wrong foot?"

"In Moira's case, I'd call it starting as she means to go on."

"That's only her manner. She's all right underneath."

"You should know. It's odd, isn't it, how differently she and Mark reacted to their unsatisfactory parents? He wants a wife and a family and a settled home."

"Why do you think she doesn't?"

"The indications are that she plans to keep herself to herself. But I don't want at this moment to discuss Moira or Mark. I'd like to learn something about you. After that, I'd like a personal view of my sister. Her letters began by being dutiful, and then became more friendly and are at last beginning to be interesting. But they don't give me a clear picture of what she's like."

"I last saw her when she was thirteen—but she was full of life, never dull, not very easy to handle. But—"

"But what?"

"I don't know what your father expected her to turn out like. If he wanted her to look and sound as English as you do, he must have been disappointed, because she doesn't. Or didn't. She was much more like your mother."

"So I gathered. Fair enough—one east, one west. And now we go on to you."

"Me? Nothing much. I'm hoping to get into Oxford at the end of next year."

"Looking forward to it?"

"Not much. My father always wanted me to work for a

degree, but somehow, with a war on, and people all round me doing some kind of war work, I feel left out."

"Would you like to nurse, like Moira?"

"No."

"Or pack up parcels for the troops?"

"No. Or knit, or make bandages? No. That covers most of the things within my scope, so what's left is study."

"At the school?"

"Yes."

"When you've got your degree, what then?"

There was a pause.

"I don't know," she said at last.

"England—or India?"

"Before you let the hammock down, I was trying to decide whether, if I went back, I'd be as happy as I was when I was a child."

"You could perhaps be as happy in a different way. Moira said that you and your father got on well. You could keep house for him. You could become a memsahib—wouldn't you enjoy that?"

"You sound as though you thought it a useless kind of life."

"It is for most of them, isn't it?"

"It isn't for all of them."

"My father said in one of his letters that your father didn't mix much with other Englishmen. Why not?"

"Because he found that many of them didn't share his views on getting to know Indians. He thought that most of the English led lives that were quite separate from the Indians, and he felt that was wrong."

"How does he propose to alter the situation?"

"He's a man of peace. He didn't go round expressing views that were different from the orthodox ones held by most of the English out there. He went his own way. The pupils he coached were mostly Indians. He liked them and they liked him."

"How many of them did you meet?"

"None. I just saw them coming and going. Shareen was the only Indian girl I was ever really friendly with. The only Indian house I knew was yours. I realize, looking back, what a lot it meant to me." She paused, and then spoke thoughtfully. "Do you ever ask yourself whether it was right to break the pattern, to tear so many children away from so much happiness and leave them in an entirely different environment? Can you wonder that so many of them felt abandoned?"

"It was a problem for the parents as well as for the children. In my own case, there was no problem at all; my father put the matter very clearly. If I stayed in India, I'd become like my uncles; if I came to England, I'd be like him. It was an easy choice." He selected a blade of grass and began to chew it thoughtfully. "If you decided to go back to India, and wanted to be slightly different from the other memsahibs, how would you achieve it?"

"I don't know. Any suggestions?"

He pondered.

"Is your Hindustani as painfully inadequate as the occasional phrases I hear being exchanged between Mark and Moira?"

"It's more fluent. Moira forgot some of hers when she was sent to England—and I don't suppose Mark can remember much of his. I don't speak it grammatically."

"Then how about trying to improve it?"

"My father speaks it grammatically—and the servants can't understand half he says."

"Are you only going to address servants? If you learned Hindi, you could talk to elevated Indians like myself. If you preferred some other Indian language, you've got a wide choice—there are two hundred and twenty-five."

"Two hundred and—!"

"Hindi's only spoken by eighty million. Do you know what India's next most widely spoken language is?"

"No."

"Bengali. If you learned Bengali, you could talk to another sixty million or so." He changed the blade of grass for a fresh one. "Then there's Bihari. Would you care to take up the study of—"

171

"No."

"Then how about Telegu?"

"No."

"Pity. Marathi?"

"No."

"You're very hard to please. Tamil? Punjabi? Rajasthani?"

"No."

"Why did you confine yourself to Hindustani, which is merely a dialect of Hindi?"

"What did you confine yourself to?"

"Hindi and Bengali in the home. Punjabi when I went north to visit relations. Would you like me to tell you about the smaller language groups?"

"No."

"Then what would you like to talk about?"

"You."

"A thumbnail sketch? A potted autobiography? Age, twenty-one. Interests, sport. Did you know that Indians play first-class hockey?"

"No."

"Well, they do. They play first-class cricket, too—myself among them. Ambition? None. Hobbies? None."

"Character?"

"In every way sound. If you're interested, I could ask my parents to send you my old school reports. Glowing. They couldn't find enough superlatives. Cooperative, intelligent, promising—and so on." He raised himself on an elbow in order to see her better. "If Shareen was here to speak for me, I wouldn't have to play my own trumpet voluntary. I'm just trying to prove to you that I'm qualified to be your second-best friend."

He was smiling. There was an answering smile on her face. She closed her eyes and lay back, letting the silence lengthen. Her mind was filled with happiness—and with gratitude: for the sunshine, the quiet little garden, the sea murmuring at the base of the cliffs, and for Chandra Prebdel, who had come to recreate something of the life she had led in her childhood.

172

A large dog of indeterminate breed trotted round the side of the cottage, went up to Annerley and licked her hand. She opened her eyes and greeted it politely.

"Hello, Flap."

"Yours?" Chandra inquired.

She laughed.

"Yes and no. When I came to England, one of the things I longed to do was own a dog—a dog of my own. And I got one. Mrs. Bray—you'll meet her when we go over to the Commodore —brought me a puppy, eight weeks old, a lovely bundle of fur. I named him Kim. I loved him and he loved me—but I wasn't his only love. His mother and his brothers and sisters paid him frequent visits, and he began to spend as much time with them as he did with me."

"He must have come back to you for his dinner."

"Not always. He often shared his family's dinner. And then he fell in love with a fox terrier belonging to the grocer, and moved in with her."

"And never came back?"

"Only to see how I was getting on, as Flap is doing now. I've had four dogs altogether—mine, and not mine."

"How about cats?"

"My grandmother doesn't like them—they give her the prickles or something. In a way, it's just as well that I haven't got an animal that'll fret when I go away."

There was another long, companionable silence. Flap decided to share the rug, and Chandra made room for him. After a time, he addressed Annerley.

"Can't you dream out loud?"

"I was thinking how differently people turn out to what one expects. Like Moira, for example. I thought she wouldn't make a good nurse because she doesn't seem to be warm and sympathetic—but her stepmother says she's wonderful. She's going to take it up as a profession. And then there's you."

"Didn't you think I'd make a good nurse?"

"I mean that I never succeeded in picturing you as you are."

173

She stopped the gentle rocking of the hammock, and spoke with an attempt to keep the reluctance out of her voice. "We ought to go and join Mark."

She had no desire to move, and something told her that he was as unwilling to leave the garden as she was. She did not want to bring the meeting to an end—but end it must, and it was better that she should be the one to end it. They would meet again. And again—and again.

He rose reluctantly. They began to walk to the inn, Flap leading the way.

"It's odd, isn't it," Chandra said, "that it's taken so many years for us to meet? Shareen thinks I should have got in touch with you as soon as you arrived in England. But that was because she hadn't realized that even in England, small as it is in comparison with the vastness of India, travelling from one place to another can take time."

"Geography wasn't her strong subject. Looking back, I don't think Miss Severn knew much about it, either. Did Shareen keep in touch with her after she left India?"

"I don't know. But I hear about her frequently from an uncle of mine who lives in London. She pays him visits because she wants to get back to India and wants him to find her a nice family with daughters to educate—preferably the daughters of a maharajah living in a nice comfortable palace. How does your grandmother get on here?"

"She's happy because she's got to know more people through her war work. She goes into Exeter most days of the week."

They were in sight of the inn. He laid a detaining hand on her arm.

"Just a moment. I'd like to ask you something."

"Well?"

"Does Moira show any sign of being worried about Mark?"

"You mean is she worrying about what the doctors—"

"You know, I suppose, that there's a fear that he may be left with a slight limp?"

"Yes. The doctors told Moira, and she told me."

"They also told Mark, and Mark told me. He didn't take them seriously. He's quite sure—at least, he was sure at one time —that the leg would heal completely. I'm not sure that he's still as certain as he was."

"He still talks about joining the Indian Police after the war."

"Let's hope he can."

When they reached the door of the inn, it was her turn to detain him.

"Will you kindly remember," she said, "that this place was built in the seventeenth century and has never really been brought up to date? If it doesn't come up to your standard of comfort, I'd rather you didn't say so out loud. Mrs. Bray is a friend of mine."

"I suppose she'll have no objection to my introducing a few comforts of my own?"

"You'll have to discuss that with her."

Mark was waiting for them in the small parlour.

"Well, did you get acquainted?" he asked them.

"Yes, we did, and now he's got to go up and see how he likes his room."

"He won't like it."

"Is yours any better?" Chandra asked.

"Not much. Go up and see."

Chandra went up and inspected both rooms. His appearance and manner were a great relief to Mrs. Bray, who, since agreeing to let him have a room, had talked to her friends in the village and had been warned to expect a dhoti-clad figure who would sit cross-legged on the floor and smoke a hookah. So much did Chandra's quiet, courteous demeanour work on her that she opened the door of a small, disused room between his bedroom and Mark's, apologized for its untidiness and explained that it was a private bathroom that her mother had had fitted up and had used until her death. If Chandra would agree to pay extra, she would clear it out, and he and Mark could use it. Chandra thanked her, agreed to the additional sum asked, and said that his uncle in London would send down a man who would do the necessary repainting without expense to her and without inconveniencing her. If the room was free, he would like to take it for the months of July, August and September. She would, he hoped, allow him to bring certain things of his own—an armchair or two—but these would remain after his departure if she cared to accept them. He added that he was a non-smoker and a non-drinker, and would be glad to pay the full sum in advance.

Mrs. Bray had by this time gauged the depth of his pocket; even the fact of his not drinking could not detract from her satisfaction. They parted firm friends.

Chandra rejoined Annerley and Mark, told them what had been arranged and then drove away to keep a luncheon appointment in Exeter and discuss the possibility of planning some cricket fixtures. Mark watched the car out of sight and then turned to Annerley.

"Everything fixed to his liking," he said. "See the way he does it?"

"He didn't do it. He just mesmerized Mrs. Bray into doing it."

"Same thing. My uncle in London. My uncle will do this or that, not in the Indian way, which means next week or the week after or not at all, but here and now. My uncle will wave his wand, and here, ladies and gentlemen, is the renovated bathroom for our exclusive use, and here are some items of furniture and a carpet or two. How did you get on with him?"

"It was wonderful. He took me back to India, and he brought Shareen into the garden. He looks exactly like his father, and for the first minute or two he had the same effect on me—paralyzing. Then I saw it was only Chandra."

"Only Chandra. When I first saw him, I thought he was going to be impossible. His looks, his seemingly unlimited money, his easy way of getting people to do anything he wanted—it was all too much. Then I found that his looks don't interest him and he takes his money for granted, and I began to understand him."

They were going slowly back to the cottage, Annerley keeping her pace slow so that he could keep up. They found Mrs. Devenish back from Exeter, watering the little plants on the windowsill of the living room. Moira had also arrived.

Mark sat down to talk to Mrs. Devenish while tea was being prepared by the girls. They asked her to lay the table, and he amused himself by counting the number of items she forgot to put out: teaspoons, jam, honey, cream. Annerley came in and supplied what was missing, and her grandmother apologized for the omissions, but not in the humble tone she once would have used. The war had changed her in more ways than one. She had by now accepted the fact that she was incompetent in the domestic sphere, and not much more useful in other departments, but the friends she had made in Exeter and her membership in a group dedicated to war work had made her very much more self-confident. With few or no domestic responsibilities, with outside interests and occupations, she was for the first time in her life developing a personality of her own.

When they sat down to tea, she said that leaflets had been left at the cottage advertising the film that was to be shown that week at the church hall. Mark and Annerley decided to attend the performance, but found that the audience for the afternoon show—the only one he was able to attend, since there was a time limit to his outings from the hospital—was made up of small boys and girls from the village, whose shrieks of excitement drowned the music being thumped out by the local Mrs. Fernandez. They decided to go into Exeter, and he took her after a cinema show to a café which provided a generous tea and was patronized for the most part by troops on leave. For Mark, this outing was quiet enough, but for Annerley it was brimful of excitement. She enjoyed the films, good or indifferent, with a wholeheartedness he found refreshing; she enjoyed pouring out tea for him and sharing the toast and sandwiches. His enjoyment came from watching her. She was good company, she was undemanding. The more time he spent with her, the more he marvelled at his initial failure to realize how attractive she was, with her delicate skin, large, grey-green eyes, hair in soft waves round her forehead, and total lack of self-consciousness.

Moira seldom joined them unless they were going on a picnic. Chandra sometimes took them for a drive, but a great deal of his time after he had taken up residence at the Commodore was spent meeting cricketers who were on leave, and arranging matches. Mrs. Devenish agreed to meet them sometimes for tea, but like Chandra, had little free time.

But Mark had nothing to do but convalesce. He knew that it would not be long before the doctors gave their verdict as to whether his leg would heal completely, or whether he would be left with a limp, but he did his best to forget what lay ahead, and gave himself up to enjoying the warm summer days.

Annerley, so often alone with him, came to be completely in sympathy with his moods, but she was happiest on the occasions on which Chandra joined them.

One day, Chandra took her to a cricket match in Exeter, between senior schoolboys and men on leave from the front. On the way there, he questioned her to find out how much she knew about the game.

"Not much," she confessed. "My father used to play some-times, and I used to go and watch, but—"

"But you thought it was all pretty slow?"

"Well . . . there's more action in football, isn't there? In cricket you have to wait for the ball to get back to the bowler, and then he takes a long walk and it adds up to a long wait."

"The batting, the bowling, the fielding—you missed it all?

"Yes. Very sorry. Mark says you're good."

"Of course I'm good. Would I be playing for Oxford if I weren't? I'll expect you to be able to discuss some of the finer points of play with me while we're having lunch. What's in the picnic basket?"

"Everything you asked for. I wish—"

"You wish?"

"It's such a heavenly day. I wish I weren't just going to sit and do nothing."

"You are not going to do nothing. You're going to learn to understand your national game."

Watching, she could not have said whether she was learning or not, but it did not require knowledge of the game to tell her that every movement made by Chandra, batting or bowling, was grace itself. When he ran, she knew that he was running swiftly, but there did not seem any undue haste to reach the ball. Seeing him, tall, slim, with upraised bat after a beautifully played stroke, she wished she had the skill to capture the pose on paper.

They lunched on the grass, other picnickers round them. When the game was over, they drove home slowly, stopping on the way to finish the last of the picnic. Then he took her to the cottage and they sat in the garden, saying little, watching the sun dip slowly into the sea. When it grew chilly, they joined Mrs. Devenish in the little sitting room, and Chandra sat watching her sewing up the seams of a large knitted garment and listened to her occasional comments on her life in India and found it impossible to understand how a woman, even a woman with her limited intellectual equipment, could have lived for more than ten years with her eyes closed to everything that lay beyond the confines of her compound. He knew that Annerley had little real knowledge of his country—but her response to India had been emotional, and though she knew little, she felt deeply; the land had left its mark on her. He found her different in outlook from every other English girl he had met on their return from India. Her father, he thought, must be an unusual type of man. He had certainly been successful in keeping his daughter free of the prejudices held by so many of the English out there.

The simplicity, the naiveté he found in her amazed and vaguely saddened him. She was so intelligent, she knew so much about her lessons—and so little about life. Her greatest charm, he thought, was her capacity for finding pleasure in small things. She appeared to have little or no sense of material values; his car was a model that would have drawn exclamations of awe and appreciation from most girls, but Annerley was conscious only that the cushions were soft and the engine noiseless. She seemed to have few wants; she was, as far as he could judge, free from envy. The cottage, with its shabby furniture, its lack of amenities, satisfied her. For a girl with her looks, she was amazingly free from vanity. She was lighthearted—he loved the moments when her laughter rang out—but she was easily moved to compassion. A strange friendship, that between her and the sophisticated, serpent-tongued Moira.

On Annerley's next outing with Mark to the cinema, she enjoyed both the film and the tea that followed it. The café was crowded with servicemen, nurses in uniform, civilians wearing armbands or badges. She poured out tea and saw that Mark got his fair share of the sandwiches.

"I wish Moira could have come too," she said.

"Moira, being on duty, couldn't have come too," Mark reminded her. "And I would like to point out that when you're alone with a man, you shouldn't express a wish to have a third person present."

"Why not?"

"Because you'll make him feel he's inadequate."

"Two's company? That's only when it's a special two, not when it's . . . well, just two friends."

"It's not my business to take my sister out; it's my business to see that other men take her out. Which, incidentally, is something I've been wanting to discuss with you. I'm beginning to worry about her. All the patients in the hospital call her Miss Ice Cube."

"Well, you can tell them she isn't."

"Are you quite sure?"

"Of course I'm sure. She just gets tired of being chased by men, that's all. However much a girl may enjoy being admired, when she's as attractive as Moira, she can get too much attention." She reached for the toast. "But I don't understand her.

Anyone's entitled to give short answers if they're annoyed, or if they're in a bad mood, or if they don't like the person they're talking to—but the trouble is that she looks so approachable—"

"And then that soft, tender mouth opens and out come a series of snubs. It's an awful shock to the unfortunate fellows who experience it for the first time."

"She's always been like that—with strangers, anyway. But you can't say she ever—"

"Barks until she's bitten? But she does. A harmless invitation to something—a dance, perhaps—and all the poor fellow gets is three curt words of refusal. Chandra's the only man I know who's managed to stay the course and progress to what one might call ordinary conversation. He insists that she must have had some kind of love affair. Not an affair, just a meeting with someone who—let's say—gave her the same treatment she gives everybody else. Do you agree with that?"

She made no reply. A noisy group of servicemen and women were crossing the room on their way out to the road. One of the men was a naval officer. He was half hidden from her by his companions, but his movements seemed to her vaguely familiar.

"I don't know what all these naval chaps are doing here," Mark said. "This isn't a port."

She did not hear him. A deep-buried memory had surfaced, and she was staring at the man. Recognition came: it was Charles Crowther. On his arm hung an extremely pretty girl who was shrieking with laughter at something he had said to her. Annerley tore her glance away and realized that Mark was speaking.

". . . Don't really blame them for getting as much enjoyment as they can while they're ashore."

"I suppose not," she said.

The group was passing her chair. She could hear Charles Crowther's voice. The lounge, the people round her, Mark, seemed to recede, giving way to the dusty compound of a small house, a bed of cannas, stables, servants' quarters. The putter of a motorbike, her father and her grandmother upstairs, a young man, still with the freshness of an English background, in white shirt and tennis flannels . . .

She came back to the present. Mark was looking at her inquiringly.

"Sorry," she apologized. "I recognized one of those men."

"Which one?"

"The naval officer. He used to live in the flat below ours, with three other men. A chummery."

"I suppose he came to England to join up?"

"No. He was here before the war. He had to go back to England because . . . well, the firm sacked him."

"What for?"

"He used to take out Eurasian girls, and he liked going to their houses. His firm didn't like it, and after they'd warned him once or twice, they—"

"Threw him out. Yes, they would. It's a harsh rule, but my father keeps telling me there's good reason to see that young fellows keep it. Did you like this chap?"

"Yes."

"Do you want me to fetch him back to talk to you?"

"No."

That was all they said of Charles Crowther. Mark related the incident to Chandra at the inn a few days later.

"Just as well the chap didn't see her," he ended. "He might have proved a bit of a nuisance—they'd all been drinking. He didn't look an athletic type to me, but those naval fellows don't get much exercise, I suppose, except pacing the deck. Look, if I can find a tennis court round here, would you give Annerley a game?"

"If the court is good, if the balls are new, if the day is fine, if the wind is slight, if there are small boys to run after the balls to retrieve them, and if there are no gawping spectators—apart from yourself—then yes, I'll give her a game."

Moira showed no interest in the fact that Charles Crowther

had been in Exeter. Mrs. Devenish, on the other hand, wished that Annerley had spoken to him.

"He didn't see me," Annerley explained, "and he was with a lot of his friends."

A tennis court in Exeter was booked by Mark—and the booking cancelled. Chandra was summoned to London to meet his father, who had come to England on a brief visit. Annerley walked to the station with him, bitterly regretting that she could not go with him.

"You'll ask him lots about Shareen, won't you?"

"I don't suppose there'll be any need to ask."

"If you let me know when you're coming back, I'll go into Exeter to meet you."

But he did not let her know. He was away for five days. On his return, she expected him to walk up to the cottage, but he did not appear. She did not see him until three days later, when Mark came to tell her that he had once more booked a court, and they were to drive into Exeter that afternoon.

"Why didn't Chandra come and tell me about his father?" Annerley asked.

"I don't know. He came back in an odd kind of mood. I can't get anything out of him. Perhaps you'll be able to."

It was a silent drive with Chandra that afternoon. Annerley asked questions about his visit to London, about his father, about Shareen; he answered them, but did no more than that. There was no attempt to build up a picture of his visit, or to do more than politely relay the messages sent to her.

On the court, he showed the same detached air. He lost the toss, played with the sun in his eyes and without effort played Annerley off the court. For the first time in her life, she played to win, but she was not equal to the barrage of shots that came at her across the net. In three sets, she succeeded in winning only two games.

When they stopped playing and walked over to join the spectator—Mark—Chandra congratulated her.

"You're good," he said. "I wish I had time to coach you and make you even better. Your strokes, your serves, your net play— no fault to find. But why don't you run faster?"

"Why did you always send the balls to the places I couldn't get to?"

"He wanted to make sure of winning," Mark told her.

He and Chandra dropped Annerley at the cottage and went on to the inn. Mark made himself comfortable on a chair in Chandra's room while Chandra had a shower. Mark called over the banisters for a drink, and Mrs. Bray sent it up to him, with a tray of tea for Chandra.

"You're in a funny mood," Mark told him. "What's wrong?"

"Nothing's wrong. You're in a funny mood too."

"Me?"

"Yes, you. Are you worrying about what the doctors are going to say?"

"No. I've realized that worrying wouldn't do any good. What will be will be, as the Indians say."

"Or don't say. You wouldn't have a girl on your mind, by any chance?"

"Why should you say that?"

"Because you didn't take your eyes off her on the court. I suppose you asked me to play so that you could watch her playing."

"The fact is," said Mark slowly, "that I can't make up my mind whether to go on acting the part of the best friend's brother, or the older man taking a kindly interest in a young woman who's beginning to show signs of being extremely attractive."

There was a long silence. Chandra's eyes, dark and unreadable, rested on him and then went to the blue expanse of sea outside the window.

"Where's the dilemma?" he asked finally.

"In the first case, I have to share the young lady with other young ladies' brothers. In the second case, I show my teeth whenever another brother appears."

Chandra's eyes came back to rest on him.

"You mean that you're beginning to take a more than friendly interest in Annerley?"

"That's one way of putting it. The trouble is that she's still a child."

"A child?"

"She's only seventeen. She's hardly out of school. In fact, she isn't out of school."

"A child? You've forgotten that you're talking to a Hindu. She may not be as adult as your sister is—but a child? No. Are you in love with her?"

Mark got slowly to his feet. He did not answer for some time.

"Yes," he said at last. "Are you surprised?"

"Surprised?" Chandra gave a slow smile. "Yes, I am. I'm surprised that it took you so long to see what was so obvious."

After the visit of the specialists to the hospital, Mark was given their verdict. He would be left with a limp—slight, but permanent.

Chandra had driven to the hospital to await the result of the examination. When Mark was at last free, he drove him and Moira to the cottage. Annerley made sandwiches, took them with beer and coffee into the garden, and served them from the folding table. Mrs. Devenish was in Exeter.

Mark made no attempt to avoid the topic.

"All right, so now we know the worst," he said. "I suppose I'm lucky. I've at least got two legs, even if one of them won't quite reach the ground."

"You could also say you were lucky not to have to go back to the trenches," Moira said.

"Perhaps. But I'm sorry I couldn't have finished up fighting. So now where am I? Not in the Indian police."

"There's still the Indian civil service," Chandra reminded him.

"I know that. My father's been harping on it for years."

"What have you got against it?" Moira asked.

"Nothing. In fact"—his tone took on a slight edge—"how

couid I hope to do better? They'd start me off as a district officer, and I'd rule, practically single-handed, an area the size of Wales. I'd progress: sub-divisional officer or sub-collector or joint magistrate. Then I'd really be on my way to the top."

"And after twenty-five years they might even make you a judge," said Chandra.

"In the meantime, I'd live in the best houses in the best residential districts and they'd bracket me with all the other Heaven-borns and my wife would go into dinner on His Excellency's arm."

"If you didn't fancy being the governor of a province," Chandra said, "you could get one of those jobs supervising a rajah and seeing that he rules his subjects properly, and advise him on whether his sons would do better at Eton or Harrow. Then you could retire and go round lecturing on How I Ruled India."

"Quite so. What more could anyone ask?" ended Mark.

"Less talk and more coffee," Moira said tersely.

"Don't you like the picture I painted?"

"Twenty-five years," Chandra commented, "is a long time."

"Perhaps too long," Mark said. "I've been studying Indian affairs lately, and I don't like what I see."

Chandra lowered himself onto a rug.

"What do you see?" he inquired.

"That chap Gandhi, for a start."

"Ah! Gandhi. And what do you think of him?" Chandra asked.

"I think he's going to make trouble. In fact, he's already making it."

"Trouble for whom?" Chandra wanted to know.

Mark spoke sharply. "You can stop acting the village idiot," he said. "Do you think I don't know you, after all these years? Ever since you went to London and met your father, you've been . . . different. You changed while you were with him. I've been waiting for you to tell me why, but you've kept your mouth shut. You said nothing, so I said nothing. Why don't you come out

186

into the open and tell us what you and your father talked about?"

Chandra seemed to be seeking the answer on the surface of the sea.

"For one thing," he said at last, "we discussed my marriage."

"Marriage?" repeated Mark in astonishment.

Annerley said nothing. Her mind had gone back to a long-ago visit to Shareen, a day on which they too—very briefly—discussed marriage. Shareen's—and Chandra's.

"I told you years ago," Chandra said, "that I was engaged. Don't you remember?"

"Of course I remember," Mark said. "But I didn't take it seriously. You said she was . . . I forget how old, but it sounded absurd."

"You keep forgetting," Chandra complained, "that I am a Hindu."

"You were—when you came to England."

"I am still a Hindu."

"Do you mean to tell me you're going through with a marriage that was arranged when you were in prep school?"

"Why not? Such a suitable bride, so pretty, so charming, so obedient, so cooperative. My father brought me her latest photograph. I must show it to you sometime."

"Thank you. What else did you and your father discuss?"

"My professional future, of course. I told him that I would like to go back to India with him."

"Back to . . . you mean back when he went back this time?" Mark asked.

"Yes. It wasn't a good idea, and he said so. He told me I must wait until I had graduated."

"And after that?"

"After that? I told him I would go home. And to that, he agreed."

It was said simply, quietly, without emphasis, but the three listeners sensed behind the words a firm and unswerving purpose.

187

Mark spoke after an interval.

"As an Indian," he asked, "and speaking seriously for once, would you really advise an Englishman to go out to the Indian civil service?"

Chandra hesitated.

"It's a good career—while it lasts," he said. "Who can guess what's going to happen anywhere in the world after this war? Who will be able to demand a guaranteed future?" He paused. "On a personal level, of course, I would very much like to see you out in India."

Another silence followed this remark, and this time, nobody broke it. Moira looked, as usual, like a detached observer. Mark was staring out to sea. Chandra was drinking the last of his cup of coffee.

Annerley was silent because she was struggling under a weight of depression heavier than anything she had experienced since the news of her father's internment reached her. Her feelings were too confused, too uncharacteristically pessimistic to analyze; she knew only that she seemed to feel in the air a sense of doom. In these past few moments, something pleasant, something happy had come to an end. Something that she had treasured had slipped away.

She tried to regard the situation in the light of common sense. This had been a lovely, lovely summer, but summers had to end. In this small patch of garden, the four of them had met, talked, enjoyed one another's company. There would be other gardens, other sunny days, other happy meetings.

But at this moment, she could not believe it. Something told her that the end was here and now. Nothing could ever be as it had been throughout these sunny months.

As they stirred and prepared to go indoors, she knew that she was not the only one who had sensed that this was an ending. About Moira, she could not be sure. But she could read the knowledge in Mark's eyes. She did not have to look into Chandra's. She had heard the finality in his voice.

Mark came the next day in the ambulance. He found, as he had hoped, that Annerley was alone.

"I didn't expect you," she said. "All I can offer you to eat is—"

"I don't want to eat. I came to talk to you. Do you want to talk inside, or outside?"

She looked at him. He looked serious, purposeful. With a sense of mingled surprise and foreboding, she guessed what he wanted to say.

"Let's go outside," she suggested.

He elected to sit on the bench beside her. He took one of her hands in his and sat looking at it as though he had never seen it before. Then at last he spoke.

"I've never done this before," he said.

"Done what?"

"Asked a girl to marry me." He hurried on. "You see how I've made a muck of it even before I've started? I meant to tell you gradually. I meant to make a speech saying I've loved you almost from the first moment I saw you. I meant— Annerley, look at me."

She turned to face him.

"That's better. I would have said something to you before, but I wanted to wait and see how much permanent damage there might have been to my leg. And there was another thing: I thought you were too young to think about marrying anybody. But Chandra said you weren't."

"Chandra? Chandra said . . ."

"I told him I was in love with you but that I considered you not much more than a child. He said no, you weren't a child. I love you very much, Annerley. I'm not expecting you to decide anything just yet. All I'd like at the moment is to hear you say that you like me and you might—when you'd had a lot more time to think about it—feel you could grow to love me. We couldn't marry for a long time, but I'm selfish enough to want to . . . well, agree to some kind of engagement." He lifted the hand he was holding and pressed it against his cheek. "You see,

189

there's a hope that the war'll be over soon, and you'll leave this cottage and go out into what I suppose I can call the world. You'll meet other men, and other men will fall in love with you, so I wanted to feel that you felt you belonged to me."

He paused. She could find nothing to say.

"Do you love me, Annerley—just a little?"

Love? He was the only young man—apart from Chandra—she had ever known. She liked everything about him—his blunt face, his charm, his kindness, his humour. But love?

"I don't know, Mark," she said helplessly. "I honestly don't know. I like you—I can't tell you how much. But . . ."

"Don't let's go as far as love," he said gently. "Will you agree that if you meet any man you like better than you like me, you'll say so?"

"Yes."

"And in the meantime, could I pretend that you belong to me?"

"Yes."

He said no more. He took her into his arms and reflected that he had, as yet, no rivals. That there would be other men in her life, he did not doubt, but for the moment, he was safe.

He kissed her. She did not resist; nor, he noted despondently, did she respond. But this was only the beginning. For the present, this would have to be enough.

He released her, and asked a question.

"Would you rather I didn't say anything to Moira?"

"Moira'll guess. But I'd rather not tell my grandmother yet. I want to write to my father first."

"Tell him," Mark said, "that he can hand over the job of look ing after you to me."

The summer ended. Chandra went back to Oxford, the rooms at the Commodore were given up. Moira and Mark spent their time between the hospital and the cottage.

Saying good-night to her grandmother on one evening after Moira and Mark's departure, Annerley thought she seemed depressed.

"Tired, Granny?" she asked.

Mrs. Devenish, trimming the little lamps they took to their rooms each night, looked up in mild surprise.

"Do I seem tired?" she asked.

"Well, yes, in a way. Don't you think you're doing a bit too much, going so often into Exeter and doing all that work?"

"Work? I've begun to think, Annerley, that I haven't done anything. Or at any rate, so little that it doesn't really count. All the same, I thought I might go in less often." She struck a match and lit one of the lamps. "What tires me isn't what I do there in the way of work. It's . . . well, it sounds silly, I know, but I don't seem to be able to stand all the chatter anymore. If I could sit and listen, I would enjoy it. But one has to join in, has to give answers, make suggestions. I never could talk very much, at least not for long at a time, and lately I've found myself rather exhausted at the end of the day. And at first, the journey in the little train was so pleasant, so restful; I could get a carriage to myself and close my eyes and be quiet. But nowadays the train is always full, and the chattering goes on and on. But don't think I'm complaining. You don't think so, do you?"

"No, Granny, I don't."

"One of the nice things about living here has been to discover how friendly people are. They weren't friendly in India, you know. I was too old to fit into the . . . one could call it the mem-sahib circle. I was never lonely, but I did wish sometimes that I could make some kind of . . . well, background for you. You never really had a place in the kind of society you—"

"Granny, I was a child. I had school friends. What else did I need?"

"You needed," Mrs. Devenish said with unaccustomed firmness, "to be in a set where . . . it's difficult to explain, Annerley, but I think what I mean is that perhaps people like the Fernandezes were not really the right people for you to mix with so freely. Much as I respect your father, I can't help feeling, when I look back at those years, that he was rather too liberal in certain of his views. The Prebdels . . . yes, they were the right kind of people. But you can't say, can you, that I was very much help in seeing that you had nice people round you?"

"All I know," Annerley said, beginning to lock the windows and doors for the night, "is that, looking back, I don't think anything could have been nicer than it was."

"It was a happy, happy time," Mrs. Devenish said wistfully. "How lucky we were, how very lucky . . ."

"Bedtime, Granny."

"Yes, dear. There's just one thing I'd like to say, while I remember. It's about your fees and expenses when you get into Oxford."

"*If* I get into Oxford. We've got enough money for the fees, and I'll keep down my expenses."

"I know you will, dear. But in case anything should happen to me. I would like you to know—"

"Nothing's going to happen to you, Granny. There aren't any Zeppelins here, and we've beaten the U-boats, and—"

"I only wanted you to know that there will be enough money to see you through. I've put away enough to make sure of that. So you mustn't worry about money."

"I won't. Thank you, Granny."

She watched her grandmother going slowly up the narrow staircase. Then she lit her night lamp, put out all the others and went upstairs to bed.

The school term began the next day. Annerley rose early, dressed and had her breakfast, and then made tea and put it on a tray to take up to her grandmother. She knocked on the door, opened it and put the tray on the bedside table. Then she drew back the curtains. Outside was a bleak January morning. She turned and saw her grandmother lying on her back, asleep. She called softly.

"Granny! Wake up, Granny. Your tea."

There was no answering movement. Annerley, about to raise her voice, found suddenly that she was unable to speak. Something about the silence, the stillness, brought a chill to her heart. She stood staring for some moments at the still form on the bed —and then she found herself opening the door. She took two steps on the landing and then went, half stumbling, down the stairs. She snatched a coat from the hall stand, fumbled with the locks on the front door, opened it and ran down the incline into the village street. It was empty save for a few figures making their way to the station. She ran to the inn, opened the door and saw Mrs. Bray coming out of the kitchen.

"Good morning, Annerley. You're early." She stopped and spoke in a tone of anxiety. "Nothing wrong, is there, dearie?"

"It's . . . it's my grandmother, Mrs. Bray. I think—could you come?"

Mrs. Bray was in coat, galoshes and hood in a moment.

Together they went hurrying back to the cottage. At the foot of the stairs, Mrs. Bray put out a hand.

"No. You stay down here, dearie. Let me go up."

She went upstairs. Annerley sank onto the bottom stair and put her face into her hands.

When Mrs. Bray came downstairs, she spoke quietly.

"I'll stay here till someone comes to be with you," she said. "You're not going to grieve, are you? Because I don't. There's no better way to go. Just be thankful."

"I will." Annerley got to her feet. "I don't know what there is to do, but if you'll tell me, I'll do it."

"You've nothing to do but make a good strong cup of tea for us both, and then go down to the post office and get a message through to your grandmother's doctor in Exeter."

As well as summoning the doctor, Annerley sent a message to the school. Then she put in a call to Moira at the hospital. Finally, she got through to Mark in London.

He arrived before evening, left his suitcase at the inn and walked up to the cottage. It seemed entirely natural to find herself in his arms being gently cradled.

"Don't be sad," he said.

"I'm not. It's just that it was so unexpected. She looked tired last night, but she wasn't sick."

"It was a peaceful end."

He spoke soothingly, but he was deeply anxious about her. She was entirely alone. She had a home—but she had nobody to look to for companionship except Moira and himself. Moira was in Dorset, he was in London. But this was not the moment to think of the future. They would consider it when the funeral was over. Moira would be here this evening and would stay with Annerley; he would be close by, at the inn.

Chandra arrived on the evening before the funeral. He stayed at the inn, and sat up until the early hours talking to Mark.

Annerley had wanted the simplest of ceremonies, but there had been no escape from the hideous hearse, the black, plumed

194

horses and the gloomy, top-hatted undertakers. She told Moira she was glad her father was not present.

"He would have called this a barbarian spectacle."

"I know. I think that your grandmother would have regarded it as the proper way of paying one's last respects."

There were refreshments afterwards at the inn for all those who had endured the freezing conditions in the cemetery. The tea and coffee and cakes thawed the black-clad figures, and hushed voices rose to normal pitch before the guests filed away.

When the last guest had gone, Mrs. Bray told Annerley that she had something to say to her.

"I didn't say anything till now," she explained, "because I thought I'd wait till the funeral was over and done with. It's about your grandmother's letter.

"Letter?"

"She wrote one, dearie, a long time ago, and brought it to me. She said your father wasn't able to get here if you needed him, and if anything happened to her—air raids or a road accident, you never know, she said—or if she got ill and didn't get over it, I was to post the letter."

"You mean you had to post it without showing it to me?"

"That's right, I was just to post it without a word. So I did. It was to your other grandmother, a Mrs. Brooke, up in Norfolk somewhere. What your grandmother said in the letter was that it was to be posted if she died, because she felt it was her duty— that's the word she said she used, duty—to let your other grandmother know what had happened. So she wrote and told her, and she's got the letter by now, I daresay. I hope you don't think I should've told you straight away, but I made a solemn promise I wouldn't. You understand, don't you?"

"Yes. Thank you, Mrs. Bray."

At the cottage, Mark, Moira and Annerley discussed this development.

"Do you think she'll give any sign?" Moira inquired.

Annerley shook her head.

"No. She's never answered any of my father's letters."

"Did she know your father was interned?"

"If she didn't know before, Granny must have told her in the letter."

"I suppose so. Can I have a drink? I'm feeling depressed. I mean a real drink. A strong drink."

"Real drinks and strong drinks were never kept in this house," Mark reminded her. "But I brought a bottle of sherry with me, so we'll open it now."

They had it in the only available glasses—outsize tumblers into which he measured two inches of sherry. Then they sat in the quiet room and tried to look into the future. Chandra had driven from the cemetery back to Oxford, giving no more explanation than the necessity of getting back before the roads became impassable.

"I wish I knew what was the matter with him," Mark said now. "It isn't a passing mood; he used to have them, but I always knew what was the matter and I always knew how to deal with them—with him. Now I don't."

"He looked thinner," Moira observed.

Annerley said nothing. He had come; he had shown his sympathy. But he had not been the Chandra of last summer.

"What are you going to do now?" Moira asked her. "Stay in this cottage?"

"You can't live alone," Mark objected.

"Why not?" Annerley asked. "I can run it single-handed, and Mrs. Bray is just across the road if I need anything."

"You could live at the school," he pointed out.

"No. I'd hate to. I spend enough of the day there without having to spend the night too. If Moira'll come down on her free weekends, and if you'll come down whenever you can, I'll be all right."

She would be all right. But she had only now begun to realize how much she had taken her grandmother's presence for granted. This cottage without her . . .

"You're crying," said Moira. "Don't."

"Why not?"

"What good does it do?"

"None, I suppose. I only wish she'd got more out of life. She asked so little—and she got so little."

"She couldn't have gone back to India."

"I suppose not."

"What did you do with all her things?"

"I put all her clothes into suitcases—everything—and asked Mrs. Bray to distribute them to anybody who needed them. Her ornaments, her two or three little pieces of jewelry . . . I kept them because nobody would want them but myself."

She had had so little. The money of which she had spoken, the money so carefully saved, that was to help with the Oxford fees and expenses, proved to be a sum not large, but greater than Annerley, tearfully facing the lawyers two days later, had imagined. So much, saved out of so little.

Moira and Mark had gone. Tomorrow she would resume her classes at the school. Life would go on—without her grandmother.

A week later, she received a summons during one of her classes; she was to go to the headmistress's room.

She went expecting nothing more than a brief talk about her studies, but the headmistress was waiting for her at the door.

"There's someone waiting to see you, Annerley," she said. "I shall leave you to go in alone. If you want to see me later, I shall of course be happy to give you any advice you need."

Annerley opened the door. Standing by the window was a tall, thin, upright, grey-clad figure: a long grey coat, almost military-looking; a small grey felt hat, grey gloves, stout black shoes.

And the face . . . yes, Annerley thought, she would have known. Not a close likeness, but if she had passed her in the street, she would have thought: she looks like my father.

The voice was quiet. The tone was not warm.

"I am sorry we meet in this way. You know, I suppose, that Mrs. Devenish left a letter which was to be posted to me if anything happened to her?"

"Yes." Annerley indicated a chair. "Won't you sit down?"

"Thank you, no. I have a taxi waiting and a train to catch. As well as coming down to see you, I have other commitments in the district. It will not take long to say what I have to say. As you are now alone, I felt that I should come and see you and arrange something about your future. I don't know how much your father told you about our quarrel, but that is between him and myself. I have come to offer you a home until his return. You can live with me or, if you prefer, you can live here at the school and spend your vacations with me. I have talked to your headmistress; she told me that you hope to go up to Oxford in the autumn."

"Yes."

"In the meantime, you are living in your father's cottage. You cannot live alone. Which of the alternatives I offered you are you going to choose?"

Annerley answered without hesitation.

"Neither. Thank you all the same. I should like to go up and visit you, spend my holidays with you, get to know you, get to know your house because my father loved it so much. But I'm very happy and comfortable in the cottage and I want to go on living there."

"As I just pointed out, you cannot live alone."

"I'm not alone. I'm surrounded by kind neighbours. I've enough to live on. It's kind of you to come all this way, and I'm grateful, but I won't, if you don't mind, make any change in the way I live."

There was a pause.

"How old are you?"

"I'll be eighteen in March."

"What are you going to do when you've got your degree?"

"I don't know. It depends on my father."

"If you're determined to stay at the cottage, I suppose you must do so. I don't approve and I don't think your father would, either. But you appear to have inherited his obstinacy, so you must do as you please. I shall expect you to let me know if you are coming up for your Easter vacation, and I shall expect to be told the date. I cannot offer you any amusement, but the house is large and so are the grounds and there is a home farm on which you can make yourself useful if you care to. If you wish to bring a girl friend with you, I have no objection. Please don't come up wearing black. I don't care for outward manifestations of mourning. If you come, come by train and not by omnibus. You will be met at Norwich."

That seemed to be all. Mrs. Brooke moved towards the door. Annerley opened it. They walked in silence through the hall. Outside, a taxi waited. The driver opened the door; Mrs. Brooke, with a nod to Annerley, got in and was driven away.

Moira was at the cottage for the weekend.

"But is that *all* that happened?" she asked.

"Yes."

"She didn't even sit down?"

"No."

"She must be mad. To come all that way down here simply to—"

"She came to arrange my future—my immediate future. When she saw I wasn't going to leave this cottage, what was there left for her to do but to tell me she was prepared to receive me for what she called my vacations? And you, too, if you'll come. You will come, won't you?"

"It depends when you're going."

"I thought of going up for Easter. Will you be free?"

"Part of the time. But my exams are just after Easter, so I'd have to get back pretty soon. I'll go up if I can: I'd like to take a look at her. Would you have known who she was?"

"Yes. She's a bit like my father. Her features look like a copy of his carved out of an ice block. How can she be his mother? He's so kind, so . . . so warm, such *fun*, and she's like stone. She might have been interviewing someone for the post of parlour-maid. One thing she said was that I wasn't to go up there wearing black. She doesn't believe in mourning."

"Then she isn't mad."

"No, she's very sane. When you come to think of it, that's the way you behave—you don't go out of your way to dress things up. Neither did she. And after having kept up a quarrel with my father for about twenty years, it would have seemed a bit absurd to treat me as her long-lost grandchild. But when you compare her with my mother's mother . . ."

She stopped. Her mother's mother was in a newly made grave, and she missed her more than she would have believed possible. She could not bear to think of her goodness, her meekness, so far removed from the demeanour of Mrs. Brooke.

She was gone. But death had taken her gently . . .

Easter was early. It was still cold when Annerley left for Norfolk, and became colder as the train went north.

She had sent a letter giving her grandmother the date and the time of her arrival. She also said that a friend of hers would like to come, but not until a week or so later. A postcard had been sent in return, confirming that the train would be met.

Outside Norwich station, she was surprised to be approached by a uniformed chauffeur who took her suitcase and conducted her to a very large Daimler. Driver and vehicle were in almost embarrassing contrast to the drab, war-stained surrounding. The chauffeur introduced himself as Marshall and told her that he had known her father. At this, Annerley disembarked from the capacious back seat in which he had placed her, and asked permission to sit beside him in front. Before they had reached her grandmother's house she learned innumerable details of her father's boyhood. But of her mother, Marshall knew nothing.

In time they passed through an imposing gateway. The car slowed down to allow her to admire the magnificent beeches lining the drive. When they rounded the last curve, the house—Waterways—was before them.

The sight of it was a complete, almost a breathtaking surprise to Annerley. She had been prepared for some kind of mansion, but she had not expected this beautiful, spreading building standing on a rise and giving a view of quiet, peaceful, picturesque sheets of water. She had not visualized the shrubberies, the wooded walks, the terraces that led from the house to what in peacetime must have been lawns but were now acres of neatly aligned vegetables.

Marshall drove round to the other side of the building, stopped before a sweep of stone steps, got out and pulled the bell rope, and returned to assist Annerley from the car. The double doors at the top of the steps opened and her grandmother stood ready to welcome her.

It was hardly a welcome. There was no embrace, not even a cheek presented for a peck. There was merely a speech.

"I hope you had a pleasant journey. Marshall, take Miss Annerley's luggage to her room. Come in. I hope you're not cold. The house is of course not heated in wartime. This is the library. I've closed the other sitting rooms and the dining room. Please sit down. I shall tell you what our routine is and then you can go to your room and unpack. We are, here, all a part of the war, and we have done and are doing what we can to be of use. At the beginning of the war, I had most of the lawns and the flower beds turned into vegetable plots. We grow our own food as much as possible. Most of the servants joined up; some stayed to work here in different capacities. The coach house is now a communal kitchen; I feed forty people twice a day. You can work there, or you can go down to the farm and make yourself useful. I shall not have any time to spend with you. During the day, I go round making official visits. People come every day to see me, also on official matters, and I give them dinner. During dinner, we discuss the business that has brought them. When that is over, I go to my room. The visitors stay overnight and leave next morning. The house is a center for many branches of war work. I shall give you a list of the people who are expected to arrive, and which room or rooms have been allocated to them; if you undertook to look after them, it would free someone to do more useful work. Please get your own breakfast—you will find everything you need in the kitchen, which you will be shown when you have seen your room. Lunch is served in here—sandwiches, milk, beer if anybody wants it. We do not have tea, but if you want it, you can go to the kitchen and ask for it. Dinner is at seven-thirty. Please come down punctually; we meet in here." She stopped. "I think that is all. Please ring that bell."

Annerley pulled a bell rope. There was a shuffling sound outside, a knock, and an ancient maid appeared.

"Inskip, take Miss Annerley to her room and then show her any part of the house she wants to see."

End of interview. Annerley followed the witch-like maid into a corridor, along another, turn right, yet another, and then up a beautiful curving staircase. The doors on the right and left were closed. But there was enough to see without going into any of the unused rooms: carpets, pictures, furniture—a house that retained its warmth and beauty. In this house her father had been born. These were the rooms he had known, the corridors up and down which he had perhaps raced in childhood. This was the house, luxurious, gracious, that he had given up when he fell in love with Rosalind Anna Lee Devenish.

She reached her room—beautifully furnished, bleakly cold— and spoke to the maid who ushered her in.

"I don't know your name."

"Inskip, Miss."

"Is that all of it?"

"That's what I'm called, Miss, and always have been since I came here when I was fourteen."

"Is that what my father called you?"

The old eyes, watery but still shrewd, rested on her.

"We don't talk about him, Miss."

"What did he call you?"

"He called me Skippy. Not that I was, even in those days when I used to come in and tidy his room. You've got a strong look of him, Miss. But Annerley wasn't your mother's name, was it?"

"No. She was called Rosalind. Did my father talk about her?"

"To me, yes, Miss. He couldn't talk about her to his mother— she didn't want to hear. So he talked to me. He's interned in Greece, isn't he, Miss?"

"Yes. How did you know? Did my grandmother tell you?"

"No, Miss. But we get to hear things. Marshall—he's the chauffeur, he brought you from the station—he's the one who gets to know, and he tells the rest of us. And sometimes the old doctor, Dr. Picton, he says a word or two that he knows we'd like to hear. He comes here most days, Miss—you'll be seeing him. If you want anything, Miss, I'm always in the kitchen, so you can find me there."

"Thank you, Skippy."

When the door closed, Annerley went to the window and stood looking out at wintry trees and sheets of water whipped by the wind. Not a landlubber's paradise, she thought. Small boats bobbed against moorings along the shores. Her father had not spoken of sailing—had he missed this scene too much to want to recall it?

She unpacked, put her few belongings into a drawer, hung up the dresses she had brought and then went downstairs and out of the house. Snow had begun to fall lightly but steadily, and was beginning to lay a carpet on the ground. It was not difficult to find the farm, a bare mile away. The road lay through a flat expanse over which the wind blew unchecked—wind that was coming, she surmised, straight off the North Sea.

She introduced herself to the farm manager and his two assistants—both of them girls who had taken the place of men who had enlisted—and expressed herself willing to do anything except go too near the bull. She was led to the dairy, stone-floored, stone-shelved, its massive milk pails frozen to the slabs. Here she was to spend most of her days during her visit. There was a good deal of company—not only the farm people, but also the drivers of army trucks coming to take away butter and eggs to hospitals or to collect milk churns. And looking in every day to chat to her, the old doctor, wrapped to the chin in coat and muffler, hands in thick woolen gloves, a woolen cap on his head, his white whiskers yellow against the snow.

"You're Annerley," he said on their first meeting. "I'm the man who brought your father into the world. Is your work done for the day? If so, we could walk back to the house together. I shall be staying for dinner."

"Inskip mentioned you," she said as they began their journey, "but she didn't tell me you'd known my father all his life. Are you allowed to talk about him?"

"No, I'm not. Not where your grandmother can hear me. But I can tell you anything about him that he hasn't told you himself. And before you begin to ask questions"—he held up a grey woolen forefinger—"let me ask you not to judge your grandmother too harshly. People round here think that she has a stone for a heart, but in my opinion, what is lacking is not heart but imagination. She has not, has never had the smallest, the slightest touch of imagination—or sensitiveness. She is strong, in mind and body and spirit; she does her duty faithfully and efficiently. She's just, and in her own way generous—but it is quite impossible for her to imagine that other people have different likes, dislikes, feelings, passions. She, and her father before her, have always made me think of those uncompromising Biblical characters— filled with the knowledge that they were in all things right, and never aware of the effect they had on others. That's not a good way of expressing what I mean, but perhaps you understand. I'm glad you look like your father and not like your mother—it's better so."

"How long have you known my family?"

"The first member of your family I knew was your grandmother's father. He was the eighteenth in his line to own Waterways. His grief at not having a son to pass it on to . . . well, one had to guess what he felt about it. He showed nothing. Like his daughter, he was cold, cold, cold. Shall we walk more quickly? I'm very cold, cold, cold."

"My grandmother inherited Waterways, and brought her husband here, didn't she?"

"Yes. If she had been a different kind of person, she would have realized that he should have been given more share in the running of the estate. That's to say, she should, in my unasked opinion, have made him feel more like a co-owner and less like an employee. As you're perhaps beginning to realize, it's a rather big assignment for one woman. The house, the farm, the dairy, the planting and tending and sale of the vegetables—I don't know how she's managed to keep the place together. She was so sure that your father would take over the management of it when he came down from Oxford. Never, I think, did she visualize being left alone here. And it was because he left her alone that she could never bring herself to forgive him. She could never understand why he didn't feel as she herself had always felt—that this was a place to be loved, to be cared for; a place worth making sacrifices for. She didn't expect her husband to share her feeling, but she did expect to pass on her own dedication to her son. Her husband left her—and then her son left her. It's a sad history. I think much of her time is spent wondering what will happen to the estate when she dies." He sighed. "Are you going to be happy here?"

She laughed.

"Yes. It's a perfect holiday. I'm so . . . so *free*."

"Yes, we're all free here, free to do our own jobs. You won't see your grandmother—unless you catch sight of her in the distance—until we all sit down to dinner."

"What does she do, exactly?"

"She's a kind of nerve center for the district. The bulk of the dairy produce goes to hospitals. The vegetables, planted every year since the beginning of the war, go to the local markets. Groups or individuals connected with half a dozen war efforts come here—for instruction, for exchange of views, to confer with one another. You'll see them every evening at dinner. It isn't a social meal—it's business only."

This she found to be accurate. The first evening was the pattern for all future evenings. She had a bath, changed her dress and went down to the library. Here she found an elderly woman in a severe grey outfit with an armband proclaiming that she was a member of the Norfolk Voluntary Drivers Association, and a middle-aged woman with no armband but an affected voice and an arch manner, who introduced herself as Mrs. Brooke's secretary, Mrs. Thorpe.

The door opened to admit the doctor and her grandmother, who to her surprise was in unrelieved black. Black not permitted for mourning wear, she thought wryly, but allowed for evening wear.

Dinner consisted, on the first night and on every subsequent night, of canned fish mixed with potatoes, made into cakes and fried; this was followed by two thin slices of cold meat and a liberal helping of vegetables. Then came biscuits, cheese and coffee. Having the same meal every evening, Mrs. Thorpe told her later, saved reordering the menu and enabled the kitchen staff to follow an unchanging routine.

Conversation, as the doctor had said, was confined to business matters. Nobody addressed a word to Annerley—it was obviously assumed that she would have no relevant suggestions to put forward. At the end of the meal, her grandmother rose, said not only good-night but also good-bye to her guests—they stayed only one night—and went to her room. Before going, she handed Annerley a list of future guests, their reason for coming, and the room into which they were to be put. It all added up, Annerley thought, to a military exercise—well planned, well organized, well executed. By day she was free to go down to the farm, to roam round the grounds, to talk to servants who had known her father.

On the third evening, only one name appeared on the list: Lieutenant Raadick, coming to discuss the bad condition of the roads. Green Room. To arrive at 6:30 P.M.

At six, she went upstairs, bathed and changed, and came down to find an army truck coming to a halt at the entrance. A tall, lean young man got out, said "Tomorrow, ten sharp" to the driver, and took the steps in three bounds. At sight of Annerley he stopped short, his eyes widening in surprise and pleasure.

"I've never seen you here before," he told her. "Which particular branch of service are you attached to?"

"Yours, if you're Lieutenant Raadick. I have to show you to your room. My name's Annerley Brooke."

His voice dropped to an awed whisper.

"Not . . . *not* the granddaughter?"

"Yes. You can say it out loud. Will you come this way?"

He fell into step beside her talking all the way. He was about twenty-five, with no claim to good looks, but he had an eager, engaging, almost schoolboyish manner.

"Are you going to stay forever? If you are, I'll have to arrange more frequent road inspections. I'm as you might say O.C. Highways. The army lorries and the tanks and things tear them to pieces, and they blame me and shout Do Something, and then I have to come and consult your grandmother and get her cooperation for anything I have in mind about repairs. You won't go away, will you?"

"Not at once. I'm here on holiday."

"How long a holiday?"

"About three weeks."

"And then?"

"Back to Devonshire."

"Never to return?"

"I might come back in the summer."

"I shall insert a special clause in my prayers. What do you do in Devonshire?"

"I've been studying to try and get into Oxford."

"Good Lord! Oxford!"

"Somerville."

"Are you frightfully brainy?"

"No."

"That's a relief. Clever people make me recall my far-from-creditable school record—number in class, fifteen, place in class, fifteenth, that kind of thing, hardly worth wasting the fees."

"This is your room."

He followed her in and dropped his canvas bag onto the floor.

"I've gleaned a few facts about you over the years," he told her. "I live not far away, and a certain amount of gossip found its way over the intervening water. Your father didn't marry the wife his mother had lined up for him, and left home and went to India. Nobody told me anything about a beautiful daughter. Were you born there?"

"Yes. I was there until I was nearly fourteen."

"I thought all children were whisked out of the country aged eight or so."

"Most were."

"And your father . . . yes, I remember. Interned. Bad luck. How old are you?"

"I thought that was something gentlemen never asked ladies."

"Eighteen? Nineteen?"

"Eighteen—soon."

"Nice age. Do you feel life opening before you like a . . . should I say oyster or flower?"

"Flower. Is there anything you want before I go?"

"Yes. I want to know where I can find you when I've unpacked my spare shirt and socks."

"We assemble in the library before dinner."

"I know. This isn't my first visit, it's my ninth. There's almost an hour before dinner. Will you come for a quick walk down to the water with me?"

She hesitated for a moment and then nodded.

"If you like."

"Then put on a warm coat and several mufflers. See you in the hall in six minutes."

He talked all the way down to the water's edge.

"Do you sail?" he asked.

"No."

"You don't? That's odd. Your father, I'm told, was seldom out of his boat."

"I didn't know he had a boat."

"A beauty. I know because I've often taken her out—at the request of Marshall, your grandmother's chauffeur, who's kept an eye on the boathouse and the boat ever since your father left it.

If you want to go for a sail, I'll take you when the weather warms up a bit. Will you come?"

"I wouldn't be much help as crew. I've never been in anything smaller than a launch."

"Then there's a happy time ahead of you. If you're your father's daughter, you ought to make a good sailor."

"Have you always lived here?"

"No. I've lived wherever my mother's husbands were. She's on her third, and he owns this house on the water. Her first husband —my father—took her to New Zealand, and I was born there, but she found it too far-flung, so they came back and he died and she married a man who had a rather nice house in the New Forest, so we lived there for a time, and then she divorced him and married house-on-the-water, who's currently doing a kind of liaison job over in France and doesn't get home much, which suits them both, as they're much happier apart. I hope it doesn't break up, because I've got very fond of this house. You can see your reflection in the water when you look out of a window. I've spent most of my spare time in boats ever since we came here. When I joined up at the beginning of the war I thought for certain they'd put me into the Navy, but no, that would have been too sensible—I got shoved into the Army. What, incidentally, do you think of your grandmother? You may find this hard to believe, but one of the reasons people round here don't like her is because they can't find anything to say against her, apart from the one obvious thing, that she's encased in ice. She's a bit of wonder, really; there's nothing about a house she doesn't know, from the outside to the inside to the foundations. People come and ask her about chimneys, drainage, flooring, wall treatment— everything. They get the information they want, but nothing more; not a friendly word—in fact, as at dinner, not a word unconnected with the subject under discussion. Do you know, I haven't even asked how you got that unusual name: Annerley."

She told him. He walked as fast as he talked; the brisk pace had warmed her limbs and lightened her spirits. She thought him rather like a colt—long-legged, springy and delighted to be alive.

"I'm called Simon after Peter, Jason after the fleece, and Lionel after a rich uncle who was supposed to leave me money, but didn't."

"Isn't your surname—Raadick—rather unusual?"

"It's un-English. My mother thinks it's a Viking name, but that's only a guess. As a matter of fact, Raadick isn't my name. I took the name of each of my stepfathers—my mother thought it made us all sound a nice, united family. My own name was Berger. Do you find all this boring?"

"No."

She spoke sincerely; it was, she felt, exactly what was needed in her grandmother's house with its arctic, unchanging atmosphere. It was like a little bubbling stream flowing between frozen banks.

"Some people think I talk too much. If they feel that, they've only got to say so and I'll stem the flow. I only talk when I like people and want to get to know them and want them to get to know me. The polite way's too slow; in a dozen meetings, you get nowhere, whereas in this short walk, we've more or less got acquainted. I wish you could go and see my mother—she'd like to know you. How do you spend your days here?"

"I haven't had many days yet. I work in the dairy."

"Then you might see my mother when she comes to collect the milk she needs for making cheese. That's her war job, cheese-making for some of the local hospitals. She's quite recognizable: small, sort of faded-pretty, and always tailed by two or more of our dogs."

When they got back to the house, there was just time to go upstairs and get ready for dinner. Simon was waiting for her in the hall when she came down.

"Lovely house," he commented.

"Yes, it is."

"I'm all in favour of sacrificing everything for love, but in this case, it does seem a lot for your father to have given up. After being so many centuries in the family, it's a pity to see it go to whoever your grandmother has in mind to leave it to." He led her towards the library. "There won't be any chance to talk to you at dinner; it'll be road-repairing only until your grandmother leaves us. After that, we can go on getting acquainted. Thank you for coming on the walk."

Simon and Mrs. Thorpe were the only people at table besides her grandmother and herself. The conversation turned on the state of the local roads, the necessity to repair them to allow the free flow of army vehicles and, most controversial of all, where the money and the materials were to be found to effect the improvements. The Army would supply the labour. As on the previous evening, everything was pared down to the essential points of the discussion; if Simon strayed from the subject, he was brought back sharply by his hostess.

When she had retired to her room, he had several suggestions to offer for Annerley's entertainment: they could play cards—for money, as he was badly in need of some. They could play guessing games, dull for children but stimulating for grown-ups. Or they could go out into the still-falling snow and make a snowman by the light of the dining room windows. She chose to make a snowman; to her surprise, Mrs. Thorpe elected to help, assuming command of the operation and giving inept and unnecessary instructions in a girlishly playful manner which Annerley thought must grate on her grandmother's nerves. An odd secretary to choose, she thought; there were surely women with more mental equipment than this one seemed to have, who could have filled the post.

The next morning was bitterly cold, but sunny. Annerley met the departing guest in the kitchen making coffee and toast for himself. On her appearance, he doubled the quantities, and they sat at the long, scrubbed trestle table until Marshall came in to say that the Lieutenant's transport had arrived.

"Thanks." Simon snatched up his cap, stood up to finish his coffee and came back from the door to address Annerley. "I won't say good-bye. I never volunteered for these missions before, but I will in future. I can think of lots of things I shall

211

have to discuss with your grandmother. Next time I'm here, we'll go and look at your father's boat. Keep warm and keep happy."

The day at the farm was uneventful, but she enjoyed herself. There was no sign of Simon's mother. Marshall brought her a telegram—Moira would not, after all, be able to come. After the first moments of disappointment, Annerley felt that perhaps it was as well. This was not the best time of the year to see Waterways, and there was always the possibility that Moira, irritated by the military discipline, would have unleashed her tongue.

On the following day she received an unexpected letter from Moira's stepmother. She wrote to say that Moira would be staying in her London house with her for a few days—why couldn't Annerley join them on her way back to Devonshire? As well as Moira, there would be Mark, who had moved in and was going to live in the house while he studied for his Indian civil service examinations.

Annerley lost no time in posting off an acceptance. When Mark had discussed staying at the house he had not made up his mind whether it would be a good thing to do. He liked his stepmother and she liked him; she was urging him to move in—but Mark's view was that there was a hard grind in front of him, and it might be better to avoid any risk of distractions. Annerley was glad that he had decided to settle down at the house.

From thinking about Mark, she went on to think about the summer holiday. She knew that before leaving Waterways, she would have to tell her grandmother whether she intended coming back here. She would have preferred to stay at the cottage—but money was beginning to be a problem. She had become aware that she had none of her Devenish grandmother's talent for making a penny do the work of two. She had few wants, and she did not think that she had overspent, but the meaning and the value of small economies had become clear. Shutting the cottage for the summer would be cheaper than living in it. If she came here, she could save some money.

When the doctor came to see her at the dairy, she told him

that she had decided to accept her grandmother's invitation to spend the summer at Waterways.

"I'm glad. I'm very glad," he said. "You'll give a great deal of pleasure to your grandmother. She won't show it, but she'll feel it. She was looking worn out when you came here, and she's perked up. She told me herself that she's feeling better than she did. She wouldn't believe me if I told her that you're responsible for the improvement, but it's true. So I'm glad you'll be coming back."

They walked back to the house together. He stopped on the way to point to the beautiful building.

"Getting to know it better?" he asked.

"I think so."

"Wait till you see the gardens when they've been taken out of their wartime dress. Instead of potatoes and turnips, a glory of lovely colour."

She sighed.

"Will the war ever end?" she asked.

He looked at her with a smile.

"I'm not a betting man," he said, "and I hope you don't gamble. But I'd like to lay sixpence, or maybe a shilling, on the war being over by the end of this year."

"You can't have read the news."

"Oh yes, I've read the news. I know things aren't going well. 'Backs to the wall'—yes. All of us, backs to the wall. But I'm a doctor, and I know about crises. There's going to be one soon, and then you'll see: that'll be the beginning of a victorious end."

"I hope you're right."

"I'm sure I'm right. And it's going to cost you a shilling."

The company at dinner was the kind she had learned to expect: sober, well informed on their particular subject—and without exception, dull. Whether four years of war had quenched their spirits, or whether her grandmother's presence acted as a blight, she could not judge; she could only sit and eat and wait for the meal to come to an end.

Four days after Simon Raadick's visit, his mother came to the dairy. Her arrival was heralded by the sound of an engine which seemed to be in serious need of repair. A car bearing the marks of battle drove into the yard; out of it sprang three large dogs, to be immediately surrounded by those belonging to the farm. During the ensuing fight, the driver of the car sat waiting until peace and order had been restored; then she stepped out, and Annerley thought she was a sight to chase away the dreary appearance of war. She was wearing a beautifully cut green cloth coat, short, stout green-and-white Norwegian boots and a matching green-and-white woolen cap.

She waved a gloved hand to the dairy assistants.

"Good morning. I'm late, but my car didn't, so to speak, respond to the helm. I think something must be the matter with it. If, on your way to lunch, one of you girls would very kindly ask Marshall to come and look at it, I'd be very grateful." She turned to Annerley. "You're the granddaughter. I would have known; you're very much a Brooke. I've often wondered about you. It's awfully cold—shall we sit and talk in the car until Marshall arrives? Is that the milk I'm taking back with me?"

A supply had been poured into a churn which stood at the door of the dairy. Annerley rolled it to the car and with practiced ease got it aboard.

"My dear child, what strength! The new woman. I knew, of course, about the undergraduate part—Simon told me. He told me much, much more, the most surprising item being his offer to teach you how to sail. This has never happened before. He likes to sail on his own, leaving women waving on the shore, like our brave sailors. Now come and let's sit in at least partial shelter, and tell me all about yourself."

Annerley sat beside her and thought that the prettiness Simon had mentioned was not at all faded. Like him, she talked swiftly and ceaselessly; it was interesting to speculate what happened when they were together.

"Simon told me you were pretty, but he didn't say how pretty,

214

and I wondered how you could be pretty if, as he said, you were like your grandmother. But now I can see. You've got her features—the Brooke features—but like your father, you improved on them. Your father was splendid to behold, and every young woman in the county had her eye on him, myself included, only I was too old to compete—I was six years older than he was. My younger sister made quite shameless advances to him, but he wasn't a man who took much interest in women. Remind me to tell you about the time your grandmother caught my sister climbing a tree to get into your father's bedroom. But as I said, he wasn't responsive. He sailed, and he fished, and he rode, and now and then he might appear at a ball, but not really to join in, only just as it were to dabble his toes. What did you think when you saw Mrs. Thorpe?"

"Mrs. Thorpe?"

"You don't mean to say you don't *know*? Surely *someone* must have told you?"

"Told me what?"

"Hasn't anyone ever told you that . . . but how could they? I'm sure your father would never have mentioned her, and even if he had, she's had two husbands since then. It's odd how she stuck to the same letter; she was a Miss Thorold and then she was Lady Thaxby and now she's Mrs. Thorpe. So sensible not to have to unpick the embroidered initials off the sheets and pillowcases and so on."

"Do you mean . . . ?"

"Of *course*! *She* was the one your grandmother selected for him."

"Mrs. Thorpe!"

"Miss Thorold. To tell you the truth, I don't think she ever knew that your grandmother had decided she was the one for him. She wasn't often here—she spent a lot of her time up in Scotland, where she's got relations, lairds and so on. But we all knew she was chosen to be the next Mrs. Brooke, and we were all delighted when it didn't come off. Mind you, the choice wasn't as odd as it looks today. Some women wear well and some don't, and poor Miss Thorold didn't and I'm certain your grandmother realizes it. In fact, when I heard she'd actually engaged her to be her secretary, I felt it was her way—your grandmother's way—of punishing herself for having made such a bloomer. It was an error of judgment, and she doesn't make many."

"Mrs. Thorpe!"

"Yes, I know how you feel. Not the mother one would have chosen, but it's all over and done with, and perhaps if she'd married your father instead of those two stuffy husbands, she would have turned out better. Is that Marshall coming along there?"

"No."

"Good. I'm so enjoying hearing about you. Do you know, I used to feel it would have been a good thing if someone had tried to rescue your grandmother's husband. He led such a miserable life. She used to give him lists of what he was expected to do round the estate each day. One: inspect the drains; two: count the chickens, that kind of thing, so galling and also a great waste of his time, because he wasn't at all practical. He was the professor type, not at all the man you would have expected her to choose as a husband, unless of course she deliberately decided on someone rather bloodless, who wouldn't make demands on her for you know what, or perhaps you don't know what, though at your age, you should, only it's always difficult for girls who haven't got mothers. Don't you think the house is beautiful?"

"Yes. It's lovely."

"And your grandmother's kept it like that all through this war. I think it's such a tragedy that it's not going to be left to your father. But he inherited a house down in Devonshire, didn't he?"

"Yes."

"Well, that's something. Somewhere for his retirement. When you see him again after the war, you must ask him if he remembers me."

"I'm sure he does."

"It's such a long time ago—and yet when I look at you, it

seems like yesterday. Will you come and see me if you can ever get away?"

"Thank you. I'd like to."

"Are you coming back in the summer?"

"Yes."

"Then wait until then, and we can be out of doors. I hope my sister will be here; it depends whether she can get anybody to take her children off her hands. She can't bring them—they're too young; they'd fall in the water and get drowned and I'd get the blame. Here's Marshall, so we can't go on chatting. Don't give my love to your grandmother, she won't expect it. We don't meet if we can avoid it, and thank God, I've never had to attend one of her dreary dinners. Marshall, help Miss Annerley out, will you, and then see which part of the engine has given way. Don't wait, Annerley, you'll freeze to death. It's been lovely to hear your news. Goodbye."

The dinners were no longer dreary, no longer dull. There was endless opportunity for surreptitious study of Mrs. Thorpe. But it was impossible, Annerley found, to turn back the pages of the calendar and imagine what she had been like when she had been chosen as a bride for Edwin Brooke. Watching her occasional exchanges with her employer, it was easy to see how she would have got on any ordinary woman's nerves—but her grandmother, Annerley had realized by now, was not an ordinary woman. Whether she had in fact saddled herself with Mrs. Thorpe as a punishment for that long-past and costly mistake, only Mrs. Raadick would presume to guess.

Mark wrote every day. He had told her that there was no possibility of his seeing her at Waterways, but on the day after her meeting with Simon's mother, she received a telegram telling her that he had to go up to Scotland to see an uncle, and would spend a few hours with her. She retailed this information to her grandmother, who showed not a spark of interest.

Mark left London at dawn in a newly acquired secondhand car, and arrived at Waterways shortly before lunch. It was unfortunate that Simon Raadick had found himself with a free day

217

and had driven over to try and persuade Annerley to go out to lunch with him. The two men met on the drive, and showed no pleasure on being introduced to one another.

"I'm hoping Annerley will come out to lunch," Simon said. "They lay on a sort of sandwich lunch here, so you could—"

"I haven't got long." Mark addressed Annerley. "I ought to be off by four at the latest. What would you like to do?"

"I wouldn't keep her out after about three," Simon said.

"Some other time," Mark said.

"If this is your first visit to these parts, you could drive round—there's quite a decent bit of country—"

"You drive round," Mark suggested.

"I don't get many free days, so I—"

"Bad luck. Don't let me keep you."

Annerley fought her way out of the tangle of emotions caused by her tardy realization that what she was witnessing was an exhibition of jealousy. Jealousy—over her! She decided to postpone an analysis of her reactions, and turned to Simon.

"Simon, I'm sorry," she said. "Mark's only here for a little while, and I'd like to stay with him."

Simon's expression showed his astonishment at this odd preference, but he said nothing more about lunch.

"I'll come back this evening," he told her.

Mark watched him out of sight.

"Who the hell is he?" he inquired.

"He has to come here sometimes to see my grandmother. His job is mending roads."

"He doesn't seem to keep his mind on it. Do you see much of him?"

"Does it matter?"

"It matters to me. I come up here to see you, and I meet this fellow who obviously thinks he can monopolize you. Can't you see how much better it would be if you were engaged to me?"

"Yes. No."

"You haven't even said you're glad to see me."

She put her hands on his shoulders; he kissed her and then put his arms round her and held her close.

"It's awful, swotting in London without you to talk to at the end of the day. You do love me, don't you?"

"Yes."

"But not enough to marry me, or at least promise to marry me, not enough to wear my ring and tell everybody you belong to me?"

"I don't know."

"Every night, I pray for patience." He released her. "And now that we've cleared that up, where does one find these sandwiches? Or would you rather go out somewhere?"

"No. Just sandwiches, and then you can see something of Waterways."

She led him to the library. Beer, sandwiches and coffee restored his good humour.

She asked him if he had heard from Chandra.

"I've not only heard from him; I've seen him."

"When?"

"He came to London. He stayed at his uncle's house, but spent most of his time with me. I was right about the change in him; it was the result of that meeting with his father, who it seems is up to his neck in politics—a follower, or, if you like, a disciple of Gandhi. Burning with anti-British zeal—and some of the heat scorched Chandra. He wanted to chuck Oxford and go back with his father, but his father said no. Chandra's decided that as soon as his finals are over, he's going back to India. His uncle is arranging a passage for him. One interesting thing: He told me he didn't now think that the India civil service was a good thing for me to join. I said it was too late to change horses." He paused. "You'll see a change in him. I wouldn't be surprised to see him marching up and down Piccadilly wearing a sandwich board: India for the Indians. Did his sister ever mention anything of this in her letters to you?"

"No."

He looked at his watch.

"Time's going. I'd like to take a look round. Will you come?"

They explored the estate in his car, stopping to talk to the workers on the farm and in the dairy. They met Dr. Picton, who contributed facts and figures about management. When they returned to the house, Mark spoke in amazement.

"How can one woman keep a place like this going?"

"It was in good order when she inherited it. All she had to do was keep it running."

"Sounds easy—but I think she's doing a wonderful job. She's got help, I saw that, but the organization falls on her shoulders. How could your father ever have brought himself to leave?"

"He fell in love. Why did his mother force him to choose?"

"I can guess—a little. You said that your mother was the daughter of a country parson, brought up in a small village. Your grandmother would have assumed that a girl like that wouldn't know much about landed estates, and wouldn't be able to help your father in the ways he needed help. So she chose a woman who'd had a background like his."

"My mother could have learned."

"Of course. But in your grandmother's view, that would have been problematical."

"All my grandmother wanted was to make him do what he was told."

"I'm sorry I'm not going to see her."

"She could have met you, if she'd wanted to. The reason she showed no interest in the fact that you were coming, was to prove to me that she wasn't interested in me or in my friends."

He had to leave. Beside his car, he cradled her in his arms.

"How much do you think about me? All day? All night?"

She thought of his meeting with Simon Raadick.

"I don't think of anybody else," she assured him.

"That's something. I'm glad you're coming to London." He kissed her gently. "I'm not trying to tie you down—but if we were engaged, I'd feel a good deal safer."

"I've just told you there isn't anybody else, only you."

"There might be, one day. I love you so much, Annerley. When I think of you far away from me, meeting God knows who, pursued by some of those men you're going to run into, drifting away from me, I get frightened. Do you love me at all?"

"Yes. But I don't want to get engaged yet. Not yet. Please, Mark."

They stood hand in hand, and some of her serenity, her trust that all would be well with them, transferred itself to him. She wasn't like other girls, he reminded himself. She was . . . steadfast.

Patience . . .

In the next batch of letters forwarded from the cottage was one which informed Annerley that she had gained a place at Oxford. She looked for her grandmother to give her the news, but there was no sign of her until dinner. When the meal was over, Annerley followed her out of the room and showed her the letter. Her grandmother read it, folded it and handed it back.

"Congratulations," she said.

Annerley thought that the word could not have been uttered with less feeling. She wondered if her father's academic successes in the past had been dismissed in so cold, so totally uninterested a manner. It was left to Dr. Picton to voice warm and sincere praise, and to add—with a hardihood for which she felt grateful— that when the news reached her father, he would be proud of her.

When the time came for her departure, her grandmother's manner was as businesslike as it had been on her arrival.

"How long will you be staying with your friends in London?"

"Only a few days. I have to be back in Exeter for the beginning of the school term."

There was silence. Both waited for words that neither of them could find. They were both conscious of the same figure—that of Edwin Brooke. Annerley longed to speak of him, but she felt that it would be useless. He had gone. His mother had let him go —and nothing in that frosty gaze suggested that she would ever forgive him.

221

Seated in the train on the way to London, Annerley tried to argue herself out of what she felt to be a mood of foolish, even childish excitement. There was nothing to be excited about, she told herself. War or no war, people made frequent journeys to London. It was just another city; larger and more important than most, but at this moment, simply a place in which she was going to stay on her way home to Exeter.

But the excitement persisted. The explanation, she thought, lay in the fact that her life, though happy, could not be called eventful; if it had been, she would have learned to take occasions like this more calmly—she would have been behaving like an eighteen-year-old and not a thirteen-year-old. As it was, beneath the pleasurable anticipation was a feeling of shyness amounting almost to fear—fear that she could not be natural with strangers, fear that she would be self-conscious when meeting men. Mark was the only man she had ever known really well; if she had known more, if she could have had more choice, she knew that she would have had less hesitation in getting engaged to him, would have had a greater sense of security.

Moira and Mark were at the station to meet her. Chandra, they told her, was in London but had not been able to come and meet her; he would see her that evening.

Moira was not in uniform. She was wearing a coat with a large fur collar and a small cloche hat, and looked dauntingly smart.

"Skirts have got shorter," she informed Annerley when they were in Mark's car on the way to Mrs. Fenwick's house. "You'll have to put up your hems. Or don't bother; I'll lend you something to wear."

"What's the matter with what I've got on?"

"Nothing," Mark answered. "I've already told Moira that you're going to marry me one day, and I don't want her to teach you extravagant ways. I like you the way you look now."

"This isn't Torring," Moira pointed out. "Heavens, Annerley, don't you ever look at yourself in the glass? We all know there's a war on, but even so, fashions have changed a bit since 1914. And your hair . . . but you needn't bother about that. I'll take you to Bernard this afternoon."

"Who's Bairr-nar?"

"A hairdresser. Would I take you to a chef to get your hair done? You've gone round too long looking like a Pomeranian."

"Leave her hair alone," said Mark. "I like Pomeranians."

"Wait and see what Bernard does. You'll be surprised."

Annerley was not so much surprised as stunned. Nobody could complain, on her return from the hairdresser's, that she did not look at herself in the glass. She remained fixed in front of it, unable to believe that the reflection she was seeing, the slim figure in one of Moira's new calf-length dresses, with hair like a frilled, close-fitting cap, was herself.

Mark kissed her tenderly but told her that he wanted her to look as she used to look. Chandra, arriving for dinner, also said that he would like the old Annerley back. But when they went out together on two subsequent nights, it was Annerley, and not Moira, who attracted admiring glances.

On the fourth evening, they attended a party given by an

223

American general and his wife who occupied a large house and were noted for their open-house hospitality to servicemen of all nations. The occasion was the general's birthday, and was to be a more formal affair than usual, with a band and a sit-down supper.

But the host and hostess had been unable to provide the chief commodity the young men needed to make the party a success: There were far too few girls. Men who lived in the district were appealed to, and went out to fetch sisters or cousins. Mark and Chandra drove away on the search. Girls began to appear, singly or in groups; supper was served and then the general and his wife slipped quietly away, leaving the guests to enjoy themselves more freely.

Annerley was taken in to supper by two Frenchmen. At a distant table she saw Moira seated between two British airmen. Mark and Chandra had not returned.

On going back after supper to the room in which dancing was going on, she found that the atmosphere had changed. All formality, all restraint had vanished. The room was crowded to suffocation and everyone was uproariously happy. Couples set out together and were separated in the melee. The noise of the band was all but drowned by the singing of the guests.

Swept onto the dance floor, Annerley found herself in the embrace of a total stranger, from whose arms she was snatched by a tall American who had to relinquish her to a burly Australian. She passed from him to a diminutive British major, who lost her to another American. She was kissed, fondled and pinched. Suggestions for future meetings were shouted into her ears. Pressed against the jackets of uniforms, her expensive Bernard hairstyle reverted to Pomeranian.

She found that it was impossible to fight a way out of the crush and, after a while, gave up the attempt. She remembered that these were men on leave from the front, making the most of fleeting enjoyment. This was not her idea of enjoyment, but she felt that she was gaining some of the experience she had hitherto felt she lacked.

From resisting, she began to respond. She had wanted to learn about life; here she was, learning.

After a time, she found herself on the edge of the pack. Her arm was seized, and she was pulled free and dragged to the door. Her head cleared; she saw that she was facing Mark. His face was white with fury.

"Goodness," she gasped. "Let's get out."

"Out? Out?" He had to shout to make himself heard above the din. "I've been trying to get you out for the past half hour. Didn't you see me?"

"No."

"You looked straight at me—twice—and didn't take a damn bit of notice."

"I didn't see you."

"Perhaps you didn't want to see me."

"How could I—"

"You must have gone mad. I never saw you behave like that before."

"I couldn't get out."

"You didn't try to get out. I was standing there watching you. You were enjoying every minute."

"I was—"

"Naturally you didn't want to come away."

He was still grasping her arm. They had reached the head of the stairs. Here there was less noise, but every stair was blocked by entwined couples. They stepped over them and, when they had reached the hall, found Moira waiting, holding her own coat and Annerley's.

"And where the hell were you?" Mark asked her.

"On the touch line. Watching Annerley enjoying her first plunge into society." She gave Annerley a mocking smile. "You'll have to learn to fend them off."

"Fend them off?" Annerley repeated in amazement. "How? We were all practically stuck together."

"Well, let's get out of it now," Mark said. "This isn't a party, it's pandemonium."

225

Outside, snow was falling; the night looked black and bitterly cold. Inside were bright lights . . .

"It's still so early," Annerley protested.

"The time," Mark informed her, "is exactly twenty minutes to four."

Around them were men clamouring for the return of Moira and Annerley. Ignoring them, Mark took the coat that Moira was holding, put it round Annerley and led the way out to his car. His first efforts to start it produced nothing but splutters. A few more turns on the starting handle, and the car began to perform a tribal dance. He hurried round to the wheel, shut the girls into the back—like a keeper closing the cage, Annerley thought resentfully—and drove home.

By the time they arrived, his anger had cooled. Locking the front door after them, he took Annerley in his arms and kissed her remorsefully.

"Sorry," he said. "I lost my temper."

"It doesn't matter. What happened to the girls you went out to look for?"

"The car broke down. By the time I'd got it going again, it was too late to fetch girls. I took Chandra to his uncle's and went back to the party."

"And what a party," said Moira. "I want a hot drink. Does anyone else?"

Neither Mark nor Annerley wanted anything to drink. He wanted to make up for his display of ill-temper and jealousy; she wanted to shut herself in her room and sort out her impressions of the evening.

But when at last she was alone, she found that she could not sleep. She lay thinking of the confusion of the past few hours, and trying to identify the men who had shown so sudden and so unexpected an appreciation of her charms. Five nationalities, five accents, five entirely different methods of making the most of a fugitive moment. It had been less than decorous—but it had been exhilarating. And it had certainly been experience.

At breakfast, Mark was subdued and still apologetic. What

226

had upset him, he explained, had been his impression—quite mistaken—that she had been enjoying herself. Annerley, meeting Moira's amused glance across the table, said nothing.

It was Annerley's last day—she was to return to Exeter next morning—but Mark had to go to his crammer's. She and Moira had been invited to lunch with Chandra's uncle and aunt, but Moira was unable to go; she was to meet the matron of a hospital and make final arrangements for a course of study. Annerley, who had no plans, looked forward to the visit.

Chandra drove round to pick her up, coming early in order to drive her to the City area and show her a part of London which she had not yet seen.

"It's the wrong way round," he said, opening the door of his car for her. "You should be the one showing me London. You're the native, I'm the visitor."

"I'm the country cousin."

"Really?" He gave her a smiling glance. "Reports reaching me from people who were at the party last night seem to contradict that."

"Oh, you heard? I suppose Mark told you."

"How could he? I haven't seen him today. I was informed that he dragged you away, protesting. I mean you were doing the protesting. Were you surprised to find that he can be jealous?"

"He's got nothing to be jealous about."

"You've refused—more than once—to become engaged to him. Why?"

She hesitated.

"I suppose because I want to be quite sure I'm in love with him before I make up my mind."

"He's the faithful type. He won't change. He'll make a good husband." He paused. "You know, I believe in votes for women, rights for women, freedom for women—but how much simpler it would be if you gave up Oxford, married Mark and settled down to being a happy wife and mother. How keen are you on getting this degree?"

"I don't know. I like the idea, except when I think of myself at Oxford while my father's living by himself in India."

"Are you sure he'll go back to India?"

"I think he may have to. If he doesn't go back and do the work he was doing before the war, I don't see where his income will come from. Mark says you're going back after your finals."

"I would have gone before my finals, if my father hadn't stopped me. His visit to England unsettled me. It seemed to me that I ought to be out there with him. But he didn't agree. What plans have you made for the summer?"

"I'm going back to my grandmother's house—but only for September. Where will you be by then?"

"Perhaps I'll be sitting in the sunshine on the balcony outside Shareen's room, asking her to tell me what you were like when you were a child."

She said nothing. He was going. But she was glad that she had known him, glad that he had been part of the summer that she still held as a treasured memory. She had felt that it would be the last perfect summer, and she had been right.

They made a brief tour of some of the historic landmarks in the City, and then he drove her to his uncle's house. It was very large. Most of it, Chandra explained, was given over to Indians who were in London promoting various schemes for the benefit of Indian troops. His uncle and aunt were living in rooms on the ground floor.

His uncle, Mr. Chaudari, was a large, powerful-looking man with a deep voice, a loud laugh and small, twinkling brown eyes. His wife looked a good deal younger than he was, and reclined gracefully on a sofa, elegant in a mauve sari, leaving the conversation and the entertainment of the guest to her husband.

Over after-lunch coffee, he bore Annerley away to a sofa in the corner of the drawing room. Their talk was mainly of India—but it ended on a fatherly note.

"Whenever you come to London," he told her, "I hope you will remember that we shall welcome you. We have no spare rooms now, but after the war, we shall spread out again and we shall give you a room to keep for yourself, to use whenever you want to escape from your studies at Oxford. It will be your very own."

He spoke with such obvious sincerity that she found it difficult to thank him. He took her hand and patted it.

"There is no need for thanks. You are Shareen's friend. You are Chandra's friend. That means you are one of us. Please remember that. And remember something else: that if you want anything, anything that I can do for you, you must not hesitate to come and ask me. Will you promise that?"

"Yes," she said. "I promise."

When Annerley went up to Norfolk in the first week of September, it was clear that the war was in its last phase. The outcome of the fighting, for so many long and bitter years in doubt, could now be seen and felt everywhere. Victory was in the air.

The mood of the country had changed. Changes were evident, also, in the routine she found on her arrival at Waterways. Dr. Picton was in Scotland; she missed him very much. The house was still running on military lines, but tensions had slackened. Few people came to confer with her grandmother; none stayed to dinner. Those who had business to discuss were interviewed in a room which she had set apart and called her office. She had her meals alone; Annerley was left with Mrs. Thorpe.

There was no longer work for her in the dairy. Marshall, now with more leisure, drove her to see places which had been her father's favourite haunts. Simon Raadick came on his free days to take her sailing, in her father's boat or in his own. She went frequently to visit his mother, whose house was large, rambling and shabby but infinitely more welcoming than her grandmother's. Simon's aunt Psyche was on a visit—plump, slow-moving; impossible to imagine her climbing a tree in pursuit of Edwin

Brooke. They had picnic lunches on the jetty adjoining the boat-house, Mrs. Raadick on a deck chair under a large golf umbrella, Aunt Psyche on an upright wicker chair under a pretty sunshade. Simon and Annerley sat with their feet dangling in the water. Between large bites of sandwich, he outlined his future; his mother, sipping shandy, recalled her past.

"I think one of the things I might do when I'm demobbed is become a tennis pro," he told Annerley. "A chap I know was just getting started as a professional when the war came and mucked up his plans. He told me—"

"It wasn't the war, it was his parents," Mrs. Raadick corrected. "They were angry because—"

"—that one could do better abroad, France for instance. More scope there for—"

"—he threw up a perfectly good job in a jute firm and announced that—"

"—professional sport. But when I get back to civilian life I might go to New Zealand and try sheep farming, though—"

"—he was going to capitalize, that was his word, and a very silly one, capitalize on his prowess at games. He took after his mother, of course. You remember her, Psyche? Carrie Milner that was, who led poor Will Redman such a dance before she—"

"—one thing against it is that it isn't much of a life for a sheep, what with losing its fleece and being exported in refrigerators. Those Empire builders knew what they were doing, planting the flag from pole to pole. It means that one has a wide choice of jobs in far-flung places. One can be a—"

"—ran off with this young man's father."

"—tea planter or a rubber planter or a coffee planter, all on home ground, so to speak. And then there's the bush and the outback, whatever that is, and jungle or desert or snow, take your pick. I—"

"You're mixing her up with Carrie Leven. She used to run after the Smythe boys. I think that was why they all—"

"—rather fancy Burma, in a way. Perhaps, managing a ruby mine."

"Your stepfather—not this one, the last one—managed a ruby mine once."

"Did he?"

"Oh, yes."

"You never told me that."

"They all emigrated, as I was saying. You know, I—" She peered at her sister. "She's fallen asleep."

"So she has," corroborated Simon.

"It's a sign of age, dropping off like that. Is there any more lemonade?"

"No. And no more beer, either. That's why she dropped off like that."

How much her grandmother knew of these visits, Annerley could not guess. Since nothing was ever discussed between them, she could only conclude that she was as free in this matter as she was in all others at Waterways.

Mark was staying with his stepmother in Dorset. His father had returned to India and she planned to follow him when the war was over and her house restored to her. Mark drove her down to the cottage at Torring for a week, and Moira joined them. He left the two together and went up to see Annerley before returning to his studies in London.

On his arrival, she took him to see her grandmother, who was in her office. After a cold greeting, he was invited to help himself to a sandwich lunch. He followed Annerley to the library.

"Cold reception, cold lunch," he commented. "Is your father remotely like her?"

"No."

"Good. Was she always like that, or do you suppose she dried up, or froze up, after that row with him?"

"According to the people who knew her when she was young, she was always the way she is now. Her father was like that, too. Do you want to eat here, or shall we pack a lunch and go sailing?"

"Go sailing."

They went to the boathouse and he balanced the lunch basket carefully as he stepped into the boat. He watched Annerley maneuvering the little craft into open water, and expressed his approval.

"Couldn't have done it better myself," he told her. "Who taught you to be so expert? That chauffeur?"

"No. Simon Raadick."

He frowned.

"Not the chap who was here when I came up, and had the nerve to—"

"He's a neighbour."

"It must have taken a lot of time for him to get you to this pitch of efficiency."

"I was a fast learner."

"In some matters, you seem to me to be learning too fast."

She looked at him in astonishment.

"What does that mean, exactly?" she asked.

"Nothing. I'm sorry. I'm not really a dog in the manger. I know you have to meet other people, other men. What worries me, what I can never get out of my mind is the fact that there's nobody to look after you, nobody, so to speak, in charge of you. Your father isn't here, Mrs. Devenish is dead, and this grandmother here doesn't seem to care what you do."

"I'm eighteen. Do I need a guardian?"

"No. But you do need someone you can go to when you need help or advice."

"I've got somebody. You."

"I've no official standing. I would have, if we were engaged. Have you changed your mind about that?"

She shook her head.

"No, Mark, I'm sorry—but I don't want to get engaged yet, to you or to anybody else."

She brought the boat up against a grassy bank, and they got out to eat lunch.

"My stepmother," he said, "had an idea about the cottage. She thinks it would be a good place for me—and for her—to use at weekends—but not in its present condition. She wants your father's permission to put in electricity. As he's not here to ask, she wondered whether you'd agree."

"Would it cost an awful lot?"

"It wouldn't cost you anything—she'd pay for it. It's already in the village. And whatever it costs won't make much dent in her income—she's not poor. If I were you, I'd say yes and be thankful. If I'm going to spend much time there—and I'd like to —I won't want to fiddle about with lamps and wicks and candles. Will you let her do it?"

"Yes."

"Good. It's a well-built little place. She likes it because she thinks it's picturesque."

The sun was beginning to set before he left. Annerley walked with him to the car.

"I'm glad you came," she said.

He laughed.

"Can't you understand that I'm always here—in spirit? Where you are, my mind is." He kissed her, gentle little kisses on her cheeks and then one, not so gentle, on her lips. "My mind, and my heart. Bless you, Annerley darling."

He got into the car, saw a bundle of letters on the seat and gave an exclamation of apology.

"Oh Lord, sorry! These are the letters Moira brought up from the cottage and asked me to give you. Good thing I didn't drive off with them."

He leaned out of the car, took her face between his hands and kissed her. Then he drove away.

She watched him out of sight and then went upstairs to her room to change. It was tempting to open her mail, but if she did, she would be late for dinner. It was not until she had come upstairs again after the meal that she could settle in an armchair and glance at the envelopes. Moira, Chandra, Mrs. Bray, the headmistress, three official-looking letters, a postcard, and . . .

She stopped. Getting slowly to her feet, she held the last letter in her hand, staring at it in a kind of daze, a mixture of terror and hope.

Her father's handwriting. No censor's stamp. Her name, the address of the cottage. The postmark . . . Calcutta.

She found, when at last she tried to open it, that her hands were trembling. She unfolded the letter and saw that it was written on paper with the heading of the Presidency General Hospital.

Frantically, she began to read. It was a long letter, but it was confined—purposely, he said—to facts, leaving out reactions and emotions. He and twenty-three other internees had been sent back to India for medical treatment. He had been the only European in the group, but his illness was the same as those of the other twenty-two—malaria. It had been decided that the disease could be dealt with better by Indian doctors, and so here he was, in the Presidency General Hospital, which she ought to remember as she had passed it so many times. He was in the care of no fewer than three doctors, all of them expert in this field. He must, they had told him, have carried the disease for some time. It had shown itself at the beginning of his internment, but only recently had necessitated urgent treatment. She was, he said firmly, not to worry. He was still weak, but he would be cured in a month or two. He was in good hands, and he was glad to have come to India to be treated. All she had to do was be thankful that for him, the war was over, and would soon be over for her too. He looked forward to hearing from her, letters long and frequent and news-filled. If she had not left Waterways, he would like her to give his love to his mother. He was her ever-affectionate father, Edwin Brooke.

5

It was only on looking back, some time later, that she understood that as soon as she had read the letter—perhaps even while she was reading it—she had made her decision. There was no hesitation, no need to reflect; she knew what she was going to do.

But she had no idea, that evening, of the battles that lay ahead.

The first was against her grandmother. This was perhaps fortunate, for though it was brief, it was the most bitter, and it hardened her against the struggles to come.

She looked for her early the next morning, after a night spent between fitful sleep and agonies of impatience. Mrs. Brooke was not in any of the places in which she could be expected to be found at this time—not in the kitchen, giving orders for the day, not outside in the gardens. Annerley found her at last in the office.

Passing through the hall on her way there, she saw through one of the windows the army truck that provided transport for Simon Raadick. Simon was coming swiftly up the steps. She did not want to meet him, but it was too late to escape. He entered, closed the door behind him, came up to her and took both her hands. His words came in a rush, breathless and eager and with a desperate earnestness.

"I prayed I'd find you alone—I thought I was too early. . . . Annerley, I've only got a few minutes, but I had to come. I got my marching orders at midnight—we're entraining in an hour for God knows where, and I didn't know when I'd see you again, if ever, so I had to come and tell you before I went that I love you very much, and I know it's awful to throw the thing at you like this, but if you could give me just one small glimmer of hope that you could ever care for me, I'd—"

"Simon"—she freed her hands—"I can't tell you how grateful I am for—"

"But that's just what I was afraid of—that you'd say thank you for teaching me how to sail, good-bye. I haven't time to put this properly, Annerley, but I've got to tell you before I go that you're the only girl I've ever—"

"Oh Simon." She broke into his passionate speech. "Oh Simon, no, no, no"—and she burst into tears. Sobbing, fumbling unavailingly for her handkerchief, struggling for self-control, she pressed her hands to her eyes in an effort to stop the flow of tears. "I'm so sorry, Simon. Please . . . I'm so sorry . . ."

He took her hands gently from her face, shook out his handkerchief and mopped her wet cheeks, murmuring endearments, apologies, pleas for forgiveness.

"Don't be upset, Annerley darling. Just forget it for now. Pretend I haven't said anything. Pretend we're just good friends. Only . . . please think of me, and write to me, and don't forget me."

"I won't. Oh Simon . . ."

"I love you. This wasn't the time, in fact there wasn't the time to tell you properly, and I was mad to expect to be able to explain how I felt. Say good-bye. Just good-bye for now.

"Good-bye, Simon."

He kissed her cheek, took up his cap and ran down the steps to the waiting truck. She stood watching it as it went out of sight, his handkerchief still crumpled in her hands, tears still falling.

She went up to her room, washed away their traces and then sat on her bed trying to regain her composure. She would need a clear head before confronting her grandmother.

When she entered the office, her grandmother looked up from the papers she was studying, nodded good morning and gestured in the direction of a chair. Annerley remained standing. Asked to state her business, she did so in brief, simple and straightforward terms. Her grandmother's cold, level gaze showed no change as she listened. When Annerley had ended, there was a pause, and then she spoke.

"You can't be serious."

"I'm quite serious."

"Then you have taken leave of your senses."

"I don't think so. All I've decided to do is go out to India to join my father. I realize that getting a passage will be difficult, but people have been going and coming throughout the war, so I see no reason—"

"You are seriously contemplating throwing away your chance of a university degree?"

"For the moment, yes."

"If you don't go now, you will never go. Don't you understand that this is the chance of a lifetime? Didn't your father himself want you to go?"

"He probably still does. But I'm not going. He's ill, and he's alone."

"You said that he wrote telling you that he went back to India in order to get the best treatment, and he is apparently getting it. What do you imagine you can do for him that isn't already being done?"

"Medically, nothing. But when he comes out of hospital, do you think I can stay in England while he lives alone, with nobody but servants to look after him? He'll go back to our house, our flat, where we were all happy, he and my grandmother and I, and there'll be nobody, nobody to talk to, to turn to. So I'm going back."

"Do you suppose he'll welcome you, knowing that you have thrown away the prospect of getting a degree?"

"If he doesn't want me—which he will—he'll send me back —which he won't. Nothing, *nothing* is going to keep me here while he's ill and alone out there."

The glacial gaze remained on her for some moments. Then her grandmother picked up the papers from her desk.

"In that case," she said, "there is nothing more to be said."

"Yes," Annerley said. "There is."

"I think not. You have made your decision—rashly, but I shall not waste time trying to make you see reason."

"I want to thank you for inviting me here. I'm glad to have seen my father's home."

"It is not your father's home. He abandoned it with the same blind obstinacy as you have thrown away a university career."

"His reason was the same as mine. He loved my mother. I love my father. You didn't understand then, so I don't expect you to understand now. You have the fortune, or the misfortune, to be able to subdue or control your emotions, to look at a thing from the standpoint of reason. But sometimes reasoning doesn't help much. There are times when people are driven by something stronger than reason. I don't know what you had against my mother, but whatever it was, she loved him enough to marry him when he had nothing, to live in India on very little, and make him happy. He gave up a good deal more, in going to her, than I'm giving up in going to him. He gave up a home that he loved and a mother he loved, and how you could let him go, and ignore every letter he wrote to you afterwards, is something I shall never understand, however long I live. Do you want to send him any message?"

"No."

"Then I'll say good-bye. Will you allow Marshall to drive me to the station?"

"Yes."

"Thank you. And thank you for having me here. I enjoyed it

239

and I'm grateful to you and I'm sorry it had to end like this. Good-bye."

As she closed the door behind her, she saw her grandmother opening a file and beginning to study its contents.

She went to her room, finished her packing and then went down to the kitchen to find Skippy.

"*Ill*, Miss? Very ill?"

"I think he has been, Skippy, but he's going to be all right."

"I'm glad you're going to him, Miss. Will you tell him we all still remember him?"

"I will, Skippy. Good-bye."

The drive to the station was a silent one. Only when Marshall had found her a seat on the train and put her suitcase on the luggage rack did he voice his sentiments.

"It's a shame, Miss, that you're going like this, without a kind word. You'll send us news, won't you?"

"Of course, Marshall. I'll write to Dr. Picton. Good-bye, and thank you."

The train bore her away, and she sat looking out at places which she had seen on her journey to Waterways. She had considered and rejected the idea of going by way of London; she wanted to get back to the cottage and begin the process of leaving it. The journey seemed interminable; she ceased at last to stare out of the windows, and took out pen and paper and began to make notes of what she would have to see to before she left England. The cottage: there would be no need to look for a tenant. Mark and Moira and Mrs. Fenwick would use it and keep it in good condition. There were letters to write: to the headmistress, to Oxford, to Mark. To Moira.

Getting a passage. . . . A shipping company in Exeter, or if that failed, in London. There would undoubtedly be a long waiting list, but she would get one eventually.

She got no reply to her communication to Oxford. Her headmistress wrote as she had expected to write—a scathing letter full of reproaches and warnings, none of which had any effect on her.

Mark's reply was to come straight down to the cottage. He left his suitcase at the inn and walked up to see her. His first words were a question.

"What in hell do you think you're up to?"

Tears sprang to her eyes.

"Oh Mark, please! Don't begin like that. Come inside and sit down and try at least to understand."

He came inside, but did not sit down; he looked for and found a drink, in a cupboard which had once held books and now held bottles. He gave her sherry, and decided on whisky for himself.

"I need something strong," he said. "Now you can sit down and explain why you've lost your head."

"Is there anything extraordinary in a daughter going out to join a sick father?"

"Your life, for the next few years, is here in England. You can do nothing in India but hang about. Your father doesn't need you. He's got malaria, which they've apparently checked or even cured. He might even be sent to this country to complete the cure. You'll get out there, fall into his arms and then realize you've gone out for nothing, and chucked away everything you worked for here."

"But I—"

"Annerley, you mustn't do it. When I read your letter, I couldn't believe my eyes. I know you've had a shock, and you reacted in perhaps an entirely normal way—but you've had time, since getting your father's letter, to think, to reconsider. You can't rush out to him in this hysterical way, this headlong way. The war isn't even over."

"The war is almost over."

"We're on top, thank God. But who knows how long it'll drag on? Go to Oxford, get your degree, and then—if your father is still in India—go out and join him. I'll be going out myself in two or three years. We could go together—engaged, I hope. If your father had said anything about wanting you to go out now, he would have—"

"Mark." She spoke with an effort at calmness. "This decision isn't as—what did you call it—headlong as you think. For years, I've looked forward to going back to India and—"

"I know. But what you think you're going back to, isn't there anymore. You were happy—I know that. What you didn't tell me about those days, Moira filled in. Your life was all sunshine and servants and sahibs and gallops on the Maidan and flying kites. A child's life, sheltered, pleasant, something to remember and be thankful for. But you can't recreate it."

"I don't want to recreate it. I want to go back and live with my father and run the flat for him, and try to be useful. If we were a family, it might be different—but there's only himself and myself. When we came to England, I accepted the fact that I'd have to stay here and only see him when he came to England on visits—but he wasn't going to be cut off, isolated. I can't bear the thought of him alone out there."

"If you faced the truth, wouldn't you say you've never really wanted to stay in England? Haven't you always regarded your life here as an interval to be got through before going back to what you've always thought of as home?"

"Perhaps. I honestly don't know. I tell myself all the time that it's good to be English, to live in England, get to know spring and summer and autumn and winter, hawthorn buds in May, holly in winter, skipping lambs and St. Paul's and the Thames and Shakespeare and . . . oh, everything about England! But I've never felt *rooted*. Every time I've closed my eyes to think, what I've seen is not England but India."

"How much of India? Seymour Street?"

"Not much more," she confessed. "A small part, if you like, but for me, a wonderful way of life."

"So are you going out to be with your father, or are you going because you've found an excuse for going?"

She stared at him for some moments, fighting back tears.

"I knew you wouldn't exactly encourage me," she said slowly, "but I—"

He spoke more gently.

242

"You didn't expect me to make you examine your motives?" He put down his half-emptied glass, came over to her and drew her out of her chair into his arms. "You must have expected me to fight," he went on. "But I'm not only fighting to keep you here; I want you—now and always—to link up what's in your heart with what's in your head. Go out to your father if you have to—but ask yourself exactly why you're going, and don't be afraid of the answers. Act now as you acted, as you're acting in the matter of becoming engaged to me. You love me—don't ask me why I'm so certain of that, but thank God, I am. You love me, but you've reasoned, rightly, that you need more experience, more experience of men, before agreeing to marry me. So apply the same sense to your present problem. Think instead of merely feeling. And then, whatever you decide, I'll try to help."

"Thank you."

He laughed.

"But you'll go, and deep down, I don't blame you. Kiss me, long and lovingly, and swear you won't forget me."

Later, over coffee, they spoke of other things. Moira, he said, was going up to Scotland for three weeks to do a spell of duty in a hospital. Chandra had ceased to write letters.

"So has Shareen," Annerley told him. "Not a word."

"She'll write soon enough when she hears you're going back."

"They dined at the inn, Mrs. Bray fussing over them, and insisting on their accepting a bottle of wine—to wash down the wartime food, she said. Then Mark got into his car and drove away. His last words, as he kissed Annerley, were to assure her that he would do his best to help her to secure a passage, and wished her luck in her own efforts.

But this, she discovered, was all but impossible. There were ships going and ships coming; people obtained berths. But they were people with official reasons for travelling; those going on missions, those making urgent journeys. There was nothing for anybody like herself.

The weeks went by and all her efforts came to nothing. She

tried first in Exeter, and then further afield. She wrote to every shipping company she had ever heard of. When an answer came —and not many did—it was the same: nothing.

She came near to despair. It was one thing to plan; anybody could make plans. What she needed was someone who was in a position to help her to cut through the barrier between planning and sailing. But she knew nobody—and, it transpired, Mark knew nobody—who could help. She thought of the officials who had come to consult her grandmother at Waterways and who had been present at dinner. Important people all; people of influence who might have helped, but it was too late now to ask them. There was nobody.

October came—and went. Her spirits fell to their lowest level. Her father's reply had come; she was unwise, he thought, to have given up Oxford, but he was too far away, and they had been parted for too long, for him to judge. He did not think that she would get a passage before the war ended, or even for some time after it had ended. She must be patient. He added that she was old enough, independent enough, sensible enough by now to be entitled to plan her own future.

She reread the letter in bed, lying staring miserably at the low ceiling. She had cut her moorings, but she had not been able to do more. She was not even drifting; she was motionless. There was nobody who could help her. Nobody . . .

She sat upright, her heart beginning to beat faster. Nobody? Yes, there was somebody. If appearances went for anything, he would be kind. If rumour had not lied, he was immensely influential. If he had told the truth, he would be glad to see her whenever she cared to visit him and his wife. And he had offered his help if she ever needed anything. She needed something now.

She caught the mid-morning train from Exeter to London. She ate a sandwich at the station when she arrived, and then looked for a bus to take her to her destination.

Chandra's uncle.

Chandra's uncle, who could do anything . . .

244

He was even kinder than she had hoped. He was as glad to see her as he had said he would be. The extent of his influence was yet to be tested, and at first it seemed that in this matter, he might prove to have none. But his hesitation, she found, was not due to any doubts as to his ability to get her a passage; it sprang from another cause.

"Surely, my dear Annerley, you do not propose to travel alone, unaccompanied? Surely your father would not allow it?"

"What could happen to me? I'm quite independent."

"It is not what could happen to you that I am thinking about. A young lady like you cannot go on a long voyage like this without somebody to . . . what shall we say? Protect her, help her, chaperone her, any term you like, but the thing is that no, you cannot go unaccompanied."

"How could I find anybody I know who's travelling? It's going to be hard enough to get a passage for myself—how can I expect to find someone I know going on the same ship?"

"It is almost impossible, I know this. But if you wait, if you go later, when the war ends, which any day it is going to do, then many more people will be going, and among them . . ."

He paused, frowning. She waited.

"An idea has come to me," he said at last. "Do you remember, by any chance, somebody who is called Miss Severn?"

"Shareen's governess? Yes, I remember her."

"She was the last. When she left Shareen, she came to England. Now, like you, she plans to go back. She has visited me frequently, to ask if I knew anybody who needed a governess, and at last I found somebody, a maharajah who is a friend of mine. He is arranging her passage. If I tell him that a young lady wishes to find a travelling companion, he will—"

"No."

"No?"

"Thank you very much, but no."

"You did not like her?"

"It isn't that. It's just . . ."

"You feel that you do not need a governess?"

"You could put it like that."

"In that case, I must recommend you to be patient."

She had intended to see Mark and then return to the cottage, but history intervened. The armistice was signed, and Mrs. Fenwick insisted on her staying with her during the subsequent celebrations. Moira came down from Scotland, and the four—Mark and Moira, Annerley and Mrs. Fenwick—found themselves on the roof of a taxi moving at snail's pace through shouting, cheering, delirious crowds, singing and waving miniature Allied flags. Mrs. Fenwick threw open her house to a host of passing strangers. Mark and Moira and Annerley ended the evening at the house of Chandra's uncle, who was dispensing champagne to several dozen friends, relations and celebrating servicemen. They toasted victory, they toasted the future, they drank to Chandra and Shareen and to Edwin Brooke, soon to be reunited with his daughter.

Moira had intended to return with Annerley to the cottage, but changed her mind.

"I'll go down later," she said, "when I'm free. At the moment, I'm still tied up with this hospital. What made you think of asking Chandra's uncle to help you to get a passage?"

"Despair. I'd almost given up hope of getting out before the end of the century—and suddenly I remembered him, and his reputation for being able to work miracles." She paused. "The war's over. What are you going to do? Will you go out with your stepmother when she goes out to join your father?"

"No."

"You will go back, won't you?"

"Of course."

"It would be . . . different, if you weren't there."

"Why? You'll still have your great friend, Shareen Prebdel."

"She hasn't written for ages."

"Perhaps she's busy getting married. Let me know when you hear about your passage."

But she was at the cottage when the summons came. It was sent by telegram to Annerley—would she go and see Mr. Chaudari at once?

She and Moira went up together. This time, Annerley did not stop for a sandwich on arrival. They went straight to the house.

Mr. Chaudari was alone. His wife, he told them, was visiting friends. Without saying more, he led them into the drawing room, walked to a desk, opened one of the drawers and took out a long envelope. He handed it to Annerley.

"Your ticket," he said. "London to Bombay. P and O—Peninsular and Oriental—the *Hindustan*. Before the war, a nice ship, but now, I don't know. You sail on December the eighteenth; you will have Christmas on board, which is a pity, as I think you would have liked to spend it with your father."

She was staring at the envelope in her hand, struggling to find words in which to thank him.

"Mr. Chaudari," she began, "I—"

But he held up an outsize brown, fleshy hand and stopped her.

"Wait!" he said. "I have forgotten something."

He went to the desk, but before opening the drawer, had to wait until he had recovered from a prolonged fit of laughter. Shaking, roaring, gasping for breath, he tried to utter a word or two, gave up and shook his head. Then, taking out a handkerchief and wiping his eyes, he opened the drawer and took out an envelope identical to the one he had given to Annerley. But this time, it was to Moira that he handed it.

"Your ticket," he said and, turning to watch Annerley's reactions, burst into laughter once more.

"Oh, this I am enjoying," he said when he could speak. "Do you know, Moira my dear, I actually advised against her travelling without a companion. I actually . . ."

Annerley was looking at Moira. Once more she was trying to find words.

"I don't understand," she said at last. "You're . . . you're coming?"

"I am." Moira was as calm, as matter-of-fact as ever. "I'm going out on a double mission. My stepmother is sending me out to keep an eye on my father. My brother is sending me out to keep an eye on you. He and she are going to keep an eye on one another. If you've anything to say, keep it until after lunch." She turned to Mr. Chaudari. "We're both more grateful to you than we can express, Mr. Chaudari. Would you perform a further kindness and take two hungry girls out to lunch?"

He spread his arms wide and then crossed them over his heart and bowed.

"My dear young ladies, I shall be honoured."

PART THREE

1919-1929

The S.S. *Hindustan*, awaiting her passengers at Tilbury docks, looked very different from the trim liner she had been before the war. Years of troop-carrying, hazardous voyages in convoy over dangerous routes, had left their mark on her. The low wooden shacks that had been built on her decks had not yet been removed; passengers in the first and second classes would have separate dining saloons, but the available deck space had been made common to all. Thus Annerley, who had insisted on travelling second class, and Moira, who had refused to go anything but first class, were not separated after all.

Mark and Mrs. Fenwick drove them to the docks, but visitors were not allowed on board. When he left, Mark took Annerley into a hungry embrace. She found herself weeping uncontrollably, and he dried her cheeks and reminded her that she would soon be with her father.

"I know. But I hate leaving you."

"It won't be for too long. The harder I work, the more quickly I'll be with you. You won't fall in love with anybody else, will you?"

"Oh Mark . . ."

"Find out why Chandra hasn't written. He's up to something. Find out what it is and tell me. Darling, I've got to go . . ."

She stood at the rail with Moira, watching him limping beside his stepmother. She could scarcely see them through her tears.

"Why cry?" Moira asked. "If you need him all that much, you should have stayed with him. But getting away from him is going to make you see that you made a mistake in not getting engaged to him before you left."

"Do you think he'll be very lonely?"

"Yes. I wish I could be sure that he really wants this job he's working for."

Annerley dried her tears and faced her.

"What makes you say that?" she asked.

"I've got a feeling my father pushed him into it. Or perhaps not. Perhaps it was because you were going to be in India that he decided to go out there too."

"Don't you think Chandra might have had something to do with it?"

"Chandra tried to put him off—in the end. Mark would have made a good policeman—but after his leg injury, he wasn't left with much choice." She turned from the rail. "Let's go down and see what they've given us in the way of cabins."

No cabins had been allotted before the ship sailed. They now found that they were on different decks and in widely separated cabins. Annerley was in a cramped two-berth with a woman who was rejoining her husband in Bombay. Moira was led to a spacious stateroom with a window overlooking the promenade deck. She was preparing to unpack when the door opened and she found to her fury that her cabin companion was to be none other than Miss Severn.

Not, however, the Miss Severn who had so often and so humbly sought the help of Chandra's uncle in finding a post as governess. This was a new Miss Severn, haughty, smug and oozing patronage. She was going out, she informed Moira, to teach the two daughters of a maharajah. The gentlemen standing

252

outside the cabin superintending the disposal of her luggage were His Highness's agents, who had permits to come on board to see that she lacked nothing.

"I am so glad," she told Moira regally, "to find myself with someone of my own kind. I was a little anxious, I confess. One never knows—"

Moira, who had been counting the pieces of luggage being carried into the cabin, interrupted her brusquely.

"You can't possibly bring all that stuff in here."

"I beg your pardon?"

"I said I'm not going to have all that stuff in here."

Miss Severn drew herself up and put on her pupil-pulverizing expression.

"This is my cabin luggage. Would you kindly inform me where else it should be put?"

"In the baggage room."

"Most certainly not!"

"You couldn't possibly need all those things for the journey."

"They are the things I shall require on the way. The rest of my luggage has been put elsewhere."

"If you think I'm going to spend the next three weeks falling over your suitcases, you're mistaken." Moira addressed the cowering agents. "Take those things away."

"These gentlemen"—Miss Severn halted them with upraised hand—"have been sent by His Highness to see me safely on board. His Highness—"

There was no point in continuing. Moira had stepped over the intervening obstacles, scattered the attendant gentlemen and was on her way to Annerley's cabin. She found her alone, unpacking.

"Who've you got with you?" she demanded.

"Somebody called Mrs. Nixon. Who've you got?"

"It's no use asking you to guess. I've got stuck with that ghastly creature Severn."

"Miss Severn!"

"The same—only different. She's going out to teach the unfortunate daughters of a maharajah and she's suffering from *folie de grandeur* and she's stuffing the cabin with luggage and I'm not going to stand it."

"So what do you propose to do?"

"Change with you."

"This is a second-class cabin. Where's your pride?"

"This is no time to try and be funny. I'm not going to breathe the same air as that woman. You'll be able to put up with her—you're the putting-up type. Will you change?"

"What if this Mrs. Nixon is ghastly, too?"

"She won't have fifteen pieces of cabin luggage."

"How about throwing Miss Severn out of the porthole?"

"No porthole. Even if there were, I'd never get her through it —she's too big in the bust."

"I'll change if you like—I don't mind poor old Miss S. But we'll have to ask the purser."

"No, we won't. We'll just change, and if he objects, he can say so and I'll deal with him."

The change was effected, the cabin stewardess made a report to the purser, who began a protest to Moira and then changed his mind and wisely decided to let well alone. Mrs. Nixon thought that one girl was the same as another, and only learned better as the voyage progressed.

The journey was not a lively one. Even the calm seas, the unexpectedly good food and a brave display of Christmas decorations could not put the passengers into a festive mood. There were few young people travelling; the majority of the passengers were middle-aged businessmen returning to their firms or wives rejoining their husbands.

The Mediterranean was cold, but sunny. At Port Said, coats and scarves were consigned to the baggage room and exchanged for light attire. As the heat increased, Annerley found that she had not brought out enough dresses, and spent a good deal of time washing and ironing those she had. Moira, in a succession of flowing skirts and sleeveless jackets, left washing and ironing to underlings and lay on a long chair on deck, reading the books she had brought on the journey, and ignoring or repelling all friendly approaches.

When the ship arrived at Bombay, the transition from boat to train was made in conditions that reduced Moira to almost speechless rage. Confusion was at first limited to the cabin she had shared with Mrs. Nixon, into which flowed as soon as the ship docked a mob of visitors. Mr. Nixon had come to meet his wife, and with him had come his colleagues, his and her friends and a number of acquaintances who came merely for the pleasure of getting on board. Moira's luggage was carried out with Mrs. Nixon's and only retrieved in the customs shed. Annerley was all but lost in the group of gorgeously attired officials sent by the maharajah to meet Miss Severn.

On the dock, matters were even worse. Mr. Fenwick had arranged for his daughter to be met and seen onto the mail train. The opportunity to gain favour, not to say promotion, had been seized by several junior members of the service, who came bearing baskets of fruit, Indian sweets and bottles of highly coloured mineral water. These were carried into the compartment she was to share with Annerley, leaving little room for the luggage. As soon as the train left the station, she opened the window and hurled out all the offerings. Then she sank onto the seat and gave a sigh of relief.

"Thank God we won't have to fight off any welcoming committees when we get to Calcutta. All we'll have to do is say hello, and be taken home."

When she stepped out of the train at Calcutta, Annerley was all but deafened by sounds that took her back to her childhood. Bells clanged, coolies shouted, officials argued, disembarking passengers called to those who had come to meet them. The hiss of steam rose over the cries of tea or *pan* sellers. And above the sounds were smells—the smell of India, smoky, spicy, garland-scented.

She stood looking in vain for any sign of her father. She saw

Mr. Fenwick approaching, far off, a servant clearing a way for him. He greeted Moira, and she stood a little apart, feeling lost and lonely.

And then a hand fastened on her arm and she was turned slowly and found herself facing her father. The next moment, she was in his arms.

She fought the desire to burst into tears. When she had conquered it, she raised her head and looked at him.

"You're thinner," she said.

"You're taller. And prettier. Do I look prettier, too?"

"Your hair's a bit grey at the side."

"And a bit thin on top. Did you have a good voyage?"

"No rough weather. Not like going home."

Mr. Fenwick and Moira joined them.

"I see we've both managed to find our offspring, Brooke. Welcome back, Annerley."

"Thank you."

Edwin had not yet greeted Moira, but his pleasure at seeing her was evident.

"It's nice to see you again, Mr. Brooke," she said. He took her hands lightly in his own.

"I must keep reminding myself that you're just one of my ex-pupils," he told her. "Otherwise I might mistake you for a beautiful stranger. Did you ever manage those square roots?"

"Yes. I forgot them as soon as I'd done my exams. How many pupils have you got now?"

"More than I can manage, and applications are still coming in. But several eminent doctors are keeping an eye on me to see that I don't take in too much."

He freed her hands. Mr. Fenwick paused berfore leading her out of the station.

"I take it you've got your own transport, Brooke—or can I take you home?"

"No, thanks."

They went away, followed by a long line of coolies bearing

Moira's luggage. Edwin counted the cases and then looked at Annerley's modest pile.

"You don't seem to have done as much shopping as your friend," he remarked.

They were walking to the exit. She kept his hand in hers; they were together, but she had an odd feeling of fear that he might slip away from her once more. His appearance had shocked her. Not only was he thinner, not only was his hair beginning to go grey, but his skin looked transparent, and his eyes had an exhausted look. For the first time, she realized how ill he had been. She felt thankful that she was here, that she was with him, that she might perhaps hasten his return to health.

On the drive to Seymour Street, in a rattling taxi driven by a speed-crazed Sikh with long strands of hair escaping from a loosely-wound turban, she sat looking out at sights that were a mixture of the old and the new—things that she remembered, things that she had forgotten. She saw with amazement the teeming humanity in the streets round the station; she noted that taxis had largely taken the place of gharries. Tenements lined the narrow streets; the taxi threaded a way between trams and bicyclists and humped sacred cows which roamed listlessly across the lines of traffic.

Park Place. The houses along it looked to her very large and very luxurious. They turned into Seymour Street, and the driver slowed down to read the numbers. Ten—the Fenwicks' car standing in the drive, the servants unloading Moira's luggage. Nine, eight, seven, six. They were home.

The taxi circled the bed of cannas and came to a stop in the porch, below the room in which she had spent so much of her childhood. They got out to see a tall figure in snowy uniform salaaming in welcome.

"Abdul!"

His face was alight with affection. Besides him was a shorter, sturdier figure—his son, Ali, Abduh explained. He was to be Annerley's bearer; Abdul would continue to look after Edwin.

Farther away, peering round the corner of the house, were other figures. One by one they emerged: the cook, diminutive and grinning. The cook's mate, a fourteen-year-old newcomer from Allahabad—and lastly, the sweeper, gaunt, humble, with two half-naked children clinging to his knees

In the hall waited the Leesons, to welcome Annerley and to show her their new baby—four months old, a girl, with something of the rosebud look her mother had had on arrival in India but which, Annerley noted with regret, had faded.

Upstairs. And as soon as she entered the large, sparsely furnished, echoing rooms, Annerley felt that her decision to come had been the right one. There was no comfort here, no homeliness. Her heart ached as she thought of her father alone here for months, years, with only the servants to look after him.

He was watching her expression.

"Disappointed?" he asked.

She turned to him and smiled.

"No. But it all looks . . . bare."

"Five years is a long time. The curtains and the covers we left all wore out. The Leesons replaced them with things of their own, and naturally they've taken them away with them. I decided to leave these rooms as they were until you came."

"I'm glad you did. Didn't we have more ornaments than these?"

"No. Most of the ones we had belonged to your grandmother —I suppose they're in the cottage?"

"Yes. I wish I'd thought of bringing them out with me."

They walked slowly round the rooms. Her father's bedroom— austere as she remembered it. Her grandmother's.

"As you see, I've made this into a sitting room—for myself," Edwin said. "You'll be making friends and inviting them here and you'll need a room to entertain them in. You can have the porch room and I shall retire to this one."

Her bedroom, stripped of everything that had made it hers, that had made it home. There was, she realized, a great deal to do, a great deal to buy before the old comfort and homeliness could be restored. Her spirits, which had been falling lower and lower, rose at the thought of undertaking the work. This was her job; this is what she had come to do. Rugs, curtains, pictures; colour—above all, colour to relieve the monotony of white walls.

She walked out onto the verandah and gave an exclamation of surprise.

"What's that new building?" she asked.

"That was where numbers one, two and three once stood."

"Number three? But that was where the Stanleys—"

"They had a long lease. The two houses at the end had been demolished—as you must remember. But there wasn't enough ground to build this school, so it was decided to wait until the Stanleys left."

"Where did they go?"

"Up to Kurseong. They've opened a photographic studio there, and it's doing well."

"What's the school?"

"They call it the Zenana College. It's for women in *purdah*. I'd be happy if I thought they were learning with a view to throwing off the veil, but I fear it's just an attempt to make them less illiterate."

"That's a start."

"As you say, it's a start."

He left her to unpack. They met again to talk—throughout dinner, over coffee in the porch room, far into the night. He told her something of his experiences in the internment camp. She talked to him about Mrs. Devenish and about his mother. She did not, for the moment, speak of Mark.

She asked him what their financial position was.

"Are we as poor as we used to be?"

"Were we poor?"

"We didn't seem to have as much money as most of the English people we knew. It wasn't until Granny died that I realized how good she'd been at managing."

"Lack of money won't be a problem. I was uneasy for a time after I returned—I found things very unsettled out here, and I thought there might be fewer young Indians wanting to go and study in England. I was wrong; they're going in greater numbers than before, and while they go, I'll be able to make a good living. Any more questions?"

"Lots. Are all the neighbours the same?"

"No. There are new people in number nine—name of Kier. Old man Kier founded the firm—Kier and Sons—and died; the elder son is now running the business. He's married—it was a rather grand wedding, I'm told—the bride was the cousin or the aunt or the something-or-other of Lord Somebody, and they were married from Government House and Seymour Street is considered very lucky to have them occupying number nine. The younger brother had just come out—he's staying with them until he can find a couple of men to share number six with him."

"Number six? Aren't the Ronsons here anymore?"

"No. They went to England, couldn't settle, and ended up in Australia."

"Number eight?"

"Still Monsieur and Madame Maule. Remember their daughter?"

"Of course. She used to rap me on the knuckles every time I played a wrong note."

"She married a teacher at the Conservatoire and they're living at number seven and giving piano lessons. So we've become quite a musical community."

"Is Lady Parrish here?"

"No. She spent the war years in Scotland. She's back in India, staying with friends in Bombay."

"Is her club still running?"

"More successfully than ever."

Silence fell for a time, and she sat listening to the sounds outside—little traffic at this late hour, but the distant howl of jackals, the voices of the servants in the compound. The room was dark, illumined only by the light from the dining room. The bearers had been sent away.

"Did you find my mother very forbidding?" Edwin asked.

"Yes. But everyone I talked to at Waterways said that she had always been like that, even when she was young."

"That's not quite accurate. I remember her when she wasn't like that. It was only after my father left that she seemed to . . . to close up. How did you find the courage to tell her you weren't going to Oxford?"

She smiled.

"I don't think I would have been able to face her if there had been time for me to simmer down. But after I'd read your letter, I didn't do much thinking."

"Have you written to her?"

"Yes. In fact, I've written three letters. She won't answer them, but at least she'll know where we are and what we're doing. How could you give up that lovely, lovely house?"

"Is it still a lovely, lovely house?"

"Yes. I met the girl you left behind."

"The girl I. . . . ?"

"The one your mother picked out for you to marry. Mrs. Thorpe."

"Mrs. Thorpe?"

"Miss Thorold that was. She married twice after you turned her down. First she was Lady Thaxby and then she was Mrs. Thorpe. She was rather awful."

"Then I had a lucky escape."

"Mrs. Raadick thinks your mother engaged her as her secretary to punish herself for having made such an error of judgment. Do you remember Mrs. Raadick? You'll remember her as Mrs. Berger."

He threw back his head and laughed, and for a few moments became the father she remembered, full of life and strength and humour.

"She was the sister of someone called Psyche."

"Yes. She married the man who owned that lovely house on the water."

"Oh yes, I remember her first husband had run off to New Zealand, and she had a small boy named Simon to raise on her

261

own. And he grew up and asked you to marry him and you cried. Was Raadick his name? It couldn't have been."

"He took his stepfather's name. In fact, he took the name of his first stepfather, too. He's going to New Zealand as soon as he can get himself demobilized."

"Sheep farming?"

"No. His stepfather's back. Mrs. Raadick loves the house, but she doesn't love her husband. She had to have both or neither, so she's decided to go to New Zealand with Simon. He's not going to farm; he's going to work in his father's office—his own father."

"It all sounds rather complicated. Did you like Dr. Picton?"

"Yes. But I'm glad he wasn't there when I went up to Waterways in September. Telling him about Oxford would have been even worse than telling your mother."

"Do you remember the Cole-Hardys?"

"Yes."

"He died two months ago and she decided to sell up and go home. I bought one or two things at the sale."

"Were the horses sold?"

"Yes. Mr. Fenwick bought one for Moira." He looked at his watch and got up and went to the light in order to see better. "It's late," he said. "We'd better continue this tomorrow."

She did not respond at once. She wanted to stay up a little while longer—to talk about Mark. She would have liked to tell him the story from the beginning—her hesitations, her doubts, her refusal to become engaged. She wanted to confess that since leaving him at the docks at Tilbury, each day that passed had made her miss him more. But this was her father's evening. This was not the time to confess that she had come out to him leaving a part of her heart in England.

She rose.

"First thing tomorrow," she said, "I'm going to walk round and see Shareen."

"Are you prepared for a number of changes?"

"In her?"

"In them—the whole family."

"What sort of changes? She hasn't changed much in looks. She sent photographs from time to time. I know what she looks like now."

"Did you know that her grandfather, old Amrit Prebdel, died three or four months ago?"

"No. Do you think that's why she and Chandra haven't written?"

"I don't know."

She thought that there was an odd hesitation in his tone, but she did not ask the reason. She would find out tomorrow when she saw Shareen.

She went over to kiss her father good night. "I had something to show you," he said, "but it'll have to wait until morning."

"*Chota hazri* at seven?"

"Six-thirty."

"When do I take over the housekeeping?"

"You can't take it over—I never took it on. I gave Abdul carte blanche."

"Then I'll have to inspect the carte and see how much he's been making out of you. Do I give out the stores every day, as Granny used to?"

"I wouldn't advise it. Let the cook tell you what he needs, and if you think it's reasonable, let him have it."

When she was settled in bed, she read her mail. Letters from Mark; village news from Mrs. Bray. A long letter from Dr. Picton, to be shared with her father. A longer one from Simon Raadick, outlining his plans for bringing his mother and father together when the three met in New Zealand.

She reread Mark's letter with a heavy heart. He said frankly that he was lonely and that he bitterly regretted not having persuaded her to become engaged to him before she left England. He was writing this letter because it would travel out on the mail boat with her and would follow her across India and be put into her hands in Seymour Street. He had nothing to look forward to but her letters, and he was hers forever.

She joined her father for early-morning tea on the verandah outside his room. Then she went to make her first inspection of the things the cook had brought from the bazaar. She ordered the meals for the day, and then returned to Edwin.

"You said you had something to show me," she reminded him.

"You'll have to dress first; it's downstairs."

When she rejoined him, he led her down to the compound and then turned towards the stables. Surprised, she followed him. Looking in, she saw an occupant very different from the cast-off ponies of her childhood. Head uplifted, watching her suspiciously as she approached, was a beautiful chestnut mare.

She went to stroke it.

"Whose?" she asked.

"Yours. With love from Mrs. Cole-Hardy."

She stared at him, too surprised to speak. The mare nuzzled her hand. A syce came in, and she recognized him as one of those who had worked for the Cole-Hardys. Edwin said that he had engaged him, and the man gave a respectful salaam.

"You mean . . . this horse is mine?"

"Yours. It's inadvisable to look a gift horse in the mouth, but I must explain that Mrs. Cole-Hardy couldn't get a decent price, so she decided to give it to you. The name is Shalimar."

"Why couldn't she get a decent price?"

"Because Shalimar is the result of a misalliance. Her mother fell in love with a handsome hack. Shalimar is their daughter—beautiful to behold, but with none of her mother's speed or fire or pride of performance. She'll give you a good ride, but that's all."

"Have you ridden her?"

"Only lately, when I was fit enough."

"Can we afford to feed her, and pay the syce?"

"Would I have accepted her if we couldn't?"

She smiled happily at him, and he smiled in return. The likeness between them could be very clearly seen.

"Well?" he asked.

"This," she told him, "is what I call a homecoming."

When her father had begun his day's lessons, Annerley set out for the Prebdels' house. She chose to go by the roads, avoiding the back lanes and the bazaar; she was not ready, as yet, to face further proofs that there were aspects of India that she had not understood, had not even seen, as a child. The drive from Howrah station had opened her eyes to poverty and destitution which in the past she had accepted as part of her surroundings, and had not troubled to question. She realized that a period of readjustment lay before her, and she knew that some of it would be disillusioning—and painful.

She walked slowly along familiar streets, the sound of taxi horns mingling with the clip-clop of horses' hooves. When she reached the Prebdels' gate she stood waiting for admittance, a flood of memories filling her mind.

The durwan, recognizing her, exclaimed in surprise and pleasure and shouted for a servant to conduct her to the house. She did not wait for him; she walked up the drive and turned the corner of the house and then stopped to look about her.

There seemed, at first glance, little change. There was less noise from the courtyard—perhaps the children were resting.

The lawns did not look as sleek as she remembered. Then she saw, to her astonishment, that—as at Waterways—they had been truncated to make room for a spreading area of vegetables. The intrusion of rows of carrots and cabbages into this magnificent garden seemed to her extraordinary and inexplicable.

She turned towards the steps—and then a sound from the balcony above made her raise her eyes. Standing looking down at her was an Indian girl who looked very much like Shareen—who might have been Shareen but for the fact that she was dressed in a coarse white cotton sari.

And then a voice, loud, well known, well remembered, hailed her.

"Annerley! My God, Annerley, it's you!"

Annerley stood frozen, her head tilted back, her eyes staring, her mouth open.

"Shareen?" she managed to utter.

Shareen's shout of laughter floated down.

"Oh Annerley, you look so funny, as if a thunderbolt had hit you. Wait—I'm coming down."

Annerley waited at the top of the steps. Through the entrance hall came a tall, thin, striding figure—Shareen. But not the Shareen of the tinted photographs, in delicate rose-pink saris with silver edges.

But Shareen for all that—hugging her, holding her at arm's-length to study her, attempting to speak but almost helpless with laughter.

"Oh Annerley, stop looking so . . . so stunned! I tried to write —I began letters and then tore them up. How could I explain it all in a letter? Chandra told me to wait, you would understand better when I could speak to you. Come inside. Come upstairs. I'm dying to talk to you."

But as they moved to the stairs, Annerley halted, gazing round her in bewilderment.

"The furniture—" she began.

This caused Shareen so much amusement that she sank onto the bottom step until she could recover her powers of speech.

Then she rose, seized Annerley's hand and pulled her up the stairs. A few moments later they were in her room.

Annerley looked at it. Gone were the expensive English chairs. Gone was every sign of the western way of life that Shareen's father had so proudly and painstakingly created. There were rugs, cushions, a low divan, the bed, and nothing more.

Shareen sank onto a rug.

"Come and sit by me," she said.

Mechanically, Annerley took off her shoes.

"That's right," Shareen said. "You'll be a good Indian yet. Sit down. And *talk*. First, is your father better? We heard he had been ill."

"He's fairly well—not fully recovered. How are you all?"

"Never mind about us for the moment. Let's talk about you. Moira came out with you?"

"Yes."

"Why? Didn't she hate everything about India? Didn't she become a nurse and work in a hospital?"

"Yes. You know her father remarried? I met his wife—she's very nice."

"Did you hear that my old governess is back again?"

"Miss Severn? Yes. She was on our boat."

"I didn't know that."

"She was in Moira's cabin, but Moira couldn't stand it, so I changed with her. I didn't see much of her—of Miss Severn, I mean—on the journey. She's rather grand now. She spent most of her time telling the other passengers about the maharajah."

Shareen laughed.

"Poor old Miss Severn. My mother told me that when she was here, she was always wishing for a husband—but she didn't find one. Why aren't you married?"

"Why aren't you?" Annerley asked in her turn. "Shareen, why are you wearing white? Isn't that mourning? For your grandfather?"

"No. What I'm wearing . . . but before we go into that, do you want to eat something, drink something?"

267

"No, thanks. I'll be going back to lunch."

"You used to say tiffin, now you say lunch."

"The first lunch I've ever ordered."

"You're going to be the housekeeper?"

"Yes."

"Have you forgotten your Hindustani?"

"No. But I've realized how inadequate it is. Now tell me about yourself. Why are you wearing white?"

"What I'm wearing," Shareen told her, "is *khadi*. Have you ever heard of *khadi*?"

"No."

"You'll hear a lot about it in the future. You . . . you know, Annerley, you haven't really changed at all, in yourself."

"Neither have you. Go on about this khadi."

"Our family," explained Shareen, "isn't the family you used to know. The people are the same; most of us are still here, my grandmother and my mother and father and two of my uncles and aunts and cousins and all that—but there's no more nonsense about copying your western ways. All that—" she swept her arms in a wide circle—"is gone. Finished."

"Why?"

"Because my father has become—we've all become—followers of Gandhi."

"Gandhi?"

"You're not going to tell me you haven't heard of him?"

"Gandhi, yes. But followers?"

"Gandhi is our leader. At last India has got one—a leader to make the whole country into one, to unite us for the fight."

"Fight? Fight what for?"

"For independence. We won't get it unless we fight for it. But we're going to fight for it in the way that Gandhi has shown us. There isn't going to be violence. We're simply going to resist, that's all."

"But—resist what?"

"The government, of course."

"But—"

"But what?" Shareen, smiling, rocked to and fro on her heels. "Don't you believe we can fight?"

"I can see the political—"

"Ah! But what I'm talking about, what you've got to listen carefully to, and try to understand, isn't politics but people. Have you ever heard of the Indian Congress Party?"

"Of course."

"My father has joined it. Chandra has joined it. My cousins are all junior volunteers. Even the small boys are wearing Gandhi caps. Did you notice them in the street?"

"Yes."

"Two of my aunts went to stay in Gandhi's ashram. I'm going next month. I won't like it, but I've got to learn to . . . I've got to prepare for what's ahead. Many people think this family has gone mad. There aren't many of our friends who are prepared to give up anything—yet. They want freedom, but they don't want to fight for it. They'll stand by and watch, and enjoy it when we've won it for them. Does it sound to *you* as though we've gone mad?"

"No. I can see . . . but how can one family start a movement to—"

"One family? I told you—this is spreading, Annerley. The whole nation is being taught how to prepare itself. We don't expect anything to change yet, but we know what we have to do. My father—you only remember him, if you remember him, as a very expensive copy of an Englishman. If you saw him now, if you knew what he'd done to spread Gandhi's teaching, you'd realize a little bit what is happening."

"Are you talking about your whole family? Your aunts, your uncles—?"

"Only two of my uncles. The others thought that my father was going too far, so they went away, taking their wives and children. The other two are working with my father—and Chandra, too. Chandra is in Lahore—he went only yesterday, but he will be back soon. And my grandmother is with us. I mean she's with us in this. And so is my mother."

"Your grandmother . . ."

"You see? Still you don't believe. You still expect to see my mother in silk saris, ordering her carriage. Finished, Annerley, *finished*. Look at me—the way I'm dressed. Would I wear this, look like this, if I didn't wear it as a kind of uniform? I'm proud to wear khadi—we all are. And now do you see how impossible it was for me to write to you, or for Chandra to write to Mark? How could we have begun? So we decided that it would be easier to explain everything to you when you came back. Now I've explained, and you won't believe me."

"I do believe you. Only it's . . . it's hard to take in."

"I suppose it is. I'm beginning to forget how things used to be." She got to her feet and held out a hand to Annerley. "Come and see the others. I told them what ship you were coming on, and they're longing to see you."

They went to the door. But before following Shareen downstairs, Annerley walked to the end of the balcony and stood looking down at the courtyard. Shareen, beside her, waited for her comments.

But Annerley found nothing to say. Gone were the rich carpets, the colourful rugs and cushions. No servants bore silver trays of food to and fro. Children still played, and ayahs still guarded them, but the women of the house, without exception dressed in coarse khadi, sat at spinning wheels, working busily, cheerfully, calling to one another and pausing now and then to arbitrate between quarrelling children. Annerley recognized Shareen's mother and old Mrs. Prebdel—frail-looking, khadi-clad, with a look of perfect serenity.

Nobody looked up and saw her. She did not call to them. Her mind was in confusion, and she needed time to adjust to the situation.

"Well?" Shareen asked.

Annerley turned to face her.

"You're really . . . really serious?" she asked.

"Serious? My God, you ask if I'm serious! Serious? We're

going to fight—don't you understand? Gandhi has sent out a call for non-violent civil disobedience, and we've answered it. We've hardly begun, but we won't go back. We'll all become a nation of spinners, spinning khadi and wearing it. We'll go on protest marches. We'll picket shops that sell English goods. We'll face *lathi* charges from the police. We'll go to prison—and in the end we'll force you, force the British to give us our independence. We're all in it, all our family. Soon all India will be in it. Perhaps you think I don't know what's ahead for us all—but we all know. We're not afraid."

Annerley said nothing. They walked downstairs and through the house, stripped of western influences, no longer the home of a wealthy family. In the room of Shareen's mother, the casket which contained her jewels had gone from its shelf. There were no gold and silver and filigree ornaments, no little Hindu shrines.

Standing at last on the steps to say good-bye, Shareen spoke.

"You'll come often, as you used to do?"

"Yes."

Her eyes were on the rows of vegetables. These were the grounds in which Shareen's parents had held garden parties. Where cabbages now sprouted there had strolled Cabinet ministers, Indian officials, wealthy Indian princes. Women in gold-trimmed saris had walked gracefully over the lawns. Bands had played, champagne had flowed . . .

"Yes," she repeated. "I'll come again. But I might feel in the way. You're not as free as you used to be."

Shareen laughed.

"What did we do, all those long days together? How did we pass the time?"

"Playing. You remember?"

"Yes. Eating pistachio nuts, putting ice into dolls' bathtubs on the balcony and waiting for it to melt."

"Flying kites with your cousins."

"Trying to make my hair into plaits and yours into curls."

"Roller skating up and down the balcony when it got cool."

271

"Pasting pictures into scrap albums."

Shareen raised her arms above her head. "*Aie, aie, aie,* playing, playing, playing."

There was a soft scurry behind them. From the hall came a small figure—a young Indian girl of perhaps seventeen, thin, with a face whose flawless skin and beautiful, dark, long-lashed eyes gave it a delicate beauty. She was not wearing khadi. Her sari was the colour of aquamarines. There were rings on her fingers and on her toes, and her nails were vermilion-tipped. She took Shareen's hand and stood waiting to be introduced.

"This is Kamala," Shareen said. "She's been dying to meet you. She has heard all about you."

The girl pressed her hands together and, holding them against her breast, gave Annerley a brief, smiling greeting.

"She doesn't speak any English," Shareen said, "but she's beginning to understand a little."

"Hello," Annerley said.

Kamala smiled enchantingly.

"Yes," she said.

Annerley turned to Shareen.

"She's sweet," she said. "Who is she? A relation?"

"Of course! You haven't guessed?" Shareen exclaimed in surprise. "You should have. But perhaps you can guess now."

Annerley shook her head.

"No. Who is she?"

"She's Chandra's wife," said Shareen.

Annerley could not have told by what route she walked back to Seymour Street. She had a vague sense of moving along familiar streets. The trees, the houses looked the same, but there seemed to be a slight haze over everything, and a heavy mist seemed to be clouding her mind.

She found after a time that she had made a detour and arrived at the Maidan. Here, almost alone on the vast, grassy expanse, the sounds of traffic along Chowringhee muted, she struggled to get her thoughts into order. Chandra's wife . . .

Gradually, as she walked, she forced herself to face the truth. The truth was that she had allowed herself to live for too long on the memories of one brief summer. It had been a period of almost perfect happiness; when it ended, she had schooled herself to accept the fact that the factors which had combined to give it its perfection—the peace, the sunshine, the indolent Chandra, the hopeful Mark, the independent Moira, her carefree self—would not be found together again.

But schooling was one thing. Learning was another. She now realized that she had been clinging to a vain hope—the hope of staging once again a scene from which the actors had disappeared.

In the cool, dry breeze that blew now on her cheeks as she turned for home, she recognized that the time had come to look not to the past, but to the future. Mark had given up his early ambitions and was preparing for a new career. Chandra . . . Chandra had a wife and a vocation. Moira would amuse herself for a time, and then would perhaps turn her mind to marriage.

She herself? For the first time, she understood fully what she had thrown away when she turned her back on a university career. She knew that given the same circumstances, she would make the same decision: to return to India—but as she quickened her pace and made her way back to Seymour Street, she thought it was a pity she could not have had both—Oxford and India.

She found her father in the porch room.

"Moira came in just after you left," he told her.

"Anything special?"

"No. Chiefly to complain that I hadn't installed a telephone."

"They've got one?"

"Yes. How about ordering lunch?"

While it was being brought, he drew her attention to two large, thickly bound photograph albums on the table.

"You can go through those at your leisure," he said. "I collected all the loose snaps that were lying about in the drawers of my desk, and assembled them for you to look at. You may have seen one or two of them, but I kept most of them out of sight because many of them were of your mother, and I didn't want to upset your grandmother by keeping them on view. She never really got over your mother's death."

Nor, Annerley, thought, had he. But she realized that the presence of her grandmother had meant that he was faced with a constant reminder of his—and her—loss.

"And now," he said, as they seated themselves at the table, "tell me about the Prebdels. Was it a shock?"

"How much did you know?" she asked him.

"Only what my pupils told me. Some of them are pro-Prebdel. Others—the majority, I'm afraid—are anti-Prebdel."

"The house . . . it's completely different. Not only Shareen's side—the other side, too."

"Everything thrown out but spinning wheels?"

Tears sprang to her eyes.

"That's about it," she said shakily.

"You're upset," he said. "You'll feel better when you've eaten. Then we'll try to get the situation into focus."

"How?" she demanded. "For all those years, Shareen's father was determined to adopt a western style of living. In Shareen's part of the house—as you must have seen—you couldn't believe you weren't in an English atmosphere. I hardly ever saw her father in Indian dress. Their clothes, their furniture, their food —it was the same as ours, only richer. And now, suddenly, this."

"Not suddenly," Edwin said.

She looked at him for some moments.

"You could have prepared me," she said.

"Not really. You had to see for yourself. Isn't that why Shareen and her brother didn't write? They knew that seeing was believing. If I had told you that Zumeer Prebdel had become one of the first leaders of the nationalist movement, how much would it have meant to you? Now you can understand better."

"I can't understand anything at all. I could understand if there really was a nationalist movement—but all I can see is those Gandhi caps that some Indians are wearing—and one family, the Prebdels, suddenly deciding to lead India to independence. What good are they doing, sitting there spinning this khadi and looking drab and sending away most of their servants and selling the car and those lovely carriages and telling the British to go away? What can they do, just one small group?"

"They can make a start. Didn't you understand that they've dedicated themselves to a cause?"

"I saw the dedication. What I can't see is the cause."

"Then I'll try to explain. I'll try to make you see what your friends the Prebdels are up against."

"I'm listening. What's this Congress Party?"

"The Indian National Congress. It was formed in the eighteen-eighties. Eighteen eighty-five, to be exact. The original members were mostly professional men, English-educated, who met annually and discussed Indian affairs and aired Indian grievances and reported their findings to the viceroy."

"Hindus and Muslims?"

"The Muslim League wasn't founded until nineteen hundred and six. The following year, the Muslims demanded separate electorates, and the Indian Councils Act granted them. In nineteen sixteen, separate electorates were introduced in the United Provinces, even for local elections. Are you clear so far?"

"Yes. Go on."

"What you saw today at the Prebdels is the result of the disappointment and dissatisfaction—the bitterness—felt by Indians over the poor response given by the government to their magnificent war effort. Between nineteen fourteen and nineteen eighteen, India recruited more than a million men. While the war was going on, things out here deteriorated—trade slowed down, industrial projects were shelved, the transport system suffered. There were shortages of all kinds, and there was a great increase in debt. When the war came to an end, the Indians naturally hoped for some return for the sacrifices they'd made."

"You mean political return?"

"Yes. The Indians now feel that progress towards self-rule is too slow and too uncertain, and they've decided that something must be done to force the government to speed up the process."

"Where does Gandhi come in? Who is he, exactly?"

"He's a lawyer from Gujerat, considered by his followers to be a saint. He became known in India when he fought for the rights of Indian workers in South Africa. His method of fighting for the cause of self-government is by peaceful non-cooperation. *Satyagraha*, which means, roughly, leaning on truth."

"Peaceful non-cooperation doesn't sound very effective."

"It can be very effective indeed. It means boycotting firms which sell English goods. It means handing back titles and

276

honours and resigning from the police. It means boycotting government institutions—including schools. What you saw today was only the beginning—one family jettisoning superfluous cargo and preparing for the storms ahead."

"You think there'll be more and more families?"

"The Prebdels are among the leaders. There are already signs that the movement is spreading. It's going to unite the nation."

"Why are young Indians still coming to you to cram for English degrees?"

"Because they want to equip themselves to rule their own country—one day. Have you got a sort of picture now?

She did not reply at once.

"I know one thing, at any rate," she said at last. "I know which side you're on."

"Didn't you always know?"

"Not so clearly. Now I can see."

"Then you can also see why I never mixed much in English society out here. I came to this country with a viewpoint that I've never seen any reason to change. I found that my ideas were unacceptable to almost every Englishman I came across—and their views seemed to me narrow and ignorant and prejudiced. The men in the Indian civil service—with some exceptions, like our friend Mr. Fenwick—are the men who see the Indian on, so to speak, his own ground, and understand the Indian problems and pressures. That's why I'm glad that young Mark Fenwick is joining them. I've learnt from what you've told me in your letters that he isn't cut to the same pattern as his father." He paused. "Do you want me to go on lecturing on the Indian question?"

"I think I've got enough to go on."

"Then let's go and have coffee."

In the porch room, she handed him his cup.

"Did you know that Chandra Prebdel was married?" she asked.

"Yes. Didn't you?"

"No."

"It couldn't have been a surprise to you. Hasn't he been a prospective bridegroom since he was a schoolboy?"

"Yes. But he was so completely . . . well, English, that I couldn't believe he'd agree to an arranged marriage. None of us thought he would—Mark, Moira, myself. Though when the subject came up," she admitted, "he reminded us that he was a Hindu."

There was something in her tone that made him give her a keen but wary scrutiny. She had not written much about young Prebdel, he remembered; her references to him since her return had been confined to speculation as to why he had not written. But something had hurt her. Chandra's failure, Shareen's failure to keep up the correspondence? Or perhaps she was depressed because she had realized on her visit to the Prebdel house that there would never be the same carefree, happy atmosphere there that she had known in the past.

It was no use guessing. If there was anything more than he could see in the situation, perhaps she would enlighten him. Or perhaps she wouldn't. He had never forced, never would force her confidence.

She opened the photograph albums. He rose to go back to his work.

She spoke out of a long silence.

"Don't go for a minute."

He sat down again.

"I'd like to talk about Mark," she said.

"I'm listening."

She told him how matters stood between Mark and herself, and in the telling, found that many points that had not been clear in her mind were falling into place. Edwin did not interrupt her; he sat listening, watching, picturing events as she described them.

"And that's all," she said at last.

He smiled.

"That's rather a lot."

She made a restless movement.

"I wish I could be more like Moira. She knows exactly what she wants. What's more important, she knows exactly what she *feels*. Until almost the last moment, every time I asked myself if I was in love, the answer was 'Yes, *but* . . .' Why should there be a but?"

"Because you were on territory you'd never trodden before. You were wise to go warily."

"Could you picture him at all, from my letters?"

"Very clearly. I had a bad moment or two wondering whether —when you were told that he'd been left with a permanent limp —you would be filled with compassion and mistake it for love."

"I wish you knew him. It'll be such a terribly long time before he can come out."

"Which is sad for you—but not sad for me. I'm glad that—"

He stopped at the sound of footsteps on the stairs. A moment later, Moira appeared. She was wearing a foulard silk dress and looked as finished as a fashion plate.

"Hello, Mr. Brooke. I thought you'd have finished lunch by now."

"We have."

"I've been looking at that mare of Annerley's. Annerley, let's ride tomorrow."

"All right."

"Seven o'clock." She held out an envelope to Edwin. "My father's going up-country for a few days, and can't use these tickets for the charity ball on Friday in the grounds of Government House. He says will you please use them?"

"Me—go dancing?" Edwin asked in surprise.

"He thought you might agree to take Annerley and me. If you don't go, we can't go."

"Blackmail?"

"In a way. Please take us."

Edwin looked questioningly at Annerley.

"I'd like to go," she said. "It'll be moonlight."

"I'll take you on one condition," Edwin said. "That is, that I'll spend the evening on the sidelines with the chaperones. No leading you out onto the dance floor. Agreed?"

They agreed. He left them and Moira waited until he was out of earshot and then turned to Annerley.

"Could I have dinner here?" she asked.

"Of course. Is your father going out?"

"No, he's staying in. He's invited a horde of his friends to dine tonight, to welcome his daughter home."

"Then hadn't you better be present?"

"No. They're not my friends and I didn't ask them and he didn't ask me if I wanted to meet them. So I won't. Don't tell your father—he'll say I can't come here." She joined Annerley at the table. "Photographs? Is that your mother? She looks—looked—lovely. Who's this?"

"My mother's mother, taken before my mother met my father."

"*Not* Mrs. Devenish?"

"Yes. Wouldn't you have known?"

"Not in a thousand years. Is this your father in his boat?"

"Yes. All the other snaps on this page are of Waterways. That's the house."

"Nice. I'm sorry I didn't see it."

She seated herself on Edwin's long-sleever, found it too long and too slippery, and transferred herself to a chair.

"You went to see Shareen Prebdel?"

"Yes. They—"

"Don't tell me. I've had it all from my father. He says they've committed themselves to the so-called nationalist cause, which only means, he says, that they'll all land up in jail. They've cast off their rich attire and got rid of all their English furniture and they're going about in cotton they've spun themselves. Old grandfather Prebdel is dead, Shareen's father is leading the fight and Chandra . . . my father said that Chandra was married. Did you talk to him?"

"He wasn't there. I saw his wife. I couldn't talk to her because she doesn't know any English."

"He must have married her almost as soon as he got back to India. What does she look like?"

"Very young, very thin, very small, lovely face, pretty ways."

She spoke without emphasis, but Moira looked at her keenly.

"You mind, don't you?" she asked. "You think he shouldn't have done it. He kept telling you he was a Hindu, but you wouldn't believe it. I believed it because Mark knew him better than anyone, and Mark always said that underneath the veneer there wasn't much western influence. What's Shareen like now?"

"The same. Full of enthusiasm and—"

"Crusading spirit. She'll be the first one they'll throw into jail. The whole of this movement, I gather, is non-violence. Moderation. She'll lose her temper and let fly, and that'll be that. Speaking of your old friends, who do you think passed me as I walked round here just now. In a car, no less."

"Who?"

"Your next-door neighbour. One of that Fernandez lot. Not Edna—the middle one. What was her name?"

"Myrtle. She married a doctor."

"Yes. Called Millet. My father says he's very successful. He's got a surgery in Park Place, but he and Myrtle live next door."

"I'm going to see them. Want to come?"

"God no."

"Then you'll have to go home because I'm going to see them now. Abdul told me that the doctor comes home every day about this time, between his hospital work and his surgery hours, to see his family. So he'll be there now. Sure you don't want to come?"

"Absolutely certain. See you at dinner."

Annerley, on reaching the gate of number 4, found the house almost unrecognizable. There was no sagging wooden gate—it had been replaced by a neat iron one. The compound, once dusty and littered, had been paved; the ferns had vanished and scarlet cannas had taken their place. There was no structural change in the house, but its walls and windows had been given a coat of paint, and the verandahs on which dirzhees had once sat and sewed were empty, except for a pram and a playpen, each of them occupied by a small brown baby.

As she approached the steps, a bearer appeared, only to be brushed aside by a plump, pretty young woman in a flowered, flowing garment that was half dress, half negligee. A voice hailed her, and she recognized Myrtle's nasal, singsong voice.

"Anner-lee! Oh my! How nice! I said to Victor, she's back but she won't come to see me, she'll have forgotten me. And now you've come so soon and you look just the same only naturally you're older and you look a very grand lady. Come inside, come. Victor will come soon. He comes only for an hour, just to have some tea and see the children, or else when does he get a chance? Sit down, come, sit here in this chair. I made all the antimacassars—you like them? I like to do crochet when I'm sitting with the children. Oh my, I'm talking, talking all the time and you haven't said anything. You like the house now?"

"I think it's very pretty."

"I changed everything, when my mother died, only some things I kept because they were my mother's and I didn't like to throw them away, you know? I copied this room from a magazine. You like it?"

Annerley said truthfully that it was very bright and colourful. She would not have believed that so many items of furniture and so many large ornaments could have been fitted into so small a space. In a corner was a folding table, opened and set for tea.

"Could I see the children?" she asked.

"You want to? You're not just saying? Then come—they're on the other verandah, where it's shadier. The babies are out here—that's Bobbie, the youngest, and that's Eunice, she's nearly two, and so clever already. And here"—she led the way around the verandah to the other side of the house—"this is Bernard, but we call him Buddha, he's four. Buddha, come, give this lady a nice kiss."

282

Urged by the ayah, Buddha advanced unwillingly, proffered a cheek and returned to wind up his toy.

"And this is my eldest, she's just five. Her name's Victoria, but we call her Poojee. Poojee, come and kiss this lady."

"They all look so healthy," Annerley remarked.

"That's their father, he's wonderful for children. You've heard about him?"

"I've heard he's a very successful doctor."

"Maternity, really, but lots of children come also. More and more, he has been a success here in Calcutta, and more and more patients come. He rented a house in Park Place for his surgery— it was big enough for all of us to live, but he said no, he wanted to keep his work separated from his home. Of course he gets calls to this house, daytime and nighttime too. We've got a telephone. Have you got one?"

"No."

"Not many people have, only offices and what-all. Victor," she said, leading the way back to the drawing room, "is saving up to have a maternity home of his own."

In the drawing room, seated on a straight-backed chair behind a tea tray, they found a small, thin woman with a dark, leathery face, a sharp nose, firm lips and an air of dignity. She was wearing a high-necked blouse through the neck of which was threaded a narrow black ribbon.

"This is Mrs. Millet, my mother-in-law," said Myrtle. "She lives here with us."

This piece of information provided Annerley with the explanation for the great change that had taken place in Myrtle's ideas of tidiness. This old lady, she had no doubt, ran the house, and was the reason for its neatness and order, the respectful bearing of the servants, perhaps even the well-being of the children. She spoke in a voice that was rather nasal, but her words were carefully enunciated.

"I know about you, Miss Brooke. For many years I have heard. You have just come back from England."

"Yes."

"When you were there, did you see Ruby and her husband?"

"No. I think I caught sight of Mr. Crowther once, but he wasn't near enough for me to talk to him."

"Please to sit. I will order the tea. Myrtle, there will not be enough sugar for all. Take my keys, take, open the dooley and give out more."

Myrtle departed, and her mother-in-law looked after her with an expression midway between affection and exasperation.

"She was brought up badly," she confided. "I knew her mother for many years, and always I saw in this house the same thing—servants who didn't listen, didn't work properly, everything out of place and the girls thinking only of dress."

"Did you come to live here when Myrtle married your son?"

"At first, no. While Mrs. Fernandez was alive, I didn't come. But then she died, and the first baby came, and I was a widow and Victor is my only son and he said to me that his wife was a good girl but she didn't know how to keep a house nicely, and also she didn't like to do the housekeeping, so I must come and do it. I came, and it was arranged for Myrtle to look after the children and I would look after the house, and that is how it is. I am the one to give orders, but Myrtle doesn't mind this, and everything goes all right. You see? Here is Victor now."

The doctor came in with Myrtle, and Annerley took in details that she had not noted at his wedding. He was tall and immensely broad, sallow rather than dark-skinned, with a smooth skin, a deep voice with very little trace of accent, and a calm, pleasant manner. Myrtle, she thought, had done well.

They spoke of Charles Crowther. He was still in the Navy, but when he got out, Myrtle said, he was going to start an office.

"An agency," her husband corrected. "A theatrical agency."

"And why?" pursued Myrtle. "Because in the war he met heaps and heaps of chaps who were good at acting and singing and dancing, and they wanted to go on the stage, and so he's going to be an agent, like Victor said, and find jobs for them."

"Did Edna go to England?" Annerley asked.

"Edna?" Myrtle gave a sniff. "No, she didn't go. What she did, she married this chap called Frank Ellis, and went off to Singapore. Not a proper wedding, like mine."

"He didn't want it," Mrs. Millet explained. "He only wanted to go back to Singapore. A lot of money he's got."

"Yes, rich as a rajah," Myrtle confirmed. "So now she doesn't write to us, only to talk about her big house and her servants and all."

Her husband rose and shook the crumbs from his trousers.

"If you'll excuse me," he said to Annerley, "I'll leave you and go and look at my children."

He walked onto the verandah, picked up two babies and, holding one under each arm, went round to join the other two. Shrieks of laughter floated back to the sitting room, and Annerley smiled.

"He seems a very good father," she said.

"And a good husband," Myrtle added. "You needn't think I don't know how lucky I am. When I think of Ruby stuck with that Charles Crowther—you know he goes chasing after other women? She has a time of it, I can tell you."

She walked with Annerley to the gate.

"I saw your friend Moira going to your house just now. Is it true she was a nurse in the war?"

"Yes."

"She did a training?"

"Yes. She's fully qualified."

"I can't imagine her at it. So rude she used to be, so insulting. The things she used to say!"

"She still says them."

"How can you like her?"

Annerley laughed.

"Friends are friends," she said. "Remember me to Edna."

The ball was an outstanding success, resulting in the handing over of a large sum to charity. As usual, there was a scarcity of girls; for every one present there were half a dozen young men. Among these was the elder Kier, who had brought his bride, and his younger brother Arthur—the latter newly arrived from Scotland. The trio did nothing to enliven the proceedings, staying for most of the evening within the Governor's orbit, and wearing expressions of weary boredom. Edwin, watching them, felt that they were going to be far from neighbourly. He was not surprised that the haughty bride, in the course of a single brief meeting, had succeeded in leaving Mrs. Leeson dazzled by her social eminence.

Arthur Kier's sole effort to take part in the dancing came when, after studying Annerley for some time, he asked for an introduction. An A.D.C. led him up to her; Mr. Kier bowed and requested the pleasure, learned that her program was not only full but overflowing, and retired.

On the following day, Mrs. Leeson came upstairs to tell Annerley that she had heard all about the dance.

"I hear you made a great hit with young Mr. Kier," she ended. "You know why he came out, of course?"

"No."

"He was engaged to a girl who let him down. She was"—Mrs. Leeson lowered her voice respectfully—"an earl's daughter. He was terribly cut up, and so his brother suggested his coming out to India. You're the first girl he's taken any notice of since he's been here. He rides every morning—he's sure to ask you to go with him. Did you know his chaprassi had come with a letter?"

This was by no means the only chaprassi waiting patiently in the compound for answers to letters they had brought. The young men had lost no time in sending round invitations to future functions.

Moira employed her own ruthless methods of dealing with the flood, merely signing the letter books and informing the chaprassi that there was no answer. Annerley, less hardened, fell back on a policy of evasion and ended by entangling herself in a net of half-promises.

"You're mad," Moira told her in exasperation. "Why don't you do as I do—choke them off?"

"They're only trying to be kind."

"Kind! Oh God, Annerley, you do talk bosh sometimes. Some of these men haven't seen girls like us—girls just out from home, decent looking, wearing dresses that didn't go out in the eighteen-nineties—for *years*. Naturally they want to take us out. But we can't go out with them all, so all you have to do is to be firm and say no. It's quicker in the long run—and kinder."

"But it's so hard to write a—"

"Refusal? You couldn't have read those invitations properly. Woman-starved or not, they all breathe the kind of brass-bound assurance that makes me want to be sick. Under all that I-hardly-dare-to-hope, and if-I-may-presume and so on and so on, you can see that they expect you to be bowled over. Why do men think they're so . . . desirable?"

"You mean irresistible."

287

"What makes them imagine that they've only to pay us a few compliments and we'll fall into their arms?"

"I don't know. Couldn't you write out a not-too-rude letter that I could copy?"

"No. There aren't enough girls to go round, so you'd better get used to refusing."

"But—"

"But nothing. All you've got to do is say no—convincingly."

Lady Parrish returned a week later. Edwin, walking over to see her, found her alone. As she welcomed him, it did not seem to him that the years that had passed since their last meeting had left any mark on her.

"You haven't changed," he said.

"You have. You don't look ill, but you're not the man you were. You'll have to get to England, Edwin, before you really get rid of those malaria bugs."

"I feel all right—and the doctors seem satisfied. Are you glad to be back?"

"Yes. For a time, anyhow."

Over drinks served by the Goanese butler he remembered, they exchanged views. He was not surprised to find that she had already learned that the Prebdels were playing a leading part in the campaign for independence.

"In England," she said, "it didn't sound important. But out here, I found that it's . . . well, ominous. You can see it in the streets. You can feel tension—at least, I can. But I can't say I've met anybody, since I returned, who thinks it's to be taken seriously. Do you think they'll get this self-rule they're after?"

"Eventually, yes."

"Not in my time, I hope. I can see that a number of our ministers sitting in Whitehall know little or nothing about India, and won't learn until they're made to. All the same, I'd like to finish my time here under British rule."

"You probably will."

288

"And now tell me about Annerley. I hear you actually took her to a dance."

"Her and Moira Fenwick."

"And Arthur Kier asked her to dance. I hope she was impressed."

"He looks pretty heavy-going."

"But he's a great catch, all the same."

"I thought you didn't care for Scots."

"There are Scots and Scots. I'm not impressed by the kind that make such a fuss on Burns' night and pipe in the *haggis* at the St. Andrew's dinner and go first-footing at Hogmanay. I prefer them when—like the Kiers—they own a distillery or two, shoot over their own thousand or so acres of grouse moor and live in historic castles on off-shore islands. Does Annerley keep in touch with your mother?"

"She wrote to her and gave her what news there was. There's been no acknowledgment—and there won't be."

"She knew that young Prebdel—I forget his name—in England, didn't she?"

"Chandra? Yes. He's a friend of Mark Fenwick."

"Extraordinary, isn't it? Years of English prep school and public school and university, and then he comes out and sheds it all and joins the Congress Party, and marries that little daughter of some millionaire or other from Lahore. You won't find her family giving up anything in the cause of self-government. They'll look to their purses and let patriotism go hang. What are you getting up for?"

"I have to go."

"Already?"

"I'm afraid so. I'll drop in again when I can. I only wanted to see how you were."

She went with him to the terrace.

"Where's this wife of Mr. Fenwick's?" she asked. "She's due out here soon, isn't she?"

"In about ten days. Annerley met her and liked her."

"Horsey, they tell me. Like that Mrs. Cole-Hardy. Well, good-bye. Give my love to Annerley. Oh, wait. As you emerged from your seclusion to attend a charity dance, could you make another public appearance and dine here next week? Thursday. A musical evening with the Maules and their daughter and her husband and that Italian pair who are performing with that opera company that's out here."

"Sounds nice. Thank you. I'd like to come."

"Wonder of wonders. I shall order a gala dinner."

Mrs. Fenwick arrived, and to Moira's relief showed no desire to act as chaperone. She spent her mornings riding and her evenings playing bridge. She brought several dresses out for Moira, and an evening dress for Annerley, who received it gratefully, having discovered that her wardrobe was totally inadequate for the round of engagements upon which she was now embarked. She appealed to Myrtle Millet, and a file of dirzhees appeared, settled themselves with their sewing machines on the verandah and proceeded to copy the dresses that she had brought out from England.

Edwin pursued his usual tranquil routine, seeing little of Annerley, becoming used to the presence in the porch room of a series of young men whose names and occupations he found it impossible to remember. He also learned to sleep through the sound of cars entering the compound at all hours of the night.

With the approach of the hot weather, the pattern changed. Most of the women made preparations to depart to a hill station. Mr. Fenwick, his wife and Moira were to go to Simla. Moira came round to ask Annerley if she would go with them.

"It's nice of you," Annerley said, "but no."

"Why not?" Moira demanded.

"I don't particularly want to go away in the hot weather."

"What do you want to do—stay down on the plains and fry?"

"I didn't fry before."

"Because you didn't notice the heat. Now it's different.

You've got used to English summers. Besides, you can't stay down here—everybody'll be going away."

"Not my father. I'm trying to persuade him to take me away in September. The hot weather isn't so bad, and I like the monsoon—it's only September that gets so sticky."

"What do you expect me to do if you don't come with us—get stuck in Simla with all that ghastly government lot?"

"Have fun."

She half expected Moira to refuse to accompany her parents, but by the end of March the three had departed. They were followed by most of the English mothers and daughters: those that remained were in ceaseless demand, assailed by pleas to attend the social events planned for the hot weather.

This situation forced Annerley at last to give refusals that were firm and unequivocal and in some cases almost as brusque as Moira's. She had had all she wanted of dances and parties and picnics, and she longed to leave herself free to lead the life she enjoyed: days spent with Shareen, rides with her father, who was exercising Moira's horse, occasional visits to the Millets next door. She had come to like more and more the equable, burly doctor, she liked the children and she enjoyed listening to old Mrs. Millet's stories of her youth.

Less frequent were her visits to the Leesons. She had never cared for Mr. Leeson, but she had had a childish liking and admiration for the pretty Miss Highfield. This had faded as the pink-cheeked, engaging schoolteacher merged into the pale, ever-complaining wife and mother, whose conversation was an unending list of the things she found lacking in life: an English garden with shady trees, a good English nanny, drinking water flowing from taps, milk from sleek, well-fed cows, a mild English sun under which one could sit.

"We'd like to move," she confided to Annerley. "We miss that lovely porch room. The downstairs flat isn't nearly as bright as upstairs. But I haven't heard of any place we could afford, except one or two houses in districts we wouldn't dream of living in.

Another thing is that I wanted to ask my mother to come out this cold weather, but there really isn't room for her where we are now—I made one of the bedrooms into a nursery for the baby. And another difficulty is entertaining." She sighed. "I'd like to ask people who would be useful to my husband, but how can I give dinners to important people in the small space we've got?"

"I've got an idea," Annerley said. "But perhaps it wouldn't appeal to you."

"What is it?"

"Well, you want a bigger house but you say you can't afford it. Mr. Kier—Arthur Kier—wants to take over number six, but can't find anybody to share it with him. Couldn't you take the house and ask him to move in as a paying guest?"

Mrs. Leeson stared, first in astonishment and then in speculation. Annerley could follow her thoughts; the house was large, the garden had grass and shady trees, paying guests out here had a status far more elevated than they had in England. The neighbours—Edwin and Annerley on one side, and on the other the Maules, cultured, well known, respected. And, above all—Annerley could read the thought on her face—the prospect of a connection, however tenuous, with the local grandees—the Kiers.

"Annerley," she said, "that's a wonderful idea. I'll ask Mr. Kier what he feels about it."

The suggestion was made. Mr. Kier, after giving the proposal serious consideration, assented. Mrs. Leeson's conversation became a crescendo of joyous planning. The move was to be made in June.

"Having robbed me of my income from the downstairs flat," Edwin said when this plan was made known to him, "how do you propose to make up the loss?"

"I hadn't thought of that," Annerley confessed.

"So I noticed. Any ideas?"

"No. Except that Professor Maule keeps saying that he wished he had extra practice rooms. So does his daughter. How much would we be able to charge them for letting the downstairs rooms to them?"

"I don't know. But it would mean having to listen all day to beginners thumping on the piano or squeaking on the violin. I don't think that would help my pupils to concentrate."

"You could let it to some young men as a chummery."

"No. No more chummeries. No more young men."

"*You* think of something," Annerley suggested. "If you haven't already."

"All I thought was that it would be a good idea if I took the flat over and used it for myself."

"You mean—move down there?"

"Exactly. Nothing gives me greater pleasure than to see you going in and out with all your friends—but nothing can be more distracting for a busy man. I could shut myself away quietly downstairs and your young men could come and go without causing me the smallest inconvenience. Isn't that a better idea than scales and arpeggios and chummeries?"

"Yes. Would you really be happy down there?"

"I'd be quiet. At this moment, I feel that to be quiet is to be happy."

This move, too, took place in June. The Leesons left, Edwin moved downstairs and Annerley spent two happy weeks settling him with all the furniture that could be spared from upstairs. Thereafter, peace reigned, to be broken only by Annerley's comings and goings. There was a certain loss of income, but then—Edwin pointed out serenely to Annerley—money wasn't everything.

The hot weather ended, the monsoon brought rain and relief. Annerley received a message from the convent: would she go and see Mother Superior? Going the next day, she was asked if she would take, on a temporary basis, one of the kindergarten classes.

It would be a mixed class, the ages between three and seven, the hours mornings only. She agreed, was offered and accepted a

293

minimal salary, and went to inform Edwin of the new development.

"If it's what you want . . ." he said.

"It'll give me something to do—and some pocket money."

"Won't it interfere with your social life?"

"No. But I'll be able to pretend it does."

"Surfeited already?"

"Yes. I'm just tired of rushing from one function to another with a series of uninteresting men, that's all."

"Most young women seem to enjoy it."

"It isn't what I like doing. I'm forever pretending to enjoy myself when I'm not enjoying myself at all, running round but not really liking it. You see?"

"Of course. You put it so clearly."

"What I'm trying to say is that at all those parties, you meet the same people over and over again, but in different places. Nobody talks about anything except what happened at the last party, and who's going to the next. I'm tired of telling people that yes, my grandmother is Mrs. Brooke of Waterways and yes, we had a cottage near Exeter, and I'm sick to death of explaining how I got the name of Annerley and trying to think of things to say with tongue-tied men and trying to get talkative ones to shut up. I know now that I'm like you—I want a quiet life. I don't seem to be able to manage numbers. I like time to myself, and time to get my breath between things. All I want is you, this house, Moira and Shareen now and then, other people like perhaps the Millets next door. But what I'd really like," she ended in a sudden burst of candour, "is to have Mark here."

"Ah."

"There's no 'Ah' about it. I miss him. I didn't dream it would be like this."

"You didn't dream that—?"

"That being without him would be—so empty. I don't know how I ever brought myself to leave him. I don't miss him less; I miss him more and more and more." She paused. "Perhaps it's the climate."

"Among all the other young men you've been meeting lately, haven't you—?"

"Haven't I come across one who measures up to Mark? No."

"Well now," said Edwin.

"What does 'Well now' mean? I thought you'd say something helpful."

"This is a situation I haven't encountered before. I'll have to look up my reference books."

"You were separated from my mother—you ought to remember how you felt. Do you think it's odd that I don't want to go to parties all the time?"

"No."

"Couldn't you say that I was like you—disinclined to get involved in a lot of time-wasting activities that they call enjoyment, but isn't?"

"At your age, I wasted as much time as the rest. It was only when I met your mother that—"

"That you realized you could only like things if she was with you. That's how I feel about Mark."

"Well now."

"Stop saying that. I'm not rejecting social life. I just can't keep up, that's all. It confuses me. I think I've got a lazy streak, like you. I hate having to think of the right replies. And another thing: When I've been to a particularly vapid party, and go the next day to see Shareen, and watch them all practicing to go to prison and giving up everything . . . then I feel ashamed of how little I've ever done or am ever likely to do. So now you know how I feel."

"Well now," said Edwin.

Annerley had come to be as frequent a guest at the Prebdels' house as she had been before her departure to England. After her morning ride and bath and breakfast, she walked to the convent. She returned for lunch, and after it went to see Shareen, sometimes joining the aunts and cousins but more often seated on the floor of Shareen's room, watching her as she wrote circulars, arranged meetings, or sat spinning. On the ground floor of the house, more and more followers of Gandhi forgathered, and more and more calls for help came from those who had given up almost all they had to help the cause. All were dressed in khadi, which had become their uniform. Chandra was still in Lahore, organizing meetings there.

Looking on, Annerley had no sense of involvement, but her admiration for Shareen began to hold a measure of anxiety. There had never been any half-measures about anything that Shareen said or did, and it was becoming clear that she was now preparing to go into action. Gandhi had recommended women to undertake the picketing of shops that sold foreign goods. It was to be peaceful picketing, but the picketers were rebels and the police would soon begin to deal with them. Shareen had already led groups of women in protest marches through the crowded Howrah district, and was planning further acts of provocation.

"Couldn't you leave it to the men?" Annerley asked.

"Why?" Shareen spoke indignantly. "Did your suffragettes leave it to the men?"

"No, but they were after one definite goal. Your aim seems so . . . so wide, so far-reaching, so . . ."

"So slow? There has to be a *beginning*, Annerley, and someone's got to make a *start*, don't you *see*? What's the use of talking to the British government, or to the government of India, about our aims? They're not interested, and anyway they're all mad. If it's left to them, we'll get self-government in two hundred and fifty years, or not even then. Stop looking so worried and come and eat. It's time."

They seated themselves on the floor in the cool recesses of the room that had been Miss Severn's. Out on the balcony, the light seemed almost incandescent, and the marble floor was hot to the feet.

A servant—one of the few survivors of what had once been an army—brought trays of food—but food that was no longer spicy and pungent and appetizing.

"Eat," Shareen urged. "I know you don't like it, but eat. We now eat only vegetables cooked together without flavour. Kamala has, of course, special food. She is not preparing to go to prison. I wanted to prepare special food for my mother and grandmother too, but they refused to take it. They want to do everything as the rest are doing." She scooped up a small mound of vegetables and conveyed it to her mouth. "All the same," she went on, "I must get them away. But what authority do I have over them? If my father were here, if only Chandra would come—he should come today, but he is always putting off—then they could make them go away."

"Where to?"

"To my mother's people in Kashmir. They would be safe. This life will kill my grandmother. My mother, too, I think, but she at least is younger. Go on—eat. I won't ask if you like it, but you must get used to it, in case when you go back to England you get put into prison." She pushed the tray aside. "It's nice to be alone, isn't it?"

This referred to the fact that they were seldom without Kamala's company. She followed Shareen everywhere. She still wore beautiful, colourful saris, which looked almost fairy-like against the general drab attire. She seemed to Annerley to be treated by everyone as half toy, half precious charge. Today she had elected to eat with the aunts.

"What does she make of all this new life?" Annerley asked. Shareen shrugged.

"Who knows? I told you—she doesn't have ideas."

"Is she in love with Chandra?"

Shareen rocked to and fro—her habit when convulsed with amusement.

"You don't change, do you?" she said. "You were asking that —and about Chandra—when you were thirteen. Is he in love, is she in love, are they in love?"

"Well, are they?"

"They are married, and when he's here she clings to him and he's kind to her. What's below the surface, if there's anything, is

297

hidden from family view. Chandra never tells his feelings—didn't you learn that when you knew him in England? The only worry I have is her parents. They don't like what's going on here. I don't think she would have been allowed to marry Chandra if her father had known that we were going to become followers of Gandhi. But all he saw was that my father and Chandra were making some changes, to be more in line with today's ideas, throwing out western influences. But now—"

"Now?"

"I think he's beginning to see what's happening. Chandra has been to see him. Before he left here, he told me he thought her father wouldn't make any objection to his daughter staying here until things became more difficult—even more, you may say, dangerous. Myself, I think he'll object very strongly."

"So then what?"

"He'll remove her."

"You mean—take her away? How can he do that?"

"Simply by coming down from Lahore with a few attendants, and taking her back with him."

"But a husband's rights . . ."

"Override those of a father? In the ordinary way, yes. But Kamala's father doesn't want to see his daughter surrounded by militant women who are engaging in activities that will soon bring the police down on them in lathi charges."

"But if she sympathizes with her husband's aims . . ."

"Annerley, please to *think*. What does Kamala know about aims?"

"But if she loves him? If he loves her? Does he?"

"How do I know? He accepted the engagement from when he was a boy. When he came back to India, he had time to withdraw if he had wanted to—but he saw her, liked her, married her. If her father considers that his daughter is living in an atmosphere of unrest or even danger, he can take her back to her home, and if you're going to say will she go, then I can tell you that she will. She'll go home and it will be just the same for her there as it is here—she'll be petted and spoiled and protected

298

and perhaps quite glad not to to see any more spinning wheels and khadi. There would be no complications; she isn't pregnant and therefore there's no question of children. And now that we have got onto the subject of love, why haven't you ever told me anything about you and Chandra's friend Mark? I expected you to tell me everything; you told me nothing. Are you going to marry him?"

Annerley hesitated.

"If you'd asked me that when I first came back," she said, "I would have said, 'Yes, one day.' Now the answer's yes, but not one day; just as soon as he feels he's in a position to marry."

"You're in love with him?"

"Yes."

"I didn't ask if he's in love with you. Chandra told me."

"Chandra?"

"Chandra was the first to know. Mark said to him—I think it was that summer when they stayed in the village where you lived —he said that he was falling in love with you, but that you were a child still. Chandra said no, you weren't a child and that if Mark loved you, he should tell you so. It was so silly. Mark saying you weren't ready for marriage—saying it to a person like Chandra. Chandra always liked to joke and say that Hindus invented child marriages. So you see, I knew something. Now you can tell me more."

"I've told you. I love him. Now we can talk about your own affairs of the heart."

"Mine?"

"Do you remember Starup?"

"Starup?" Shareen, remembering, threw back her head and laughed. "Have you kept him in your mind for me all these years?"

"You only mentioned one possibility."

"Well, there isn't even that one now. He—there's an English word—he jilted me. He didn't want to marry a girl who—he says —has lost her sense of values. He meant his values. Like you, I'd like to marry. I'd like to find a man as dedicated as Chandra, and marry him and have sons who would fill key posts in the future Indian nation. If you hear of anyone, let me know."

The servant came to remove the trays. A message was brought to Shareen that the members of the community were beginning to arrive. She rose.

"Don't go," she said. "I've only got to show them where the meeting's to be held, and then I'll come back. Chandra should have been here to attend this meeting—it's quite important."

Left alone, Annerley rose and walked out onto the balcony. The evening breeze was scorching. She put on her shoes and went slowly to the end and stood looking down into the courtyard. It was almost empty. Two women were standing in the shade of the aunts' verandah. A child ran out and was carried back into the house by an ayah. In a negligent pose at the foot of the flight of steps that led down from the balcony stood a man, an Indian, wearing a Gandhi cap, the now-familiar long shirt, dhoti and slippers. She thought the uniform, if uniform it could be called, unnecessarily ugly. Gandhi had chosen to dress like the humblest in the land, and his followers had adopted the simplicity of his garb. It was doubtless patriotic, but nobody, she thought, could call it becoming. The man down there, for instance . . .

The man looked up. It was Chandra.

For some moments she could not move. She could only gaze downward, rigid with shock.

Chandra. Chandra, whom she had last seen in an English spring, wearing a suit of impeccable cut, burnished shoes . . . Chandra of the flannels and blazer, Chandra the fastidious, the faultlessly groomed.

He was coming slowly up the steps. He stopped two steps from the top, his face level with hers. His expression was the one he had worn when she had picked herself up from the ground in the cottage garden when the hammock had inexplicably descended: bland, with a slightly mocking look.

"Why are you all alone in the heat?" he asked her.

She made an effort to speak in the easy, natural tone he had used.

"I only came out for a moment. I was waiting for Shareen."

"Shareen is waiting for me. She told me you were up here, and I was bracing myself to come up and confront you in these clothes. Did you recognize me?"

"Yes. No. It was . . ."

"A shock?"

"In a way. I liked you in English clothes."

"But you don't like me in these?"

"Not much," she confessed. "It's just a matter of getting used to them. On you."

He came onto the balcony and turned her towards the room she had left. In the shadow of the doorway, he looked at her with a smile.

"You look paler than you used to at the cottage. Have you written to Mark to tell him why I didn't write?"

"Yes. But he was—he is your friend and he would have understood what you're trying to do."

"Would he? Very few people do." He picked up her left hand and held it lightly. "No ring? Why are you keeping him waiting?"

Shareen appeared at the end of the balcony and called to him. He released Annerley's hand gently and turned away. He joined Shareen and did not look back.

She did not wait for Shareen to rejoin her. She wanted to get home, to think, to adjust. Two images—the Chandra she had known, the Chandra she had just seen—were circling bewilderingly in her mind. She had thought of him often, but she had never pictured him as anybody but the man she had watched on the cricket field, the man who had played tennis with her, the man who had been as English as Mark. What she had remembered was a dream. The figure in the dhoti was the reality. And facing reality, she was experiencing a devastating sense of loss.

When she got home, she stayed for a time in her bedroom. When she came out to join Edwin at his after-dinner coffee, he looked at her, looked away, looked again, hesitated and then spoke.

"You've been crying. Should I pretend not to notice, or could I be allowed to share your misery?"

The tears began to course slowly down her cheeks. She shook her head angrily, but was unable to check them. Her father unfolded a large handkerchief and handed it to her.

"Some people like salt in their coffee," he said gently. "I don't. Shall I make a guess at what's upset you?"

"I'm not upset. I saw Chandra, and it was . . . it was just a shock, that's all. I don't know why. I mean, he never stopped stressing that his English appearance was just a sort of veneer, a top layer, but if you saw him now . . ."

"You've forgotten. I have seen him. He came to see me when he arrived in India, to tell me about you."

"But he wasn't wearing a dhoti."

"No. But I knew that he would soon be wearing one. I would have thought that after seeing Shareen, seeing their house, you would have been prepared for another Gandhi follower."

"That's just the point—I still can't believe it. I know they're deadly serious. I know—or I'm beginning to know—what's ahead of them, what they aim to do, what the cost is going to be —but even seeing them, hearing them, I don't seem able to take it in."

"You think it's something they'll do for a time, and then give up?"

"No. Nobody who looks at Shareen could doubt how deep it goes. But somehow I . . ."

Her father handed her his cup.

"If you'll fill that," he said, "I'll explain."

"No, I will. I don't want to see, that's my trouble. I'm beginning to think that my one talent is for hanging on to things that are dead and gone, just because I want to keep them alive. Isn't that what you were going to say?"

302

"In rather more polished English, yes."

"You're not like that. Was my mother like that?"

"No. But her mother was. You were too young to understand, but in all her twelve years or so in India, your grandmother continued to look at it through English eyes. She applied English standards and looked for English solutions. I used to wish sometimes that I could do the same. But I've always seen this country from the Indian angle—and that's what's made life very difficult at times."

"Holding unpopular views, you mean?"

"Yes."

"Won't Mark think as you do? Look at all the years he was Chandra's friend—always being presented with the Hindu viewpoint. Won't he come out here sympathizing with their aims? Won't he?"

"If he does, he'll have to keep a check on his tongue." He paused. "I wish I knew him. I wish we could talk about him. But I know so little about him that it would be a one-sided conversation. Has he given you any more or less definite date for coming out?"

"Yes. The spring of nineteen twenty-two."

"A long time to wait," he said sympathetically.

"A long time? A lifetime," she answered.

Mark returned to India seventeen years after he had left it as a small boy bound for an English preparatory school.

His father had retired two months before his arrival, and was living with his wife in her house in Dorset. Moira had refused to accompany them, and had been left behind. The car was also left behind; on her parents' departure, she assigned the chauffeur to the back seat and took over the driving. They had also left, to Moira's fury, a meek little semi-retired governess named Miss Clowers, to act as combined chaperone and companion. She, too, had been given a back seat, and had come to realize that the key to a pleasant and comfortable life at number 10 Seymour Street was to assist Moira in the pretense that she was not there at all.

Now a member of the Indian civil service, Mark had been recruited to the province of Bengal. He had not asked for it and had not wanted it, but he derived some comfort in knowing that he would not be far from Annerley.

He came out to a Bengal rent by racial divisions, alive with terrorists and in the forefront of the ever-widening Nationalist movement. The campaign had gathered momentum; his friend

Chandra Prebdel was deeply committed to it, and was now engaged in going round the villages preaching the doctrine of Gandhi and setting the women to spin khadi.

"Not," Edwin observed on his introduction to Mark, "a peaceful place to come to."

Mark agreed, but he was not thinking very clearly. Although Annerley's letters had made him increasingly aware of her feelings for him, he had not been prepared for her whole-hearted capitulation. He was in a state divided equally between joy at being with her, and despair at the prospect of leaving her.

Between him and Edwin there was instant liking and—on the part of Edwin—reassurance; here was a young man who had nothing of his father's overbearing manner or, as far as he could tell, narrow prejudices.

"I don't know much about things yet," he told Edwin. "My father told me—I saw him in London just before I sailed—that he was glad to be out of it all."

"I gather your stepmother was sorry to leave India."

"She felt she hadn't seen anything of the country. She hopes to come back one day."

There was an interruption: Moira had brought the car round and was coming up the stairs to meet Mark.

"I didn't go to the station to meet you," she explained, "because I didn't want to watch Annerley crying over you. I suppose you howled?" she asked Annerley.

"No, I didn't."

"Didn't you tell him what's been obvious for some time—that you're longing to marry him?"

"Yes, she told me," said Mark. He addressed Edwin. "It seems a bit late to ask you, sir, if you have any objection to my marrying your daughter?"

"How does he know?" Annerley asked. "Wait until he knows you better, and then ask him."

"I've done enough waiting," Mark told her. "And I've no time to waste—I'm leaving tonight."

"Any details about the job yet?" Edwin asked.

"Some. I'm going to be under a fellow named Overton—he's the district magistrate and I'm the assistant magistrate of this place I haven't yet learned how to pronounce. What I've got to do, exactly, I won't know until I get there. The idea seems to be that I have to pass some examinations—law, languages, that kind of thing—and I've got to learn how they run district offices, and I have to do some touring, and before they take me off the leading rein I've got to spend a few months in something called a settlement camp doing surveys of the fields and straightening out the rights of the landlords and the tenants and the subtenants. When I'm not under a tent, I'll be on top of a horse. But the most important thing is that whenever I see a chance of getting away for a bit of leave I can—with your permission—find my way here. I shall sleep at number ten and spend my days with Annerley. We can't be married until I get a job in Calcutta, which is on the cards for the distant future. As far as I am able to make out, as soon as the monsoon starts, the whole of the part of Bengal I'm in will disappear under water. The roads vanish and you have to build your own private jetty in order to get into your bungalow. That doesn't really sound any life for a woman."

"I like water sports," Annerley said. "If there aren't any roads, how do you get round?"

"By launch."

"I'd love that."

"The launch would be for me, not for you. You would have to sit on the verandah of the bungalow and fish for my dinner. And no neighbours. And no other white faces probably, although I'm told that one or two jute families have bungalows there and can be visited. And speaking of visiting, if we went round to see Chandra, would he be there?"

"No. Nor would Shareen. She's spending a month in Gandhi's ashram, learning how to live a spartan life. She gets up at five and sweeps the floor and cooks ghastly messes—vegetables without salt—and what help all that's going to be in winning self-government for India, I still cannot understand. And never will.

306

I ordered dinner for four, Mark. Can you stay, or do you want to go up to number ten?"

"I'd like dinner first. I'll have to leave immediately after it. Are you quite sure Chandra isn't at home?"

"Quite sure."

"Then I shan't be able to get in touch with him for some time. There's nothing as civilized as a telephone in the places I'm going to be in for the next month or so. Will you ask him to send me news of what he's doing?"

"I can tell you what he's doing," Moira said. "He's giving the police every opportunity to send him to prison. I don't think he'll feel like a real Gandhi-ite until he's been—"

"Incarcerated? It's funny, isn't it, the way I thought I knew him so well when I didn't know him at all?" He looked at Edwin. "Do you think he's going to get himself into serious trouble?" he asked.

"It depends. I think he'll go a lot further towards it than his father would recommend. The whole point of Gandhi's teaching, it seems to me, is making haste slowly—but although I've only seen young Prebdel once, and although most of our conversation was about the summer he spent near the cottage, he struck me as . . . would seething sound too strong? He—and, from Annerley's account, his sister too—are the type who need action."

"What's given Gandhi this hold over them all?" asked Mark curiously.

Edwin smiled.

"Gandhi's had all the help he needed from the government," he said. "The issue of self-government would have remained fragmented, separated, flourishing only in certain widely separated parts of India. But there have been a series of what the Indians see as betrayals—and with every broken pledge, the sense of injury spreads. What Gandhi has done is to recognize that the time has come to launch a popular campaign that'll draw all sections of the population together. Annerley thinks that what's

307

going on in the Prebdels' house is a feeble effort directed at a powerful government—an effort so feeble that one could compare it to a bee buzzing round a sleepy British official taking his ease in his garden. No, not bees—this is a rash, and its spreading fast. 'Swaraj' has become a battle cry. The non-cooperation policy has reached a stage at which it's seriously affecting government administration, and the authorities are soon going to go after the leaders. And when they do, it'll be the beginning of a long-way-off end. The more martyrs, the more heroes. The more heroes, the more leaders and the more fervent followers. And so it'll go on."

There was a pause.

"A nice welcome," Mark commented, "to my new job."

Edwin regarded him in silence for a few moments.

"Annerley gave me the idea—which has grown stronger since I've met you—that your sympathies might well prove to be on the side of your friend Chandra Prebdel. If this is so, perhaps I needn't warn you that if you air views which are directly against those held by most Englishmen in this country, and in your service, you'll end by getting yourself into trouble. Serious trouble."

"I'm going to be discretion itself," Mark told him. "I heard enough on the ship coming out to give me an idea of the kind of thing I'll be hearing more of. Some of the older fellows holding forth in the bar of an evening should in my opinion have been shipped straight home again."

"Well, be careful," said Edwin. He rose and Moira looked at him.

"If you're going to pretend you've got papers to correct," she said, "I'd like to come and help you."

He laughed.

"Don't let's make our withdrawal too obvious. We'll have our pre-dinner drink down in my part of the house."

They went downstairs. Left with Annerley, Mark drew her to the cane-seated sofa, pulled her down beside him and took her in his arms.

"We're alone," he said with satisfaction. "We're not on a crowded railway platform, we're not in the taxi with a speed-drunk driver, and we're not being eyed by my boss. This is the only opportunity I'll have to hold you in my arms for God knows how long. I love you. Now a question: among all that lot of men you've been going around with out here, did you ever meet anyone you liked specially?"

"No."

"Moira wrote and told me that some of them had the damned nerve to propose to you. Are you sure you didn't give them any encouragement?"

"Quite sure."

"Are you prepared to marry me the moment I'm free to marry?"

"Yes."

"Leaving you is hell."

"Think how much nearer we are to each other now than we've been for years."

She rested quietly in his arms, resigned to his going, happier than she had ever been in her life. She loved him—and she was proud of him. She knew that during the time she had known him, he had developed, matured. He was very much a man; he had seen war, he had been wounded, he had been faced for a time with the prospect of losing a limb. He had been forced to give up the career he had chosen. He was gentle, kind, considerate, utterly trustworthy. She could not imagine life without him.

"This may sound silly," she heard him saying, "but perhaps you'll understand. It's about an engagement ring. I went to buy one. I actually chose one I thought you'd like. But then I thought that I'd like you to choose one with me. Is there time to go out and get one now?"

"Yes."

Mark drove the car to the station. Moira drove Annerley back to Seymour Street.

"I want to ask you something," she said. "It's been in my

mind for some time, but I wanted to be sure before I asked you. I don't know what you'll think of the idea."

"What is it?"

"I want to ask Shareen Prebdel to let me go with her to some of those villages she goes round. I want to take a look at the women. I'm not setting out to be a health officer; it just struck me that the women might need something more than political speeches. And it seems a waste not to use my nurse's training. Would you ask Shareen out-with-the-British Prebdel if she'd take me on one or two of her tours?"

"Of course. But I can't imagine you and her together."

"She doesn't like me any more than I like her—I know that. But we'll be directing our efforts to two separate ends. Ask her, and see what she says."

"I will. How's poor Miss Clowers getting on?"

"I've no idea. I only see her once a week, to give her the housekeeping money. Let me look at your ring again. Any idea when you can marry? And when you do marry, how is your father going to feel about being alone?"

"We won't be far away."

Moira said nothing.

Mark and Annerley were married in October of the following year. It was all very well, they had discovered, to make long-term plans, to decide to put off marrying until Mark had a settled home—but his need for her had become ever greater—and each time he snatched an opportunity to come and see her, she found him thinner, paler, more exhausted. She worried about him when he was away, missed him more than she had thought possible, and when he begged for an early marriage, unhesitatingly agreed.

It was a quiet ceremony. Edwin gave away the bride, Moira acted as sole bridesmaid, and the only invitations sent out were to old friends or close colleagues. But the oldest and closest—Shareen and Chandra—were missing. They were both up-country, picketing cloth shops. By the time Shareen returned, Annerley was staying in Mark's bungalow on the banks of a river which, she learned, made a habit of changing its course and causing untold confusion between those who had owned the old, submerged land and those who claimed the new. She learned to spend long days alone, to adjust herself to housekeeping under difficulties; she met and became friends with Mark's Indian subordinates. On his longer absences, she returned to Seymour Street.

There was no perceptible change in Edwin's routine, but it was strange to discover Moira and Shareen meeting in apparent harmony. Neither had lost the suspicions that each had felt for the other since their childhood, but a new quality—respect—had entered their relationship.

"She's just as rude as she always was," Shareen confided to Annerley. "You remember how I used to wonder how you could stick her? Talking to people, she still says what she likes—but you know what? She's a good nurse. That's a surprise for me. I thought nurses were gentle and sweet and—"

"Ministering angels?"

"Yes. She's certainly not sweet. You'd think she'd put the women off, but she doesn't. They like her. They can't understand much of what she says—she calls it Hindustani, but it's rubbish, really."

Moira was scarcely more complimentary.

"I got a shock when I met her again," she told Annerley. "She was never much to look at, but now, wearing that awful cotton stuff and looking half-starved . . . it hasn't improved her looks. And she still shouts, but I suppose if she's going to harangue the multitudes, then all-the-better-to-hear-you-with. But . . . I don't want to worry you; I know you cherish an exaggerated regard for her, but she seems to me to go out of her way to ask for trouble."

"What sort of trouble?"

"Police trouble. Have you seen those women sitting in groups in the middle of a busy traffic jam?"

"Yes."

"The police have seen them, too. They disperse them; the women move on and settle at the next road junction. All very peaceful-looking, *but*."

"You never saw the Prebdels' house as it used to be, did you?"

"No. You can't forget it, can you?"

"No. If I could forget how things *were*, I'd find it easier to understand how things *are*."

"That's your trouble with Chandra, isn't it?"

"Yes. He's become two people, and I can't separate the two. Behind this Hindu patriot I see the almost-English undergraduate. Watching him with all those men who fill the house now, coming and going and planning and going further and further along this self-government road, I see the cottage and the view of the sea and the four of us having tea. The two pictures won't separate—I can't think of one without getting confused with the other."

There was a pause. They were walking across the compound to the gate after one of Moira's visits.

"Chandra had a very odd effect on you," Moira recalled. "Perhaps it was because he was so good-looking. The two of you made friends very fast. You skipped the getting-to-know-you period altogether."

"He was easy to know—then. Now he isn't. And his marriage."

"Yes—his marriage. Why did he marry her? Such a *useless* kind of partner. I asked Shareen. Her answer was that he married her because there didn't seem any reason not to. If you're going there tomorrow, I'll drive you round—I've got to go and see Shareen about something."

She put a hand on the gate, and then paused to watch Dr. Millet's car going by.

"Which reminds me," she said. "If—one day—you have a baby, you're not thinking of having it at the Millet Maternity Home, are you?"

"Yes. Why not?"

"Wouldn't you rather have an English doctor?"

"If I knew an English doctor who was better qualified than Dr. Millet, then yes, perhaps. But I think—my father thinks—he's a good doctor."

"Yes, he is. But there are still people who prefer not to go to him."

"The anti-Fernandez?"

"Well, yes. But it's your affair."

When the time came, eighteen months later, Doctor Millet was only too pleased to reserve a room for the arrival of Mark and Annerley's first child. It would be, Annerley said, a girl, and was going to be named Victoria. Moira would be its godmother and Shareen would be coopted as a kind of deputy.

Her pregnancy meant that Annerley could spend less time at Mark's bungalow, but he developed a talent for swift travel; he would appear at any time of the day or night, pass a few hours at Seymour Street and vanish back to his waterlogged place of work.

It was a time of quiet happiness for Annerley, but her visits to Shareen began to fill her with a kind of dread for the future of the family. The year was marked for them by bitterness and unrest. Passive resistance was now a nationwide fact and force. The injustices of the Rowlatt Act, the Viceroy's insistance on disregarding Gandhi's pleas, and putting the act into force; above all, the imprisonment of Gandhi, his release and rearrest swept into the nationalist movement most of those who had hitherto hesitated. Shareen spent a good deal of her time encouraging and assisting the Association of Hand Spinners. Chandra came and went, Mr. Prebdel was seldom seen. Moira continued to visit outlying villages when Shareen could go with her.

As the political tension mounted, Annerley began to feel that there was something unreal about her visits to the house. Once there, she could see the struggle that was taking place, sense the dedication of its inmates. When she left it, she found herself with people who had little idea of what was taking place in the country, and even less desire to find out. The riots in the city, more and more frequent, were merely a signal for young Englishmen to leap into their cars and find out whether there were any fringe dangers to be faced. Balls, parties, receptions, picnics went on as before.

On a wet, sullen day about two weeks before the baby was

due, Annerley paid Shareen a visit.

"You didn't walk?" Shareen asked anxiously.

"No. Moira drove me round. She's calling for me in half an hour. I've got an appointment with Dr. Millet—she's taking me to the maternity home."

"Come inside and sit down—it's beginning to rain. Wait—I'll put another cushion."

But Annerley remained standing, gazing at the corner of the room in which Shareen's bed had stood.

"It's gone!" she exclaimed.

"What's gone?"

"Shareen, don't be silly, you know quite well—your bed. Where is it?"

"Where you said—gone."

"How can you do without a bed?"

"I'll let you know in a week or two. So far, I've only been without it for two nights."

"Without it? Why?"

"Because I'm obeying orders. No, that's wrong—I'm taking advice."

"What advice?"

"The advice to prepare ourselves to spend some time in prison. It won't be so bad if we prepare ourselves, learn to do without, go without, that kind of thing."

"You're sleeping on the floor?"

"No. On a nice rug. Sit down, sit down, sit *down*."

Annerley sat down and leaned against the cushions.

"I suppose you know what you're doing," she said helplessly. "It still seems to me that—"

"That someone else should be doing it? *That*," Shareen said, "is the fatal weakness of all movements. People won't join because they think that other people, not themselves, should do the fighting. But I can tell you something that will please you: at last, my father is sending my mother and my grandmother away."

"Thank Heaven. Where will they go?"

"To Kashmir. He's been trying to get them to go for a long time, but they wouldn't listen to him. But now they understand that they're too old for this hardship we'll all have to face, so they've agreed to go. And now tell me how you're feeling. Are you well?"

"I'm bored. Why does this business have to take nine whole months?"

"Why didn't you go on with your teaching at the convent? It would have made the time pass more quickly."

"I thought I was looking a bit too conspicuous. Small children have a way of asking awkward questions. And walking about among the nuns, looking as I look, made me feel self-conscious. Is Chandra away?"

"He comes back today. I thought he would be here by now. Perhaps you'll see him before you go."

"And Kamala?"

"She went for a drive in someone's nice new motorcar. You know, Annerley, I feel sorry for her. This isn't a very cheerful atmosphere for someone like her."

Moira, to whom Annerley repeated this remark on the way to the maternity home, said that if Kamala had had an ounce of spirit, she would long ago have given Chandra a choice: herself, or Gandhi.

"But I feel sorry for her, too," she went on. "She's got herself sandwiched between the British lion and the Bengal tiger—I wouldn't be in her shoes, if she wears shoes, for anything. Would you mind if I stopped for a minute when we got to Chowringhee? I want to go and buy some face powder. I won't be long."

She stopped the car outside the shop. Rain was pouring down; she ran swiftly across the pavement. She was longer than Annerley had anticipated; she came out carrying not one parcel, but several.

"Sorry," she said, as they drove away. "I always seem to get the assistant without any brains."

316

"You're soaking wet."

"Only my shoulders."

The rain increased. Under the car's canvas hood the mica windows were obscured by the water coursing down them on the outside. Moira slowed down at the corner of the road that led to the maternity home.

As she began the turn, a taxi drew level with the car. At the same moment, a cow that had been sitting near the tram lines heaved itself to its feet and placed itself directly in their path. Moira, unable to avoid it because the taxi was still alongside, swerved and braked. The back wheel of the car slithered along the tram lines. The car went into a skid, swung round and overturned.

Dr. Millet fought for twelve hours to save Annerley's life. His efforts were successful—but Victoria was stillborn.

Mark, urgently summoned, sat hour by hour beside the unconscious Annerley, speechless, motionless. Shareen paced the corridors outside the room. Chandra came and went, and came again.

In the room adjoining Annerley's, Edwin watched over Moira. Uninjured, she had spent the waiting hours standing before one of the windows, staring out into the gathering darkness. Edwin had tried without success to rouse her—and then at last she turned and made a blind movement towards him. He took her into his arms and held her, saying nothing, rocking her gently. And little by little, he found his own pain easing. Her body was warm and clinging; mature. It was not a child that he held in his arms; this was a woman who had grown up under his eyes and who, until now, he had failed to recognize as an adult.

He knew that the accident had not been her fault—but she blamed herself, and others would blame her, for she had a reputation for fast driving. He could think of no words of comfort. He could only hold her and let her find what strength she could in his arms.

She grew quiet, but she did not free herself. Together they

317

waited until news was brought, and Edwin was allowed to go in and see the still unconscious Annerley and his little stillborn grandchild.

On the following morning, Mark, Edwin and Chandra drove with Dr. Millet to the cemetery, where Canon Tremblett awaited them. In the pouring rain, after a brief prayer, the tiny coffin was placed in its grave, and the damp earth covered it. Then the men returned to their cars.

At the maternity home, Annerley opened her eyes to find Mark on one side of her and her father on the other. Only Victoria was missing.

Life went on for Annerley as it had done before the months of pregnancy. The tiny grave marked the end of the hopes that had lightened the period of waiting.

There was a possibility that Mark would in the foreseeable future be transferred to Calcutta. He decided to ask for leave and take Annerley away for a time. They had spoken frequently in the past of going to see Burma; now they would go.

Their first plan was to travel on one of the British-India boats to Rangoon, but Edwin advised an extension of the journey, to include Penang and Singapore. They asked him to go with them, but he refused on the plea of work. Moira, too, refused to join them. She had decided to go to England for three months—in an attempt, Edwin thought, to escape from the sense of guilt that still haunted her. In her absence, he would look after number 10. Miss Clowers was thanked for her services, given a handsome bonus and seen off to her next post, which was a residential one at the convent, taking over the kindergarten duties that Annerley gave up.

The voyage was quiet, but healing. Between ports of call,

Mark and Annerley kept a joint diary; he confined himself to statistics and politics while she described people and places. On their return, Mark had some copies typed, with spaces left for appropriate snapshots and postcards. He posted a copy to his parents, presented one to Edwin and kept one for Moira.

Edwin treasured his copy as an interesting memento. Moira, on her return from England, sold her copy to the *Times of India* and, to Edwin's indignation, pocketed the proceeds.

"That money," he pointed out, "wasn't yours. Only a quarter of it belonged to you. I could have bought a new dinner jacket with my share."

She lit a cigarette—the latest act of provocation directed at her critics—and eyed him through the smoke.

"Who thought of publication? *I* did."

"It was a distinct breach of copyright. What are you going to do with the money?"

"Not buy you a new dinner jacket. I need it for my work in the villages."

"You're going on with that?"

"Of course. Shareen thought I wouldn't stick to it; now she knows better."

Annerley paid occasional visits to the Millets, but it was with Shareen that she spent most of her time. She thought that she and Chandra were growing thinner and more gaunt, but there was no diminution in the dedication they showed to their cause.

Going to the house one morning, Annerley found Shareen looking less buoyant than usual. She took Annerley up to her room; Annerley settled herself against the divan and asked what was the matter.

"Why should you ask that? What should be the matter?" Shareen countered.

"I know you, and I can see that something's happened. What is it?"

Shareen did not answer at once. She sat with her hands for once idle on her lap, staring out at the sun-warmed balcony.

"This morning," she said at last, "Kamala's father came. I told you he would, didn't I?"

"To take her home?"

"To take her back."

"Has she gone?"

"Of course. I told you that, too."

"Was Chandra here?"

"No. He's away. That's why her father chose to come today. But Chandra here, Chandra there, what difference does it make? In the end, she didn't want to stay here. What was there for her here? Don't say 'her husband.' Don't translate this into English terms."

"Do you mean that she'll never come back?"

"Never. It's finished. And you know, in a way I think her family has been patient. They expected her to be surrounded by luxury, to live as we used to live. When all that went, I thought they would come and take her away. But they didn't. They waited. They waited until they saw that things would never change with us. They realized what lengths we were prepared to go to, to defy the government, defy the police. They know that nothing is going to stop us. So they came—her father came—and took her away. She's gone."

"Without protest?"

"The only protest she made was that she didn't want to leave until her new saris had arrived. They promised her more when she got to her home. Her things were packed while her father waited. Then they drove away. She said good-bye to us all, just as if she was going to take a drive along the Strand Road, an airing before coming back to eat. I think that by the time she reaches her home, she will have forgotten she ever left it."

"And Chandra?"

"Chandra? He'll come back, he'll learn what has happened, he'll say nothing. He will go and see her, see her parents, because he cannot accept the situation without making an attempt, real or not, to get her back. They will refuse, he will return and he will give all his mind to the future of India."

Annerley found nothing to say.

When she became pregnant once more, at the beginning of nineteen twenty-six, Dr. Millet persuaded Mark to send her up to Murree for the baby's birth.

"It is a long way," he said, "but look: It is a new place for her, no unhappy memories, and a first-class maternity home, one for which I can personally speak. She should not stay on the plains for the hot weather. She should go up before May, and stay until the baby is born. The air is very bracing—it is over seven thousand feet. If you like, I can arrange for you to take a bungalow for six months. There is a club, there will be many English people. Please consider what I'm saying. I am giving good advice."

Mark decided to take it. After some correspondence, a bungalow named Chota Koti was rented for six months. Both Mark and Edwin promised to go up on visits—and Moira elected to go up with her.

"Six months is a long time," Annerley warned her.

"If I can't stick it, I can always come back here. You need a change of climate. I'll see that you eat well and take exercise."

It was a long six months. Moira had known that Murree was a hill station whose maternity home attracted pregnant women from many parts of northern India. What she had not known, she told Annerley indignantly, was that every woman in sight would be pregnant, and that the only males to be seen would be sheepish-looking husbands who made brief appearances and then vanished. Nor had she expected conversation at the club to be exclusively of forthcoming confinements, or that a woman like herself, flat in front, would be considered an object not of envy but of scorn.

At the gate of every bungalow there waited, day and night, a rickshaw with its attendant rickshaw-wallah, ready to speed to the maternity home when Nature gave the word. Moira, in desperation, sent to Calcutta for paints and canvases and filled in time by painting hillscapes which she exhibited at the club and sold for steep prices. She wrote daily reports to Mark and to Edwin. The latter, sensing her boredom and impatience, felt that this was her way of making up in small part for the loss of Victoria.

Twin sons were born to Annerley in October—as fine a pair, the presiding doctor told her, as he had ever seen. They were named Edwin Francis and Anson Victor—and Annerley, looking down at the two small forms in her arms, whispered a promise that one day they would have a little Victoria to play with them.

Mark came up to make the return journey with the precious cargo. With him came Annerley's old ayah, who had reappeared from nobody knew where and had haunted the compound of number 5 until Edwin wrote to Annerley and suggested reengaging her on the principle that the devil she knew would be better than the devil she didn't know.

It was number 10 Seymour Street to which they returned. Edwin was waiting to inspect his grandsons. He stayed to dinner, and the evening seemed a happy one—but when they were seated over coffee in the drawing room, he told them that he had some bad news to break to them.

"What is it?" Annerley asked.

"It's something you won't want to hear."

"I've got to know, haven't I? Tell me."

"It's Shareen and Chandra."

"What about them?"

"They're in prison."

She could only stare at him in horror. Chandra, perhaps—but Shareen? A young girl? She had listened often enough to Shareen's talk of arrest, but she realized now that she had never taken it seriously.

"Why?" she asked at last.

"Picketing. They were warned. Mr. Prebdel was up north. Shareen insisted on going with Chandra. Eight people were arrested—Shareen and Chandra among them."

"Where are they?"

"He's up-country. She's near Calcutta, but she's not allowed any visitors yet. When she is, they'll be close relatives only."

"Can I write to her?"

"Yes."

"How long . . ."

"Four months."

"Can she write to me?"

"I think she'll be allowed to write once a month. But letters in and out will be censored."

For this reason, perhaps, Shareen said little in the letter that eventually arrived—but she said that she did not want to see anyone. Chandra did not write.

The thought of Shareen and Chandra in prison was not the only weight on Annerley's mind; she was also seriously worried about Mark.

There was no doubt that he was delighted with his two infant sons, but beneath his pride in them and his relief at her safe delivery, Annerley sensed that something was missing. She watched him for some time without making any comment; then one night when they had said good-bye to Moira, who was going to a party, she broke the peaceful silence that reigned in the room.

"Mark, are you over-working?"

He looked up from his book.

"Not more than usual," he answered. "What makes you ask?"

"You've seemed tired lately. Is your leg giving trouble?"

"No."

The next probe was deeper, more painful.

"You're not disappointed, are you? I mean, you don't wish that one of the twins had been a . . . a girl?"

"No. God, no. There'll be another girl—one day. In the meantime, we've got two splendid sons."

"Then am I just imagining that you're depressed?"

He laid aside his book.

"I'm not depressed. I'm a bit worried, that's all."

"About . . . ?"

"About my work. My job."

"Isn't it going well?"

"As far as the eye can see—the eye of my superiors—it's going very well. But—since you've asked—I wish I didn't have so many reservations about it."

"Reservations?"

"Reservations about what I'm doing—and why. I wish I could rid myself of this feeling that I'm . . ."

"That you're what?"

"It's too vague to put into words. I feel I'm treading water. I work hard, my colleagues work hard, my subordinates work hard, but I don't feel that we're getting anywhere."

"But you like the work."

"Yes. I've always liked the work. It's always been interesting. I like going round remote villages inspecting wells and drains and houses and schools—if there is a school. I like doling out justice. I like settling the fights and the feuds that spring up when a river changes its course and leaves one fellow with no land and another fellow with more. It took me some time, in the early days, to get used to the watery conditions—working in the delta of the Ganges—but once I got myself fitted with webbed feet, I enjoyed it. So did you, on the few occasions you could come and join me."

"Yes, I did."

"I liked the thought of being not too far away from you. A launch trip, a short train trip, and you waiting to meet me. I liked the challenge of having to administer an enormous—by English standards—area, at an age when most of my contemporaries at home were licking stamps in London offices. I've felt proud to belong to a service with so many fine traditions, even though it wasn't the job I chose in the first place. But when I've said all that, then I find myself turning the coin round, and what I see on the other side makes me uneasy. Makes me restless."

"Why?"

"The reasons," he confessed, "are a bit vague."

She left her chair, carried a footstool across the room, and sat at his feet.

"If you bring them out into the open," she suggested, "you might find them getting clearer."

"I doubt it. What I'm worried about is that there's tension growing everywhere I look, and nothing seems to be done to ease it. The results of the infiltration of the Gandhi-ites into the villages frighten me. They're a new breed—educated, tough, with clear-cut aims. It's all very well to talk about peaceful non-cooperation, but there's nothing basically peaceful about it. It used to be a kind of experiment—children thumbing their noses at policemen and seeing how far they could go without getting caught and dealt with. But now it's got far beyond that. The children are adults who know all the risks and who—like the Prebdels—are willing, are eager to take them. We're still the rulers, but the system's paternal: you are our children and we're doing what's best for you."

"Well, aren't we?"

"Yes. But something more, or something less is needed now." He paused, took one of her hands and held it absently. "What one has to remember is that we've made some ghastly mistakes in recent years, and we're not going to be allowed to live them down. In one village I visited, there were two women whose husbands had died in that Amritsar massacre—shot by the troops when General Dyer ordered them to fire on a peaceful mob—a meeting organized by the National Congress. Twenty thousand people trapped in an enclosed space. Nearly four hundred killed, over a thousand wounded. My own private, probably worthless opinion is that that order to open fire was the match that set a slow fire burning. The two widows in that village . . . I can't forget them. They came at me like avenging witches. It's quite an experience to come out to India thinking of the Raj as a benevolent paterfamilias, and run into Indians who are only waiting to throw the old gentleman back where he came from."

"Have you talked like this to any of—"

"The people in the service? God, no. Every fellow I've met is

326

convinced we're right and always have been and always will be. Your father warned me when I first came out that I must keep my mouth shut, so I've been careful." He moved restlessly. "What I want is a long talk with Chandra—but he won't talk, either. Not to me. He cut himself off not only because he'd joined Gandhi, but also because he realized that it wouldn't do me any good to be known as his friend."

"Have you talked to my father about this?"

"I've said some of it to him. He's the only man I can talk to with absolute frankness. I haven't said much to you because I haven't wanted you to worry, especially during the past few months. But I'm glad to be able to tell you how I feel."

They sat in silence for a time. Then, "I wish I could help," she said.

He laughed.

"Help?" He stood up and drew her up into his arms. "Help? What do you think I'd do without you?"

When Shareen was released from prison, Annerley was waiting for her at the Prebdels' house. She found her thinner, but unsubdued. Throughout her imprisonment, she told Annerley, she had been upheld by thankfulness that her mother had not been with them at the time of the arrests.

"You're so thin," Annerley moaned. "Didn't you get enough to eat?"

"I suppose so. Next time I go to prison, I'm going to take more books."

"What did you do?"

"Weaving, cooking our meals, seeing to the children of the women who were in jail. I thought of you all the time, wondering how you were getting on. Why didn't you bring the twins to see me today?"

"I'll bring them tomorrow. Have you news of Chandra?"

"No. At least, none lately. One of my uncles went to visit him and said he was well. How do you like living at number ten?"

Annerley smiled.

"I live in both houses," she said. "I leave Moira to do the

328

housekeeping at number ten while I go and supervise things at number five."

"You think it's a good thing to have Moira living with you?"

"It's better than good. We don't see much of her. She'll be coming round to see you soon—she wants to go out to some more villages with you."

"I can't go while my mother is here."

Annerley looked at her in astonishment.

"Your mother? But you said she was going away with your grandmother. Didn't she go?"

"She went, yes. But when she heard her children were in jail, she came back. We're all insisting on her going back again, but she wants to wait until Chandra's released. I'll be happy when she's gone."

Chandra was not released until June. Annerley found him more withdrawn, more remote than she had ever known him. Between him and Shareen there seemed to have been created a kind of unity that had no need of words. Their dedication to their cause was absolute.

There was a discussion between Mark and Edwin on the advisability of sending Annerley and the twins to England to escape the hot weather. This met with so much resistance from her that Mark agreed to a compromise—that she would spend the hotter months in Shillong.

Moira went with her. Neither she nor Annerley joined the club, and neither joined in the ceaseless round of amusements available to those on holiday. They went for long walks, watched the steady development of the twins and learned to ignore the frequent earth tremors that were a feature of the station. There was reassurance in the thought that they would not be buried under piles of masonry, the walls of their bungalow being—like the walls of all their neighbours—constructed of lath and plaster.

They returned to Calcutta in the middle of June. The monsoon had broken early, and with storms of even more violence than usual. Annerley went to see Shareen, but found that she was away. Chandra was also away, but they were expected back at the end of the week. She went home and waited for news of them.

It came on an evening when peals of thunder were alternating with vivid flashes of lightning that illuminated the streams of water running along the pavements and dripping from roofs. Annerley was with her father, waiting for Mark to appear in their newly acquired car, to take her dry-shod back to number 10.

A car drove into the compound and Annerley and Edwin went downstairs—but it was not Mark's car; it was Moira's. From it leapt a figure who was almost unrecognizable, and Annerley saw to her horror that it was Chandra. He was mud-covered, his face scratched, his shirt torn, his arm pouring blood from a wound. He ran towards the steps shouting Edwin's name.

"Mr. Brooke! Mr. Brooke!"

Annerley and Edwin were beside him in a moment, heedless of the storm and the pouring rain. He spoke in a hoarse gasp.

"Where's Mark? For God's sake, where's Mark? He isn't at the house—I've just come from there."

"He's coming to pick me up—and here he is," Annerley said.

Mark stopped the car behind Moira's, got out and stared in disbelief at Chandra.

"You're hurt," he said. "What's happened?"

"You've got to come with me," Chandra said. "You've got to come at once. I can't get her away. She won't leave. For God's sake, hurry!"

"Who won't leave?"

"Moira. Your sister. She won't leave Shareen. I got my mother away, but Moira . . . the police . . . you've got to hurry."

He turned back to Moira's car. Edwin put out a hand and caught his uninjured wrist.

"Wait a moment, Chandra. You've got to tell us what's happened. Where are they?"

"Near the station—Sealdah station. There was a group of women sitting in the road, and the police told them to move on. Shareen and Moira and I were passing—and I recognized my mother. And just then, the police charged with lathis. I got my

330

mother out. She and two of my aunts . . . I sent them home. But Shareen . . . Moira wouldn't leave her. We carried Shareen into a side street and I came to fetch Mark."

He got into Moira's car. As it approached the gate, Annerley opened the door on the passenger side and jumped in.

"Annerley!" Mark shouted.

She leaned out to call to him.

"I'll be all right. They won't hurt me."

"Annerley, come back!"

Her reply was carried to him on a gust of wind.

"Bring Doctor Millet."

Mark rushed next door. The doctor, preparing to return to his surgery, followed Mark instead to the car and got in. Edwin went with them. After driving for some minutes, they saw ahead of them Moira's car.

In it, Chandra, speaking in jerks, filled in a few details for Annerley. Water was streaming down his face—she could not tell whether it was rain, or tears.

"I was at a meeting near the station. Moira and Shareen were driving back from a village and they came to pick me up."

He paused as a peal of thunder cracked almost overhead.

"We saw the women in the road, and the police telling them to move on. Shareen wanted to stop, but I didn't want to involve Moira in any trouble, so I insisted on going on."

The flash and the crack came almost simultaneously. The car seemed to be moving through a sheet of water.

"And then I saw my mother. She was in the middle of the group, struggling with the police. Moira stopped the car, and Shareen and I ran out to help my mother. We got her out—unhurt. Two of my aunts were with her. I stopped a taxi and put them in and sent them home, then I went back to get Shareen. She . . ."

Once again, he paused. She waited.

"Moira helped me to get her into a side street. I told Moira to leave us. I begged her. She wouldn't go. So I went to fetch Mark . . ."

The car was slowing down. It was not difficult to guess that they had reached the scene of the disturbance. A crowd was being dispersed, a police van was driving away with prisoners. Chandra turned into a deserted side street. Some distance along it, Annerley saw two figures by the wall of a house. Chandra stopped the car and they got out.

Mark's car was not far behind. Mark and Edwin and the doctor got out and walked a few paces and then stopped, looking in horror at the scene on the roadside.

Annerley was seated on the pavement, Shareen's head pillowed in her arms. Kneeling beside her was Moira, endeavouring to smooth back from Shareen's forehead the loosened, blood-matted hair. Shareen's eyes were closed. From above one temple oozed a trickle of blood. Chandra was crouching beside Moira, holding his sister's hands.

Moira made room for Doctor Millet. He knelt beside Shareen. His examination was brief. His eyes met Moira's and she read in them the knowledge that had not yet penetrated to Chandra and Annerley. He got to his feet and addressed Mark.

"We must carry her to the car," he told him. "The police will be here at any moment."

Annerley looked up at him. There was a question on her lips, but she could not voice it. Nor was there any need. The truth could be seen in the limp form, the dead, closed eyes. She could read it, and she could see that Chandra had read it too.

The four men gently lifted the lifeless body into Moira's car, and Annerley cradled it in her arms. They took Shareen home and laid her on the floor of the hall, where her mother, in torn and mud-streaked sari, awaited her. There were no words. There were no tears. Round the body knelt those who had loved her best. The only sound was the low moaning of Shareen's mother.

Mark took Moira home; Annerley begged to be left for a little while longer. The doctor went away, and Chandra and his mother and Annerley were left with Shareen, whose fight was over—a fight that was to continue and be won. Through Annerley's mind went a series of pictures of the years that had gone.

Shareen would never again storm at dirzhees because they made her dresses badly. She would never again rail against Edwin or speak scornfully of the Fernandez sisters. Those childhood years were gone—but it was the Shareen of those happy years that Annerley knew she would remember longest. Shareen the arrogant—the rebel. Shareen of the loud speech and the loud laugh, Shareen who had loved her, Shareen whom she had loved.

Mark came to take her home. Chandra rose and stood in the doorway, watching them go. Annerley put her arms round him and laid her head on his shoulder.

"Cremation?" she managed to say after a time.

"Yes. A funeral pyre. Will you come?"

"No. Oh, Chandra . . ."

"Don't worry. This was her way."

"Yes."

She went away without a backward look. When she and Mark reached number 10, her father was waiting with Moira. She went past them, went into her room and closed the door.

Mark's application for leave was granted in December; he and Annerley and the children were to go to England in April.

There had been a possibility that Edwin would be with them, but Annerley had begun to wonder whether it would ever be more than a possibility. He had, he explained, lost touch with his old friends. He had become used to the life he was leading, he had become used to the climate, he saw no reason to pull up the roots he had put down.

But in mid-December, to his disappointment and dismay, he had a bad bout of malaria, and Doctor Millet came over to speak seriously to him.

"You've got to get away—to England," he told him. "The disease is in your system and it'll stay in your system while you stay in this climate. You'll keep thinking you've got the better of it, but believe me, it'll end by getting the better of you."

"I've been free for years. Why—"

"Look, Mr. Brooke, you're thinking that I'm only a woman's doctor, so you won't take any notice of what I say. Let me make an appointment for you with a friend of mine, a man who's the leading doctor on your trouble, a specialist, and hear his verdict. Will you agree to that?"

"If you think it's necessary."

"I know it's necessary. And will you agree to do whatever he says you ought to do?"

"Let's wait and see, shall we?" Edwin suggested.

The specialist's advice, more strongly worded, was the same as Victor Millet had given: get out of India.

Edwin discussed the problem over a drink with Mark.

"It's all very well to tell me to go," he said, "but at my age, one can't think in terms of going and coming back. I can't shuttle for the rest of my life. At the same time, I can't see myself settling down forever in England. Especially as my daughter and my grandchildren will be out here."

"Perhaps," said Mark quietly.

Edwin, about to take a sip of his peg, put the glass down and looked at him.

"What do you mean by 'perhaps'?" he asked.

"I said perhaps," Mark answered, "because I've been working up the courage to tell you that when my leave's up, I don't want to come back here."

"Come back where? To Calcutta?"

"To India."

There was silence.

"Good God," said Edwin at last. "How long have you had this in mind?"

Mark, drink in hand, turned the glass round slowly, gazing into the untouched whisky and soda.

"The truth," he said slowly, "is that I should never have come out. It wasn't the career I wanted. I thought I was right in taking it on when my leg put me out of the running for the police."

"Feeling as you do," Edwin said, "you wouldn't have liked the police job any better. In fact, you would have liked it a great deal less."

"Looking back," Mark said, "I suppose that what I was

335

doing, without realizing it, was making sure I'd be where Annerley was. From the start—I mean from the start of my work out here—I've had a struggle to try and bring my thinking in line with the other fellows I met in the service. But eight out of ten of them—and nine out of ten of the Englishmen I met outside the service—held views that seemed to me not only ignorant and arrogant, but in the present climate dangerous. You're one of the only men, the only Englishmen I've met out here who seem to me the kind that should be out here. I've watched, in clubs, conceited young upstarts just out from home snubbing Indians who had twice their background and breeding and education. I've seen wives of officials humiliating timid young Indian wives and keeping their children away from anything that smacked of the country. I'm not competent to judge—I'm merely telling you what I've seen. And I've come to the conclusion that I don't want any more of it."

"Have you said this to Annerley?"

"Yes. There was a time when she couldn't contemplate leaving India for good—but Shareen's death changed her."

"Yes," said Edwin. "Shareen's death changed her. Just as Victoria's death changed Moira." He paused. "What about Moira?"

"I don't know. One can't get much out of her. But it looks—doesn't it?—as though we're all due for a change?"

"If you give up your job, what will you do in England?"

"I don't know. The prospect isn't too bleak. I've got relations with what's called influence—who can pull a few strings. I'm still young enough to start again."

"Where would you live?"

"That would depend on the job. You'd go to the cottage, I suppose?"

"Yes. You haven't touched your drink.

Mark finished it and rose.

"Sit down," Edwin said. "I'd like another."

"I thought your limit was one."

"I want to drink to the future. You said it wasn't too bleak, but I'd like to see it a bit more clearly."

Mark raised his refilled glass.

"To the future—to all our futures," he said.

Solemnly, they drank the toast. Then Mark rose and walked home, thinking less of his own future than of Edwin's. A young man could begin again. But Edwin . . . ?

They were to go. Not only for Mark's leave; not a few months in England and then a return to his work here. They were packing, but there was no separation of things to take, things to leave until their return. There would be no return. The house, theirs for so long, would be given up. Their heavy possessions would go into the packing cases now being assembled by a carpenter in the compound. The servants would be found other employment and would be given pensions. The furniture would be sold, the horse, the car. They would travel by sea all the way, taking all their worldly goods.

The house had already lost its lived-in look. Mark came home to find that more and more items had vanished, taken from their accustomed places and fitted into the places prepared for them in the trunks. He watched Annerley, unhurried, calm, making lists, checking lists.

He found her busy one evening in their bedroom, dressed for a dinner engagement they had made, but still finding small things to occupy her until he was ready.

"I hate the house the way it looks now," he said.

"So do I."

"I'll be glad to get away."

She made no reply. He turned from the window and stared at her across the room, his forehead lined with a worried frown.

"And what about you?" he said.

"Well, what about me?"

"You haven't said much."

"About what?"

"About going. About leaving this country."

"There's no problem, is there? Where you go, I go."

She had been folding the children's small garments. She sat on

337

the bed, still holding them, looking down on them unseeingly.

"Yes," she agreed. "I love India. But I've been asking myself lately what it is, exactly, that I love about it—and there doesn't seem to be a clear answer. I love, I've always loved the life out here—but is that India? I love the sun and the colours and the feeling that I belong here—but I've found out that I don't know much about the land and even less about the people. India, for me, was my father and grandmother and the servants—and Shareen and Moira. And then you were added. But now? My father's going. Moira won't stay here alone. Shareen's dead— and you don't want to stay out here. So what's left?"

"India. I could find another job out here."

"No. If you did, we'd have to face separations when the children are old enough to be sent to school in England. You'll never be happy here—and my father will never be fit. So on the whole . . ."

Her voice died away. He came and sat beside her and drew her close to him.

"You're unhappy," he said gently. "I can't bear to see you like this."

"I'm not unhappy. That's one thing I know very clearly: If you're with me, I won't be unhappy." She lifted her head to meet his eyes. "I don't know when I realized it, but I know that I couldn't do without you. I fell . . . what are you smiling at?"

"You. You make such a small world for yourself. You should have been a bird, safe in a little nest with your chicks under your wings and your bird-mate close by. You're not going to be much use, are you, to these new women who are advocating . . . whatever it is they're advocating. Suppose I don't get a job, at first, in England, will you be prepared to, so to speak, live on our fat for a time?"

"There's quite a lot of fat, isn't there? You can't call us poor."

"Wait until my salary ceases to be paid, and see how far my income will stretch."

"There's always the cottage."

"*All* of us?"

"A bedroom for my father, a bedroom for us, a cubbyhole for the babies."

He looked dubious.

"All right for a week." He laughed. "It'll be odd, won't it, to live there again?"

They were not, however, to live there again.

The telegram came a week later, and was delivered to Edwin. It was from his mother's lawyers. He read it, reread it slowly and then, with it in his hand, walked to number 10 and handed it to Annerley.

Her grandmother was dead. The telegram contained the information that she had left her house, Waterways, to her son, Edwin Anson Brooke. She had left her fortune to her granddaughter, Annerley.

Seated round the dinner table at number 10 a week later, Edwin put an end to the arguments, the persuasion and the pleas that Annerley had directed at him since the arrival of the news from Waterways.

"No," he said, for perhaps the twentieth time. "For the last time, no. I will not go and live at Waterways."

She looked across the table at Mark, and from him to Moira; she saw that they, like herself, recognized the finality in his tone.

"I don't know why you won't," she said helplessly. "You love it, it's the most perfect house, it's healthy, and you can watch your grandchildren growing up there."

"Why can't you see," asked Edwin in his turn, "that it's the perfect place, not for me, but for you and Mark? He needs a job, the estate needs a man to run it. He'll be kept busy, God knows. The place is geared to making money, and he'll have to learn how to make it go on paying. If he gets into difficulties, he can come down to the cottage and ask my advice."

There was silence—the silence of acceptance. Then Mark spoke.

"That seems to take care of us all—except Moira," he said. His eyes rested on his sister, and then went to Annerley. "How many times have we tried to get her to tell us what she intends to do?"

"I haven't counted," Annerley said.

"You mean that you've lost count?" He addressed Moira. "There must be some reason why you're dragging your feet in this way. Are we to take it that you've made other plans? Have you?" She made no reply, and he continued. "I've tried to make it clear, and so has Annerley, that we want you at Waterways. You haven't said no, on the other hand you haven't said yes. Could we know what you've made up your mind to do?"

"I'm going to live at the cottage," she said.

"Cottage? What cottage?" Mark asked in bewilderment.

"The cottage Edwin is going to live in."

Three pairs of eyes became fixed on her. Mark was holding a serving spoon in the air while the bearer, puzzled but patient, waited at his side.

"You're joking of course." He put a large helping of pudding onto his plate. "What, seriously, are you thinking of doing? You know you're always welcome wherever Annerley and I are."

"Thank you. Thank you both. But Edwin proposes to live by himself at the cottage, which I think is an absurd idea."

"What's absurd about it?" Mark asked.

"Living there alone is absurd. He'd be miserable." She took a mouthful of pudding. "So miserable," she continued, "that he'd be driven to look for a woman to share it with him. I'd like that woman to be me."

Mark spoke in bewilderment.

"You mean that you're proposing to—"

"Not proposing to," she interrupted. "Merely proposing." She looked from him to Edwin. "For years," she said in an even tone, "it should have been obvious to you that you were the only man whose company I ever showed any desire for. I would have thought it would have been obvious not only to you but to"—her glance swept Mark and Annerley—"you two. But for years, you've all been so absorbed in other matters that nobody has had

340

time to sit down and wonder why I refused so many offers of marriage. If one refuses offers of marriage, it doesn't necessarily mean that one doesn't want to marry. But for years I've had to endure being treated"—once more she was looking at Edwin— "as Annerley's friend Moira. I'm Moira Fenwick, who at the age of thirteen, or was it fourteen, went to your house to sit for an examination, and fell in love with the proctor. He was kind—so kind, that I realized he wouldn't have let me go through the farce of that test paper without doing something, anything, to get me into that school. I knew that all my father's boasts about influence were nothing but his usual empty claims to be able to pull strings. All through that examination, I sat with a growing feeling that nobody had ever taken an interest in me before, nobody had ever tried to help, nobody had ever understood. I thought you were wonderful. I went on thinking so. The hard work I did at school was for you. The work I did during the war was to make you feel I was trying to be useful. I—"

"Look, Moira," Edwin broke in, "you—"

His voice was husky. He stopped to clear his throat, but she had gone on speaking.

"I came back to India, not to run this house for Mark, but to be near you again. I've been waiting ever since for a sign that you thought me a woman and not a child. Now I'm tired of waiting. I would like to marry you, if you like me well enough to take me on. And somehow, I think you do."

Edwin was struggling to speak.

"Moira, my dear—"

"You're not going to say something puerile about being old enough to be my father?"

"Yes . . . that was what I was going to say."

"A young man's mistress, an old man's nurse—haven't you heard that? I'll be your nurse—for a start. And once you get over feeling fatherly, we'll be very happy. I couldn't marry anybody else, ever. You know me; you know the worst and you can bear it. I love the cottage. I'd like to think that this proposal came

341

from you, but you've proved as blind as Annerley and my brother. So now you know. I'd rather you didn't say anything until you've had time to think things over. Not marrying me—you can take that for granted. All I'd like from you at this moment is an assurance that you love me like a father. I didn't like my own father, as you know. I'm sure you'll make a better one—until you get used to living with me and understand that I'm not your daughter, but a woman very much in love with you."

She stopped. Staring across the table at her, Edwin put unsteady hands up to his head.

"My hair," he began, "is—"

"Beginning to go grey. Anything else?"

"Yes. You're young, strong, at the beginning of life."

"Anything else?"

"To consider shutting yourself up with an old man and—"

"Not shutting myself up. Looking after my husband and being happy visiting Mark and Annerley and going on trips abroad and seeing all those parts of the world I've never seen, and you've never seen. Anything else?"

His eyes went in appeal to Mark.

"Make her see what she's doing," he begged.

"I know what I'm doing," said Moira calmly. "Why don't you say something about May and December—you left that out. Will you please say something constructive? Something like, 'Yes, I've loved you secretly for years and you have made me the happiest man in the world.' Go on—say it."

Edwin groped for his glass, took a long drink and then looked slowly round the table. His gaze rested finally on Annerley.

"You . . . you heard what she said?" he asked in a dazed voice.

"Yes, I heard."

"Tell her she can't do it."

She shook her head, smiling. She had heard—and listening, she had felt the shadow that had lain over her heart ever since Shareen's death begin slowly to disperse. She drew a deep, grateful breath. Shareen had gone—but this other friend would remain. Moira would always be there, one of them, bound closely to the family. And while Moira was there, Shareen would never seem very far away.

Edwin appealed to Mark.

"Make her see what she's letting herself in for," he begged.

Like Annerley, Mark shook his head.

"Do you think she'll give up—after all these years? Your best course is to climb down gracefully. She's waiting for you to say something constructive."

"You'd let her marry a man of my age? She's vital and warm-blooded and fresh and . . . and desirable and—"

"And has been for years," Moira ended.

Mark looked at her.

"You really love him?" he asked.

"Yes."

"You want to marry him?"

"Haven't I just said so?"

Mark turned to Edwin.

"Take her. She's yours," he said.

They were to sail in twenty-four hours. Annerley had tried to make herself go to the Prebdels' house. Several times, she had set out; each time, she had returned before reaching the end of Seymour Street. She could not face the house without Shareen—the empty shell, the empty room giving onto the balcony. She wanted to say good-bye to the family, to see them for the last time, to tell them that they would be in her thoughts. But she shrank from meeting them.

Chandra came on the day she was to leave. He stood in the doorway, silent, unmoving, his eyes taking in the signs of departure—the locked trunks, the nailed-up packing cases, the children's toys in a corner awaiting distribution to the children of the servants.

She broke the silence.

"I tried to say good-bye," she said "I couldn't. I started out to

343

go to the house, and I turned back. It was no use."

He smiled—the smile she had first seen in the cottage garden, gentle, friendly.

"Perhaps," he said, "your sons will return one day."

"Perhaps. You know better than I do what there will be to come back to."

"India."

She looked at him. His wife had been taken from him. His sister had died for the cause. His mother had been removed from the battlefield, his father was continuing the struggle in the north of the country. He was alone.

"I didn't come to say good-bye," he told her quietly. "I came to ask you to remember—always."

"Remember? Do you think I could forget?"

"You will remember Shareen—I know that. But there are other things to remember. There was a summer that seems long, long ago. Will you remember that?"

"Yes. Always. Oh Chandra—always . . ."

"I'm glad. And I'm grateful, too. Are you happy?"

"Yes. But you?"

"I will be. 'Some future day, when what is now is not,'" he quoted softly. "I think there will be other summers."

She turned away for a moment, unable to speak, groping blindly in a drawer for a handkerchief to wipe the tears that were streaming down her cheeks. She found one, and dried the tears, and turned back to face him. But he had gone.